Thirteen Forty-nine

Jane Anstey

A Wings ePress, Inc.
Historical Novel

Wings
Press, Inc.

Wings ePress, Inc.

Edited by: Jeanne Smith
Copy Edited by: Joan C. Powell
Executive Editor: Jeanne Smith
Cover Artist: Trisha FitzGerald-Jung
Gravestone Image: Pixabay

All rights reserved

Wings ePress Books
www.wingsepress.com

Copyright © 2021 by: Jane Anstey
ISBN 13 : 978-1-61309-558-4

Published In the United States Of America

Wings ePress Inc.
3000 N. Rock Road
Newton, KS 67114

What They Are Saying About

Thirteen Forty-nine

An evocation of village life in the medieval English countryside, at a critical point in time: the Black Death is on its way...a sorrow and woe upon all. Two hundred years in history after the medieval life portrayed in Ellis Peters' Cadfael novels, Jane Anstey takes us further on the journey through time.
—Dr Janice Rossen, author of Women Writing Modern Fiction
(Palgrave Macmillan, 2003)
and Epiphanies in Literature (Madcap Press, 2011)

Striking in its timeliness, the novel plays out against the backdrop of a rampaging virus, which comes from overseas to race through the country, sparing no one from death and grief. Sound familiar? The Black Plague isn't even Alys [the heroine]'s biggest problem. The pandemic will pass, but once it does, she'll still be stuck in her feudal society, in a position of powerlessness, ruled by her absentee husband and the self-serving lord of the manor. Anstey presents all of this with the expert eye of an historian, and as you can imagine, the story is far from a nostalgic one about days gone by.
—Chris Boucher, author of Pivot Move
(Wings ePress, 2021)

Jane Anstey's carefully researched account of medieval life in pandemic in a small Hampshire village paints a vivid picture of the dislocation of life, whether in the monastery or the fields, that the Black Death caused. But above all it shows the indomitable human spirit, the caring and the resilience, brought out by adversity. A tale for our times!
—Liz Anslow, MA (Oxon)

Another page-turner from Jane Anstey, this time set in 14th century England where fears, daily uncertainties and tragedy strike to the heart of all, from the grandees in the manor down to the poorest families in their hovels. Their experiences resonate with ours as we battle Covid-19 in the 21st century, and the novel serves to bridge the intervening 650 years in the most uncanny way. The plague casts a long shadow over the varied cast of characters from the beginning, but there is also hope, love and strength in the face of adversity, making this a readable and ultimately uplifting novel, with a clever twist at the end to delight the reader.

—Dr Jane Santo-Warner, retired psychologist

Dedication

To the key workers of the 2020 pandemic

***

A note on language

Medieval speech was significantly different from modern, so much so that the story might be incomprehensible if I used proper Chaucerian dialogue between my characters. I have tried instead to give a flavour of the difference in rhythms of speech by using some archaic forms of words and syntax.

One

"Is it the pestilence that ails him, master?" The innkeeper's wife crossed herself as she spoke.

An anxious silence fell on the inn yard, for the mysterious disease that had been sweeping across Europe for a year was already raging in Caen and Paris to the west, and tales of its terrible symptoms and the swift passage of the infection from town to town had lost nothing in the telling.

Steven ran his fingers through his thatch of fair hair. "Nay, I think not. You're safe for the present, goodwife. I've seen folk taken ill with the pestilence when we were travelling in the East, and I'll never forget it. My lord has an ague of some kind, nothing more."

With a collective sigh of relief, the grooms, carters and other assorted frequenters of the yard resumed their bustle, though some followed the inn-wife's example and crossed themselves piously first as a precaution.

"You've journeyed in the East, master?" The inn-wife's voice was respectful at such adventure, and the kitchen maid beside her stared.

Steven noticed for the first time that she was speaking English rather than Artois French, and with very little accent.

She met his glance with a smile. "Aye, I can speak your tongue pretty well, master. We were in Gascony when we were young, my man and I, and had an English lord. But my husband's father died a few years ago and we came to take over the inn here. Did they have the pestilence in the East then?"

A persistent woman, Steven thought with some irritation. "We were at the siege of Kaffa, two years ago," he answered shortly. "Half the town was dead of it before the Tartars broke in. They threw the bodies over the walls with catapults to hasten the end. I know what people look like who've died of plague."

"Did you have the sickness yourself?" asked the inn-wife in awed tones.

"Nay, would I be here talking to you if I had?" he retorted. "Not many live who get the black swellings – nor the circle rash, either."

"I – I did not know," she faltered, flushing. "I ask your pardon."

"No matter," he said, turning away. "You'll see for yourself soon enough, I fear."

She followed him as he walked across the yard to the stable. "Will you run home to England, when your master recovers, and hope to escape the pestilence?"

He shrugged. "It is as God wills," he replied, turning the question aside, though he resented the implication that they were cowards who'd flee at the first sign of trouble. He feared there was no escape from the pestilence, even across the Channel. But she didn't want to hear the true answer any more than he wanted to give it.

Besides, there was still hope. Perhaps the poisoned air really would not cross the water, as many believed. Some, he knew, thought England would be protected, that God was on their side, just as He had been in the war with France, as their recent victories at Crecy and Calais proved. Steven himself had little faith in that idea. He couldn't see why the English shouldn't suffer for their sins like the rest. But it would be better to face disaster at home in their own village than here among strangers, caught between war in Flanders on one side and pestilence on the other.

"My lord has a high fever," he reminded the inn-wife, before she could ask any further questions. "I should fetch a physician to him as soon as I may."

Not that he had much faith in physicians, either. Most of them were big on theories that dated back centuries and terribly small on practical cures. But there was always the faint chance that the local representative of the profession might be some use, and at least he would be doing *something* to help his master. He had his own very good reasons for wishing to prevent Sir Thomas's death, besides the call of duty and affection.

His mind ran anxiously over the events of the previous night. They had slept at the inn east of Calais, with the intent of pushing on the last few miles to the English-held town first thing in the morning. Sir Thomas, the leader of the expedition, had certainly looked tired as he dismounted in the September dusk, but Steven had thought little of it until Toby, their lord's bodyservant, had woken him in the early dawn with the news that his master was seriously ill with a raging fever and cough.

"My lord needs a physician," Toby had told him. "And quickly."

Steven had hurried after him into the knight's bedchamber, where the sick man lay tossing restlessly. "We'll have to send to Calais. There'll be no one but a barber-surgeon in the village, and he won't understand English, I'll warrant, even so close to the town."

Toby was wiping Sir Thomas's sweating brow tenderly. "'Tis no use asking these Frenchies to help us, anyway. They're scared shitless now the fighting in Flanders is so close. You'd best go into Calais yourself."

"Aye." It might be a dangerous journey, with the French army in the vicinity, but danger was more to his taste than staying here to share the sick-nursing with old Toby. He'd shut the door of his master's bedchamber behind him with guilty relief. The air of the inn yard was thick with the smell of horse droppings and the stench of refuse from the kitchen, but it seemed fresh after the foetid atmosphere of the sick room – though he could have done without the insistent questions of the ignorant innkeeper's wife.

Alan came towards him as he turned to the stable, light on his feet, with a longbow slung across his back and a short sword at his side. "They say the French have cut the road to Gravelines. You'd best go on to Calais – and be quick."

Steven clapped him on the shoulder. "You'll guard Sir Thomas while I'm gone." It was more than a question, but not quite an order—he had no authority over Alan.

"I will that," confirmed the younger man. "And Toby can wield a weapon at need." He glanced contemptuously round the inn yard, where men had begun frantically saddling, bridling and harnessing their charges for a hasty departure. "These sheep will scatter, I warrant. There's precious few will make a stand."

"They've little trust in the defences," Steven agreed.

He didn't blame them. The village was notionally within the circle of English defences around Calais, but in practice these consisted only of rough palisades around the southern edge that offered little protection against any kind of determined French attack.

"Take my mare," suggested Alan. "She's fast, and tis only a few miles."

It was a generous offer. Apart from Sir Thomas's destrier, who had fallen lame on the previous day and delayed their arrival at the inn, the other horses were steady cobs, suitable for carrying equipment and travelling gear, but not designed for swift errands where speed was of the essence. The mare, however, was Alan's own property, given him by Sir Thomas after the archer had saved his master's life during an encounter with bandits. She was both beautiful and valuable, but a lightweight, like her owner, and not really big enough for Steven.

"You're sure, man? She'd go faster still if you ride her."

"Aye. But you'll deal with the Calais garrison better than I will. They'd likely shoot me for a Frenchie, before I got within hailing range."

It was said lightly, but the point was a grimly realistic one. The English garrison would be on the lookout for enemy movements and might shoot first and ask questions afterwards. With Steven's height and his fair colouring, he would not easily be mistaken for a Frenchman. He grunted acceptance of Alan's offer and hoped the mare wouldn't founder under him, even on such a short journey.

They pushed their way past the frantic stablemen running hither and thither in response to loudly voiced demands from the inn's clientele. Alan's mare was stabled towards the back of the block, in a stall with Sir Thomas's own horses. She nickered when Alan spoke to her, and nodded her head in welcome, but she was shifting around anxiously in response to the ferment around her.

"There now, my beauty," he said, his voice as gentle as his hand on her neck. "Go well for Steven. He has need of all your speed today."

He saddled the mare himself, soothing and encouraging her as he did it, while Steven checked the knife in his belt and adjusted his sword and buckler to hang comfortably while he rode. His leather travelling clothes were stained and worn, and had not been removed for days, for they had ridden at speed through the County of Flanders to avoid what was rapidly turning into a state of civil war.

He swung up into the saddle and steered the mare out through the chaos of the yard on to the main road. She moved uncertainly but not unwillingly under him, and once out on the road Steven urged her into a canter. Calais lay three or four miles to the west, and if Toby's view of the severity of his master's illness was to be relied upon, time was short.

Within a mile, their pace had slowed to a walk, for the road was choked with refugees and panic-stricken travellers from the east streaming westwards. The truce between England and France, which had lasted almost a year after the fall of Calais, had expired in July, and negotiations for a fresh one had not yet begun. After the heavy rains that had fallen all summer, the low-lying ground on each side of the causeway was impassable. The road to Calais was the only route for refugees with the French army close behind them.

The mare sensed Steven's frustration and began to fret, sidling and snorting, throwing her mettlesome head up and down against the bridle. He swore and used the flat of his sword on the pedestrians in his path. They scattered before him and the mare picked up her pace again, her hooves splattering mud over any who came too close.

A few hundred yards further on, the road cleared and they made better speed. Signs of English occupation could be seen along the roadside here, and he expected at any moment to be challenged by sentries. He passed what remained of the wooden buildings of Villeneuve-la-Hardie, the town thrown up by the besieging army to house troops, stores and hangers-on. It lay disused now that the army was based in Calais itself and was slowly mouldering away in the damp atmosphere. He must be near the boundary of the Pale, the area around the captured town that was directly controlled by English forces.

The challenge came at last, from a group of guards at the crossroads where the causeway from Gravelines intersected with the road south to Guines. Steven answered it and explained his mission. His English accent and bearing, along with the guards' recognition of Sir Thomas's name, brought acceptance, and the soldiers directed him towards the town.

"What hour is it, d'you reckon?" he asked them as he turned the mare's head northward. A mass of cloud obscured the sun, and it was difficult to estimate how much time he had spent on the road.

"It wants two hours or more to noon," answered one of the sentries. "Lose no time, my friend, if you wish to find a physician and return eastwards. There'll be reinforcements joining us soon, to hold the Pale against the French if they come. The townsfolk will be preparing as well as the garrison. The king wants the port held at whatever cost."

"We may be under siege ourselves before long," agreed another, clearly relishing the prospect of a fight. "You'd best get on your way, man."

Steven gestured a farewell and dug his heels into the mare's side. He could see the high walls of Calais in the distance, murky in the mist but in reality solid and able to resist anything the French could throw at them. The English refugees behind him on the road would be safe enough if they could get this far, and for the moment the road was clear in front of him.

By the time he reached the town gates, barred against an imminent French attack, heavy rain was falling again. The mare was breathing hard, the froth from her mouth flying back into his face. Sentries challenged him from the far side of the ditch as he drew near.

"My lord is sick, back there," he yelled, pointing in the direction of Marck, and hoping they would hear him clearly enough. "I need a physician."

There was no response for a minute or two. Surely there must be someone with medical knowledge here, attached to the garrison? For the first time he wondered whether he had come on a fool's errand. But there had been no choice, anyway. He had had to make the attempt.

The gates swung open for him to enter. Clearly the garrison saw no possible threat from a lone lightly armed man. The bar rattled down into its slots again behind him, making the mare throw up her head. One of the sentries ran to hold her while Steven dismounted. "A physician, you said, for your master?"

"Aye, and quickly. My lord's in a high fever. He lies at an inn on the Gravelines road. The French are on their way, we heard."

The sentry nodded grimly. "We know they're on the move." He gestured behind him, to where a troop of horsemen were mounting up. "We're well prepared, though, and there's a sortie going out. You'd best bring your mare in out of the way. They'll be off directly."

Steven drew the mare into the small courtyard beside the sentry tower. He heard the clatter of hooves as the mounted troops rode out, followed by the steady tramp of booted foot soldiers marching across the cobbles behind them. A blond giant of a man entered the courtyard, bending his head to negotiate the low archway. He was in half-armour, a sword at his side.

Steven blinked. He hadn't seen this man for more than five years, but there was no mistaking him. "Wat Chesil, by the Virgin. How come you here?"

The giant turned, then strode over to clap him on the shoulder. "Steven the Woolgatherer," he laughed, using Steven's village nickname. "You left home so long ago I thought you were never coming back. I'm with the garrison—I'll explain later. What brings you to Calais? An ill wind, I judge, with the news this morning."

"We heard the French had cut the causeway, but they hadn't reached Marck when I left the inn."

"They captured Coulogne two weeks ago," Walter told him. "We've been on high alert ever since. You heard the sortie party go out just now?"

Steven nodded. "Sir Thomas has a high fever," he said, recalling his errand. "Can you direct me to a physician, Wat?"

"There's only one in the town," said Walter. "Unless you want one of the army's surgeons. I wouldn't advise it—no better than butchers, most of them."

Steven's heart lifted with relief. "One physician will do. Which street, Wat? Can you direct me? I need to take him back with me, so he'd better have a mount he can use."

Walter looked doubtful. "He won't want to go out of the town this morning," he observed. "Horse or no horse. I expect he's got some kind of nag hidden away somewhere, but he'll have no stomach for trouble, especially if it means any risk to his own skin."

Steven took the mare's reins and prepared to mount again. "He'll have trouble from me if he won't come," he said grimly. "Where do I find this cowardly physician?"

Two

"Let me speak with my commander in the guardroom here," suggested Walter, "and I'll take you to the physician myself. It's no more than a step, and near my own house. You can have a bite to eat with me while the man gets himself ready."

"That's kind of you, Wat, but I've no time to lose. Toby takes a poor view of Sir Thomas's chances."

"Toby was always one to think the worst," Walter reminded him. "And you'll have to wait for M'sieur Arouen," he added, giving the French name its correct pronunciation. "He'll not get ready the quicker for having you standing over him breathing fire, however you may feel about it."

Uneasy at the delay but unable to think of any alternative, Steven led the mare to drink at the stone water trough built into one corner of the courtyard, while his friend spoke to his commanding officer.

Walter was swift with his errand, and within a few minutes the two men were walking briskly along the street towards the centre of the town, leading the mare. In spite of his anxiety, Steven looked about him with interest. The town was built on a rectangular site, wider from east to west, with a regular grid of intersecting streets. Since King Edward had made no attempt to destroy it during the siege, preferring instead to starve its inhabitants into surrender, the place was in a reasonable state of repair. Many of the houses Steven passed looked empty, however, some still bearing the signs of forced entry during the looting that followed the surrender. Comparatively few seemed inhabited, but those that did were freshly painted.

"Did the townsfolk flee, at the end?" he asked. His information on last year's siege was sketchy, but they'd heard that Calais was now an English town full of English settlers as well as a garrison, and likely to stay that way.

"Most did," Walter replied. "But the king has encouraged English folk to come over and settle here, and there's talk of having a Calais Staple to handle all the wool trade."

Steven pricked up his ears at this. A Calais Staple would reduce wool merchants' dependence on Continental buyers and give them better profits. His family's prosperity was based on wool and what served the merchants would benefit them.

"He means to hold Calais at all costs, then."

Walter nodded. "It looks that way. We need a bridgehead if we're to get anywhere in this war. The garrison here is large for a town this size, and many of the houses are used by men at arms. The rest are camped at the castle." He pointed towards the north-west corner of the town, where Steven could see the outline of the keep above the house roofs.

"And where is this physician of yours?" he asked. They had already been walking for several minutes, and he was growing anxious. The morning hours were passing and Sir Thomas might be dying for want of treatment.

Walter pointed to a house on the corner of a street a few paces ahead of them. "There's his lodging. And mine is across the road there, just before it."

He knocked boldly on the door of the physician's house with the hilt of his sword, and spoke loudly in a foreign tongue that Steven assumed must be Artois French, the local dialect. He looked at his friend in surprise. How had Wat learned so much local French in less than a year?

After a moment, a torrent of words in the same dialect came floating back.

"He's in bed," Walter told Steven, with the hint of a smile. "And doesn't want to be disturbed. Stale drunk, belike."

"Tell him to get up. I'll not wait on his convenience while my lord is grievous sick."

Walter grinned and relayed something of these sentiments to those within. The door opened and a man confronted them, broad and squat with powerful shoulders and thinning unkempt hair, a servant, from his dress. His face wore a surly expression and after a brief colloquy with Walter of which Steven could make nothing, he turned his back on them rudely and stalked off, muttering, into the interior of the building.

Walter touched Steven's arm. "Come across the way and break your fast with me while M'sieur Arouen makes himself ready. The servant understands the urgency, however little he may wish to exert himself. He will pass the message on, and his master will not lightly refuse the chance of a fee."

Steven followed his friend into a pleasant cob-built house a few paces across the street, and was surprised to find himself being greeted by a small, slender woman with a wife's coif over her hair. From the way her eyes sparkled when she saw Walter, and her murmur of pleasure, it was clear their relationship was warmer than that of master and housekeeper.

"My wife, Giselle," Walter enlightened him, and introduced him to her more formally, in English. "This is Steven, an old friend of mine from my younger days, *ma chérie*. We grew up on the same manor—I was esquire to the son of his lord, and we boys played together." This was, Steven thought, a delicate way of informing her that though he was not of the same social standing as her husband, he was acceptable as an equal in friendship nonetheless.

Steven bowed to her as gracefully as he could, uncomfortably conscious of his stained and travel-worn attire and his clumsy manners. He wondered how Wat had come to marry a Frenchwoman but wasn't sure whether it was appropriate to ask.

"*Venez*," she said at once. "Come inside and have some food. Walter has been on duty and he will be ver' hungry, I know. He is always hungry," she added, her eyes twinkling.

Steven bowed again, and was ushered into a long room set up with trestle tables and benches. Servants were already laying a meal at one end, and at their mistress's command they set an extra place for him.

Walter explained to his wife the need for haste, and sent a servant to keep an eye out for the physician and take steps to hasten him if he did not appear. He poured ale for Steven and a maidservant brought them a bowl of water in which to wash their hands. For a garrison town, Steven thought, it was all very civilised.

"Where is Sir Richard?" he asked, sitting down and accepting a trencher of bread and a slice of beef. "Is he in Calais?" By all the conventions, Sir Thomas's son ought to be fulfilling the family obligations to fight for the king, and if he had been at the siege the year before, he might still form part of the garrison, like Wat. If so, it would be politic to get word to him of his father's sickness.

"Nay, he went home six months and more ago," said Walter. "He was here briefly near the end of the siege, but he's taken a wife while you've been away and the children are young. She is ailing, so she doesn't like him being from home too much." The words were said compassionately, and held no trace of criticism, but Steven remembered Richard from their youth and thought it quite likely that his wife and her ailments were a handy excuse to avoid danger. The son didn't have his father's love of action, nor his soldierly instincts.

"So he sent you to the muster in his stead."

Walter nodded. "But I stayed on my own behalf. I was knighted at Creçy, by the king himself."

Steven drew in a breath. "Well done," he said. "Sir Walter."

"Nay, just 'Wat' will do well enough still, between friends."

Steven said nothing, but thought their friendship even more unequal than before. "Your lady is French, I think?" he said, turning the subject into what he hoped were more pleasant channels. "How came you to take an enemy to wife?" He laughed at his own joke, and bit into his trencher hungrily, reaching for his mug to wash the mouthful down with ale.

Walter's face darkened. "Do not speak of her that way, I pray you, Steven. She is an Englishwoman now."

Steven made haste to apologise. "It was meant as a jest, no more."

"Her father was one of the townsfolk here," Walter explained. "This is his house, where she grew up. He had to go, with all the rest, leaving his belongings behind. She was only allowed to stay because of me, and I had to beg her hand in marriage as a boon from the king himself."

Steven saw that Walter's high favour with royalty had stood him—and Giselle—in good stead. "She must feel her father's absence," he said, awkwardly. "What happened?"

"They surrendered at their last gasp, when King Philip failed to send help. The citizens held out as long as they could, and suffered loss as a result." He paused for a moment, shaking his head in disbelief. "Philip never tried to raise the siege in all the time we were here. We met with skirmishers, but no full assault. They deserve his bounty now. He has found homes for them all in towns across this region, so they say, out of guilt perhaps. None are to be punished for surrendering the town."

Steven chewed his beef thoughtfully. It must have been a strange end to the siege, with no fighting, only the abject surrender of townsfolk betrayed by those who should have come to their aid. For the first time since he had heard of the victory, he was glad he hadn't been there.

"That physician," said Walter, getting up from the table, "should have been here by now. I'll go and roust him out for you."

"Thanks," said Steven. "'Twill be a slow journey back, I fear. We'll have to fight our way through the crowd that's fleeing in this direction in the hope of succour."

"The sentries won't let them near here. We've enough to deal with to keep the town in English hands without taking in folk from the Flemish countryside. As you say, that may cause some chaos on the road."

"The French villagers won't be in much better case," Steven observed. "They have a choice: they can welcome French forces with open arms and risk being punished for their dealings with the enemy this last year, or they can throw in their lot with the English conquerors and save their skins, at least for now. Or they can run away until things settle down again."

Walter nodded. "Your mare will be at the door directly, and M'sieur Arouen will follow, if I have any say in the matter."

He strode out into the street and Steven heard his voice shouting orders, its volume fading slightly as he crossed the road to the physician's house. Steven drained the last of his ale and wiped his mouth with his hand. He thanked the lady Giselle for his meal as best he might, his rough country voice framing the courtesies awkwardly.

Outside, Alan's mare was standing waiting for him, stamping her foot and looking, to his relief, refreshed and ready to carry him some further miles at speed. Across the road, Walter was stooping in the low archway of the door to the physician's house. After a moment, he ushered into the road a small, thin, expensively clad man with a pointed black beard and carefully combed hair, who was protesting volubly at their intrusion.

"Have you told him we need haste?" asked Steven quickly. "How can I speak with him if he has no English?"

"I can speak your uncouth tongue," the physician told him in a thick Artois accent. "An I must. Have you a horse for me?" He looked at the mare hopefully.

Steven opened his mouth to respond angrily, but Walter laid a hand on his arm. "Let M'sieur Arouen ride the mare, Steven—she'll go faster under him. I will mount you from my own stables." He gave a sharp command to the groom who was holding the mare's head, and the man ran back into the stableyard behind the house.

Steven stammered his thanks at this generosity, and wondered what kind of mount he would be offered. Neither a heavy cart-puller nor a spirited war horse would be a welcome mount on this errand. But he need not have worried. A sturdy but tall cob appeared within a surprisingly short time, and the groom held it while Steven mounted. The physician was already aboard the mare, and in a few minutes they were ready to start.

The beginning of their journey was accompanied by a continuous litany of complaints from the physician, a comprehensive range of grievances that included the unseemly haste of their departure, his unnecessary summons to what was no doubt a simple case of fever, the risk of being captured by the French, and demands that his fee be paid before he approached the patient. Steven ignored it all, and concentrated on persuading his horse to keep up with the mare, who was making good speed along the causeway towards Gravelines under the physician's light weight.

The road was still busy with westward-bound traffic but there was less sign of panic, which was encouraging. It looked as though the French had followed their usual practice of beginning an attack and then melting away rather than pressing it home. He breathed a sigh of relief as they neared the inn at Marck without encountering any sign of the enemy. With luck, Sir Thomas could be attended to without further delay, if the physician turned out to be a worthy member of his profession, that was. Steven was not impressed with what he had seen so far, but to his credit the man had come with him, however reluctantly, and surely any medical help was better than none.

But when they reached the inn, the yard was empty and silent, deserted by its owners and their customers alike. Steven jumped down from his borrowed horse and ran to the door of Sir Thomas's chamber. He flung it open and found Alan and Toby kneeling beside the bed where their lord lay still, hands composed across his breast in the final peace of death. His fever had run too high for his weary body to overcome, and the rescue party had come in vain.

Steven stood stock still, unable to speak.

Alan got up from his knees and went over to him. "Tis all over," he said. "An hour gone, he died. We could do nothing more."

"Damn that cursed physician and his delays," said Steven in disgust. "May he rot in hell."

Alan looked up, surprised at the violence of his companion's reaction. "Tis scarcely noon," he pointed out. "You could not have come sooner."

Steven shook his head, his mind full of regrets. He might be blaming the physician aloud, but he knew that if he hadn't stopped to break his fast with Walter, they could have reached the inn earlier, even if it had meant dragging the physician out in his night attire. He remembered with shame his enjoyment of their meeting, when he should have thought of nothing but his lord's need.

He flung out into the innyard, angry and frustrated with the turn of events. He was grieved at his lord's death, certainly, but sick at heart also for his own loss, for Sir Thomas had promised him freedom from the bonds of villeinage as a reward for five years' loyal service. All was to win again, and who knew what Sir Richard would be willing to do for him when they arrived home?

The physician was still astride Alan's mare, turning her this way and that as he tried to catch the horse that Steven had abandoned in his haste, and looking extremely harassed. Steven cornered the cob by the stalls and led it over to the physician. "You may ride back into Calais on Sir Walter's horse, and return it to him with my compliments. I will take the mare now."

The other man bristled at this ingratitude. "I am not your lackey," he said, his anger thickening the heavy Artois accent and making his words all but incomprehensible. "Where is the patient I was summoned to help?" He held out his hand, palm uppermost. "And first I will have my fee."

"My lord is dead," Steven told him. "We were too long on the road, or rather waiting for you to ready yourself to come with me. You have not done anything to earn a fee."

"Bah! A vain errand, then, and I'll be paid for my time and the danger you brought me into, or I'll take this mare and sell her in Calais market."

It was probably an empty threat, and Steven knew Walter would stop the sale if he got wind of it. But even so it made him pause, for the mare was not his to lose.

Behind him a voice spoke up calmly. "Sir, the mare is mine, loaned only to my companion here for his errand of mercy." Alan had emerged from the sick-room in Steven's wake, and overheard their exchange.

He looked disapprovingly at the stranger. "You certainly have no right to sell her," he told the physician, "but we will pay you for your time and the wasted journey. Let me have the mare now, and I will find you something to eat and drink before you return."

"You may ride Sir Walter's horse back to Calais for him, if you wish, and save us the trouble," added Steven.

"Or if you prefer," suggested Alan, "you may wait for us to ready Sir Thomas's body for travel, and we will accompany you."

Steven stared at Alan. "For travel?" he repeated.

"We thought to take Sir Thomas home for burial," Alan told him. "Toby reckons our master would not want to be buried here in France where he's unknown, but in his own chantry chapel that they were building for him when we left home. Tis surely the truth."

Steven nodded slowly.

"The innkeeper and his wife have fled," went on Alan, "and so have their servants, but we will find a bier and Toby's horse or yours can draw it, as far as Calais at least. There we must be able to find passage across the Channel, surely?"

Steven shook his head. "I don't know. Sir Walter—that's Wat Chesil from home, Alan, knighted at Crecy. I met him by the gate into the town and he found me this...this apology for a physician." He indicated the dapper Frenchman contemptuously. "Wat will know what we should do. The town must be supplied from the sea, so there will be ships going back near-empty to England that can bear us."

Alan took the mare's reins. "Come, sir," he said to the outraged physician. "It is a fair offer. Await our escort, or go alone."

"Never fear but we will check with Sir Walter that his horse comes safe home," added Steven. There was a hint of menace in his final words, and the physician saw that he had no choice but to dismount and hand over the mare to her rightful owner.

"I will await your escort," he replied stiffly. "There is safety in numbers, they say, though as a Frenchman I do not, of course, fear my own countrymen. Where is the innkeeper? I must find wine and bread if I am to keep body and soul together. You were in such haste to set out that I did not have the chance to break my fast."

"Pray go into the inn parlour, sir," Alan said, ignoring Steven's expostulations. "The innkeeper and his staff have fled your countrymen's approach, but there is food aplenty in the larder. Let me attend to the needs of these horses, and I will come and serve you."

Mollified, the physician made his way into the inn.

Steven laughed suddenly, a short mirthless guffaw of derision. "Tis no wonder he goes in fear of the French," he said to Alan, "whatever he may say to the contrary. He's living in Calais under English protection and offering the new townsfolk his services. That won't suit French notions of loyalty, I'll be bound."

"You'd do better to save your breath, my friend. Go and bear vigil with Toby over my lord's body. He is in need of our prayers."

Steven looked questioningly at him. Every man needed the prayers of the faithful in the hours after his death, that was well known. Why was Alan making such a point of it?

"My Lord had no time to make more than a brief confession to the priest from the village. He had the viaticum, but only at his last breath, and in much distress, for the priest spoke no English. He seemed anxious, though neither Toby nor I could think of any mortal sin he was guilty of."

"Who knows what burdens another man's soul?" growled Steven.

Alan shrugged. "I reckon my lord now needs all the prayers we can give him, at least until his chantry priest is able to take over the task. I will deal with this Frenchie, and while he eats, we will get ready to leave."

Not a 'good death' then for Sir Thomas, and lacking even the comfort of an English priest, never mind a notary to write his will. Without a word, Steven turned on his heel and went into his lord's chamber.

Three

As they rode northwards through the sodden English countryside, Steven was aroused from his unhappy recollections by a shout from Alan, who had ridden ahead a few paces, impatient with the slow progress made by the tumbril.

"There's Winchester! I can see the cathedral tower!"

Steven ignored him and pulled the hood of his cloak further over his head to keep out the rain.

"There'll be pies to buy in the city. My stomach's rumbling, I don't know about yours."

"Never mind pies," growled Steven. "I could do with getting out of this downpour. Can we persuade Toby to stop at St Cross, d'you reckon?"

They both looked towards the third member of the party. Toby seemed impervious to the discomforts of rain and chill, all his attention focused on the body of his dead master. Trudging on foot close beside his master's coffin, his head bowed against the rain, he watched the precious cart attentively in case its tattered covering should slip or a wheel become mired. Grey-haired and tight-lipped, his whole demeanour spoke of his grief at the loss of Sir Thomas, in whose service he had spent most of his life.

"Toby!" Alan called to him, as they came under the shadow of Twyford Down across the river, with the mound of St Catherine's Hill beyond. "St Cross will give us the wayfarers' dole, surely? And we can still get home before nightfall."

"If the gates are open as we pass, we could take the dole," Toby agreed, removing his gaze for a moment from the tumbril. "But they couldn't accommodate us. St Cross is a hospice for old men, not a pilgrim's inn."

"Hyde Abbey, then, if you think we should rest for the night," offered Alan, thinking the older man might be tired. "Tis only a step off our route."

Toby shook his head. "Nay. We must press on."

In truth, he doubted whether it would be possible to reach home today, at their current rate of progress, but the dogged attempt to do so suited his mood. Sir Thomas had died so close to home, after all the distant Eastern lands they'd seen in their travels. Another day or two and they would have been across the Channel on English soil, within easy reach of home.

Toby took no comfort, either, from the paltry nature of the funerary cortege they had been able to provide for their lord. It was a shamefully down-at-heel affair, the tumbril drawn by a single horse and covered with a threadbare black cloth. Five years of holy soldiering had worn out Sir Thomas's gear as well as himself, and they had had to sell his best horse to help pay the Calais tolls and buy their sea-passage to Southampton. Even the coffin was of inferior wood and workmanship, knocked up in a hurry to make the journey home. In the face of dire rumours of pestilence in northern France not far to the west of them, they had not dared to wait for funds to arrive from Sir Thomas's manor to bring him back in style. Instead they had caulked the seams of the coffin, wrapped it tightly in oiled cloth, and hurried to make the sea journey—bier, horses and all–– leaving behind (they hoped) the unhealthy air of the Continent that bred the pestilence. Necessary, perhaps, in the circumstances, Toby sniffed to himself. But not fitting. Not how things should have been done. He only hoped they would not incur censure from the family when they arrived home.

The gates of St Cross Hospital stood open, and Alan requested the wayfarers' dole from the porter's lodge. There was no question that, as travellers, they were entitled to it, though the porter insisted that each of them come to the lodge individually to receive the horn of ale and morsel of bread.

Alan had some difficulty in persuading Toby to leave the tumbril in his care while he went for his share. "You're on foot," he reminded the older man, ignoring the fact that it had been Toby's own choice to walk beside the bier the whole way. "If we're to reach home today, we don't want you to founder on the way. Tis little enough they're handing out, and not too willingly given either. No one will steal Sir Thomas's body while you fetch some food, and I promise I will keep guard. Be sensible, man!"

With bad grace and a frowning brow, Toby allowed himself to be steered in the direction of the lodge. He drank quickly from the horn and came back to the tumbril with his bread in his hand. When Steven had partaken of the dole, too, they moved on. A small queue of wayfarers was forming at the lodge and Alan wondered how the porter was able to distinguish genuine travellers from hungry Winchester folk trying their luck. But no doubt anyone local who came more than once or twice would be noticed.

They walked in single file through the south gate of the city and along the narrow streets. It was unusually quiet, and no piemen offered them food along the way, as Alan had anticipated. Few inhabitants of any kind were abroad; those they saw doffed their caps respectfully and made the sign of the cross as the tumbril and its contents passed them, but no one made any attempt to converse with them.

They passed the end of the cathedral close, where the new west wall of the great building was covered in scaffolding, the masons and their labourers perched high above the ground as they hurried to cement in the last stones before the summer building season came to an end. It was the only evidence of conspicuous expenditure they had seen: the streets showed signs of neglect, with grass growing between the cobbles in places. Clearly the city's merchants had been hit hard by the heavy taxes levied by the king for the war. Wool exports were always an easy target for taxation, though wool levies had to be agreed formally by parliament. In view of King Edward's military successes at Crecy and Calais and his consequent national popularity, no doubt parliament would refuse him nothing and even the taxed would pay up with alacrity.

They crossed the High Street into the maze of streets where once the city's Jews had lived and kept shop, before an earlier King Edward expelled them from England. Alan looked about him curiously, but it was more than fifty years since any Jew had lived in the Quarter, and English settlers had replaced them long ago.

"Whither away, masters?" asked a bold damsel in a canary-coloured dress, eyeing Alan with more than a little interest. Her clothes were gaudy and expensive, but he thought she was not the lady she appeared.

Toby looked up angrily, and Alan made speed to answer her before the older man could speak. "We're bound north, mistress. My master died near Calais a sennight past and we are taking him home for burial."

She blanched. "Ye've come from France? Please God you have not brought the pestilence with you."

Alan pulled up his horse for a moment, letting the others move ahead of him. "There was no pestilence in Calais when we left."

"Calais!" she said. "They say that's where it came from."

"What d'ye mean, came from? There's none in England surely?"

She crossed herself. "We've heard there is great suffering in Dorset. We fear it may come here soon." She gestured at the empty streets. "People stay in their homes and wait."

Alan glared at her angrily. "I don't believe it."

"Travellers brought it," she retorted. "By ship, or so I'm told."

Alan shrugged. "Believe idle rumour if you will, mistress. I prefer to believe God protects England." He touched his heel to his horse and trotted on.

"You should not bandy words with such a trollop," Toby said to him when he rejoined them. "Tis not fitting on a holy journey, especially in the presence of our master's coffin." He crossed himself.

Alan scowled. "She was fearful of the pestilence. Tis fitting enough to put a woman's fears to rest."

"Especially a pretty one," Steven teased him, aroused for a moment from his abstraction.

Toby's face condemned them both, but Alan grinned as they moved on slowly past the walls of Hyde Abbey and turned north-eastwards along the old road which once had carried troops and goods bound for the Roman town of Calleva. Though it was not the most direct route they could have taken, the road was straight and the ancient paving still gave grip, in the wet and slippery conditions, to their underpowered tumbril and its horse. In spite of the incessant rain that had accompanied them across the Channel in a chartered vessel only just big enough for the tumbril and their horses, and then up the dilapidated Roman road that led northwards from Southampton, Alan was still anticipating with relish their homecoming to familiar haunts and families who had probably given them up for dead.

"'Twould have been very different," he commented to Steven, "an we had come home with the king after they took Calais."

"Aye," agreed Steven. It was a pity Sir Thomas had taken it into his head to go on pilgrimage in 1343, before ever King Edward had set out for France to pursue his claims to the throne of that country. He too wished they had been part of the great army that had followed King Edward and his iconic young son to war in 1346, rampaging across northern France to lay siege to Calais, though the siege itself seemed to have been a tawdry business, as he had heard from Wat.

On the other hand, only knights and nobles were enriched by war. Ordinary soldiers—even much-prized archers like Alan who could lose ten arrows a minute and hit the target at the butts every time—more often came back maimed, and sometimes penniless into the bargain. Their wages might be left unpaid if funds ran short, or at worst, if their lord were captured or killed, they might be abandoned to fend for themselves in France. At least he and Alan and Toby were coming home safe.

Under the grey English skies, the light began to fail early, and Toby called a halt at an inn serving the junction of two roads. This time it was Alan who was keen to keep going.

"God's bones, man, we're nearly home," he protested. "I thought you were in a hurry. Don't you want to sleep in your own bed tonight instead of sharing one with all the fleas in Christendom?"

"'Tis a pilgrim's inn," Toby reminded him. "The beds will be clean."

Alan snorted, thinking of the monastic hostelry near Southampton that had enjoyed their custom the night before, where the beds had been anything but clean and the welcome less warm than might have been expected for the mortal remains of a crusading pilgrim. He waited for Steven to contribute his opinion, but his companion merely shrugged and got down from his horse.

"'Twill be dark soon," he observed.

"Nay, Steven," Alan pursued. "With only three miles further to go? There's another hour's light, at least, if we press on."

"Three miles is far enough, especially with no moon and the rain falling. You may think you know the lanes from here like the back of your hand, Alan, but tis tempting Providence to travel them in the half-dark if we don't have to. Besides, I'd sooner arrive home in the forenoon to a welcome, not in the dusk when most folk will have closed their doors for the night."

He had his own reasons for preferring to put off their homecoming for one more day, but he wasn't about to share them with Alan while Toby was listening. As they had neared home, his regrets had grown that he had had to leave Calais. Archers and men-at-arms were needed in a town placed almost permanently on a war footing. But he had agreed with Alan that they couldn't leave Toby to take their master's coffin home alone, and in any case his own service to Sir Thomas would not be at an end until they reached Northchurch.

Alan sighed. "Very well." He slid down from his horse and began negotiations with the innkeeper, who had bustled out to greet the prospect of business.

"Two beds," he demanded briskly. "And space for the tumbril in your barn. One of us will guard the body overnight."

The innkeeper's enthusiasm abated somewhat. He clearly did not recognize his guests, which was perhaps not surprising after five years' absence. He crossed himself. "Whither bound, my masters?" The respect in his voice due to a coffin was mixed with consternation.

"Northchurch," Steven answered tersely. "We accompany the body of Sir Thomas LeClerc on his final journey home."

The innkeeper bowed. That name was clearly known to him. "I will clear a space for the tumbril in the barn," he said. "I have nowhere suitable for a coffin within. You will wish to stay near your master, I expect. There are pallets in the room above." He seemed to have a superstitious dread of allowing even the dead man's attendants inside the house.

Steven was outraged. "We'll have a bite and some ale inside first."

The innkeeper swallowed hard. "I will prepare some bread and cheese," he offered, not altogether hospitably, and scuttled off into the house.

Steven scowled. "Call it a pilgrim's inn!" he exclaimed as they brought the tumbril under cover. "They can't even offer us beds in the house!"

Alan shrugged. "Fear drives out hospitality," he suggested. "Pestilence or no."

Steven did not reply, but the memory of the Winchester woman's words hung in the air between them. Could the pestilence truly have arrived in England?

Toby had ignored the interchange between his two companions. "I'll bed meself down in the straw here beside the bier," he told them. "You can bring me out a bite to eat when you have your own. Mind you don't drink too much," he added. "And no whoring."

Steven scowled. Whoring was the last thing on his mind, even if chance had offered, though a few pints of home-brewed would go down nicely. He tried to remember whether he'd visited this inn before, and what the ale was like.

Alan patted Toby's shoulder affectionately. "I'll bring you some ale and a pie," he said. "You can give your old legs a rest for a bit."

Toby bristled. Old legs, indeed! It was true he had felt his years on occasion during their journey, especially after they had arrived in England and he had felt obliged to walk while the others rode. But even mounted, five years of hard travel had seemed long indeed to a man who was middle-aged to begin with. No doubt his master had felt the same, though he had given himself no rest. Now he was dead. Toby shivered.

He sat down on a straw bale and wondered what the LeClerc family would find for him to do when he got home. Sir Thomas's son Richard had his own bodyservant and wouldn't want another. But Toby was too old to take on manual labour in the fields or the mill, and he had no family to support him. His wife had died in childbirth when they were both young, along with her baby, and he had never remarried. All his devotion had been given to Sir Thomas, and without his master, he felt lost and directionless.

He pulled the coffin covering straight again, then bent to untie his bootlaces and stretch his aching feet. There were holes in his stockings, he saw, and the shoe-leather was wearing so badly that soon there would be holes in the boots, too. They were his last pair. No matter; he would be able to buy new ones when he got home, and hose to go with them. His purse just now was empty, for like the others, he had been paid no wages for the last few weeks, and the three of them had had to pool what resources they had to get home. But Sir Richard would pay him what was owed, even if there wasn't any work for him at the castle.

Inside the inn, having supplied Toby with his promised meal, Steven and Alan settled down with ale and dice to while away the evening, a proceeding to which fortunately the innkeeper made no objection. Neither gave much thought to the rumour they had heard of folk suffering from the pestilence in nearby Dorset. They had encountered plenty of scare stories of one kind or another on their journey and they were prepared to discount this one, for wild rumours were common in an age where reliable reports were few and far between. Yet the possibility had unsettled them, and they were glad to find diversion from their thoughts in the roll of the dice.

"Why did Sir Thomas take us so far, think you?" said Alan, as they played. The journey had been ostensibly an individual pilgrimage, blessed by the parish priest with much pious fanfare, and Sir Thomas's coat of mail was adorned with a crusader's surcoat, red cross on a white ground, but Alan knew the adventuring they had actually experienced had not always been in sympathy with that aim. And in any case, why should Sir Thomas, not especially known for his piety, have decided to go on a solitary pilgrim crusade with all the trimmings rather than serving his king in France like most men of his age and rank?

Steven directed a hard, shrewd glance at him from beneath his eyebrows. "Why d'you ask that now?"

Alan shrugged. "No reason. Just that I've often wondered. His wife died a few months before, didn't she? Mayhap that upset him so much that he couldn't stay at home."

Steven grunted. "Could be. Who knows?"

Alan opened his mouth to pursue the subject, because Steven was older than he, and might have been trusted with the secret, if secret there was. But then he thought better of it. Toby would know more, for he'd been Sir Thomas's bodyservant for years. He'd pump Toby another day, and hope to get some answers.

"You owe me," Steven said half an hour later, gathering up the dice with an expert hand and reaching for his mug of ale.

"Too much," agreed Alan ruefully. He turned out his pocket and grimaced. "I've lost count. You'll have to play me for love if you want to go on."

"I'll play you for your horse," Steven offered. He didn't particularly want the mare, but she was the only thing of any value Alan possessed, and he wanted to go on gaming.

"Nay, she's not up to your weight."

"If I win her, she can be a wedding gift for Alys."

"And what would Alys do with her? She's no fine lady to go riding abroad."

Steven shrugged.

Alan looked at him speculatively. "You're truly going to wed Alys when we get home? I began to wonder whether you might leave the maid a-sighing forever."

Steven laughed shortly. "Alys a-sighing? You're far off, man, and you know it."

"Yet she's waiting for you, I'll be bound."

Steven sighed. "Aye, she'll be waiting. She'll always be waiting, however long I take to come home. Her father and mine agreed to the bargain and she'll stick to it. Nothing else she can do, poor maid, perhaps," he added after a moment.

"We've been gone five years," Alan reminded him. "Maybe she'll have tired of waiting and married the miller. He had an eye for her even when she was a little girl with her skirts kilted."

Steven smiled rather sourly. "That old man? Nay, she'll be waiting." He held out the dice. "Will you throw?"

Alan shook his head. "And risk the mare, with my luck tonight? Reckon I'll stay with my debts as they are. I'll pay you when we get home. Tis getting late and I'm for my bed."

Steven shrugged. The money wasn't particularly important to him, but he would have liked to have gone on dicing to keep the thoughts at bay. He didn't relish the prospects ahead of him when they reached home.

He had agreed to the marriage contract with Alys before he left to journey East with Sir Thomas, and they were to marry when he returned. His father had had it all worked out. Their own prosperous wool business would be enhanced by an alliance with the village weaver, for local sales attracted no tax, and cloth exports bore much lighter duties than wool. The grazier would give Alys's father a discount on his purchases of wool as part of the deal. How better to make that alliance a permanent one than to marry his eldest son Steven to the weaver's eldest daughter Alys? The girl was not ill-favoured, even if not exactly a beauty, and it was a good match, especially as the weaver had no sons and Alys and her younger sister would inherit his property.

It all made sound economic sense, and Sir Thomas himself had approved it. Indeed, Sir Thomas's promise of freedom on their return had been made partly as a marriage gift to the couple, and a valuable one, at that. There were no limits on what they might achieve as free tenants rather than churls, without fear of interference from their lord. If there had been a will, Sir Richard would have to follow its instructions. But most men left will-making till their end was in sight, and Sir Thomas's end had come all too suddenly.

Steven wondered, watching the firelight flicker on the beams, whether the failure of his hopes of freedom would make a difference to the marriage plans. It had been a fair bargain when it had been made, but in the circumstances, would Alys's father change his mind? He wouldn't want his daughter marrying a villein, when he'd been promised to her as a free man.

He smiled suddenly. If Weaver John couldn't or wouldn't keep the bargain, he, Steven, would be free to look around him for someone else. There was no harm in Alys, but she aroused no longing in him to take her to wife. There must be better fish to fry.

Seeing his companion's thoughts had turned inward again, Alan clapped him on the shoulder briefly and went away. He knew without being told what was biting his companion, but to him a marriage arranged on the grounds of family economics seemed a small price to pay for the prosperous inheritance Steven looked set to enjoy. Alan's free status availed him little when his family were always scraping the barrel to make ends meet. Their landholding was small, much of it marginal land that had been brought into cultivation when famine stalked the land. The soil was poor, exhausted by years of use, its yield dropping until these days it was almost uneconomic to till. No one of Alys's economic and social standing would be looking at him as a prospective husband, free or unfree.

Not that he envied Steven Alys, whom he remembered as a prosy little thing, competent and brisk and independent. Even as a young girl with her hair just plaited, she had a habit of looking at a man with a kind of lofty disapproval that did nothing for his self-esteem. Spoilt, he'd thought her, with parents who indulged her and no brothers to curb her pride, only a younger sister whose admiration was as uncritical as it was boundless. Brown-complexioned, too, and slightly pock-marked about the face, as so many were. Nay, Steven was welcome to her.

In spite of his family's poverty, Alan was convinced that he would make his fortune, somehow or another. He was a more sanguine individual than Steven, exuberant when times were good, cheerful and uncomplaining when they were not. His handsome face, good temper and pleasant voice had gained him the best of the comforts and pleasures on offer on their travels, and he had come back richer than he went out, in goods if not in gold. His luck would hold, when they returned.

In the attic above the barn, he found three straw pallets stacked in a corner, ready for use. He pulled one out and shook it. Dust rose from it, but mercifully no insects. He pummelled it into a more comfortable shape and laid it down well away from the draughty window opening, then stripped off his tunic and folded it up as a pillow. He pushed his boots into the corner of the room, under the eaves, and lay down, casting his cloak over him. Hands behind his head, he stared up at the sloping beams above him and went peacefully to sleep. When Steven came up an hour later and laid his own pallet against the other wall, Alan never stirred. Like all seasoned campaigners, he had learned to sleep, and to sleep deeply, whenever chance allowed.

Four

"Have you a meal prepared, Alys?" called Ellen from the doorway. Her tone was querulous and her expression anxious. "Your father will finish work soon and be hungry."

"Yes, Mother," replied Alys. She spoke patiently, for her mother responded badly to any sign of annoyance. But the patient words were followed by a covert sigh. Her father had finished his last piece of work more than a year ago, and had been buried in the churchyard for ten months, but her mother lived in a fantasy world where these events had never happened. "The meal will be ready soon and I will serve you your share here at the table."

Her mother nodded, her expression relaxing into its normal vacancy. She liked to sit outside the cottage door in fine weather, distaff in hand, and watch her neighbours as they went about their business, but Alys didn't think she took much notice of their movements anymore. All her thoughts were turned inward to a happiness that was past.

Alys shrugged and went to stir the pottage, made of pease and a few vegetables and seasoned with a little mutton and herbs, which was bubbling by the fire. She dipped the ladle into the pot to taste it, then took some bowls down from the shelf and put them to warm in the big hearth. It was hot beside the fire, and she pushed the damp tendrils of hair off her forehead as she hung the ladle back on its hook. James, the hired labourer, would have to be paid today, as he was at the end of every week, as well as being entitled to food at their table and a place by the fire in the evening. He would arrive soon and he really would be hungry after a morning's work ploughing. Probably hungry for attention, as well. She was as distant with him as she reasonably could be, but it was becoming increasingly difficult to ignore his advances. Even if she were not already long promised to another man, she would consider him a poor match. She shuddered when she thought of being forced to accept the hand of such a man. He was strong and healthy, it was true, but also uncouth and stupid, and she felt she would rather die than wed him. But her father's looms lay idle, and with not much income coming in, and that mainly from her sister's earnings in service at the castle, their resources were dwindling. Would the betrothal her father had set such store by five years ago survive the downturn in their financial circumstances that had resulted from his death?

Her eyes strayed to the big linen press in the corner of the living kitchen. Deep at the bottom of it, in a small locked casket, lay the money to pay her dowry. Without that money, she was afraid Steven might repudiate the arrangement, especially now that the economic advantage his family had thought to gain by the alliance had died with her father. His parents had always been kind to her, and since her father's death had treated her no differently than before. But Steven was not a child. It would be his decision to make, whatever his father thought. Somehow, in spite of the difficulties, she must preserve her small stock of coins against his return.

She turned at the sound of a step at the door, and her mother's murmured greeting.

"Alys!" It was her sister's voice. "Lady Eleanor has gone to visit Sister Margery, so I have an hour free."

They exchanged a warm embrace. Rosamund always came in to visit them when she had an hour or two to spare from her duties, and her visits always cheered her sister.

Alys pushed her to arm's length gently. "How are you? We haven't seen you in days."

"I'm well," Rosamund replied, but Alys was not altogether convinced. There was a bloom on her sister's fair skin, it was true, and her flaxen hair, plaited into a coil beneath her headdress, was looking soft and silky as it always did. But there was a guarded look in her blue eyes, which usually sparkled with humour and fun. Something had happened to upset her.

Alys knew better than to challenge her openly. With her mother listening—as much as she listened to anything in the real world these days—Rosamund wouldn't open her heart to her sister.

"I have an errand to the mill," she said instead. "There's time before dinner if I go now. Will you come and bear me company?"

"As long as you don't want me to carry the flour home," said Rosamund, smiling.

Alys laughed. "James fetched it yesterday. But I need to pay the miller what I owe."

She saw Rosamund looking at her curiously, clearly wondering whether the debt was a large one.

"Nay, tis only for this last bag," Alys assured her. "I wouldn't trust James to carry the money——he might spend it at Widow Brewer's on the way." She gathered up the small bag of coin from the cupboard and put it in a scrip at her waist.

"Mother," she said to Ellen as they reached the door. "Ros and I are going up to the mill. The meal should be ready when I come back. If James returns before I do, ask him to cut up some wood for the fire while he waits." She didn't want James wasting his time, or, worse still, going off to drink ale with his friends, as had happened once or twice recently, leaving the afternoon's work undone as a result.

Whether her mother would give James the message was uncertain, but she had done her best. Perhaps it was unwise to go and leave her in charge of the house, yet the temptation of a walk with Rosamund was too great to resist. Besides, the miller might not be willing to let James bring home the flour sack next time ahead of payment. The money was owed to their lord, and would be passed on to his bailiff by the miller, but the latter was always strict about payment on his master's behalf.

She led the way down the narrow path that skirted the outbuildings and led on to the lane. The rain had stopped, she was glad to see. There had been more than enough of it this summer.

"Is Matt Miller causing you trouble?" asked Rosamund as they walked along briskly, enjoying the unaccustomed sunshine. The unpaved lane was muddy and had been churned up by the hooves of oxen and the wheels of the carts they drew, but the women picked their way along the edge where the going was better, lifting their skirts carefully to keep them clean.

Alys shook her head. "No. But he seems to think he might have a chance with me, if Steven...if Steven doesn't come back soon." She swallowed. "Tis difficult to manage everything, I can't pretend otherwise. Mother is no help, as you know. Not that I blame her," she added quickly. "Tis not her fault. And Steven's parents help as they can, but taxation has been heavy for them with the war, and Cicely is sickly."

Rosamund squeezed her arm sympathetically. "Tis hard for you, I know."

Alys sighed. "I sometimes feel I have to do everything and be everything, and even then I don't succeed. James only does what I tell him. He doesn't seem able to think for himself. Except for making eyes at me, which I'd lief he did not!"

"He sleeps at Widow Agnes's still, I hope?"

Alys nodded. Agnes, the wheelwright's widow, lived in a tiny cottage attached to the old forge a few yards down the street from the weaver's house, and was glad of the few pennies Alys paid her to keep James away from her at night, now that her sister was living in at the manor house. Her mother's presence in the cottage should have been protection enough for her daughter, but Alys and

Rosamund both knew that James had scant respect for Ellen and would not hesitate to take advantage of Alys's situation if he could.

"I've no wish to be force-put," Alys said with a shudder. It was a real fear. If James forced himself on her, she might then be expected to marry the labourer in disgrace, perhaps with a child on the way. Better to wait forever for Steven to return, as she seemed like to have to do.

They walked in silence for a little, passing the greybeards supping their ale outside Widow Brewer's house, no doubt debating whether the morning's sunshine might provide a window of opportunity to get the meagre harvest in before the crops rotted in the damp. Sir Richard had already called on bonded labour to do the manor harvesting, but much of the tenants' barley stood ungarnered in the big field to the south of the river. As they crossed the wooden bridge that led to the northern part of the village, where the mill lay, the river ran deep and brown and turbulent beneath them. Sir Thomas had had the bridge built when he inherited the land from his father, as a service to the community as well as for his own convenience when visiting different parts of his manor. Not for the first time, Alys was glad they no longer had to use the old ford which had served previous generations as a link between the two halves of the community. It had always been deep, and in earlier generations, the southern section of the village and its arable fields were often cut off from church and manor house for weeks, though the houses, built as they were on the incline on the far side of the road, were seldom actually flooded.

"Steven should be home by this time." Rosamund said this carefully, as though fearing to make matters worse. "It's too bad you have to deal with everything."

"He should," agreed Alys with feeling. "Until he comes, I can't decide anything or change anything. I knew, of course I did, when he left home that it would be a long time before I saw him again. But not this long." *Dear God, not this long.*

She looked up at her sister. "D'you think we would have heard, an the whole party had perished somewhere out East in those heathen lands? What if they've just vanished without trace? They could have been murdered by Saracens with great curved swords."

"I'm sure they have not," Rosamund consoled her. "You mustn't give way to such thoughts, Alys."

"Has Lady Eleanor heard anything?" As maid-companion to Sir Richard's sister Eleanor, Rosamund often had news of events affecting the lord and his family before anyone else.

"If she has, she's told me naught of it, and I'm sure she would. She knows you must be worried, and it's been months since we had word. Though truly, that means nothing," she added quickly. "With Sir Thomas on the move all the time, and out in the East too, it wouldn't be easy to send a message home."

"Cannot Sir Richard send someone to look for them?"

"Not him! He won't take too kindly to Sir Thomas's return, if you ask me. He likes being in charge, and having things the way he likes them."

There was something in the way she said this that made Alys look at her more closely. "What kind of things?" she asked.

Rosamund shrugged and walked on. "Oh, just everything, I suppose."

Alys grabbed her arm. "Don't try to pretend with me, Ros."

"Well, he's not the first lord to stray," her sister said.

"You mean he's tried something with you." Alys's voice was fierce.

"I'm growing up, aren't I? Tis natural, I suppose. He says I'm beautiful, though I expect tis what he says to any girl he fancies."

Alys snorted. Her sister *was* beautiful, it couldn't be denied. Men were bound to be attracted to her, but it was a worry.

"Lady Eleanor has warned him off, but she can't always be there when he comes sniffing around me like some randy dog."

Alys looked round to make sure no one was listening. It was not wise for Rosamund to say such rude things about the lord of the manor's son, especially out in the street where anyone might hear her. "You sleep in the lady Eleanor's bedroom, though, don't you?" she pointed out. "You're safe enough, surely."

"Aye. I've a cot in her chamber. Tis what may happen at other times that worries me. He is the master, and he can go where he pleases. Do what he pleases, too, as I said."

"I'd rather have you here at home," Alys told her angrily, "than see you in trouble." Having her younger sister off her hands and earning something had made a difference to her financial position, but she didn't like the sound of the situation Rosamund described.

"I know, Alys. I know. But I love serving the lady Eleanor, and I wouldn't leave her. If I'm really frightened, I'll speak to her. She would take steps to protect me."

"Surely she could tell her sister-in-law what is going on?"

"Lady Maud wouldn't be able to stop her husband from doing anything he wanted to do. She's used to his eyeing up her maidservants, and he has her cowed, like everyone else."

"Except you."

Rosamund laughed. "Except me. And his sister. Lady Eleanor speaks of going to live with Sister Margery for a while. She says there is no peace at the manor while Sir Richard is trying to persuade her to marry Lord Fitzwilliam, though he won't succeed, I think. She plans to be a nun, or even an anchoress like Sister Margery herself."

Alys digested this as they reached the mill. In her anchorhold attached to the parish church, Sir Thomas's sister Margery lived a life of prayer and contemplation, never leaving the little house for any but the most exceptional reasons, though those who came for advice and succour were never turned away.

"It would be well for her to be with Sister Margery. Her aunt will be glad to support the lady Eleanor if she wishes to stay for a while." She frowned. "Though how would you serve your mistress then? There is no room for another servant at the anchorhold, surely?"

"Sister Margery's servant would look after them both." Rosamund was trying to sound cheerful, but given what she had said about Sir Richard, Alys wondered how much she feared what would happen if the lady Eleanor were away. "But mayhap I will have to come home then."

"I don't like the way the LeClercs treat the church like a private chapel," Alys observed, turning the subject tactfully. "Parish folk have a right to attend service there, but sometimes you'd think they were only let in on sufferance."

Rosamund smiled at her indignation. "Father Edward really annoys you, doesn't he?"

"He hears confessions with his nose in the air," answered her sister. "And hands out penance with a heavy hand."

"It can't be easy trying to be both the lord's chaplain and the parish priest," pointed out Rosamund. "The bishop should appoint another incumbent and let Father Edward concentrate on his work with the family. Though I suppose it might be even more difficult if there were two priests in competition."

"'Twould have been better if Sir Thomas had built a chapel of his own up at the manor house," retorted Alys, "instead of paying for a chantry to add on to the parish church, and training a priest to say Masses in it for him when he's gone. Then we could have had our church to ourselves."

Ahead they could see the big mill-wheel turning as the water poured through the mill race. Matt Miller was his usual graceless, grumpy self. He accepted Alys's coins without thanks before turning back to his work. Others were waiting for their flour, so the two sisters bade goodbye to the miller's unresponsive back and went out into the sunshine.

"How you could even think of marrying that man," muttered Rosamund, as they walked back towards the bridge.

"Oh, I never did. The thought of marriage was always his, not mine. But I don't like to quarrel with folk an I can help it."

"You could tell him 'no' plainly," suggested Rosamund. "I don't see how that could make him behave worse than he does already."

"I have tried. Several times. That's why he's so surly. He knows in his heart that I'll never marry him. But until Steven comes home, he'll go on hoping. He's got plenty to offer a woman, after all, if I were mercenary-minded enough. A house and a thriving business, the lord's favour—oh yes, I can see that some would put up with his manners and his ugly face for that."

"But not you," smiled Rosamund.

"Not me. Steven will come home soon. I know he will."

Rosamund said nothing, but she pressed her sister's hand.

"I'll come with you up to Sister Margery's," offered Alys as they reached the bridge. "'Tis a long time since I've seen her, shut away as she is."

The main road turned left in a dogleg, but the sisters took the smaller road leading northwards, then turned right into the narrow-rutted lane that served the church. Above them up on the hillside, Alys could see the white dots of sheep grazing. Most of them belonged to Steven's father, which was a comforting thought when it was hard to make ends meet and still keep her dowry from erosion. She had only to hold on until Steven returned, and all would be well. That is, if he hadn't changed his mind while he was away. She imagined Steven riding in with a foreign wife up behind him on the pillion or reclining in a horse-drawn litter. Five years was plenty of time to have met many women with exotic clothes and customs, plenty of time to have found a wife well-endowed with beauty as well as wealth to supplant her own dowdy little brown person.

Or if he hadn't changed his mind while he was away, he might do so when he came back and found her father dead and his family impoverished. Alys didn't flatter herself that she had any beauty or grace that would keep him faithful to his promise. His father wouldn't—nay, couldn't—force him into the marriage if he didn't want to go through with it. But she never expressed this fear, even to her sister. It was better left unsaid, and if possible unthought.

The church lay directly ahead of them now, its grey bulk shutting out the vista of sheep-strewn hillside. They passed the long cemetery that stretched westwards towards the village, capacious enough for the dead for a century to come, guarded by its yew trees and girded by a stone wall. Sister Margery's anchorhold and garden were attached to the south side of the church, just beyond the lych gate. Alys paused to enjoy the garden, where the flowers and herbs were making the most of the fine day to release their pleasant scents into the air, in a final burst of vigour before the autumn frosts brought their summer bloom to an end. She grew some of the same herbs in her own garden beside the cottage, some to use in cooking, others as medicine for the commoner ailments. But Sister Margery was an expert in their use, and clever at getting them to flourish, perhaps assisted by the south-facing aspect of the garden, with the stone wall of the anchorhold behind it to keep it warm.

Old Thomas Chapman was snipping off the dead blooms of the marjoram and tidying up the lemon balm bushes as they walked past. He no longer went from village to village selling goods from a cart, but had retired to a cottage near the church, leaving his son to take on the business. A bad cough afflicted him in the winter months, and forced him to stay inside by the fire most days, but in the summer he loved to help Sister Margery with the garden.

"Morning, Thomas," Rosamund greeted him. She couldn't help wondering how much help he really was to Sister Margery.

Thomas nodded to her. "Lady Eleanor be inside, with Sister Margery," he told her. "Waiting for you, I b'lieve."

At once she began to hurry, anxious that she had caused her mistress delay, but Alys put her hand on her arm. "Take no notice," she said quietly, so the old man did not hear. "Tis nowhere near the hour you said she'd given you. She can't possibly be waiting for you yet. And even if she is, she won't mind, especially if she's with Sister Margery."

"He does it every time," exclaimed Rosamund with annoyance. "Always wants to make me feel guilty, the nasty old wretch."

"It makes him feel important, I guess. Not much in his life does that these days."

Rosamund sighed. "You're kinder than I am, Alys."

"I've lived five years longer. And I've learned patience. Especially with the elder folk."

Rosamund thought of their mother, addle-brained and useless since their father's death, and still only middle-aged. No wonder Alys had learned patience. She would have spoken the thought, but just then her mistress came out of the little house and down the path towards them. Sister Margery waved from the door, then turned back inside. To avoid old Thomas, wondered Rosamund, or to resume her life of prayer? Perhaps both.

"Alys!" exclaimed Eleanor. "You are a stranger these days."

Alys opened her mouth to protest, and closed it again. It was true. She hadn't seen the young noblewoman for weeks.

"Alys has so much to attend to," Rosamund faltered. "My mother...the house..."

"I meant no blame!" Eleanor responded, holding out her hand to Alys. "You have indeed much to do, Alys, I know. More than it is fair to expect of you," she added. "It is good to see you out this morning with your sister. What beautiful weather for a change, don't you agree?"

Alys curtsied and touched the outstretched hand briefly. It was bad enough comparing her dull brown hair and slightly pock-marked complexion to her sister's flaxen curls and sparkling blue eyes. Against Lady Eleanor's patrician beauty, even Rosamund's prettiness faded into insignificance. Alys looked up into that pale poised face, the cool grey eyes smiling but veiled, the golden blonde hair smoothly wound into a coil beneath her wimple. Eleanor's gown was simple, even old-fashioned, flowing around her feet from a girdle at the waist, but the surcoat she wore over it was richly coloured and decorated, in contrast to Alys's brown kirtle.

"There are strangers in the village," Eleanor exclaimed suddenly, looking beyond Alys's shoulder down the lane to the river.

Alys turned. A murmur of voices could be heard from the village green where a group was quickly gathering around two horsemen and a dusty cart drawn by a cob. No such equipage had left the village in recent weeks, for the solitary pedlar carried his goods on an ox cart, so these must, as Eleanor had said, be strangers. And although they were unlikely to be the returning wayfarers she sought, strangers might have news of other travellers encountered on their way. She picked up her skirts. "We should go and see who they may be."

Rosamund moved to go with her, then halted, remembering her service to her employer. "Should we go, my lady?" she asked. "You will be expected home, perhaps and..."

"But I am interested in the strangers too," Eleanor interrupted her gently. "For they come our way too seldom. Come, Ros, let us go and see whatever there is to see."

Rosamund nodded. The road that passed through Northchurch, crossing the river on its way west, was the main route from Basingstoke to Whitchurch along the River Test, but most who travelled it were local folk going to market or merchants passing through with goods for the Cistercian monastery to the north. Those on longer journeys took the major routes through Newbury towards Bristol, Oxford or London. Although occasionally local villagers travelled as far as Winchester to buy special goods and hear the news, most people's needs were met by a weekly visit to the market at Whitchurch. Strangers from further afield, whether friars, mendicants, pedlars or chapmen, were always welcome with their stories of the wider world.

She let Alys hurry on ahead, and followed with her mistress in a more stately fashion.

As Alys crossed the bridge, Goodwife Joan ran towards her, greasy hair tousled and pale blue eyes glittering. "Dark-faced strangers from across the water," she announced. "'Tis a wondrous sight. And they have a great box with them, under a black cloth. Some foreign magic, perhaps." She crossed herself as she spoke, presumably to ward off the dark powers of the foreign box.

Alys paid scant attention to this superstitious utterance, but made her way across the main road and out on to the green. The group surrounding the visitors hid the cart and its contents from her sight, but she could see that one of the men had dismounted and was mingling with the crowd, while the other still sat his horse, expressionless amid the tumult. As Joan had said, his skin was dark, but Alys thought it the darkness of deep sunburn, layer upon layer laid down through years of weathering in sunnier climes. A stranger perhaps, but an Englishman, not a foreigner born far across the seas.

Maybe not even a stranger. For as she stared at him, recognition dawned. The face was older and harsher as well as sunburnt, but there was no mistaking the man. Steven had returned at last.

Five

Their eyes met, and for a moment Alys thought Steven hadn't recognised her, though surely she couldn't have changed as much as he had. Then he raised a hand, acknowledging her, she thought, with sombre formality. But he still sat his horse and his expression didn't change.

Well, what had she expected? Did she imagine he would rush over to greet her with love and longing? Romance had never been part of the bargain, after all: they had not been lovers of any kind, their betrothal a matter of form and family arrangement as much as if they'd been nobles. No doubt he would come to visit her when he was ready. When he'd seen his father, probably. She looked around to see whether Reeve Paul was in the crowd. Cicely would be at home, probably ailing as usual, while her housemaid did most of the work. She rarely came down into the village these days, poor thing.

She gave thought for the first time to the tumbril and its contents. No foreign magic, as Goodwife Joan had surmised, but surely a coffin. She recognized old Toby standing beside the bier, unmoved by the bustle around them. Alan was mingling with the crowd, so whose coffin could it be but Sir Thomas's? She noticed how tattered was the black cloth that covered the coffin, how travel-stained their clothes, how dirt-spattered their boots and the hooves of their horses. What an end to their pilgrimage, to return thus. She wondered how far they had come with this sad load.

She glanced behind her, to where Lady Eleanor stood with Rosamund, and saw that she too had made the deduction. Her face was paler even than usual, flesh stretched tight across the high cheekbones with shock. Alys remembered how much Eleanor had always loved her father, how she had missed him when he left, though of late, Rosamund told her, she had said little about it. This homecoming was not what she had dreamed of.

Alys turned her back on Steven and joined her sister beside the bereaved woman.

"It must be my father who has died. We should go and tell my brother." Eleanor spoke with effort. "There will be arrangements to be made."

She made no attempt to approach the bier, so Alys made her way back through the press of people and spoke to Toby. "I take it you have brought our lord home for burial?" she asked him.

Toby looked up. "Is that you, Alys? I scarce recognised you." Perhaps, then, Steven hadn't known who she was.

"Is it Sir Thomas, Toby?" She indicated the covered tumbril. "Why have we had no word? It is such a shock to the lady Eleanor to see her father's coffin like this."

Toby sighed. "Aye, tis Sir Thomas. We have brought him only from Calais," he added. "There was little time to send word ahead when he died." He paused for a moment. "And we were short of money to pay messengers."

"You should take the coffin up to the castle. Lady Eleanor says Sir Richard must be told at once of Sir Thomas's death."

Toby put his hand to the cob's bridle and began to lead him forward slowly, through the crowd, leaving Alan talking merrily with all who had come to greet them, his handsome face smiling but his hand firmly on the rein of his mare.

Alys looked up at Steven, still sitting his mount, but he took no notice of her. Seeing Toby moving forward with the bier, he nudged his horse into a walk and followed them across the bridge. His family home lay that way, hard by the upland pastures where they kept their sheep.

Rosamund came up behind her. "I'm taking Lady Eleanor home," she said. "The family must give Sir Thomas's body all the respect it is due, and she will want to be part of that."

Alys nodded. "I don't think he knew me," she told her sister.

Rosamund looked at her. "Steven? Of course he knew you. Why would he not?"

Alys shook her head. "Toby didn't recognise me at first. Am I so changed, Ros? Tis not so long, surely, that he would forget?"

"Did he not even speak to you?"

"I thought he acknowledged me at first," allowed Alys. "But then he made no other sign, spoke no word. Perhaps he did not recognise me, after all." Her distress was evident. "Ros, what shall I do?"

"Talk to him. You're his betrothed. He won't expect you to ignore the fact that he's returned."

Alys shook her head. "I'll wait until he comes to me," she stated with decision. "Or sends for me."

"I'm sorry, Alys. I can't stay. I must go with Lady Eleanor." Rosamund turned away, and put her hand under her mistress's elbow.

Alys looked at Eleanor, whose face was a mask of calm, though who knew what emotions were surging beneath it. She smiled absently and began to follow the bier, leaning a little on Rosamund's arm. Alys stood back and let them pass. She would have liked to follow the bier, and Steven, back to the castle, in the hope of a word from him. Any word that might give her a clue as to his thoughts. But first she must give James and her mother their dinner. She could see James mingling with the crowd around Alan. Clearly, he had been distracted from his tasks, and her mother left to tend the pottage. She would separate him from his cronies and go home.

~ * ~

Rosamund stayed silent for a while as the two women began their melancholy journey towards the castle.

"I am so sorry, my lady," she ventured at last. Their formal relationship did not allow for much expression of sympathy, but she felt it nevertheless.

"They have been gone such a long time," Eleanor reflected. "No word of them, even, for months. I half-expected that something had happened. Alys felt it too, surely."

"But they have come only from Calais with the coffin," Rosamund reminded her. "I heard Toby say so to Alys. Your father died little more than a sennight ago."

As they halted to wait for the porter to open up and let them inside the curtain wall, they saw that Steven had dismounted and was speaking to Toby.

"Take him to the stables with you," they heard him say, as he tied his horse's reins to a ring on the cart. "I will walk home." He shouldered his tattered pack and turned away.

Toby nodded acknowledgement, and Steven strode back the way they had come. He passed quite close to the two women, but only nodded a brief courtesy as he turned off down the lane that led to his father's house.

"Did not Steven wait to speak with Alys?" Eleanor asked in surprise, watching him striding briskly along the lane. She kept her voice low, though he was soon well behind them, out of earshot.

Rosamund shook her head. "I thought that strange too, not to greet his betrothed properly, when she has been waiting for so long."

"He will speak when he is ready, I suppose. There must be matters to be discussed with his father." Eleanor paused for a moment, and then went on: "It is a shock, not to have one's father to turn to, isn't it? Even though I have not had that privilege all the time Sir Thomas was away, I still hoped for it again. I know you understand."

Rosamund nodded and pressed her lady's arm. Her own father's death had been unexpected, so there had been little time for him to prepare his family, or to say goodbye and leave his affairs in order.

But at least she and Alys had been at his bedside. She tried to imagine what it would be like to wait and wait for your father to come back from a long journey, only to find him returning in his coffin.

The porter was leaning out of the gatehouse, airing his doubts as to the wisdom of opening up to such a cortège, but the sight of the lady Eleanor walking close behind it changed his mind. He unbarred the heavy wooden doors and the bier rumbled over the stones to pull up in front of the house. Northchurch Castle it was called, but with the baronial wars long past, and the French not yet presenting any immediate threat of invasion, it was a castle only in name. Sir Thomas's father had remodelled it, converting the original outbuildings into stables, dairies and other necessary appendages to a comfortable life, and retaining the Norman keep as barracks for the soldiers. Meanwhile the family lived in a newly built stone house in comparative luxury, and––at least since Sir Richard and his lady had taken the reins of the establishment—dedicated to conspicuous expenditure.

As he drew nearer to his parents' house, Steven's pace slowed. Coming home after years of travel had proved more disturbing than he had expected. On the village green an hour ago, while Alan had responded so easily to the villagers' avid interest, he himself had felt an alien. He wished he could have joined the Calais garrison, as Wat had invited him to, or taken service with one of the English bands of mercenaries hired by the various warring factions in the Low Countries. But as a bonded villein, he was not free to make that kind of choice. Northchurch was where he belonged, the land to which he was tied, and it was where he would have to stay.

His family home lay at the end of the lane, set back in its own curtilage. Steven stopped as he reached the gate, observing that his father had made more improvements to the property while he had been away. The fence that enclosed the messuage had been replaced and extended, and some of the scattered and tumbledown outbuildings had been replaced by a massive barn some distance from the house. A new waterbutt had been set up at one end of the cottage, and the firewood stack by the door had been given a roof of sorts to keep it dry. The house itself, built of wattle and daub on a timber frame, had been extended. It was larger than the other villein houses in the village, with a room at one end to shelter the domestic livestock in the winter, and a big living kitchen at the other. Sleeping accommodation lay above in the rafters under the thatch, where the rising warmth from fire and animal bodies served to stave off the cold at night. Steven could see that a new single-storey section had been built on to the living end of the house, though he couldn't immediately think why. But its presence reassured him that his father was still prospering from the sale of wool and other produce, in spite of government taxes and levies.

He noticed smoke filtering through the thatch at the apex of the roof and blowing away in the light breeze. His mother was probably preparing the midday meal. With luck, his father would be out on the land somewhere harvesting the last of the fodder crops or in the wool barns counting over the clip, if any were still awaiting sale. A meeting between them could not be avoided forever, but Steven preferred to greet his mother first.

He pushed open the door and entered the dim interior. A fire was burning merrily in the centre of the room on its hearth of stone, on which stood a cooking pot that gave off a rich smell of stew. Steven felt saliva forming in his mouth. Breakfast at the inn had been a sketchy affair.

"Mother." He spoke the word softly, hoping not to startle her.

"Trenchers are on the table," she said, not looking up from stirring the pot. "The meal will be ready soon."

"Mother," he repeated. "It's me. Steven."

She turned quickly and he thought for a moment she was going to faint with shock. She blanched and dropped her stirring spoon on the floor. Steven moved swiftly to catch her, but she steadied herself, looking up at him doubtfully in the dim light.

"Steven, is it really you?"

He put his arms round her. "None other. Home at last."

She gave a great shuddering sigh and let her head rest against him. Then she drew him to the bench set against the wall and made him sit down, still holding his hand as though fearful he might disappear before she had had a chance to speak.

"You didn't believe me dead, Mother, surely?"

"Nay, not that. But no word, no news—it has been hard to bear. The doubts crept in sometimes, I admit that. Oh, Steven, tis good to see you. You're in good health?" Her eyes searched his tanned face anxiously.

"I'm well enough. But Sir Thomas is dead, Mother. We brought his body home for burial."

"Sir Thomas dead? That is ill news, son...both for his family and for us."

"Why 'for us'?" Steven thought of his own calamity, that Sir Thomas had died without giving him his freedom. His mother hadn't heard about that yet. What else could make this ill news for them?

"Sir Thomas was a fair man," she explained. "We knew where we were with him. Now Sir Richard will have things his own way more than ever. And we've seen where that will lead. More depredations, harsher terms for new leases. He likes his comforts, and tis clear we are the folk who have to pay for them."

Steven was saved from answering this bitter comment by the arrival of a young woman, carrying a bundle of firewood on her hip. She stopped in the doorway at sight of him, her eyes wide, her jaw dropping with surprise.

"Tis Steven back from his travels at last," Cicely told her. "Steven, you remember Mary, Timothy the cottar's girl? She was a little wench when you left, younger than Alys. She does the heavy work for me now."

Steven nodded to her politely, but either she had changed out of all recognition or he had forgotten her completely.

"Speaking of Alys," his mother continued. "Have you seen her?"

"Not yet," he said. "Not to speak to. I want to see Father first." He didn't want to discuss his betrothal, even with his mother, in Mary's hearing.

She nodded. "That's best. Come in, girl," she said sharply to Mary, who was still hovering in the doorway. "The fire's burning low and needs that wood you've brought."

"How have you been keeping, Mother?" Steven asked her. It seemed to him that she looked paler than he remembered, and moved with less vigour. "And Jack and the girls?"

"The girls are wed, all three, and out of the village. Jenny has a couple of babes, too. You'll see Jack when your father comes in... they're out harvesting. He works hard, young as he is, though he doesn't always manage to please your father, of course."

"And you, Mother?" Steven asked again.

"Go and fetch your master," his mother said to the servant girl. "Tell him the meal is ready, and that Steven is home!"

Mary obeyed her quietly, but Steven saw her break into a run as she left the house.

"Mother?" He persisted, wondering why she had sent the girl away before she answered his question.

"I'm fine and well, Steven. Mainly. Tis only that I found I could not do the household work the way I used to. My heart would beat right up in my throat sometimes, and I'd feel faint."

"Mother!"

"Nay, all's well now, son. Mary works hard and she's willing. I do what I can, but I'm much better now that I have her help." She got up and began stirring the pottage again, as though to prove that her ailments were minor.

Steven knew better than to pursue it. His mother had never recovered fully after the birth of his brother, more than ten years before, and this new problem probably had the same cause.

"Father's been building again, I see," he observed, indicating the new room behind her.

"Just this last summer," she nodded, coming to sit beside him again. "But tis a waste of money, to my mind. He thinks to have a solar, like the grand folks. But where's the sense in that? Villeins we are, working folk, and what point is there in aping our lords?"

"Villeins we are," echoed Steven. "And villeins we remain. Sir Thomas died before he could give me my freedom, Mother."

"That is a pity," his mother answered after a moment. "I know how high your hopes were. But your father and I have done well enough as bond tenants. What difference does such freedom make, after all?"

"You sound like his echo, Mother. Father never could see why it meant so much to me."

"But mayhap he's in the right of it, Steven. You know what he says—as long as the wool clip makes money, tis easy enough to pay others to carry out our work dues on the lord's demesne. Sir Richard has not altered that arrangement, even though he's had a free hand while his father was away. Wool is doing well, and we have our own grazing."

Steven sighed. His father had always seemed to accept their rather complicated social status philosophically. Paul had found his own route to affluence by making shrewd purchases of freehold land, always waiting to buy until prices were low and other less provident folk were forced by hardship to sell. The DeClercs had generally accepted this entrepreneurial activity, especially after Paul was elected reeve. But Steven still felt a sense of humiliation that the family's personal serfdom remained, with all its tiresome obligations. Many landlords these days were accepting money payment instead of enforcing labour dues, and relinquishing of their own free will the feudal relationships of the past. They seemed not to care much about the legal aspects of the matter as long as the money flowed in from their lands. But Sir Thomas had always preferred the old ways, and refused to follow suit.

"Didn't your uncle run away to find his freedom?" he countered. "He clearly didn't want to be a villein. Not everyone in the family is as philosophical about it as you and my father."

She shook her head. "Does it matter that much to you still, then, even after these years away?"

"Aye. It chafes me to come back to it, that's for sure."

"Speak to Sir Richard," she urged him. "Remind him that Sir Thomas promised you your freedom. Toby and Alan will bear witness to your service abroad that was the basis of it, surely?"

Steven nodded. "I'll do that." But privately he doubted anything would come of it.

"Alys, now," Cicely went on. "She'll be glad to see you, that's certain. If you haven't spoken with her yet, you'll not have heard the news from that quarter. John Weaver died a year back, and Ellen's been away with the fairies ever since. Poor Alys has had it all to bear alone, for Rosamund is maidservant to the lady Eleanor now."

Steven stared at her, while his mind revolved around this new situation. "John Weaver dead?" he echoed at last. Then, hesitantly: "Does the betrothal stand, think you?"

Cicely shrugged. "No reason to suppose not. You'd best ask your father about it when you see him. He doesn't see fit to consult with me about these things. Your marriage is his business, not mine, he says."

My business too, Father.

"But with this news about Sir Thomas's death, and you still being unfree," Cicely ran on, "well, who knows?"

"Who indeed?" agreed Steven.

There was the sound of running footsteps outside the door, and Mary burst in breathlessly. "The master is here."

Cicely rose slowly to her feet. "We will serve the meal now," she said. "Fetch me the ladle, wench."

Steven looked up as his father came into the room, fearful suddenly that five years would have brought devastating change to him too. But Paul looked much the same as he had when Steven had left the village––a little greyer about the beard and balder about the head, maybe a little stooped, but nothing beyond that.

He bowed a formal submission. "I hope I see you well, Father?"

The reeve looked him up and down and he felt the old paralysing fear of his father's criticism creep over him. He reminded himself firmly that it was he and not his father who had gone adventuring successfully abroad. If his father wasn't proud of him now, he never would be. He made himself raise his eyes and look his father in the face.

"I'm certainly the better for seeing you at last, my boy. Took your time, though, didn't you? Not made your fortune, either, I see." He looked pointedly at Steven's rather ragged attire.

"I ask your pardon for my travel stains," Steven replied formally, striving not to sound defensive. "I will buy new apparel as soon as I may."

"There's good cloth aplenty in the clothes press," broke in Cicely. "We can measure you for a new suit of clothes in no time."

"Nay, Mother." He laid his hand on her arm. "I've not come home to depend upon you for my clothes, or my keep. I am owed wages by my lord, and I've no doubt they will be paid promptly now we are home."

"Sir Richard has summoned us both to the castle on the morrow," his father told him, seating himself on a stool at the table and drawing a trencher of bread towards him. He drew his knife from his belt and laid it on the table beside him, ready for use. "You're not fit to appear before him as you are."

Steven sat down opposite him as his mother served the food. "These clothes are all I have at present. Sir Thomas was beggared by the end, and Alan and I had to use what we had of our own coin to bring him home from Calais. There was no money for smart clothes. Sir Richard will have to receive me as I am, if he wants me at all. Or wait until I'm paid the wages I'm owed."

Sir Thomas's son was one of the new breed of knights, he thought, a man who preferred domestic virtues and luxury to the discipline of a military life. He smiled sourly. Sir Thomas had despised such knightly choices and would likely rise from his coffin to condemn his son had they not fixed the lid down firmly.

But he did not speak the thought, for it augured ill for Steven's relationship with his own father that they had clashed first about such issues of respect. Instead he smiled at his younger brother, who had crept unseen into the house in the wake of his father and was now eating his dinner voraciously, while covertly watching Steven as he talked.

"You've grown, my lad," he said. "But you're not as tall as I am, not by a long shot, not yet."

Cicely smiled at him, happy now that she had her family around her. "There's no one like our Steven. Jack knows that."

Six

When Steven and his father arrived at the castle, they were ushered into the manor hall by a liveried servant, who guided them to a position in front of the raised dais on which the adult members of the DeClerc family were seated. Steven noticed to his surprise that Alys was also present, with her sister beside her. She was looking down at the floor and made no attempt to meet his eyes. Alan, too, was standing near the centre of the hall, looking as tatterdemalion as Steven himself. Clearly he had not acquired new raiment for the occasion either, but that was not preventing him from paying a great deal of attention to Alys's sister Rosamund, who had changed radically in five years from the scrawny child whom Steven remembered. She was ignoring Alan's admiring gaze, Steven noticed approvingly, although perhaps only because of their formal surroundings.

Somewhat to his surprise, he saw that no benches had been set out to sit on, not even for the women, though the family were seated. Courtesy towards those of lower social status was something on which Sir Thomas had prided himself, but it was obvious that in the new regime this was going to change, like so much else. He remembered his mother's earlier disquiet at the news of the old lord's death.

A sound from the dais drew his attention to the group seated in state before them. Sir Richard lounged at his ease on a tasselled cushion in a carved armchair, a goblet of wine to hand. His wife and sister sat each side of him, each in a chair slightly less ornate and padded than his. Whilst the women were chastely clad in the traditional robes appropriate to their status, Sir Richard was dressed fashionably in a long-sleeved gipon tunic with a jewelled belt slung around his hips, showing off his shapely legs in their pale-yellow hose. His cloak, rather warm for the mild day, was richly lined with fur and cut with an elaborately jagged edge. The whole outfit had clearly cost a great deal of money.

"My father left detailed instructions regarding his retainers Steven and Alan before he left home for the Holy Land," Sir Richard began, his tenor voice declaiming the words precisely as though reading from a legal document. "Of course, these will be dependent on the will being proved in court. But there should be no difficulty. The document was properly drawn up and signed. I have summoned you here today to hear these instructions and to make arrangements to implement them."

Steven swallowed. Perhaps he should have realised that, going into danger for who knew how long, Sir Thomas would have made his will before he left home, rather than when his end was imminent, like most men. Out of the corner of his eye, he caught a glimpse of Alys turning to look at him for a moment, and Alan reached out a hand to touch his shoulder briefly, aware of the portent of Sir Richard's words. His father, however, stood still as a stone, his face impassive.

"You, Alan," said Sir Richard, turning to speak directly to the archer, "if you have given good service, my father awards you rents from land on his manor of Beaconswell in Kent, you and your heirs in perpetuity, together with the office of bailiff at the said manor."

Kent? Steven almost laughed out loud. Generous though the bequest appeared—and Sir Richard had not sounded too pleased about its alienation of family income, however minor—there must be a catch. A pension for life, with a job appointment to go with it? Was Sir Thomas wanting to get rid of Alan for some reason? He could see his bewilderment mirrored in Alan's face as the latter bowed formally in response.

"And you, Steven: Sir Thomas gives you your freedom from villeinage in return for your service to him overseas, as you requested and he promised. He judges, however, that you will have made money from your adventures, and asks a money payment for the manumission if you stay here in Northchurch. If you leave, however, as you are now free to do, no payment is required." Sir Richard paused, awaiting a response.

"A money payment, my lord?" queried Steven. "I did not seek to buy my freedom. Sir Thomas offered it to me as the price of service."

"I have read my father's will, and you have not, Steven. I merely report what he laid down."

Or as much of it as it suits you to divulge, thought Steven savagely. "How much does Sir Thomas require?" he asked, keeping his temper with difficulty. He could hardly demand to see the old lord's will, even if he could have deciphered it, but he felt sure that Sir Richard was capable of inflating the price beyond what Sir Thomas had specified, if indeed he had given a figure. Steven had no intention of leaving the manor permanently. Why should Sir Thomas want to give him an incentive to do so? It made no sense, when it was service to Sir Thomas that had won him the concession.

"Thirty shillings," Sir Richard replied smoothly.

Steven opened his eyes wide. "My lord, that is a small fortune to a man in my position, as you must know."

Sir Richard smiled. "I feel sure your father will help you with the sum required."

There was some kind of unpleasant humour involved here, Steven felt. The lord was clearly enjoying the prospect of bleeding his richest villein of money that he disapproved of him having, though it was legally acquired.

"Nay." Paul spoke decisively. "I'll pay no silver for something that brings me no benefit. Manumission is your pipe dream, not mine, Steven, as well you know."

"Father!" hissed Steven.

"You wanted to pay your own way, son," his father reminded him, in a quiet but forceful aside. "Now is the time to do it."

Steven swallowed hard. He should be overjoyed at achieving his dream of freedom, against the odds, when he had thought it lost. Was it sensible to challenge Sir Richard further and risk a change of heart? The knight held all the power in this situation, even if it might be expected that he would respect his father's wishes. He hesitated, not wanting to risk the promise of manumission, even if the price being asked was outrageous. He wished his own father were in a more generous frame of mind.

He made an effort to be polite. "May I ask, my lord, did Sir Thomas himself mention this sum?"

Sir Richard smiled, his narrow lips stretching a little for the purpose but his eyes remaining cold. "He did not, of course, know what sum would be appropriate when the time came. Indeed, I feel sure he had not foreseen the will being implemented in these circumstances. He was not an old man, and though he took the precaution of writing his will before he left home, he clearly expected to come home safely. He would have thought to discuss the matter with you himself at that time. In this sad situation in which we find ourselves, however, I have thought carefully on this matter, and this seems to me to be a suitable amount."

"My lord," Alan spoke up before Steven could find measured words to express his consternation. "You may not know that we are both owed a considerable sum in wages, as is Toby. And Steven and I paid for Sir Thomas's coffin, the cart to carry it, and the sea passage home. We had to sell your father's destrier and the pack horse to do so, and were out of pocket ourselves besides. Tis you who should be paying Steven, instead of demanding a sum from him for something that everyone believes Sir Thomas promised him freely in return for service."

Sir Richard seemed somewhat disconcerted at Alan's uncompromising speech. He had obviously underestimated both of them, had thought of them as the untried youngsters they had undoubtedly been when he last saw them, but were no longer. He smiled thinly again, and favoured the archer with a less-than-friendly glance.

"What is owed will of course be paid in due time," he assured him, waving a hand airily. "I believe you yourself received much from my father in goods, which might be set against such expenditure as you were forced to make."

"He gave me my mare, sir, if that is what you mean. She was not payment, and I used her as a saddle horse in his service for two years and more, saving Sir Thomas the cost of a mount. I will not have her worth discounted from what you owe me in Sir Thomas's name."

"Richard," put in Eleanor quietly. "This haggling is not worthy of you, nor of our honour as a family." Her lovely face was set with anger at her brother's duplicity, though she spoke coolly and obviously wished to make little of the acrimonious debate that had arisen.

"Well, well, we will not argue over a few shillings." Sir Richard waved away both his sister's comment and Alan's arguments. "Bailiff Michael will settle up with you if you apply to him. You will have to justify your expenses, of course," he added. "And prove the wages you were owed."

Seething, Alan and Steven both remained silent. There was nothing to be gained by reacting to this provocation. Michael had been the manor bailiff for many years and they knew him well. He was a fair man and they could trust him to pay them what was owed, whatever Sir Richard thought about it.

"I will arrange the manumission ceremony," Sir Richard went on. "But it will have to wait until we have buried my father, of course."

Steven nodded, accepting this, though with some anxiety. Any delay might allow Sir Richard to find some loophole, some reason to cancel the concession or raise its price.

"We cannot wait for Piers to arrive from Oxford," Sir Richard added with irritation, as though the young man whom Sir Thomas had chosen for training as a chantry priest should have somehow foreseen the need to return in time for his patron's unexpected funeral. "Father Edward will receive my father's body into the chapel this afternoon, and we will bury him on the morrow."

"Yes, my lord."

"There is one other matter. Reeve Paul, now that your son has returned, we should finalise your marriage plans for him. As I'm sure you've been told, Steven, Weaver John has died, and in the absence of a male heir, his daughters will inherit his property jointly when they are of age. Alys's marriage is now in my wardship. What say you, Paul? Does the betrothal stand?"

Both Paul and Alys glanced swiftly at Steven. There had been no opportunity before the meeting to speak about the changed circumstances. Even for Sir Richard, this was a high-handed way of proceeding. They wondered what he had to gain by it.

"It might be best for this to wait as well, my lord," ventured Paul at last. "My son returned only yesterday and we have had no chance to discuss the matter."

There was silence for a moment. Sir Richard continued to wait, his gaze fixed on the reeve, so Paul replied. "But if you insist on an answer now, Steven must speak for himself."

Thanks, Father. That's just what I need. Steven's immediate reaction was frustration at being faced with making a binding decision, and in public, that he had not yet fully thought through. Yet to be fair to his father, he would not have wanted the decision made for him either.

He hesitated. The pieces of the betrothal puzzle no longer fitted together as they had done: he must pay for his manumission, and unless he could persuade his father to help, he would then have little left to marry on. The joint venture agreed upon with Alys's father, that the latter should weave woollen cloth exclusively from their fleeces, was no longer a possibility.

Steven looked across at Alys, whose face was white with strain. She had not sought this forcing of his hand. He imagined what her life must have been like for the last year since her father died–– uncertain of his return, and trying to keep the family afloat in the face of her mother's abnegation of responsibility. Whatever the result, whatever his private misgivings, he could not repudiate her in front of his father and Sir Richard.

"The betrothal stands," he declared, and was dismayed to see how her colour changed with relief. She hugged her sister, and he thought he saw tears on her face. *God grant we can make something of it, after all this time. For I hardly know the girl, nor she me.*

His father turned to him and shook his hand. "You are doing the right thing, boy," he said, gruffly. "Life doesn't always work out how we expect."

Steven turned back towards the dais. "Is your business with my father and myself completed, Sir Richard?"

The narrow lips no longer smiled. The knight's face was veiled and inscrutable. Steven wondered whether the decision to retain the betrothal had displeased him. He hoped so. It would be a small victory, at least.

"The business is completed, Steven," he confirmed at last. He turned to Alys. "My wife will assist you and your mother with the marriage arrangements. I will myself let Father Edward know." He paused. "I suggest you make all speed to finalise this, now that Steven is home."

Was there an implication that Steven and his father might change their minds? Likely she seemed to him a bad bargain, whom no one else would want. Steven found his fists clenching in anger. How dare that mincing popinjay hint that he would go back on his word?

Alan, who had been watching this byplay with some concern, took Steven's arm and ushered him out of the hall before he could start trading words with Sir Richard again. He understood his friend's anger, but now was not the time to give it rein.

"Hold up, man," he advised, as they went out into the courtyard. "You've got what you wanted, and nothing comes free in this life. Your family can find the funds, surely, at need, for your freedom? Whatever your father said in there, he won't force you to miss this opportunity."

"I'll have little left of my earnings if he does. Besides, I wouldn't let my father pay the manumission price, even an he wanted to, when it's I who want my freedom. Alys will have to wait a while for her wedding ring, for I've a mind to go soldiering abroad again—there's money to be made by a free man in that. Or mayhap we'll start over somewhere else, where my father won't be looking over my shoulder. I could get out of paying the price then, it seems." He frowned, wondering whether Alys would be willing to move away.

Alan shrugged. This seemed a fruitless speculation to him, not worth spending time on. He had enough to think of on his own behalf, with Sir Thomas's legacy, which Steven had ignored, though congratulations might have been expected. He grinned. He would be a franklin, with money to call his own! Just as well he had learned his letters under Father Nicholas's tuition with the other boys in the village when they were all young, though he would certainly make use of whatever clerical help was available to a manor official such as a bailiff. On the other hand, he would be forced to spend most of his time in Kent from now on, overseeing the manor administration, which would not have appealed to him even if he wanted to leave the manor where he had been born, which he did not. Particularly not when he had just set eyes on Rosamund.

He turned as the two sisters energed from the hall.

"Give you good day, Alys," he said to the older girl, bowing slightly. "Tis long since we last greeted each other. And I would not have known your sister," he added, smiling at Rosamund. "So sweet a flower from so unpromising a bud!"

"I thank you, sir," she said, twinkling demurely at him from beneath her lashes.

"Tis hardly a compliment, Ros," Alys pointed out. "Alan scarcely noticed you when you were a child, before they went off gallivanting."

Alan ignored this. "I would know you better now, though, if you can bear it." He indicated his tattered tunic ruefully. "I swear I will look more seemly when I've been paid my dues by Bailiff Michael." With his newfound status, he thought, he would be able to wear something more luxurious than basic peasant garb.

Ros smiled, and it seemed to him that the sun shone upon him as it never had before. "Our worth is not in our clothes alone, sir," she reminded him. "But I must go and look after my mistress now."

She turned and walked away gracefully, her kirtle swaying as she moved. From the way she had spoken to him, perhaps closer acquaintance would not be too repulsive to her. He hoped not. The acquaintance could not be close enough for him. Even imagining her in his arms made his heart race.

Alys turned to Steven. "I am grateful." Just how grateful, he would probably never know. "The betrothal stands, but I do not ask for a speedy marriage. That was a piece of spite from Sir Richard."

Steven sighed. "I know. But the worse spite was in the manumission price. I had given up thought of my freedom with Sir Thomas's death, so his will was good fortune unlooked for. But I had not bargained for paying for it and that changes everything."

"It need not," she told him.

"Why? I won't ask my father for that kind of sum. Mayhap we will have to wait a while to get married. Will you mind that, Alys?"

She put out her hand to him. "No. But come and visit with my mother, and I will show you why we do not have to wait."

She curtsied briefly to Alan and tucked her hand into the crook of Steven's elbow confidently, as though they had not been parted for five years.

He walked with her along the lane and across the bridge, her springy step matching her pace to his in spite of her short stature. Young she had been when he left her, but she was much as he recalled her, both for good and ill. A small brown maid, his father had called her, though not unkindly. Far from beautiful, not enchanting or romantic like her sister, but she might make a good wife, perhaps. He saw, when they arrived at her house, that she was at least a good housekeeper. The place was spotless, and her mother, feeble-minded as she now was, looked clean and well cared for, sitting by the door with her distaff in her hand.

"Good morrow, Mistress Ellen," he greeted her.

She turned her vacant eyes on him without recognition.

"Tis Steven, Mother," Alys told her gently. "Steven the reeve's son, remember? He and I are betrothed, and he is returned from his travels after many years."

Ellen nodded, but Steven thought she had understood little of what was said. He left her to her spinning and followed Alys inside.

"She will come in when she is hungry, or if it rains," Alys assured him.

She went over to the trunk and took out the casket. "You need not worry about the manumission price, Steven. This is my dowry that my father left me for our marriage." She handed it to him. "There is enough there to pay the price, and more."

He gaped at her. "Dowry?" With her father dead, and the difficulties she had clearly encountered in the wake of that, he had not expected her to possess anything much, never mind a bag full of coin to the value of thirty shillings. Her inheritance would have been dowry enough.

"Tis yours. Take it and give it to Steward Roger for your manumission, and we can start afresh. This house is half mine, as is the land." The house in particular was valuable, being solidly built and commodious. "In time we can pay Rosamund her share in money, though if we live here we will have to bear my mother's presence, I fear. You don't want to live with your parents, do you?" She looked up at him, as though checking that her assessment of the situation was correct.

"I would rather live here on this side of the river than under my father's eye, that's for sure," he agreed. "And your mother is welcome to make her home with us. Your sister, too, should she wish to leave the lady Eleanor's service."

He thought privately that Rosamund would not remain long unwed. He had seen Alan's besotted gaze, and thought that even if the archer could not offer her enough to tempt her, someone else soon would. The only problem was that they would have to find a dowry for her, unless John Weaver had given a suitable sum to his younger daughter as well. But now was not the time to ask.

Alys smiled suddenly. "Paul and Cicely have been more than kind to me since my father died. But you and I want to build something of our own together, do we not?"

Steven frowned, wondering what she had in mind.

"Paul's fleeces, and my weaving business," she explained. "Just as your father and mine planned it."

He stared at her. "But I am not a weaver," he protested. "And nor are you."

"Not fully trained, no. My father died too soon. But I learned much along with his apprentices. I know how cloth looks when it has been well woven, I can design the fabrics and I have kept my father's looms safe in the workshop. The apprentices we had are long gone, of course, but I thought to employ a master weaver—mayhap some journeyman without the money to set up for himself—when we have the means. I would be able to finish my training then."

Steven raised his eyebrows. "As a married woman? What of the children you'll bear?"

"That will be as God wills," she told him. "There are enough girls in the village who would welcome work as a nursemaid."

Steven tried to digest this and failed. His mother would never have entertained the idea of trying to run a business and bring up a family at the same time. Those women who attempted it were usually widows and did it out of necessity.

"And we'll employ another labourer," she went on. "One who doesn't have his feet under the table."

He grinned at this. "James doesn't please you, I trow."

She shuddered. "No indeed. I will be glad to be rid of the man. He may be strong, but he is also shifty, lazy and lecherous."

Steven blinked, taken aback by this comprehensive denunciation. "You are harsh!"

"You do not know all," she retorted. "I have not had the means to hire anyone better since my father died, and he has my mother's confidence. He accepted a low wage in the hope of winning my hand, I think. But as soon as you and I are wed, James will be on the road, for he will not be able to make a living here unless I—we—employ him. And that I will not do."

Steven shrugged and wondered what kind of marriage he was letting himself in for. He was damned if he would let this 'small brown maid' rule the roast. On the other hand, his father would welcome her business ideas. His mouth twisted with wry amusement. At least if she's busy with weaving, he thought, she won't expect me to be at home, and perhaps Wat would welcome a man at arms in his retinue, over in Calais. His heart lifted. Freedom would bring those choices, though he could imagine Alys's reaction if he told her that he would rather be abroad soldiering than helping her run a weaver's business at home!

"Let's see how much money we have when Bailiff Michael has paid me what is owed," he suggested. "At least that will give us a start, as your dowry will have to go for the manumission payment. Until then our plans for the future will have to wait."

He was grateful for the money she'd offered, and his commitment to the betrothal was unaltered. But his ambition to leave Northchurch and go soldiering elsewhere was strengthening by the minute.

Seven

The funeral of Sir Thomas DeClerc was a magnificent one. Rather too magnificent, Alys considered, for a minor knight with neither pretensions to nobility nor ambitions beyond his own manor and its concerns. But of course, it wasn't he who had made the arrangements, and Sir Richard had pretensions and ambitions aplenty.

The procession exited the castle precincts in the late afternoon, led by a much smarter hearse than the one that had carried Sir Thomas home from Calais. It was drawn by two black horses wearing his tournament livery, and followed by twelve poor men, also clad in black but with their cloaks enlivened by contrasting white-lined hoods. Steven and Alan were among them, as Sir Thomas had decreed in his will, but the other ten were selected from among the cottars, landless peasants tied to the manor by feudal bonds, most of them in the service of the family. They would be expected to pray fervently, and forever, for their lord's soul as part of the bargain. At least, Alys reflected, the mourners would probably be allowed to keep their funeral suits, to do duty for many years as Sunday best and be bequeathed in time to their descendants.

The coffin was a large one, made of oak with brass accoutrements. It was covered with a piece of fine black cloth, overlaid by another showing a red cross on a white ground to demonstrate Sir Thomas's crusading credentials.

"They didn't open the coffin he came home in," Rosamund whispered to Alys as they stood together in the lane watching the procession go past. "They just put it inside this larger one." There was no need to discuss why this decision had been made, but Alys couldn't repress a shudder at the thought of the decomposing body within its double container.

"Why isn't Toby walking with the procession?" Alys asked her sister. "Shouldn't he be following the coffin with the poor men, like Steven and Alan? Surely he would want to do that?"

"He has gone to fetch Piers from Oxford, I believe. The lady Eleanor thought he should have been given a rest, but it seems he volunteered to go."

"What else would he do?" was Alys's practical response. "No family left, no home to go to, no land to till. I expect he'd rather be doing something he can be paid for."

"Mayhap that's true," her sister replied. "And if it is for Sir Thomas himself, all the better. But to miss the funeral Mass, not be included among the mourners...I think that seems unlike Toby, don't you?"

Alys shrugged. "If he chose it himself, then I judge he didn't want to be here."

Sir Richard and the ladies rode behind the bier in an open coach drawn by black palfreys, and when they alighted at the church Alys saw that, like the poor men, they were dressed in keeping with the occasion. Seamstresses, she thought, must have spent many wakeful hours creating funeral garb by candlelight in order to have it ready in time. She and her sister had no official part to play in proceedings and had simply donned their woollen Sunday kirtles. They formed part of the crowd that lined the lane from castle gates to church to watch the main procession as it passed, before following it in twos and threes, in respectful silence for the most part. Sir Thomas had not been greatly loved before his departure, but distance had given them a fondness for him. He had been the lord of their daily lives for as long as most could remember, and his passing would bring changes that none could predict.

Father Thomas met the cortège at the door of the church. Beyond, where the anchorhold abutted the church wall, Alys could see Sister Margery standing patiently, waiting to send her brother on his way to the next world with prayer. The chantry priest would take up this role when he arrived, and perform the daily Masses that popular piety demanded and for which he had left provision. Alys knew no harm of the chantry priest, whom she remembered as a boy of about her own age and a member of her own class of free peasants before Sir Thomas sent him off to Oxford to be educated. But she thought God would be more likely to take note of Sister Margery's simple prayers than all the Masses that Father Edward and his ilk might offer up.

The grooms unharnessed the horses from the hearse, and the poor men drew it into the chantry chapel that had been built to the north of the church, balancing Sister Margery's anchorhold on the south. It was a tiny space, created only to shelter the body of Sir Thomas himself. He was to lie here overnight in his open coffin, ahead of the funeral Mass which was to be said in the morning. His family followed the hearse into the church, together with six of the official mourners, who would help to manoeuvre the heavy coffin in the confined space, while the rest of the villagers waited outside, listening to the rise and fall of the priest's voice through the open door as he said the proper prayers for the occasion. Behind them the black horses stamped and fidgeted beside their grooms.

At last the mourners emerged, and the hearse was pulled back through the doorway, revealing to bystanders the magnificent tomb Sir Thomas had constructed for this hour. Alys noticed that the lady Eleanor had not come outside with the others, and imagined her standing beside the tomb grieving.

"Shouldn't you go and look after her?" she asked her sister in a fierce whisper. "Surely she shouldn't be left alone."

"Tis not my place," muttered Rosamund. "Not with the family there."

"But they *aren't* there," persisted Alys. "Not in the chapel with her, neither of them. If you ask me, the lady Eleanor is the only one who truly cares about her father's death."

Ros shook her head. "Mayhap that's true. But she will prefer to be alone with her father, at least for now." She touched her sister's arm. "I feel as you do, Alys. But I know her. I will wait outside the chapel with the rest. When she has spent a little time alone there, she will come out. That's when she may want me with her, unless Sir Richard and Lady Maud wait for her."

"My lord will take his wife home at once, Ros," said Alys, impatient with such optimism. "You know he won't wait." She looked across the churchyard to where Sir Richard was already handing his lady into their vehicle.

"Lady Maud is sickly," Rosamund reminded her. "But in any case, mayhap Sir Richard will send the coach back for the lady Eleanor." She took a breath. "Surely even he is not so forgetful of what is right that he would leave his sister to make her own way home on foot today. It will be dark soon. But anyway, as you said, tis my job to be there for her, within call." She picked up her skirts and set off along the path.

She encountered Steven and Alan coming from the chapel, their hoods thrown back in the early autumn sunshine. Behind them the grooms were re-harnessing the horses to the empty hearse for its journey back to the manor house, and she saw that the villagers had already begun to wait by the chapel door for the moment when they could file in slowly to pay their respects to the mortal remains of their lord.

Alan halted to exchange a word with Rosamund, but the latter shook her head and moved past him to stand beside the chapel door and watch for her mistress. Before he could move on, another villager had button-holed him, presumably to quiz him about their adventures abroad. It struck Alys, watching them, that there had been little opportunity for anyone to ask about their journey, and there must be so much to tell.

Steven left Alan fielding questions smoothly and moved to Alys's side. "I have had no chance today to see my lord about the manumission ceremony," he told her. "But after the funeral there will be a manor court, and I mean to ask formally then about it."

"There is no hurry, surely?"

"Then we will arrange a day for our marriage," he went on as though she hadn't spoken. "There is plenty of time for banns to be read before Advent."

Two months, thought Alys. No marriages could be formalised during the church seasons of Advent and Lent, and she was happy that he had not sought to put the wedding off into the Christmas season, joyous though weddings during the festival always were. But would two months be enough time for them to get to know one another again after his long absence? He seemed to have lost much of the youthful exuberance she remembered and which she had found so exciting and attractive. She wasn't sure what it would be like to be married to this dour, grim-faced stranger whose face she had yet to see graced with a smile. The betrothal stood, and she was relieved that it did, but she would have preferred to wait a little longer to take her marriage vows.

"I am not sure how soon I can be ready," she prevaricated. "There are changes to be made to the house, and I have little ready in the way of wedding clothes."

"Nay, there's no need for that, Alys." He looked at her, taking in her simple worsted kirtle. "This is your best homespun, I take it? 'Twill do well. I've no taste for finery, and no money to spend on a wedding suit with all the trimmings, either. And you have household goods enough, surely?"

"I have a piece of fine cloth in my trunk," she told him, "waiting to be made up into a gown for my wedding. Father wove it for me two years ago. But 'twill take a little while to sew it, with all the rest of the preparations."

He sighed. "So I must find a way of making myself presentable, must I? I hope you do not expect me to become a fine gentleman, Alys, and dress to impress. Free man I may be now, but there are limits."

She took a breath to reply indignantly, before she realised that his eyes were twinkling, though his face was as grave as ever. She tapped him sharply on the arm in reproof, but she was smiling. Perhaps it would not be so bad to be married to him after all.

When all the villagers who wished to do so had passed by the coffin, Father Edward called them together for the usual Friday penitentiary procession, led by himself and one of the junior clerks who assisted him with parish work. The clerk carried a censer, which he swung as he walked, to scatter the sweet-smelling incense fumes, while the priest intoned the penitential psalms and the villagers joined in at the appropriate places. It was only as she followed them that Alys found herself remembering the other deaths they had all heard of in the last few weeks, not so far away in the neighbouring county of Dorset. The Friday processions had been inaugurated by Father Edward a few weeks ago in the hope of keeping the pestilence away from their community. But it seemed that, in other places, similar fervent public prayer and devotion had not had the desired effect. How long would it be before other, humbler, Northchurch people were buried in their turn? Plague funerals were being held in haste, it was said, and with little respect for the bodies of the dead or time to mourn and feast in memory of them. Would Northchurch look back on Sir Thomas's funeral not only for its magnificence but for its orderliness? She shivered as she walked, and wished Steven had stayed to walk with her in the procession.

~ * ~

"What is happening about the Michaelmas Fair, Mother?" Steven asked, breaking his fast the following morning before attending the funeral Mass for Sir Thomas. "I thought to come back to all the final preparations for it, but I haven't seen much sign of those. It isn't to be cancelled because of Sir Thomas's death, I hope? Tis surely too late to send word to everyone not to come."

Cicely sighed. "Nay, Steven, tis not my lord's death so much as fear of the pestilence."

For a moment Steven's heart ran cold. Had his mother heard news of plague in the neighbouring villages?

She looked up. "Don't look like that, son. All I mean is that your father and Sir Richard reckoned it best to cancel this year because holding the fair would mean so many strangers coming to the village from who knows where. They thought it wasn't wise in these difficult days. Word was sent to all the regular merchants a week or two back. But we are celebrating our patronal feast as usual."

Steven digested this in silence as he ate the last of his breakfast. "No fair will mean tighter belts come winter," he observed at last. "Folk will have to store their surpluses instead of selling them, and do without what they would have purchased, too."

Cicely nodded. "We ourselves won't lose by it. This year's wool clip is already in the warehouses in London, ready to go to the Staple. But yes, tis true that others may find it difficult to make ends meet."

Steven wondered whether Alys had produce to sell. How generously she had offered him her bag of coin, her dowry. She was bringing much more to the marriage than he had realised, with the land and her cottage, even if in theory they were shared with Rosamund as joint heiress of their father. He wondered how easy it would be to find a master weaver to employ so she could finish her training. Most of them had their workshops in London, where the craft guild had its headquarters, and they wouldn't relish exchanging urban amenities for a country village. She might be biting off more than she could chew there, even if he approved of her working, which he did not.

"Alys and I mean to marry as soon as we can, Mother. Next month probably, if we have the means, or early November. We will live at her cottage, and she has plans to revive her father's weaving business and mayhap employ a master to teach her."

"Aye, she was sore disappointed when her father died before she had completed her training. Seemed to mean a lot to her, though how she thinks she can go on with it when she's married is a mystery to me."

"I said that to her," agreed Steven. "But you know Alys!" As he was beginning to do, he reflected.

His mother smiled. "Alys is a good lass, Steven. She'll suit you well, you'll see. And your father's plans to link our business with hers can bear fruit at last."

"As long as she doesn't expect me to become a weaver," he said. "I've other fish to fry."

Eight

"Piers! Piers! Rouse thyself, slugabed," came the muffled voice from beyond the closed door. "A messenger from home. Th'art wanted urgently."

Piers turned over on his pallet and pulled his cloak over his head. It wasn't only that he hated being woken in the morning before he'd had his sleep out. There was also the instinctive fear that a messenger from home might bring bad news. He remembered vividly the time three years before when his mother had died of fever and the news had been brought belatedly, weeks after the event. Nothing could be so bad as that, perhaps, but just the same he didn't want to know whatever tidings this messenger brought.

"Piers! Art deaf as well as stupid?" His fellow student John burst into the room, the oak door flying back against the stone wall. "Toby's come to fetch thee home."

Piers peered out from under the cloak. "Toby?"

"Aye. He says—"

"But Toby's been away these five years. How can he be here?"

"The family hath sent him. He came home with Sir Thomas yesterday and th'art needed." John's northern accent became more pronounced as his voice rose. "Cum on. Don thy hose and come talk wi' 'im. E'll cum up 'ere an roust thee out thy bed else."

Mystified, Piers pushed his covers back and pulled his hose on under his shirt. His friend, whose tall graceful form was already clad in the dark robe he always wore except in bed at night, waited for him with impatience as he fiddled with the fastenings.

"John, cease hopping up and down like a flea, and go and tell Toby I'm on my way. Give him a draught of ale and a bite, as well, will you?"

"Aye. Tha's a good thought. And thou will have summat too? Sounds like Toby's expecting thee to pack thy belongings and go with him straight. Says he arrived in Oxford last night too late to find lodging and has been rolled in his cloak in a stable with his horse. No wonder he is in haste to see thee." John ran off down the stone stairs to attend to Toby.

"I can't imagine why it's so urgent," Piers grumbled as he pulled on his tunic and hunted for his shoes in the clothes press that stood under the high window. He left his cloak lying on the pallet and his hat hanging on the peg. If he had to go with Toby, he would come back for them. He'd need his boots, too, for the road. But he would try to avoid leaving if he could. Even here in unworldly Oxford they had heard of the pestilence raging in the south of the country. He had no wish to court its horrors without good reason.

He was more than a little dismayed when Toby explained the reason for his summons home, for Sir Thomas's death would cut short his studies and put on hold many of his other dreams. His lord's passing might be unexpected—though there were always dangers attendant on travelling, especially such long and adventurous travelling as Sir Thomas had undertaken—but Sir Thomas had paid for his university education in return for his services as chantry priest when the need arose, and he must honour his part of the bargain. He wondered whether the chantry chapel itself had been completed. And also why Sir Thomas, not a notably pious man in the past, had suddenly felt the need of such petitions in the first place. It was a question he had often asked himself. What secret sins had the man committed, that made him fear his time in Purgatory so greatly?

As it turned out, it was impossible to set out immediately, as Toby had wanted. The man had ridden almost without rest on the way to Oxford, it appeared, in the hope of their returning in time for Piers to take the funeral service for Sir Thomas, and had arrived just as darkness fell the previous evening. But by the time he ran Piers to ground in his student house the following morning, and Piers had settled his affairs in Oxford, explained his departure to his tutor, paid his dues at his lodgings, and acquired a horse to carry himself and his possessions home, it was well after noon. Unless they were prepared to ride through the night, with all the risks that entailed, there was no possibility of their arriving home before the funeral.

They decided after some argument to break their journey at Abingdon, where there were a number of decent hostelries, rather than risk damp beds and voracious insects further along the road or, worse still, being benighted somewhere lonely and dangerous.

"The evenings are drawing in," Piers pointed out to Toby. "Unless you bespoke beds at an inn further south, it will be folly in the extreme to press on for the sake of an hour or so's further progress." He thought privately that his companion, well-travelled as he was, should have known this harsh fact only too well. Even as it was they had to make do with the hay loft over the stable in the Abbey guesthouse, and put up with the lumpiest of pallets, the main rooms all being full of better-prepared and better-funded travellers. But Toby was in such haste that Piers had to promise they would start out early the following morning.

Piers woke first, as it happened, and lay for a while thinking over the change in his fortunes. He turned over on his pallet and stretched before looking across to see whether Toby was awake. But the old man was lying flat on his back on the other side of the loft, snoring gently, one hand cushioning his head. Piers got up and felt himself gingerly around the buttocks and thighs for bruises. Horse riding was an unaccustomed activity, and although he had enjoyed the luxury of the experience yesterday afternoon, his nether parts had protested loudly when he dismounted. He was not sure how they would respond to climbing into the saddle again this morning, but Toby had been adamant that they should return to Northchurch as soon as humanly possible. He could see the sky lightening outside the window, yet Toby was showing no signs of waking. To be honest, he was glad of a little time to make sense of all that had happened. It had been a shock to him to be summoned home so suddenly.

Even if there had been no pestilence to avoid, the last thing he wanted at this juncture was to go home with his university education half-finished. Sir Thomas had left money for him to study the quadrivium for six years, and then to specialise in theology or medicine as he chose, always on the understanding that he would act as chantry priest when required. That education would have given him in the long term the chance to make a career out of the church, or as a physician if he preferred, for the duties of a chantry priest could be farmed out to a lesser cleric for very little outlay—there were always plenty of half-educated priests looking for a job. His patron wasn't an old man, and it hadn't seemed at all likely that Piers would be needed in a priestly capacity yet awhile, especially while the knight was far away on a holy pilgrimage of some kind. He hadn't even attained his Master of Arts degree yet, being still only a humble Bachelor, and there had been the glories of medicine to look forward to once he had finished the quadrivium. He'd taken minor clerical orders as was expected of him and had been ordained deacon less than a year ago, though Sir Richard would expect his father's soul to be supported properly with Masses which only a full priest could celebrate. He supposed the bishop of Winchester would arrange his full ordination once he arrived home.

He could hear the abbey bells ringing for Lauds. It was time to wake Toby and get themselves on the road.

~ * ~

In the event, although they arrived too late for Sir Thomas's funeral Mass, they were in time to join the feast that followed it. The road from the north took them past the castle, where Sir Richard's servants informed them that the family were still feasting in the village.

"Let's go and join them," said Piers. "I could do with some food." He was ravenous, for they had ridden hard from Abingdon and had stopped for little in the way of rest or refreshment. But Toby was such a dour, phlegmatic character that it was hard to tell whether he suffered from such human pangs as hunger and thirst.

"Nay, I've no wish to feast over the body of my master," was Toby's initial reaction. "'Twill be for rich folk and such, too. Not fit for me. Nor for you, come to that, though I suppose now you're a clerk you'll be rubbing shoulders with the lords and ladies."

"The feast is for poor folk, too," pointed out Sir Richard's groom, still within earshot on his way to the stables with Toby's horse. "Those that were invited, that is. Steven, the reeve's son, is there, and Alan Archer. They helped to carry my lord's coffin yesterday, and followed him in the procession. Twelve poor men in all. You'll be in good company, Toby."

"There," said Piers. "If Sir Thomas's other travelling companions are invited, you will be welcome, too. And I'm sure Sir Richard will expect me to present myself to him immediately. Come on."

Toby grunted. "I suppose I'd best come and introduce you. Sir Richard will only remember you as a scrubby lad. Come to think on't, you haven't changed much, even if you do wear a cleric's robe."

Piers laughed. "I shan't need introductions," he replied cheerfully. "But you should come and join the feast, not skulk in some corner like a man with nothing to say for himself."

"We'll see," was all Toby would promise.

When they arrived, they found Steven and Alan holding court with tales of the East, to which even the high table party were listening avidly, while the half of the village who had not been invited to the feast had gathered to listen. The weather was still fine, so food had been set out on trestle tables on the village green near the bridge. After the first respectful murmurings with regard to Sir Thomas's death, conversation had become more cheerful and more general, especially once the bereaved family, augmented by some distant cousins who had ridden over from a manor near Reading, had betaken themselves to eat at a separate table.

Alan was in full flow, describing the events that led to Sir Thomas giving him the mare. "I shot the bandit leader," he said, "and the rest fled, leaving my lovely mare in our hands."

Toby grunted. Alan seemed to be relating only the more repeatable adventures they had engaged in. No doubt he would save the more scurrilous and the raunchier for an (all-male) audience of his peers later.

He took a seat at the end of the table occupied by Steven and Alan and their families. "I'd best stay and make sure you tell folks the truth. Belike you're feeding them a lot of old wives' tales."

Piers looked at Sir Richard to see whether it was an appropriate time to report for duty, but Sir Richard waved him to a seat, too occupied with the tale Alan had begun of the winter they had spent with the Teutonic Knights in Germany to do more than acknowledge his presence. Piers busied himself gratefully with the cold meats, wheaten bread and autumn fruits that were laid out. Much depredation of these had already occurred, but there was plenty left to satisfy his hunger.

No one seemed to be suffering from plague or fearing for the lives of loved ones, he noted with some relief as he piled a trencher with food. Clearly rumour had exaggerated its terrors, or its reach, although he had the uneasy feeling that it would not be long before rumour became reality. He made the sign of the cross, and hoped that those who saw it would believe it to be a prayer of thanks for the food.

It was not until his first pangs of hunger were sated that he had leisure to look about him at the festive scene. The village green was much as he remembered it, an open space near the bridge, big enough for the fair held annually at Michaelmas and for community gatherings such as the Mayday celebrations he remembered from his childhood. Around the green, the cottages crouched higgledy-piggledy, low, half-rotten wooden hovels rubbing shoulders with more substantial cob constructions. Their doors and shutters were open to the fine autumn air, but inside, he reflected, the damp that had crept in over the rain-soaked summer would be slow to clear.

Everyone had put aside their household tasks for the day to send their lord on his way with ceremony, but he saw a woman carrying a rough platter of leftover food inside one cottage, presumably to feed an elderly relative or neighbour who was too frail to attend the feast, while another was gathering up scraps from the grass under and around the tables, putting it in a bag for the later delectation of hens or pigs.

"You are welcome, Father," said a gentle voice at his elbow. "I am sorry you were not here in time for my father's funeral, but glad that our people have supplied you with food and drink after your journey. You and Toby must have ridden hard to get here so quickly."

He looked round and knew immediately this must be Sir Thomas's daughter, Eleanor, although she bore little resemblance to the young girl he remembered. When he left home, she had been a child of twelve with her skirts still kilted, possessed of a long-legged skittishness reminiscent of a high-bred filly. She would have run wild with the village boys and girls if she had been given the chance, but of course Sir Thomas would not allow his precious daughter such dangerous freedom. He could see none of that wildness in the cool poise she presented today, though perhaps the circumstances were largely to blame. In mourning clothes, she seemed remote and dignified, the white dress robbing her face of colour, though she could not altogether hide the glorious gold of her hair, peeping decorously from inside her wimple.

"My lady!" he responded lamely. He scrambled to his feet and made his reverence to her, his heart beating wildly in his chest as his feet tried to trip him up.

"We are so grateful to you for leaving your studies at once to come home for my father's sake. To pray in his chantry."

"That is why your father gave me my education," he reminded her.

"But your studies were not complete, I think? That must have been hard, to leave learning behind."

He looked at her. There was something more to this than the obvious courtesy and sensitivity of a great lady. She had liked her books, he recalled. Perhaps she had found in those the adventures she had not been allowed to have in life.

"I loved my studies," he admitted.

"Of course! I understand that. And you must not give them up altogether. I have books...my father was always most generous to me in that. I would be so happy if you would come and read them sometimes. They have given you a cell at the castle, I believe. It would be easy for you to borrow what you want."

His heart leapt at the thought, as much for the unpriestly delight of meeting with the lady as for the chance of further study for himself. But likely her library would contain romances and tales of knightly deeds rather than the kind of theology and philosophy he had studied. Besides, it was not appropriate for him, as a deacon, more than half-way to the sacramental status of priesthood, to allow himself any unnecessary contact with a woman, least of all a beautiful noblewoman such as the lady Eleanor.

Suddenly he felt miserable and awkward. "It is a kind offer, my lady." He swallowed, trying to find an excuse that would not seem boorish or ungrateful. "I think your brother would not feel it right, however, that I should have a share in any way in books that are for your exclusive use." He was conscious that his use of the word 'share' was loaded with emotional undertones which he had not meant to express, and hurried on. "Besides, I fear we will none of us have leisure for reading or study in the days to come."

Her grey eyes dilated with shock. "Father, you speak what we have tried to avoid even thinking of. Yet you say truly. And if such a trial comes, we must bear it as best we may. But I still hope that the pestilence may be averted, if our prayers are sufficiently fervent. I beg you will add yours to ours."

He nodded quickly, eager to preserve her hope, forlorn though he thought it.

~ * ~

Awareness of the threat posed by the pestilence was brought home to everyone the next Sunday, when Father Edward read out at morning Mass a letter he had received from London, written at the king's request. "Terrible is God towards men...He punishes their shameful deeds in various ways during this mortal life so that they might not be condemned eternally," he read. "It is now to be feared that the kingdom of England is to be oppressed by the pestilence and wretched mortalities of men that have flared up in other regions."

The king, it appeared, had ordered all his subjects to redouble their efforts in prayer, together with extra Masses said by the priests, in an attempt to turn aside God's anger. The bishop of Winchester, Father Edward explained, had added his comments to the king's, exhorting his flock to search their consciences, turn from their sins, and trust that God would keep the suffering of the pestilence from them.

There was a murmur of distress and fear in the congregation. Father Edward himself looked pale with anxiety, and even Sir Richard stirred in his seat to comfort his wife, before the Mass proceeded on its familiar way. Afterwards, the knight and his family swept the priest away to the castle before the congregation had a chance to ask him any questions, and Piers found himself in the frontline instead.

"You've studied in Oxford," said one man, a young father surrounded by his children. "What do they say there about this pestilence? Is it truly a punishment from God for our sins? Why are they suffering in Dorset and Bristol, but we are still healthy?"

"We are taking steps to avert God's wrath," another man reminded him.

"Penitential psalms and processions," sneered the miller, who was listening intently. "What good did they do the folk in Dorset? They say whole villages have been left empty, and no one to bring in the harvest."

Piers shifted uncomfortably under the villagers' gaze and wondered what he could say that would help anyone, when he did not understand it all himself. Besides, he was not their priest, and had no authority to speak to them on these matters.

"Good folk," he replied at last, "I am not learned in the ways of the pestilence. It had not reached Oxford when I left there. I have heard only the same tales you have of terrible mortality and suffering. As to why it affects some places and not others, I can only tell you what the physicians say, which is that it is carried on miasma, poisonous air that travels from place to place. But even the physicians do not seem to know how to treat this sickness, if what I have heard is true. They look back to astrological omens three years ago, where a conjunction of three planets gave warning that terrible things were to come." He paused, as a murmuring of consternation broke out. "As for the ways of God, you must do what Father Edward recommends. He is your priest, not I."

"I've heard that some are driving strangers from their doors," reported a woman with a baby in her arms. "They say people bring the pestilence with them when they come from a place where it has struck."

Several people looked around anxiously as though wondering whether any strangers were hiding in the crowd.

"We came from the south but a few days ago," Steven pointed out. "There was no sign of the pestilence in the places we came through, not even Southampton and Winchester. Who is to say whether it will fall upon us or nay?"

Piers shifted uncomfortably. Reports he had heard of the way the pestilence had swept like wildfire across whole regions in Western Europe, sparing no one, did not encourage such optimism. "We simply do not know what will happen," he told them, the platitude sounding lame even to his own ears. "But it is all in the hands of God. We can only trust Him. Remember," he added more firmly, "not all suffering is because of sin."

"King Edward would be glad to hear that," commented Steven.

"With his own daughter already touched by the pestilence, and she an innocent maid."

There were sidelong glances among the group, for recent news of the death of the Princess Joan at Bordeaux in the summer had cast a cloud over even the court's determined tourneying, in spite of everyone's efforts to view it as an event that had taken place far away among foreigners, with no relevance for the spread of the plague to England.

"I've heard the king may close the ports." Tom the Hayward brought this information to the discussion like a conjuror producing a rabbit from a hat. "Why would he consider doing that unless he fears that the pestilence arrives by sea?"

"Nonsense, man!" Steven was scornful. "The king won't shut down our trade with Europe. It would be to admit defeat, in more ways than one. For one thing, it would ruin the country, and he needs prosperity if he is to continue the war with France. They were strengthening the garrison at Calais when we embarked there."

A murmur of discussion arose, giving Piers the opportunity to disappear into the chantry chapel before anyone could come up with any more questions with which to belabour him. He rested his hand on Sir Thomas's tomb, and thought it might yet become a place of sanctuary for him from such villager preoccupations. It was all a long way from the lecture halls of Oxford, where theological disputation concerned the allegorical interpretation of the Scriptures or the abstruse reasoning of St Thomas Aquinas and St Augustine of Hippo, rather than practical pastoral dilemmas in the face of impending calamity.

~ * ~

While Piers was sheltering under the auspices of Sir Thomas, Alan was practising at the butts with his bow, as was obligatory by royal command for all archers on Sunday after church. There was no shortage of men there who, convinced of their own prowess with the bow, wished to show off to the watching crowd of mothers, sisters and sweethearts that their credentials were equal to those of the famous archer who had so recently returned from his travels. Some had earned renown at Creçy with the king's forces and were keen, two years on, to remind their neighbours that they were still masters of their crafts. But though Alan had not practised at the butts for a long time, he had regularly used the bow in earnest to defend his master, and skill at target competition came back to him swiftly. By the end of an hour, his main rivals had challenged him to a contest the following Sunday, on which bets were being laid among the spectators.

"I should think he'll win easily," Rosamund said to her sister, who was standing at the edge of the crowd with Steven. Her tone was admiring, and Alys shot her a suspicious glance.

"What's it to you, sister?"

Rosamund tossed her blonde head. "I should think anyone must praise such skill," she declared.

"You watch your step," Alys advised. "He had always an eye for the girls, that one, and I don't suppose he's changed much."

"What say you, Steven?" Rosamund looked up at her sister's betrothed coquettishly. "Is Alan the man for me?"

Steven looked down at her with some impatience, aware that his relationship with Alys involved taking some responsibility for her sister. If she offered Alan too much encouragement, she was playing with fire...unless his intentions were serious this time. "Your sister is wise. A maiden should act maidenly."

She snorted and walked away from them.

Alys was troubled. "She is not usually so bold. I hope Alan has not turned her head."

"I'll keep an eye on her," Steven promised, though he didn't relish the prospect of meddling in his friend's affairs, not least because Alan would undoubtedly resent it.

Alys rewarded him with one of her rare smiles, which illumined her face from within. It did not entirely reconcile him to the prospect of protecting his young sister-in-law from the consequences of her own folly, but it pleased him nonetheless.

Nine

The absence of the Michaelmas Fair was felt by many, as Steven had predicted, but everyone agreed that cancellation was the prudent course. Tales had begun to reach them from all sides of villages and towns less than fifty miles away being struck by the pestilence, and its horrors lost nothing in the telling. No one wanted to do anything that might bring the disease any closer.

The feast laid on by Sir Richard for the Michaelmas holiday itself went some way to making up for the cancellation of the fair that normally preceded it. The weather continued fine, albeit showery, the ground was drying up after the long wet period of the summer and most of the sparse harvest had been garnered. Tables were set up in the castle grounds, for the feast was traditionally one for which the DeClercs took responsibility. It was, Alys thought as she walked through the archway on Steven's arm, a truly beautiful sight. Starched white cloths covered the trestle tables, which were laden with all manner of viands: joints of venison and beef, stuffed capons, loaves of wheaten bread and pies, and tarts and sweetmeats of every description. Tankards of ale for the villagers, and tall glasses of wine for Sir Richard's family and their guests, promised much merriment to come, and forgetfulness for those whose quarter-day rents had been hard to find, and who feared hardship as a result in the months to come.

For Steven it represented a very special celebration, for at the manor court held the previous morning, Sir Richard had performed, albeit in rather a perfunctory manner, the ceremony that gave Steven his promised manumission. In addition, his wages had been paid by the bailiff promptly and he had taken himself into Whitchurch and bought some new shirts and hose at the market, while that morning his mother had dug out a surcoat of his father's that no longer fitted its owner's ample form. Steven was conscious he had accepted this with rather a bad grace, given that she had probably saved the garment for him ever since his father had discarded it, but being beholden to his father riled him nonetheless.

Alys had attended the court with him to register formally their intent to marry, and had watched as Steven handed over thirty of her precious dowry shillings for the privilege of becoming a free tenant. The practical and administrative formalities would no doubt be dealt with by Steward Roger. But the thing was done, and when Alys saw how happy it made Steven, she was glad she had kept her dowry intact for him. He would have taken her to wife without it, she now believed, and her share of the land and the business would probably have seemed enough recompense in the circumstances, but she knew he would always remember the gift, and she hoped it would form an enduring bond between them.

The court session took longer than expected because, in addition to the normal manorial business and Steven's manumission, there were a number of land transfers to be registered. Folk selling up and leaving the village in an attempt to escape the plague, Alys realised, and cashing in their assets as best they could first.

"Rats leaving the sinking ship," was Steven's contemptuous opinion of this.

"Is that what they do?" she asked with interest. "The rats, I mean."

"So I've been told, though none of the ships we sailed on sank, so I've not seen it for myself. Nor many rats, if the truth be told."

Alys shivered. "I used to fear, sometimes, that you'd been shipwrecked and would never return. And I'd never know."

He looked down at her. "Was it hard, those years I was away? I didn't think you'd given marriage much thought, when I left. 'Twas just a matter between your father and mine."

She nodded. "That's true. But when my father died, and I was only half-trained as a weaver, and my mother became...as she is now...then I was afraid. Making ends meet wasn't easy. And I was waiting for you to return."

"Would you have married someone else, if I hadn't?"

She hesitated, but honesty prevailed. "Maybe. If I'd known you weren't ever coming. But..."

"I was the best bargain, if I came."

"Well...yes."

She held her breath, but he laughed. "Alys, you are a truthful maid, I can see."

"And you," she asked after a moment. "Did you think of marrying some fine lady on your travels?"

He laughed. "You have the wrong idea about my travels, lass. I never saw any fine ladies except when we were with the Teuton Knights last winter. And they weren't concerned with such as me. As for other women, well, young Alan would have had them all first, even if I'd had a mind for that."

"Oh, yes," said Alys, reminded of her sister. "Alan."

"Do you object to him as a suitor for Rosamund?" asked Steven, bringing the matter out into the open.

She looked up at him. "If he is a suitor, no. With this bequest from Sir Richard, he would be a suitable match for her. But I don't trust him. He has a roving eye, and he's far too attractive—I don't want her heart broken."

Steven hesitated. "'Tis true he has a way with women. But I think he's ready to settle down. He's a good man, Alys. We kept each other's back many a time on our travels. I'd trust him to keep his word."

"Ah," muttered Alys darkly. "Maybe he would, if he'd given it. She's young, Steven, and he's a hero in the village, coming back from his adventures with tales to tell, and a comely face to boot."

"And she likes him."

"Aye. I think she does. If I'm honest, it worries me."

~ * ~

Alan saw to his delight when he arrived in the castle grounds for the Michaelmas feast that Rosamund had been released from her duties while the lady Eleanor ate with her family and friends. She was seated at a table with Alys, Steven, and the reeve's family, and it seemed the most natural thing in the world that Alan should join them. His brothers and their families had taken their places at another table, but he was tired of their jolly inanities. Rosamund's face, tilted downwards with maidenly decorum as he took his place on the bench opposite, was flushed with a lovely rosy colour that he felt sure had only arisen as he approached, and he hoped it would not be long before she raised her eyes to meet his.

It's my lucky day, he thought as he began cheerfully loading his trencher from the platters before him. The sort of day when anything might happen.

After the feast, the tables were swiftly cleared, the minstrels struck up, and dancing began. The children entertained the adults first, with deep bows and curtsies carefully practised for the occasion, before their natural energy translated into exuberant dance. When it was the adults' turn, Alan ensured that he was part of a set containing Rosamund and her sister, and as they swung up and down, twirling, heying, stepping in and out, their eyes met and glanced away, seeking, questioning, inviting, accepting. When the dance ended, he claimed her from her final partner, and they walked away together unobserved.

On the lane leading away from the manor house, he took her hand, clasping it lightly, the touch a frisson that stirred in him something deeper than mere flirtation. The road was quiet, for most people were still dancing and drinking at the castle. No work would be done today, except for feeding the indoor livestock that evening, for St Michael's Day was a holiday. Most people had turned their animals out for the day, if they could, and the craftsmen had put away their tools.

They turned left at the fork, as though by mutual consent. Rosamund allowed Alan's hand in hers to guide her, though without any answering clasp, her gaze still fixed on the road in front of her. Ahead of them was the big barn that belonged to Steven's family, where the woolsacks and animal fodder were stored. Quiet it might be in the village while everyone was at the feast, but whatever was to happen between him and Rosamund he wanted to keep private. No ribald banter or lewd comments from his brothers. No disapproval from Alys or Steven or his parents. This was something serious, he knew, a world away from the casual liaisons he'd enjoyed on his travels.

He opened the wicket in the big barn door and invited her to enter with him. He didn't yet know whether she shared his feeling of awe, an excitement that went far beyond purely physical arousal. He turned her towards him and put his arms round her, slowly, gently, giving her the chance to refuse him, to pull back from the encounter, even to reject him utterly, though his longing for her grew with every moment that passed. She stood within those arms passively, not raising her eyes. Her hands were on his chest, but whether to touch him or to hold him off, he didn't know.

"Rosamund." His voice was husky.

She looked up, and her beautiful blue eyes met his ardent look at last. Their gaze was calm and accepting, the coquetry of her last meeting with him quite absent. Still gently, still tentatively, he drew her closer and touched her lips with his; and in that moment all her calm reserve vanished, as though his kiss had set her on fire. Passion blazed up between them like tinder-dry kindling, needing only one spark to start a conflagration. At one side of the barn they made themselves a bed in a pile of hay. That sweet smell filled their nostrils as they lay down together in love and desire, with kisses and caresses, with penetration and abandonment, until at last passion was spent in fulfilment.

~ * ~

Alys did not notice her sister's departure at first, although during a break in the dancing she did look around for her in vain. The feasters had broken up into small groups, chatting and drinking ale. The DeClerc family were still sitting at high table, watching the revellers, and Rosamund did not appear to be waiting on the lady Eleanor. But the whole village was packed into the castle grounds, so Rosamund might be somewhere in the crowd with friends, innocently enjoying herself.

"Piers, have you seen my sister?"

Piers was sitting on a stool near the high table, and it seemed to Alys that he was looking slightly wistful, ill at ease in his clerical role.

"Not since the dancing began," he replied. "Is she needed for something?" He looked towards high table.

"I will ask the lady Eleanor," said Alys, moving briskly past him.

Piers would not himself have dared to disturb the Family in such a way, but he had already begun to have considerable respect for Alys who, it seemed to him, was capable of anything. He watched her as she went over to speak to her sister's mistress. Sir Richard treated her with some disdain, but she took no notice.

Piers sighed and wished he had the opportunity to speak with the lady Eleanor. Her gracious welcome at the feast had left him feeling miserable and awkward, as though his mouth and his limbs didn't belong to him and he didn't know how to use them properly. Yet her sweet, spiritual smile had seemed to pierce him through, and he was conscious of her every movement, his ear tuned to each word she spoke.

In many ways, these first few days at home had been much more uncomfortable than he had expected. He had returned to his own village, to the manor where he had been born, and yet because of his education and priestly calling he felt an alien in their midst. Once he had been the boy who was always in trouble, the son of an impoverished widow who made a bare living out of growing herbs in her small garden and making potions and salves to ease the health of her equally impoverished neighbours. Only his sharp brain and the interest taken in him by Father Nicholas, Father Edward's predecessor, had saved him from getting on the wrong side of the law. But under the priest's tutelage, he had learned to love studying, so that his adventures at university had been comparatively tame and his misdemeanours minor.

He was taking his chantry duties at Northchurch seriously and genuinely longed for the day when he was priested and could say Masses for Sir Thomas as had been intended. But at the same time, between him and the villagers there was a gulf he couldn't bridge, even though they had been his friends and neighbours when he was a child. The lady Eleanor's open cordiality, in contrast, had been both a joy and a torment. Between them, he told himself firmly, there could not even be friendship. He was neither her equal in social status, nor her confessor. He had no reason to speak with her unless she initiated a conversation.

He had heard that Sir Richard had a knight lined up to wed her, though it was said the lady did not favour him. The thought tore at his heart, partly at the very thought of her wedded to someone she had not chosen, and partly because if she married, she would undoubtedly leave the manor and go to live with her husband elsewhere. Even if there could be no friendship between them, he could gaze from afar at her beauty, her purity, her loving kindness towards those she met. Yet even that was a guilty pleasure, for it fed his emotional soul, which his conscience told him should have found feminine companionship not in flesh-and-blood womanhood but only in prayer to the Virgin Mary and the female saints. Admiration for the lady Eleanor, however pure, might imperil his immortal soul and his priestly career, and would so offend her if she became aware of it that he feared she would never speak to him again.

The lady Eleanor, serenely unaware of the young cleric's conscientious self-censure, told Alys that she had no knowledge of her maid's whereabouts, but graciously disclaimed any need for Rosamund's services that day.

"Let her enjoy herself, Alys," she recommended. "It is a feast, and we will have trials and tribulations to come in the future. Let us all forget our troubles for today at least, and celebrate while we may with our friends and families. Has Steven no need of you? Now you are betrothed, he must be your first thought."

She looked over Alys's shoulder as she spoke. Alys turned and saw Steven approaching her, looking happier and more benevolent than she had seen him since his return.

"My lady has the right of it," he said, offering her his arm and bowing slightly to Eleanor. "Come and walk with me, Alys."

They sauntered around the castle wards as though, Alys thought, they were the lord and lady of the manor instead of two of its tenants.

"When will your marriage gown be ready, Alys?" he asked her, as they passed the gatehouse.

She looked at him in surprise. "It is not only my own apparel that is in question. Rosamund and my mother will also want new gowns for the ceremony."

He shook his head. "I don't want a great fuss made. I will wear these clothes—they are new, and this surcoat of my father's is bright enough for a fistful of weddings. I'll allow you the time to make that new gown you wanted from the cloth your father wove for you, and that's all. Tis your dowry that paid for my freedom, and I must do my part in return. My father has promised to make over to me some of the lands he holds free of obligations, as your dower. If we are to marry, then we should not delay. I have asked Father Edward to read the banns this Sunday."

It was almost an ultimatum, and there was a note of decision in his voice that Alys dared not combat, though the words were less than romantic. Was this really what she wanted, for him to marry her mainly, even entirely, out of obligation, because she had been generous and trusted him with the money for his manumission? And why was he in such haste now, after five long years of absence? Could it be that he did not trust himself to stick to the bargain, even though not so many days ago he had declared unequivocally that the betrothal stood?

She shook her head. The idea of planning a wedding while much of south-western England suffered and died seemed to fly in the face not only of good taste but of prudence. And even if the pestilence miraculously avoided them, who knew how long it would be before its depredations elsewhere were over, and life could return to normal?

On the other hand, she thought pragmatically, she had waited and saved and done without for just this purpose, and romantic sentiments and less-than-ideal circumstances didn't come into it. The marriage was what her father had wanted, what their parents had agreed on, and she didn't want to risk Steven changing his mind, even if he found a way to pay back her dowry honourably. The chilling thought visited her of being left with an impossible choice between the miller, James, or spinsterhood.

"I will be ready in a fortnight," she promised. Her mother would help her, if asked. Even though Ellen's wits wandered half the time, her hands had not forgotten their way with a needle. If presented with a hem or a seam to sew, she would have it done in a brace of shakes, with the smallest and neatest of stitches. She would not notice what she herself wore, but perhaps there would be time to embroider one of her everyday dresses, for she still had several, none of which was worn out—unsurprisingly, for she did little work now. Alys thought there were some pretty coloured woollen threads in the workshop that she could use. As for her sister, she had a lovely gown that the lady Eleanor had given her from her own wardrobe last year for the castle servants' Christmas feast. It was packed in the clothes press at the cottage and had only been worn on that one occasion. Rosamund would be happy enough with that.

This thought brought to mind that her sister was still nowhere to be seen, a suspicious circumstance which caused her more than a little concern, especially since Alan was not in evidence either. There seemed little doubt the two had left the feast together. While Steven rejoined the rest of the family at table, no doubt to regale the revellers with more tales of the East, Alys spent half an hour walking to and fro across the castle grounds, even poking her nose into corners where it was not wanted, but she found no sign of her sister. Instead, to her irritation she found her mother following her, querulously demanding to know what Alys was doing and why she had left the table.

"Steven asked me to walk with him, Mother. We were discussing our wedding plans."

Her mother did not seem to hear this response. "Is it time to go home?" she asked. "I am tired and the feast has finished. I do not like all this revelry when we should be in mourning."

Alys sighed. The dancing was still going on, growing more exuberant by the minute, although she felt sure those involved intended no disrespect to the shade of Sir Thomas, so lately entombed in his chantry chapel. Life was short, and especially in these uncertain days people sought to make the most of the time they had, and of good health while they enjoyed it. But she realised that for her mother, the lord's funeral had stirred up all her own grief again. She had been edgy and weepy all week, and more demanding than usual of Alys's time and attention, which Alys would have preferred to bestow on her own affairs.

Mastering her irritation with an effort, she returned to their table, her mother lagging behind her like a wayward child, and waited until Steven had finished corroborating some outlandish story of Alan's. Toby, who had cast such a workaday and grumpy shadow over their tales at the feast that followed Sir Thomas's funeral, was nowhere to be seen. She had heard he was working in the stables now, so he was probably mucking out or feeding the horses, either of which would provide him with an excuse not to attend the festivities.

"Steven, my mother wishes to go home," she told him, when he turned his attention to her.

He got to his feet. "Shall I walk along with you?"

She smiled at him, happy to share the responsibility for her mother if only for the short journey home. "We'd be glad of your company."

He took Ellen's arm and held it firmly. "Come along, Ellen," he said. "We must go and tend your animals."

Ellen turned towards home without demur. "They will be hungry," she agreed. "And I must prepare a meal for us all later."

She had not prepared a meal for months, Alys reflected grimly, and in any case seemed to have forgotten that they had all eaten their fill and more at the feast, and required no more food that day. Clearly reality had receded again, and she would be best at home with her distaff, out of the way. Alys put any thought of a further search for Rosamund out of her mind and set off in her mother's wake.

Ten

Miraculously, during October life in Northchurch continued more or less as normal, with no firm news of pestilence in the surrounding villages, though horrific tales were still reaching them of its spread through neighbouring counties. It was as though they lived in a protected enclave, the arms of epidemic reaching around to the south and west along the coast and hinterland, but not inland towards them. The weekly penitential processions gained more adherents as villagers began to have more faith in their efficacy. Perhaps, after all, they would be spared. Perhaps the pestilence was losing its virulence and would peter out as epidemics often did, leaving the bereaved to bear their grief bravely and those who had escaped to give thanks for deliverance. In the meantime, although Alys and Steven were to have the simplest of ceremonies at the church door, to which only family members were invited, the villagers were glad to be distracted from their worries by observing the wedding preparations.

By hiring a seamstress to help her prepare linen suitable for the occasion, and leaving her mother to sew the bridal gown, Alys contrived to be ready within the timescale Steven had set her.

Cicely, for her part, made do with a simple Sunday dress for herself, though she found time to sew a new and more ample surcoat for her husband, who, as father of the bridegroom, she felt should be clad as richly as current custom and law would permit a villein to dress. Father Edward consented somewhat grudgingly to bless the marriage, and it all passed off without incident, everyone playing their part correctly and the bride and groom making their vows clearly and without emotion.

The emotional sobriety of the wedding struck Rosamund forcibly, for she was living in a rosy dream engendered by Alan's frequent lovemaking, her body sensitive to his every move and look. Even Alys and Steven, she thought, must surely feel some echo of the aroused wonder she was experiencing, as each secret encounter in the barn proved more dazzling and ecstatic than the last. Perhaps when sexual intimacy began between them, there would be a change. Perhaps then they would become as lost in each other as she and Alan were...and without the need to hide it. But looking at the bridal couple, handfast before the priest, their faces betraying nothing but steady commitment and acceptance, she doubted it. How different we are, she thought. Two sisters, but worlds apart in feeling and experience.

Alys herself had thought little about her future relations with Steven other than making sure that practical matters at her cottage were taken care of––an extra chest provided for his clothes, and sleeping arrangements that gave her and Steven some privacy from her mother. She had prepared a modest feast for the family to enjoy after the ceremony, and Cicely had kindly sent Mary to help her lay it out in the main room of the cottage. But Alan, who had been chosen as best man against Alys's wishes, chose to remind her by way of ribald comments at the wedding breakfast that marriage was about more than dowries and living arrangements. She tried to take no notice, but unfortunately neither he nor his comments were easy to ignore.

She studied Steven surreptitiously as the meal came to an end. What would he demand of her that night? Would he be importunate, or rough, or would he give her time to adjust and feel safe with him? It was impossible to tell, but suddenly her imagination quaked. He had made no attempt to kiss her or hold her in his arms during their betrothal; indeed he had only returned from his journey, she realised, a bare four weeks ago. There had been no time for courtship or a gradual awakening of sexual interest.

Alan, grinning hugely at his friend, suggested the bride be bedded with no further delay.

"Tis no use prevaricating," he said. "Bedding her is part of marrying her, and as best man I'm the one to make sure you do it."

Alys wished even more fervently than before that she had been able to exclude him as a guest, but Steven had been adamant. Alan had travelled the world with him for five years and was like a brother. He could not possibly be excluded from his rightful place at the ceremony. Alys could only hope that as Steven's wife she might prevail on him to nip Alan's romance with her sister in the bud. No one else could do it, with Rosamund fatherless—and effectively all but motherless, with Ellen in the state she was—and Sir Richard not likely to lift a finger to protect his ward.

Steven lifted an eyebrow in her direction, and she saw with fury that he was rather amused at her embarrassment. "It is time, wife."

Cringing with humiliation, she nevertheless could not fly in the face of tradition. Setting her teeth to endure it all as calmly as she could, she removed her wedding gown with her sister's help and folded it carefully in the press, while their friends watched and applauded from the foot of the ladder. In her shift, under a long woollen robe her father had woven, she climbed into the big bed and pulled the covers over her, while Steven stripped to his long shirt.

"We must bid you farewell," he told the guests as he climbed in beside her. "You've work to do, for God's sake. Go and leave us alone."

With some hilarity, the guests began to leave, back to the working day and its tasks. Paul took Ellen firmly by the arm, reminding her that she was to spend the rest of the day with Cicely, and Rosamund, already changed into her working dress, set off for the manor to attend the lady Eleanor. Alan was the last to go, determined to deliver a few parting shots to encourage his friend to his marital duties. Steven said nothing, but simply waited for Alan's wit to run down. At last the front door closed behind him, and the couple were alone.

Alys looked shyly at her husband as he lay beside her, but his face gave nothing away. Although the shutters were closed in the main room below, when he blew out the candle the light still showed from without. It was not far past noon, she thought.

She smiled at him, tentatively. "It seems strange to be abed at this hour."

"'Twould be stranger still to be out about our daily tasks," he retorted.

"Y-yes," she agreed, slightly taken aback.

She waited, silent, for him to make a move, but felt no maidenly shrinking. In a farming community, where animals mated and gave birth on a daily basis, she had grown up knowing about the relations between husband and wife, at least in theory. Ellen had not, of course, given her any motherly advice, but she had expected none. It was the man's part to take the initiative sexually, and she had no doubt that Steven would do so when he felt ready.

Yet the act, when it came, was unromantic in the extreme, a matter of obligation on his part, and submissive duty on hers, in which neither of them looked for or experienced great pleasure or fulfilment. But it was completed, and for the moment that satisfied both of them. Alys, who had been up long before dawn making preparations, and on whom the burden of most of the day's arrangements had fallen, went to asleep peacefully as soon as Steven's rhythmic movements had come to a climax and ceased. She woke only to relieve herself after dark had fallen. Steven lay log-like on his side of the big bed.

She was not to know how long he had lain awake listening to her quiet breathing, disconcerted by her matter-of-fact acceptance of the requirements of marital intimacy, and wondering what kind of a marriage he had entered into. His sexual experience, unlike Alan's, had not been wide, but the prostitutes and maidservants who had serviced his modest needs on their travels had all made at least an effort to please, to respond appropriately, even, especially in the East, to tease and invite with easy and exotic sensuality. With Alys there had been nothing but a calm acceptance—without resistance or protest, certainly, but without any noticeable engagement either.

The next morning, they both arose at their normal time, ate a silent breakfast at which neither knew what to say to the other, and went about their daily tasks. Doubtless, Steven thought hopefully as he made his way to the castle, in time they would be more comfortable with each other and all would be well. But it was a pity that the easy familiarity that had begun to arise between them over the last couple of weeks of their betrothal seemed to have been lost in its consummation.

When he had gone, Alys set about to tidy and sweep the house and return it to its everyday state of cleanliness and order. Steven had folded the trestle tables before he left and stacked them in the outhouse with the benches they had been lent by friends and neighbours, but there was linen to wash, and her mother's bed to make up in the smaller chamber on the other side of the loft. Ellen would want to return home from Paul and Cecily's as soon as possible, and she would expect everything to be as it had been when she left. It was difficult to know how well she would cope with the changes that Steven's presence would inevitably bring, but at least Alys could make sure she found the main room of the cottage as she remembered it.

She began singing softly as she went about her tasks, and was surprised to find herself full of a quiet happiness that she had not expected to feel. At last, after five years of waiting and hoping for Steven's return—not to mention fearing it would never happen— she was married and her future settled, or as settled as anything could be in these uncertain times. She had not really enjoyed the experience of consummation, but it hadn't been as painful as some of the young matrons in the village had darkly prophesied. She would get used to it.

As soon as she could, she decided, trying to convince herself that the pestilence would spare Northchurch and they could get back to planning ahead for their married lives, she would look around for a weaver to take on the workshop and help her get the business back on a proper footing. Where scandal would have surrounded an unwed girl who dared to do such a thing, Steven's presence would prevent any adverse comment. Her marriage would solve her problems with James, too. Even if they had to keep the labourer on for a while until Steven could leave Sir Richard's service and take on the field tasks, the presence of a husband would ensure that James left her alone, although he had better go on sleeping at Widow Agnes's just the same. She still didn't care to have him under the same roof.

~ * ~

Alys was not alone in taking a cautiously hopeful view of the future. Piers, too, was feeling a little more content with his lot. He had begun to settle into village life, occupying his time with saying prayers to speed Sir Thomas through Purgatory, while he waited for the bishop of Winchester to bring to completion his journey to the priesthood. Only then would he be able to say Masses for Sir Thomas's soul as a chantry priest should. He was also helping Father Edward with as many pastoral duties as he could. One old villein had died and was buried with what little ceremony his family could afford, while Piers sang psalms with gusto for him as his two sons carried him in his winding sheet to the churchyard. Two babies had been born safely, though one was sickly and not expected to survive long. Their mothers had recovered remarkably quickly, given the ignorance and drunkenness of Judith, the village midwife. As the son of the previous, much-respected village midwife, Piers was outraged at her deficiencies, and made the mistake of pointing them out to her. His comments were not appreciated, and he feared she would be his sworn enemy from now on.

He still found it hard, however, even in the midst of all this activity, not to feel frustrated at the shallow triviality of his new life compared with the intellectual satisfaction of the disputations he had enjoyed with his fellow students at Oxford. But that was all over, and it was no use looking back. Tempting as it was to take up Lady Eleanor's offer of the use of her library, in the end he knew that would only lead to more frustration. Chantry priesthood is what I was trained for, he reminded himself stoutly. That was the purpose for which Sir Thomas had paid his tuition and board at university for five years. But he was dismayed to find how much more fulfilment he had found in the training than in the job itself!

He went to visit the villein's bereaved widow one morning, enjoying the brisk wind and the shoals of autumn leaves that shifted and eddied at his feet. She seemed resigned to the loss of her husband, who had been ailing for some months. Her elder son had already handed over to Bailiff Michael their best animal, a heifer, as the heriot that would allow him to take over the tenancy, and she herself planned to stay in the cottage for the time being and help her daughter-in-law to care for their growing family. All of which made visiting her a fairly cheerful affair in spite of the circumstances, and Piers was feeling light-hearted as he left her cottage and set off towards the bridge and the chantry, where he planned to put in some prayer time for Sir Thomas.

"You should have a care who you visit today, Father," Goodwife Joan advised him as he passed her front door, where she was sitting with her distaff.

He stopped. "Why do you say that?" he asked, in as gentle a tone as he could manage. Goodwife Joan was a superstitious, irritating busybody, but most of the time he believed she meant no harm.

"I've good reason, young man, as always." She paused for a moment for effect and then let her news fall like a stone. "I hear there is pestilence in the village."

For a moment Piers froze, as in panic he tried to think what he should do. He told himself quickly that it was Father Edward who held the cure of souls in the parish, and who was the proper person to decide on pastoral matters. He, Piers, would doubtless be involved in some way in helping the sick and bereaved in due course, perhaps helping to distribute the blessed viaticum to help the dying on their way to the next world. But just now his duty was plain. He must take the news to the castle. Father Edward must be informed. Sir Richard and his family must be warned—though quite what use such a warning would be, he didn't stop to think. He simply picked up the skirts of his black robe and ran.

Alan was sauntering jauntily through the castle gateway and into the wards as Piers came toiling up the hill. The young clerk had become so careful of his dignity, now that he was in charge of Sir Thomas's chantry and on the verge of becoming a priest, that Alan had not seen him run since he arrived from Oxford. Something momentous must be afoot.

"Ho, Piers!" he called. "What brings you in such haste?"

"They have the pestilence in the village!"

Alan stood still. "Who told you? Is it certain?"

"I heard it from Goodwife Joan," Piers told him.

"Did she name anyone? That woman has such a love of rumour I'd not credit anything she said."

Piers shook his head. "Nay, I believe she was telling the truth."

Alan sighed. "I had hoped we would be spared."

"Aye, I know. But it is all around us to the south and west. They are dying in their hundreds in Dorchester. You have heard the tales as well as I."

"Where do the tales end and the truth begin, I wonder. Well, we must do what we can."

"I am going now to tell Father Edward," said Piers, hurrying on. After a moment Alan followed him.

Steven looked out from the guard room as Piers passed. "Whither away?"

Piers halted for a moment to apprise him of the news.

"Sir Richard already knows," grunted Steven. "He has just given orders that the bridge be demolished, to keep the infection away from the castle."

Alan stared at him. "*What*?"

Steven hefted an axe from the pile of weapons in the guardroom. "Find yourself an axe," he told Alan. "And come with me, if you've a mind to do what we can to keep the pestilence at bay."

"Steven," Piers called after him as he strode away. "Tis foul air that spreads the infection, not contact with people."

"So they say," Steven allowed. "But I'm taking no chances. At the least we'll cut some poles and barricade the road across the bridge, keep the plague from travelling further."

He marched away down the hill towards the bridge, his axe on his shoulder.

Eleven

After a moment Alan ran after him. Destroying the bridge would cut the two sides of the village off from each other completely for all practical purposes, since the next bridge was three miles to the west, and the river itself, though not very wide at this point in its course, was running too deep to ford. Rosamund had gone to visit her mother after she had left Alan today. She would be stranded on the south side of the river, separated from him by several yards of fast-moving water, and, worse still, exposed to the pestilence.

"Steven, hold! What of Alys and her mother? Your own home's the far side of the river now, man, remember."

"Alys is with my mother today," Steven told him, ignoring the mention of Ellen. "My father will take us in, at need."

"You would condemn your own mother-in-law to the pestilence?" Alan demanded in horror. He hesitated, then added, "Rosamund is at home with her mother, I saw her go."

Steven glanced at him sideways. "I've told you before, leave that girl alone. She's not for you. Damn it, man, she's Lady Eleanor's handmaid, and Sir Richard's ward. He will give her to someone with more prospects than you'll ever have, bailiff or no, and curry favour with his tenants in the process, for no one wants to see her leave the village."

Alan was silent for a moment. Then he protested, "I'm no pauper. I sold the mare to the lady Eleanor, and she paid me a pretty penny for her, I can tell you. As she should. That's a good horse, and the lady is a rider fit for her. And I will have my income from the Kent property when it is all arranged with the lawyers."

"And where did the price of the mare go?" asked Steven savagely. "To pay your brothers' debts, I'll warrant, along with all the money you've ever earned or won. You'll never get them out of the hole they're in, Alan. You'll be penniless all your life trying, income from Kent or no. That's no life for Alys's sister."

Alan shook his head stubbornly, unwilling to admit that what Steven said was true.

"Your grandfather sold most of his land to my father to keep the children alive during the Famine," Steven reminded him. "Your father was one of those children. But without land, they'll none of them ever be worth anything now."

He took a better grip on his axe and strode away.

The younger man sighed. His family's debts did indeed go back thirty years to the Great Famine, when harvests had failed several years in a row, and his grandfather and uncles had lost almost everything they had. They had been lucky to have kin who would lend to them, or buy land from them, as Paul had done. Others had starved to death or bound themselves into serfdom. Even with Alan's new status, his brothers might drag him down financially, as Steven had pointed out.

But leave Rosamund he could not, though hell froze. For he loved her as he had loved no one before in life, and they had made vows to each other that very morning. This time, for once, there had been no passionate lovemaking, only a tender conversation, in which pledges were exchanged. If they all survived the pestilence, then unworthy of her though he might be in Steven's and Alys's eyes, surely Sir Richard would let them marry, even if he cursed his ward for ingratitude and folly. Naught would matter, as long as they were together.

He roused himself from his abstraction and ran after his friend.

"Hold, Steven!" he called breathlessly. "You have no obligation to do Sir Richard's bidding. You're a free man now, not a lackey. Are you sure these orders are the right ones?"

Steven half-turned towards him, frowning. "What d'you mean?"

Ahead of him, Alan could see that three of Sir Richard's retainers, armed with axes like Steven, had begun to hack at the wooden piers that held up the arches on the northern side of the bridge. Without pausing to argue further with his companion, Steven ran to join in, with an urgency and energy that was startling. There was nothing Alan could do to stop them. The bridge was narrow, just wide enough to allow passage for a knight in armour or a small cart, and it would not take long to destroy it altogether if the piers holding up the central span were taken out.

The miller had heard the sound of the axe blows above the sound of the mill race and came out to see what was happening.

"Hey, Steven! What are you about?" he called indignantly.

"We have had word that folk have the pestilence the other side of the river," Steven shouted back. "And that's where it stays. Sir Richard's orders. Keep out of my way, Miller, and you won't get hurt."

A crowd was gathering on the far side of the river, but so far no one had moved to challenge Steven, although they were muttering uneasily. Authority spoke louder than reason in rural communities— though it was just as likely, Alan thought wryly, that they did not want to risk the axes being turned on them. But the more he thought about it, the less he liked what his friend was doing.

"Think what you're about, man," he exclaimed in an urgent undertone.

"Sir Richard doesn't want pestilence anywhere near the castle," retorted Steven, though his blows wavered for a moment as though Alan's challenge had opened up a doubt in his own mind. "It has to be done now, at once."

He spoke more loudly, for the crowd across the river to hear. "At all costs we must block the road and keep people from taking the pestilence northwards. Tis not just about ourselves. There's Whitchurch to think of, and the monks at Whitehill Abbey, not to mention all the hamlets in the hills."

Steven and the others continued to hack mercilessly at the bridge. In the face of his friend's certainty, Alan could only watch helplessly as the piers on the northern side of the bridge weakened under the axe blows. The planks that rested on them, deprived of proper support, began to sway ominously.

Across the river he caught sight of Rosamund coming up the lane towards the bridge, clearly on her way back to the castle. The sight of her slight figure brought back all his determination not to be separated from her. At the worst, she might take the pestilence and die without him there to succour her. He ran lightly across the shaking planks just as the nearer piers fell, and leapt across the widening gap to the southern side of the bridge.

He heard Steven swearing as the last pier resisted his axe, but Rosamund was running towards him, and he opened his arms and took her into them. There would be no more secrecy or subterfuge.

"What is happening?" she asked him. "What are Steven and the others doing? Alan, they are saying there is plague in the village." She shuddered.

"Softly, dearest," he hushed her. "I have heard that news too. My lord thinks that if he prevents anyone crossing the bridge, then the pestilence cannot reach the rest of the village."

"But if he does that, I cannot get back to the lady Eleanor! She may have need of me."

"I know. But at least you and I are together, and I will not leave you."

Goodwife Joan bustled up to them, her eyes snapping with disapproval.

"You're throwing yourself away on that fellow," she said to Rosamund. "Gone five years, and from a family of wastrels to boot, promises of land in Kent or no. But there, your folly is not my business, and there are worse things to think on. This pestilence, for one. Tis Hayward Tom and his wife who've taken sick," she added.

She turned her attention to the activity on the bridge and shook her fist at the men across the water. "Fools! Traitors!" she shouted. "Who is to look after us? You are cutting us off from Father Edward and from Sister Margery. Who will care for the dying if the priest cannot reach us?"

Steven's companions stopped work at these words, and somewhat shamefacedly began to retreat in the direction of the castle.

"They are only carrying out Sir Richard's orders," Alan told her. "Though I don't like what they're doing either."

"You will have to do what you can," Steven shouted back. "What you must, as we have done. Who knows what actions we will have to take, all of us, in the days to come?"

He watched as the northern section of the bridge, bereft of its piers, began to float away down the river, leaving the southern piers standing stark and lonely in their ruin. The dark river flowed swiftly around the planks of the central span, wrenching at their fixings. It would not be long before they too were gone.

To his dismay, along the lane on the other side of the river, he saw Alys's trim figure leave her cottage and begin to walk towards him. Until that moment, he had believed her safe in his parents' cottage. What was she doing there, on the wrong side of the bridge?

Too late, he wondered whether he had in fact taken the right decision in carrying out Sir Richard's orders. Five years as a man-at-arms to Sir Thomas had inculcated in him absolute obedience to authority, however much on occasion he had been expected to act on his own initiative in the service of their little band of pilgrims. It had been instinctive in him today to do the lord's bidding, no matter what his own opinions were, even though the new lord did not have his personal allegiance as the old had done. Besides, he had seen the logic of Sir Richard's actions. Whatever the official view that infection was carried on miasma, and could travel by air across the river just as well as with pedestrians and carts, his own observations of the pestilence back in the East had suggested that person-to-person contact had something to do with it. But now, as Alys hurried towards him, and Alan walked away with Rosamund, the doubts crept in and the plight of the villagers left to their own devices on the southern side of the river became clearer to him. And it troubled him that Alan had been unequivocal in his opposition, for Alan's opinion was worth something to him.

Resisting the doubts, and ignoring Alys's efforts to attract his attention, he turned back towards the castle, where he found the wards in a state of uproar. His doubts about the wisdom of his lord's actions had grown as he walked back up the hill, fielding the anxious questions of villagers from the northern part of the village who wanted to know how they were to reach their field strips across the river, and what Sir Richard planned to do about livestock belonging to south-side villagers that was at present grazing in upland common pastures.

Sir Richard, it became plain, was too busy organising his and his household's departure from a situation of danger to have much time or attention to spare for anything else. Servants were running in every direction under the lash of his tongue, while his wife made ineffectual efforts to calm her children and keep her own anxieties from showing. The lady Eleanor stood, pale and composed, in the middle of the hall floor watching the bustle. She was making no attempt, Steven noticed, either to join in the preparations or lend her sister-in-law any assistance.

Sir Richard heard him out without comment, then shrugged. "'Twill buy us time to get away. Your father will arrange for whatever needs to be done here. I have no leisure for that now."

"You are leaving us, my lord?" asked Steven, though in truth the chaos around him could mean nothing else.

Sir Richard stared him down. "I must take my family to safety," he replied in a haughty voice that denied his need to defend a morally dubious decision.

Steven bowed slightly. It was not for him to question his lord's choices. "You are taking all your retainers with you?"

"Of course. I will need them to guard us on the road."

It was clear that Sir Richard was not leaving much behind at the manor house that would need guarding. Out of the corner of his eye, he saw that the lady Eleanor had removed herself from the scene of turmoil, presumably so as to prepare her own belongings for departure.

He considered airing his doubts about Sir Richard's actions in destroying the bridge. Then he shrugged. There was no point in questioning past orders now. What was done was done. "My service to your family is completed, my lord," he said at last. "And I would remain here."

"Certainly, certainly." Sir Richard directed a servant to carry a heavy clothes press to a waiting cart. "You are free to do whatever you wish now. I imagine you will want to stay with your wife."

Steven sketched an obeisance and left him, acutely aware of the shame Sir Thomas would have felt at his son's lack of care for the manor and its people.

He was making for the gatehouse when a page-boy stopped him. "The lady Eleanor would speak with you afore you go, if you please."

Steven halted, rather surprised by the request. "Where shall I find my lady?"

"In the solar, sir. My lord and his lady are almost ready for departure and she is all alone there." Was there an undercurrent of unhappiness, even disapproval, in the boy's voice?

Steven walked back past the loaded carts, avoiding the stamping excited horses that were being harnessed to them. Two riding horses were also being saddled, one of them Alan's mare, which Lady Eleanor had bought as a palfrey. Sir Richard was intending to take his sister with him, whatever her feelings on the matter.

Inside he found most of the baggage ready to be loaded, servants sweating and straining as they carried trunks and chests out to the carts. The boy led him up the steps to the solar, where the lady Eleanor stood waiting.

Steven bowed to her. "How may I serve you, my lady?"

"My brother and his family are leaving, as you have seen. I, however, am not."

Steven looked at her in amazement.

"There has been...some contention about the matter," she admitted. "But I refuse to leave our people here at their moment of need."

"It may be death to stay," Steven reminded her. "There is little anyone can do here. Your brother is thinking of your safety, my lady."

She said nothing, but stood twisting her hands together.

"How may I serve you?" Steven asked again. "You cannot stay here alone."

After a moment she nodded. "I have told my brother I will go to Sister Margery. Her maidservant will look after us both. Mayhap... mayhap we can help folk during this terrible time."

"I hope your help may not be needed," he said, thinking of the river flowing so strongly between them and the pestilence on the far side.

"But then again," she pointed out coolly, "it may."

He bowed. "I will escort you to the anchorage, my lady. I believe they have saddled your mare. Is there baggage I can carry?"

She shook her head. "Let the family depart first. I can send for my baggage later if I need it."

She followed him out of the solar and through the hall. The carts were fully loaded, and Sir Richard was waiting to hand his wife into the carriage. Lady Maud stood trembling by the hall door, her children clinging to her skirts. Sir Richard did not even look at his sister. It was clear there were to be no goodbyes, though he might never see her again.

Steven went to the mare and took her reins from the groom. "I will escort the lady Eleanor," he told the man quietly. He led the horse over to where she stood and helped her into the saddle, disposing her skirts around her carefully. She seemed almost in a trance, taking little notice of her surroundings, and he was afraid for a moment she might faint. He led the mare slowly along the lane, checking from time to time that her rider was still securely in the saddle.

When they reached the church, Sister Margery was watching for them. Steven helped Eleanor down and asked where she wished to stable the horse.

"Steven, would you take her back to the castle for me? Sister Margery has no stable here, and if I need to ride I can send for the mare. Please ask one of the grooms to bring my clothes later—if my brother has not taken everything with him," she added with contempt. "Where is Rosamund? She would know what clothes I need."

Steven hesitated. "Rosamund is on the far side of the river," he said at last. "She was visiting her mother, and the bridge cannot be crossed."

"What has happened to the bridge?"

Steven explained, making no excuses for his involvement. For the first time Lady Eleanor was roused to real engagement with her circumstances. "But Rosamund may be in danger."

"My lady," Steven replied. "We are none of us safe."

She nodded. "That is true. And Sister Margery and I will do what we can, but it is a long way to go around."

"You must stay here, both of you," he told her, in alarm. "The bridge has been destroyed for a reason, so that the pestilence stays on that side of the river. Your brother would not want you to be riding the countryside into danger."

"Yet my brother—and you—would condemn your wife and her family to that terrible sickness, and leave them no hope of succour?" The tone was gentle, but for a moment the eyes were steely.

"He would save those on this side of the river," he retorted. "His orders have been carried out, and it is too late to question it now." But his own doubts had resurfaced, and he bowed his head.

She sighed, and her eyes were veiled again. "We can rebuild the bridge, at least in part, so that folk can come and go. See to it for me, Steven, for in my brother's absence I will hold the authority here. And I will go and speak with Sister Margery."

Twelve

Knowing that others had already informed Sir Richard of the plague's arrival, Piers ran down the lane to the church in search of Father Edward, but the priest was nowhere to be found. He saw Sister Margery standing at the door of her dwelling, but respect for her vocation kept him from speaking to her.

The anchoress, however, called out to him. "Do you seek Father Edward?"

"Yes," he said. "There is pestilence in the village—I must tell him."

"We have already had word." Her voice was sombre. "Father Edward has gone up to the castle. Sir Richard sent for him not half an hour ago."

Piers could have stamped in frustration. "I have just now come from there! But I did not see him." He turned away. "If he knows already, then there is nothing to tell."

He went into the chantry and began to pray—not for Sir Thomas's soul, for at that moment he had forgotten Sir Thomas's existence, but for the people of Northchurch who must suffer in the next days and weeks from this terrible sickness that had come upon Europe, and for which no one, even the physicians, seemed to have a cure.

He did not know how long he had been praying when he heard the sound of horses' hooves on the lane outside the chapel. There was the chink of harness and a man's voice—was it Steven's? He waited for a moment, and to his surprise heard the lady Eleanor's clear voice calling to Sister Margery. Curious in spite of his preoccupation with the day's woes, he went outside onto the path. Steven was leading the mare away up the lane, and he saw Sister Margery open the door and draw her niece inside. There didn't seem to be anything he needed to do about these events, so he withdrew into the chapel again. But after a while he began to wonder where Father Edward was. Had he crossed over the bridge to visit the sick in the southern half of the parish? Perhaps he should go and offer help.

He began to shake with fear as he thought of it. To go among people who were suffering from a deadly disease was surely part of a priest's duties, even a cleric who was as yet only a deacon. He shouldn't shrink from it. Practical pastoral skills had not formed part of his studies at Oxford, and he had been hoping to learn them by assisting Father Edward and his chaplain. This was an ideal moment to do that, but he was crippled with terror at the thought. What if he became ill himself? Who would look after him? Was his soul in a state of grace, prepared for death?

He shook his head. *God forgive me. I know I am not ready to die. My sins are too many, and my weaknesses also.* He resolved to confess to Father Edward immediately, and be absolved. Then he could visit the sick without fear, and if he sickened and died, then he would be ready.

He left the chapel and hurried towards the castle. Ahead of him, Steven had veered off towards his parents' house, still leading the lady Eleanor's palfrey. Piers considered offering to take the horse back to the manor house for him, but thought better of it. His first concern must be with the state of his own soul, and then with the state of everyone else's. Horses were not important in this crisis.

However, in this conclusion he was wrong. For when he reached the manor house, he found it almost deserted. No one was in the hall, or the family's quarters, and the normal bustle of military activity was absent. A solitary groom remained in the stables, which were denuded of all but two of their equine occupants, and as the man approached him, he saw that it was Toby.

"I am looking for Father Edward," Piers said to him. "Do you know where he is?"

"Aye," Toby replied sourly. "He's gone with the rest, saving his own hide as usual." His tone verged on contemptuous, and Piers opened his mouth to rebuke him for such impertinence—not that Toby would take any notice of his censure.

Then he registered what had been said. "Father Edward has gone?"

Toby nodded. "You're in charge now, Father Piers. Sick visiting, last rites, funerals—they're all yours. And from what I hear, you're going to have plenty of them."

"N-no, th-that m-must be wrong," spluttered Piers. "My work is praying for Sir Thomas's soul. I'm not even ordained priest yet. I cannot do all those things. And I don't have the equipment I would need, anyway."

"Oh, Father Edward said to tell you his valise and vestments are in the church," Toby replied, confounding him. "You may use them as you will. I thought he would have spoken to you himself, but they were in such a hurry to leave, mayhap there was no time."

"But Father Edward is the incumbent," Piers protested. "It's his job to be here, to care for people. His job, not mine!"

Toby shrugged. "He's Sir Richard's chaplain, too. Seems to me you've no choice, boy. If you don't bring the comfort of the Church to our folk, who will? I reckon you need to grow up, young Piers," he added over his shoulder as he retired into the darkness of the stable. "Your student days are over. Real life begins here."

~ * ~

Steven tied the mare to the homestead gate and went inside, dipping his head as usual so as not to knock it on the low door lintel.

"Mother?"

Cicely came bustling out, pulling her shawl round her shoulders. "Those poor folk across the river," she lamented.

Steven was surprised for a moment that she had heard the news so quickly. But with Sir Richard's hasty and noisy departure, it was likely that everyone knew by now.

"Sir Richard ordered the bridge destroyed," he told her, feeling shame-faced about his involvement.

"Steven!" His mother was aghast. "Why would he do a thing like that?"

He tried to explain, but the words faltered. He shook his head. "I thought he was right at first," he stammered at last, hoping she would understand. "I helped to carry out the orders, but I only sought to keep us safe."

"And Alys and her family?" she asked him, in an echo of the lady Eleanor's objection. "Are they to be left in danger, while we are kept safe?"

He quailed slightly at her tone. "Rosamund can look after her mother," he replied. "The lady Eleanor is with Sister Margery and doesn't need her."

"Steven," his mother said, her voice gentle but firm. "Now you are a husband, you have to think of your wife before everything else."

He sat down at the table and put his head in his hands. He felt like a boy again, on one of those occasions when he had taken some impetuous decision and landed himself in trouble.

"Mother, I thought Alys was here with you, until I saw her just now, across the river."

His mother laid her hand on his shoulder in quick sympathy.

"On our journey," he went on, "It was sometimes the difference between life and death to act quickly, decide quickly. I felt I had to do this, for all our sakes. But it is Sir Richard's responsibility, not mine. He gave the orders."

There was a silence.

"The bridge is to be rebuilt. I have the lady Eleanor's orders to that effect." He was glad he could salve his own conscience by making sure her instructions were carried out. But in the midst of such a crisis as this, he wondered who would have the time or the resources to start reconstruction.

"The lady Eleanor? What has she to say in the matter if her brother—"

"My lord is busy taking his family to safety."

Cicely sat down abruptly, her concerns about the bridge fading. "They're leaving us? Now? Ah…Sir Thomas would never have done that."

"But the lady Eleanor is staying. I have just escorted her to Sister Margery's anchorage. She would not leave her people, though her brother thought she should not stay. They have quarrelled over it." He paused and looked up at his mother bleakly. "He would not even say goodbye to her."

Cicely sighed. "Tis a grim day, for sure." She pushed the tendrils of hair off her face with a trembling hand. "And no doubt tomorrow will be worse."

~ * ~

Alys swept the dirt and rubbish viciously from her living room floor and out of the door. Steven's actions in carrying out Sir Richard's orders to destroy the bridge, and then ignoring her when she tried to attract his attention, had made her both angry and frightened. Fortunately, there was someone at hand to blame. Her sister and Alan stood in the doorway.

"Send that swain of yours home to his own family, Ros, and let us get a meal on the table." She darted an annoyed glare at Alan, who looked back with equal resentment. It was not his fault Rosamund was marooned this side of the river, she told herself, trying to be fair. They all had to get on with the situation as best they could, and he was at least there with them to help.

"I will go with you, Alan," said Ros. "I would like to visit your family."

Alys shrugged. "As you please." She turned her back on them and started to set dishes on the table.

Alan's family, free folk though they were, scraped a living on marginal land at the edge of the village near the river and had little in common with craftworker families of Rosamund and Alys's standing. His brother Zack's wife, she remembered, had died some years back, not long after Alan's parents, which was why the two families had pooled resources and holdings. She had heard that the hovel they lived in was not only crowded but damp, and the children often went hungry. It was trespassing on village convention for Alan to be courting her, a craftsman's daughter, whatever his newfound prospects, not least because she was Sir Richard's ward. It might even be that their new lord would—God forbid—press her to marry someone he judged more suitable, rather than allowing her to choose. She laid her hand on Alan's arm as they left the cottage, suddenly feeling the need to touch him and maintain her connection with him even in public.

They walked together down the lane and past the mill. "I see your sister still disapproves of me."

"She's worried, Alan, as we all are, about the future. And I haven't had a chance to talk to her about you and me, either. Maybe I would scarce know what to say, even if I did."

He stopped, and turned her towards him urgently. "Would you not? What can be said, other than that we are troth-plighted?"

She pulled away from him and walked proudly along the street. Alan hurried after her. Surely, she wasn't ashamed of him now, after all the impassioned promises she had made that morning?

They were passing the row of houses where the hayward and his wife lived, and a group of women had gathered outside the open door of their house.

Alan tried to hustle Ros past the group, but she evaded his grasp and looked back.

Goodwife Joan detached herself from the group and came over to them. "And where are you two going together so secretly? Does your mother know where you are, Rosamund?"

Rosamund flushed. Alan's arms closed round her protectively, and this time she didn't pull away.

"You should know that we have pledged our troth," he told the village busybody, knowing she would spread the news, even in the current crisis. "We will be married shortly."

He looked up at the hayward's house. "Tis said there is pestilence in the village. What has happened here?"

Goodwife Joan shook her head, deflected for the moment from her moral condemnation. "I fear they will not last long," she said. "Tom has been ailing for two days and now Mary is abed too. Where is the priest? Tom may pass away at any time. He is hardly conscious now." She indicated the group of women behind her. "That is what we were discussing. Father Edward has been sent for, but he has not come."

Alan nodded. It was a serious matter. Once someone became unconscious, they were unable to confess their sins and receive final absolution.

"It will not be easy for Father Edward to get here. My lord has ordered the bridge destroyed, to stop the pestilence going north across the river. Maybe Goodwife Judith can look after them," he suggested, "until we can send for a priest from Micheldever or until Father Edward can find another way round?"

Joan sniffed. She and the village midwife had not spoken to each other since Joan's only daughter had died in childbirth under Judith's care two years before. She was not prepared to admit the woman would be able to provide any help to anyone. "I will see what I can do myself," she said at last. "But Alan, you must get a priest for us."

He nodded, thinking furiously. He could not leave Ros in the street, but this was an urgent request that needed to be complied with. He wished for a moment that he had not sold his mare, who was in her new stable on the opposite side of the river. Never had he needed her more.

He laid his hand on Ros's arm. "You'd best go home, my love. I can't take you to my brothers' house now. I must find a horse to take me to Micheldever. Their priest will come at need. Or if not, I will have to go to Whitchurch or Waltham."

She nodded, and wiped away a tear quickly.

"Do not fret, sweetheart. I will come back soon."

"I know, Alan. But it's all so dreadful. What will happen next?" Another tear escaped, and she sniffed. "I should be so happy today, and now I can't be."

He put his arms round her again, paying no heed to the stares of the women across the street

"Have patience, my own one. We will come through this." He turned her round and gave her a gentle push to set her on her way. "Go now. Help Alys with your mother. I will come later."

She set out bravely, holding her head high and ignoring the village women and their hostile, disapproving glares. Behind her, Alan ran towards his brothers' house with all the speed he could muster. He had remembered that Sir Richard pastured his spare horses in the field just beyond.

His brothers were working in the big arable field across the road from the wooden hovel that gave shelter to them and their families. He saw no one around, not even the children. Everyone must be out in the fields. He stopped briefly to find a suitable length of rope in the lean-to structure where they kept their tools and other gear, before climbing the gate into the pasture. Only a few horses were still grazing there. Presumably Sir Richard had sent for many of his spare mounts as well as the cobs and carthorses to transport their belongings. It was clear he meant to make good speed northwards away from plague-ridden Hampshire.

Alan caught the nearest horse, one that he remembered from years back. A speedy animal in its day, but now well past its prime, which was probably why Sir Richard had left it behind. It would have to do. He hitched the rope round the gelding's head to form a rudimentary bridle, and vaulted on to his back. Digging his heels into the horse's ribs, he set it at the low hedge out of the pasture on to the lane that led southwards to the nearest village, and urged it into a gallop.

Thirteen

Alys turned sharply as the door swung open. Her sister stood in the doorway as before, but silently, as though afraid to come further in.

"Ros!" cried Ellen happily. "You're home again."

Rosamund smiled at her mother and sat beside her at the table. "Yes, here I am, Mother," she said. Her voice was gentle, and Alys was aware of a change in her. "I'm going to be living here with you for a while," she went on, still talking to Ellen. "The lady Eleanor doesn't need me at the moment. She is staying with Sister Margery."

Ellen nodded sagely, but Alys wondered how much of what had been said had penetrated her permanent mental fog. She put a steaming bowl of pottage in front of her mother, and handed her a spoon. Sometimes she was able to eat quite normally, and seemed to enjoy it, but on other occasions she sat silently with the food growing cold in front of her. After a moment, Alys ladled a portion into another bowl and placed it on the table for Ros.

Ros looked up and thanked her. "I'm sorry, Alys."

Alys raised her eyebrows and ladled pottage into a third bowl.

"About earlier. About Alan. I should have told you."

Alys sat down and began spooning up the pottage angrily. "Do you think I see nothing, Ros? Do you think I am stupid as well as blind? Day after day I've heard tell of your shamelessness, or I've seen the pair of you together so lost in each other that you don't see the eyes that watch you, or hear the laughter."

Ros bowed her head. "I'm sorry," she said again. "But he is not like his brothers. And Sir Thomas has given him the chance to make something of his life—and of mine. Why should I not marry him?"

Alys looked at her sternly. "And go to Kent?" she exclaimed. She thought how far it was, and how little she would see of her sister, even if Alan did not play her false and go off on his own, leaving her behind unwed, which she thought quite likely. "Are you sure of him, Ros? So soon? When they were away so long. You have not seen him for five years."

"Yes! Of course I am. You were married quite quickly after Steven returned, after all. We will be married soon, if the pestilence does not destroy us all," she added, making the sign of the cross.

Alys rose and cleared her bowl away. "Steven and I had been betrothed for five years," she reminded her sister. "This sudden affair of yours is not to be compared with that."

She picked up a spoon and started to feed her mother, rather than watch the food grow cold and spoil. Ellen's eyes looked back without focus, but she opened her mouth for each spoonful like a baby. "You'd best wait, give yourself time to think on it, Ros. 'Marry in haste'…Well, you know the rest."

Ros nodded. "But I do not want to wait too long."

"Where is he, anyway?" Alys demanded. "Fine thing to do, sending you home to hear me scold while he gallivants off somewhere."

"He went for a priest. Hayward Tom is near death, they say."

"And Father Edward on the far side of the river, I could wring Steven's neck. Someone will have to rebuild that bridge, and quickly."

"Steven was following orders, and my lord was only trying to prevent the plague reaching the north side of the river. Besides, Steven thought you were safe with his mother, Alan told me."

Alys finished feeding her mother and cleared the table with quick jerky movements that betrayed her agitation. "I wish Widow Elspeth were still alive. Surely she would have known some herb or potion that would keep the pestilence away." Rhymes and incantations, too, if the truth were told, probably, but Elspeth had never admitted to those, for fear of church condemnation.

"Perhaps Piers knows of something," Ros suggested. "Widow Elspeth was his mother, after all. He may have learned much from her before he left for Oxford. I'm sure he would share with us anything he knows."

"But Piers too," Alys pointed out acidly, "is on the far side of the river."

"I will go and help Goodwife Joan," decided Ros, rising from the table. She could not stomach staying in the house with Alys in this mood. "Tom's wife is ill too, and has no one to care for her."

Alys whipped round, her face white. "Don't you dare go near that house," she cried. "What would Alan say?"

"I don't know," Ros admitted. "But he went for the priest. I cannot stand by and let others suffer while I do nothing. Even if you can."

She turned and walked out, leaving her sister speechless.

~ * ~

Alan found a priest more easily than he had expected, for as chance (or providence) would have it, the priest from Micheldever had been attending one of the outlying cottages in the north-west of the village and was just mounting his pony to go home when Alan came along the lane. A quick explanation, and the priest was following him back towards Northchurch at as good a pace as his pony could manage.

They arrived to find the group of village women had dispersed to their own homes, but Goodwife Joan came to the door when they arrived and had clearly been watching out for them. She ushered the priest up the ladder into the room where both patients lay groaning on the bed. A horrible stench emanated from them, and the priest recoiled.

"Rosamund was here," Joan explained, to Alan's horror. "She wanted to help me, bless her, but I sent her home. I hope you're going to do right by that maid, young man," she added, wagging her finger at him.

"Of course I am," he replied calmly. "We are to be married soon."

"And how are you to do that, with the bridge down and Father Edward gone?"

"Father Edward gone?"

"Sir Richard and his family and all the retainers," she told him. "Father Edward rode with them."

"They will return when this scare is over," Alan averred, and hoped it was true.

"Scare, is it?" Goodwife Joan scoffed. "And Tom Hayward and his wife dying of the pestilence. 'Twill be me next, I expect." On the whole, she seemed to be relishing the notoriety rather than fearing the outcome.

Alan took a deep breath. "I have seen the pestilence in the East," he said. "At the least I will be able to tell you whether this sickness is indeed something we should fear." He crossed himself. Was he still hoping they could escape, when it seemed plague was raging everywhere?

Joan looked startled. "Let the priest finish his work. Tom is dying, that's for certain. What he is dying of, well, maybe you will know better than I." Her sarcasm was unmistakable.

"I'm no surgeon," Alan agreed. "But you couldn't mistake the pestilence if you'd seen folk die of it." For the first time, he considered that what he was dealing with might after all be something much less terrifying; that they might all be panicking for nothing.

The priest came down a few minutes later and took his leave, mounting his pony to set off home to Micheldever, where no doubt there would be more work for him to do. Alan thanked him for his trouble, and found a small coin to compensate him for the extra journey, for he was only a vicar, doing the absentee incumbent's work for a pittance, and needed every farthing. Then he braced himself and went back into the cottage.

The cottage still stank horribly, of vomit, sweat and other exudations, and both Tom and his wife were clearly in considerable pain. In the darkness of the shuttered chamber, Alan could dimly see Tom lying curled on his side, one hand clutching his distended stomach. The coverlet was stained with blood or vomit. His wife was sitting up, but her face was grey and her skin stretched tight over her bones. Alan threw back the shutters, earning a muffled protest from Mary, and a louder one from Joan, who had returned at that moment.

"The cold air will kill them," she declared.

"Twill let out some of the stink," Alan retorted. "And let me see them properly."

"Why do you need to see the poor folk in their agony?" asked Joan, affronted. "Can you not leave them in peace?"

Alan ignored her.

"Mary," he said, and the sick woman opened her eyes. "Where do you feel the pain?"

"In my guts," she said. "Vomiting and purging, we've done nothing else for two days. And now Tom is failing." She groaned and bent forward.

"Have you any swellings?"

She shook her head. "Just pain in the guts...something awful. Can't even keep my own ale down." Mary was well known for enjoying ale, which she brewed herself in a little shed at the back of the house.

"Did Tom drink your ale?" Alan asked.

She shook her head. "Nay, he won't touch it. Never does. Nothing wrong with my ale, though." Her voice sounded stronger in defence of her brewing, and Alan thought she was not as near death as Goodwife Joan had thought.

"Has Tom any swellings?" he asked her. "A rash?"

"Nay. I told thee. Gripes in the guts, like me." She closed her eyes and retched but to no avail. "Ye've been abroad, Alan. Ye've seen a thing or two. I remember those tales you told at the feast. Is it...is it truly the pestilence we have, d'you reckon, the sickness that's killing everyone? The priest gave Tom absolution and the viaticum, but he said I wasn't near death. Not yet, at any rate."

"I can't tell whether you will live or not," Alan told her. "But if you die it will be of bad humours in the guts, not the pestilence. So be thankful, for the sake of others if not yourself."

He left the room to speak to Goodwife Joan.

"Tis not the pestilence," he told her, with a great deal of relief. "Swellings—buboes, they call them—or a rash like purple patches, and a fever higher than anything I've ever seen. Headaches and terrible pain in the joints. That's what folk suffer with the pestilence. This is some other sickness; I know not what."

Goodwife Joan gripped his shoulder. "Ye are sure? We have been spared?"

He nodded. "For the moment. But for how long, who knows?"

She crossed herself. "Thanks be to God."

~ * ~

Piers sat at the writing desk in his cell and dipped his quill in the inkwell, frowning. All day, since Father Edward's departure, he had been agonising over what he should do. It was one thing to bide his time as a deacon with what patience he could muster, assisting the incumbent priest and learning all that he could, besides keeping up with his prayers for Sir Thomas in the chantry, so long as the incumbent was actually in place. But it was quite another to stand by while the village lacked a priest to bring comfort and spiritual succour, especially in the midst of an epidemic to which no one had any answer.

In the end, he had plucked up the courage to consult with Sister Margery, out of respect for her holy reputation as well as recognition that she was a shrewd observer of human nature.

"Father, your time will come," she advised him. "Have patience a little longer. The bishop will arrange it, but he is busy with the king's affairs."

Piers nodded miserably, wondering how Bishop Eddington had thought he could combine being the king's chancellor with his own ecclesiastical affairs. Being a bishop ought to be enough for him, he thought with annoyance, reflecting bitterly on the way in which ambitious men accepted high office without thinking of the needs of their flock.

"What will happen," he asked, "if our people here fall sick with the pestilence?"

"Whatever is happening across the river," she replied, "where they have no priest."

He shook his head. A good death, complete with full confession, absolution, last rites and viaticum, was prized above almost everything else, and for good reason, since it ensured the least possible time spent in Purgatory. "Should I borrow a horse and find a way round?" he asked her. "I cannot give them final absolution even if I do. What is my duty?"

"There are priests at Micheldever and Waltham," she said. "They are nearer now than you are to those who need help on the other side of the river. Where people are dying it will be a priority. They will come."

"But what if those priests have too many of their own people dying?" he persisted. This seemed altogether too likely, if reports of the numbers falling victim to the pestilence elsewhere were true.

Her face fell into lines of sadness. "They will come if they can," she reassured him at last. "But we should send a message to the bishop to tell him our situation. It is his right to know what has happened here."

Her eyes met Piers' but neither said what was in their minds, that Father Edward might not be the only incumbent priest who would abandon his parish when the pestilence came, with or without excuse. Piers thought the bishop would probably be extremely angry with Father Edward when he heard that he had left them all in the lurch. He didn't like telling tales, but it seemed to him that Father Edward had deserved it.

He dipped his pen in the ink again and finished the letter, signing his name with as much flourish as he could manage, and sealed it with Father Edward's seal. He had always prided himself on his mastery of the skill, not only the elegance of his prose, but also the beauty of the calligraphy itself. But this time he gave no thought to how the letter read or how it looked.

He sat for a moment, wondering how to get the missive to London. Sir Richard not only owned most of the horses in the village, but employed a large proportion of the folk who could be sent with a message, and he had taken both with him. But Reeve Paul had servants at his disposal and, Piers thought, a horse or two. Perhaps he would spare someone to take a message at need.

At the reeve's cottage Steven heard Piers's request without favour. "My father has enough to do without sparing a man and a horse to take messages to London," he said. "And for what? Why do you not go yourself to London to find the bishop and ask him to priest you?"

Piers stared at him. This seemed an impossible suggestion as matters stood, and he wasn't sure whether Steven had meant it literally. "The next ordination will be in Advent," he explained, in case he had. "Without Father Edward, there is no one to care for the souls of the people here. The bishop should know our situation."

"We will do well enough," argued Steven impatiently. "If Mass is not said in the church until Christmas, what matter? Sir Richard will be back before then, and Father Edward with him."

Piers stared. "But Mass should be said every day," he reminded him sharply. "And you should all be hearing it, at least on Sundays, even if you do not partake of the bread above once or twice a year—especially now, with death all around us. And only a priest can hear confession and give absolution. Have you forgotten your religion, Steven, travelling all those years in heathen places?"

The other man shrugged. "I do not care so much how God is worshipped. I have seen many ways, and I deem them all of equal worth. What a man does for his neighbours is more important than what he says in church."

Piers thought for a moment. "Yes, that is true to some extent," he agreed. "Though sin is hard to shake off without the help of the church. But if the pestilence does come this side of the river,

Steven, what then? There will be deaths, and we must have a priest who can ease the dying into the next world."

"If the pestilence comes, then God help us all. If He will. If He can."

Steven closed the door on Piers' continued expostulations and sat down on the bench by the hearth. He felt restless. As a man of action, it was never easy for him to stay at home and take no part in events, and although he could see that his mother drew some comfort from his presence, that was not enough to give him peace. He and his colleagues had not been able to destroy the bridge completely, because in their haste Sir Richard's retainers had started by attacking the nearer piers rather than the further ones, thus leaving the southern section of the bridge intact. It would not be so difficult to make temporary repairs, and he had promised the lady Eleanor that he would do so. The castle, however empty of people and horses, would furnish him with some tools, and men on the southern side of the river would surely bring materials for the task and lend a hand. He got up from the bench, threw on his cloak, and set out up the lane.

Fourteen

Alan ran down the road to the bridge from the hayward's cottage. A small crowd of villagers stood around the unbroken piers, waiting. Across the swirling waters, he could see his friend standing on the far side.

"Steven!" Alan called. "What ails the hayward and his wife is not the pestilence."

Steven looked across at him grimly for a moment. "You're sure?"

"Nothing like it. No buboes, no rash, no fever. Purging and pain in the guts, but nothing else."

Behind him Steven saw Alys advancing up the lane from her cottage, her face set and determined. She began to push through the crowd, which parted to let her reach the river's edge.

"Steven!" she called across the river. "You've heard what Alan says. Hayward Tom and his wife are sick of a stomach gripe and not the pestilence at all." The words were unexceptionable, but her voice held a challenge.

He did not answer for a moment.

"You are all alone," she pointed out, indicating the crowd behind her on the southern bank. "No one supports what you have done in destroying the bridge. Whatever my lord intended; it was not for this situation. Come and see Tom, if you will, if you do not believe Alan. Come and judge for yourself."

Steven wondered how she thought he could do that, with several yards of deep water between. "If Alan says so, I'm sure tis true. We saw the pestilence at Kaffa. Neither of us will forget."

"Then give this up. What are you doing there, anyway? Guarding your handiwork?"

He had been about to tell her that lady Eleanor had ordered the bridge repaired, and that even as they spoke men were bringing materials from the southern side of the river to attach to the undamaged piers. But her sarcastic tone gave him pause.

"You are outspoken, wife," he called back, his face grim with disapproval. "Tis not your place to speak when I have chosen a course of action. I followed my lord's orders, and do not need to answer for that to you or anyone."

Their conversation, carried out in voices loud enough to cross the noisy river, was easily audible to the crowd on the southern side.

"Steven thought you at his mother's house," Alan put in, trying to deflect Alys's anger. "He did not mean to leave you unprotected."

"I know," she said. "But he was willing to abandon others to their fate. I do not lightly forgive that, I can tell you."

Alan looked at her. "Have some wisdom, Alys," he advised.

"I want to visit Sister Margery," she told him. "and I resent the fact that now I cannot. Mayhap she has herbs to help poor Mary. The priest from Micheldever has given Tom the last rites, and I fear we will be burying him before long. But there is hope for Mary, and she cannot afford a doctor, even if we could find one in these dark days, for they have their hands full with folk who are sick with the pestilence."

"Seems the maid has a mind of her own," tittered one of the crowd around Alan.

"Never thought to see Steven accept a tongue lashing," agreed another.

"Steven the hen-pecked!" sniggered a third.

Across the river, Steven moved away angrily, clearly unwilling to bandy words with his wife in public across an unfordable river. Alan could see some men from the western end of the village coming up the lane carrying heavy planks of wood, which they placed carefully on the river bank near the remains of the bridge. One walked gingerly out across the southern span, and checked the piers. Others brought the planks up and Alan assisted them to push them across the gap. Without the northern and central piers in place, no horse traffic would be able to pass, but within half an hour the bridge would be passable, with care, for foot traffic. Not too much harm had been done to communications, he reflected, but he wondered how much had incidentally been done to his friend's marriage. Steven was not known for good temper in the face of criticism.

Sure enough, next morning, Steven crossed the makeshift bridge, took his wife into the old workroom, out of earshot of her mother and Rosamund, and berated her in a low voice that yet left her in no doubt of his anger.

"Never speak to me that way again in front of others, Alys. I'll not stand for my wife shaming me like you did yesterday. As it happens, your anger was misplaced. I asked Sir Richard to release me from his service, and Lady Eleanor herself ordered the bridge to be repaired."

She exclaimed at that, at how good the lady Eleanor was, what a friend to the village.

"No matter for that," continued Steven sternly. "It is not fitting for you to question my actions as you did. You're my wife, and you need to learn to accept my ruling in everything, or feel the weight of my fist."

Alys blinked at him in amazement and wondered whether to remind him that the cottage was hers, and she not only provided food on the table for him but had also given him her dowry to pay for his freedom. Was not some consideration due from him, some acceptance that she might have an opinion?

"I welcomed your return, Steven," she said evenly at last. "You know that. But I've run this household on my own while I waited for you, and I'm used to making my own judgements and speaking for myself." The words "I'll question your judgement if I see fit" hung between them, unspoken but clearly heard by both.

For a moment she feared he might actually carry out his threat of violence, but her steady gaze, stopping just short of defiance, seemed to give him pause, and he turned and left her standing in her father's workshop, trembling with reaction.

Over the following few days, the silent stand-off between them continued. Steven kept away from the cottage during daylight hours as far as he could, and concentrated on continuing to repair the results of his earlier misjudgement with regard to the bridge. Others left their usual tasks to work with him, and although the bridge was still a temporary structure across which horses had to be led, not ridden, and too flimsy to bear the weight of a heavy pedlar's cart, commerce between the two halves of the village was beginning to return to near-normal.

He was putting the finishing touches to a new pier that the villagers had sunk on the northern side of the river when word reached him via a messenger boy from the castle that a small cavalcade had arrived there and was seeking refreshment.

"My lord and his lady being still away, and Steward Roger with him," the boy said to him apologetically, "we thought to ask you to greet the guests."

Steven straightened up. "Why come to me?" he asked with a baffled shake of the head. "I'm no retainer to my lord now. I've no status at the castle."

"Tis Sir Walter and his lady wife," the boy explained. "They have ridden from Calais, I understand, and need shelter. Sir Walter asked for you."

Steven uttered an expletive and laid his tools down. What on earth had possessed Wat to go riding about a plague-ridden countryside with his wife in tow?

"I will come and see what I can do," he told the messenger with some exasperation. "Has anyone sent north to my lord to tell him he has guests?" Steven had not been up to the castle since the family had left, but he had the impression that no one had been left in overall charge of the household in the absence of Steward Roger.

The boy shrugged. "I know not. They have not told me if so."

Steven nodded. No one of this boy's status would be told anything. He was roughly clad and his boots were badly scuffed. He probably worked in the stables normally and had been pressed into service for want of other more conventional messengers.

"I will come. Where are Sir Walter and his lady now?"

"In the solar, I believe. We have found food and wine for them, and their horses are being cared for. But tis a poor welcome for a knight with connections to the family."

A masterly understatement, Steven thought to himself. A poor welcome, indeed! How dreadful it was that Sir Richard had so denuded the household for his own comfort and safety that there was no one left to welcome chance-come guests in need of succour. It was not Steven's job to supply his lord's failures.

But on the other hand, Wat was a friend, and had given him help and provision in Calais when he was in need. He must do what he could.

He was halfway across the bridge when he thought of Alys. As his wife, she would be the appropriate person to greet the lady Giselle, even though neither of them had authority at the castle to entertain them properly. He turned back and strode up the lane to the weaver's cottage, debating with himself how to couch a request for help in the face of the recent uneasy relations between himself and his wife.

Alys was sweeping the yard when he arrived, in her workaday kirtle and a soiled apron. She pushed a strand of hair out of her eyes with a rather dirty hand and gazed up at him in surprise.

"Steven? Is anything amiss?"

"Only that Sir Walter and his lady have arrived and there is no one to greet them properly."

Alys laid down the brush and took off her apron briskly. "Have they been offered refreshment?"

"I believe so, but I know only what the stable boy told me."

"I will be with you in a moment, Steven. The lady will forgive me my working clothes, I feel sure, and it will take but a minute to tidy my hair. We must send word to Lady Eleanor at the anchorage. She will want to return home and play hostess to her father's guests."

Steven brightened. Of course, Lady Eleanor would take charge. How could he have overlooked that?

"I will go and fetch her," he said.

"No need," Alys told him. "Rosamund is here. She can walk along with us as far as the fork, then she will make haste to the anchorage to find my lady while we go on to the castle." She vanished inside the cottage, leaving him kicking his heels in some frustration in the lane. Too forward by half, she was, and bossy to boot. He wished he hadn't come to find her, though he had to admit he was glad she had taken charge of the situation.

When the two women joined him, however, he was favourably impressed by the appearance they made. Alys had not only tidied her hair but donned a fresh wimple and coif, while her best cloak hung from her shoulders, hiding the brown stuff dress. Rosamund wore one of her mistress's cast-off dresses, her glorious hair braided in a coil around her head.

He wondered where Alan was, since clearly he wasn't hanging around Rosamund at the weaver's cottage. With so many of Sir Richard's servants away from the village in their lord's train, the bailiff had been forced to pay for help from the free tenants with getting in the last of the wheat harvest. Poor as it was, after the torrential rains of the summer, every grain counted, and he felt sure Alan's brothers would be among the workers earning some extra pennies; perhaps Alan was too, in spite of his new status.

They found him, however, walking the castle wards in attendance on Sir Walter and his lady.

"It is good to see you again, Steven," the knight greeted him warmly. "I am sorry we were not able to send word ahead of our arrival. Tis clear that with Sir Richard absent, the folk here are not able to do much for us."

He looked enquiringly at Alys, whom he obviously remembered. "How are you, Mistress Alys?"

"She is my wife now, Wat."

Walter shot him a quick glance. He no doubt recalled the five-year betrothal, along with Steven's uncertainty over it on his way home, but he bowed to Alys with chivalrous courtesy. "I give you greetings, Goodwife Alys. Indeed, I guess you are still a bride, for Steven cannot have been home long."

She curtsied to him formally, yet she greeted him confidently as an old friend, for as well as growing up at the castle as Sir Thomas's foster son, he had visited the castle several times more recently, while Steven was away, and had not stood on ceremony with her and her sister. "It is good to see you back, Sir Walter. Steven told us of your knighthood at Creçy. And of your marriage." She smiled at Lady Giselle, who stood a pace or two behind her husband.

Walter drew his wife forward. She came reluctantly, feeling somewhat diffident in this unfamiliar situation.

"Come and greet my friends, my dear, and do not hang back like a child." He spoke to her in Artois French, which she knew neither Steven nor Alys would understand, but the rebuke stung her just the same. "You remember Steven," he added in English.

"I am much in your debt, my lady," Steven acknowledged, with the stiff little bow she remembered from his visit to her house in Calais.

Giselle found her tongue then, stumbling a little over the unfamiliar English syllables, but willing to make an effort for her husband's sake. "I am glad to see you again in happier circumstance, Steven. And to meet your wife." She smiled shyly at Alys.

Alys made her a curtsy too, but it was not as deep as the one she had given Walter. This woman was not a lady born, she decided. Her status as daughter of a Calais burgher was not so different from Alys's own as a village craftsman's daughter. She gave her an encouraging smile, however, for the young woman's discomfort had aroused her sympathy.

"I am taking Giselle to our own lands, in the county of Oxford," Walter explained. "I am on the king's business, to raise reinforcements for the Calais garrison swiftly, in case he decides to mount a short campaign before the season ends. He is already commandeering merchant ships to take a new army across the Channel from Sandwich, and has commanded me to raise a levy on my own lands together with any mercenaries I can recruit. But there is need of haste, for the king wishes to sail before the end of October."

Steven nodded, wondering why Wat had brought his wife with him on this recruiting drive. Was Giselle unwilling to be parted from her husband, however good the reason?

"You must understand," Walter told them, "that Giselle has not yet visited my Oxfordshire manors. We were married only a year ago, and have been busy restoring our house in Calais."

There was a slightly uncomfortable silence as all four of them reflected on the reasons why that house had needed restoring in the first place.

"Though in truth I've barely visited them myself," he laughed, to ease the tension. "For they were only granted me two years ago. "But tis too dangerous to take Giselle to my parents' manor in Dorset, as I would have wished, for the pestilence is rife there. We sailed to Sandwich," he explained, "and came overland via London and Reading. So far, we have not seen any sign of the sickness, but the fear of it is everywhere."

"And in Calais?" asked Steven.

Walter shook his head. "Not yet. But I doubt it will be long in arriving there. They say it has been raging in Paris for months, and many have died."

Giselle shivered suddenly.

"We have sent word to Lady Eleanor," Alys put in quickly, giving the girl an encouraging smile. "She is Sir Richard's sister, and she will come and arrange accommodation for you. I'm sure she will remain at the castle as long as you are here, to keep you company, for she will understand what is due to Sir Walter's bride."

"Eleanor has not gone away with Richard?" asked Walter, surprised. "I understood he had taken the whole household."

"He did," Steven replied grimly. "But the lady Eleanor refused to go. She has been staying at the anchorage with her aunt, Sister Margery, but she will be here soon. It is not far."

He looked at Alan. "Has Alan told you of his good fortune?"

"Bailiff of the Kentish manor. I'm impressed. But well deserved, from all I heard of his exploits in the East."

"And Steven has his freedom," Alan told him in his turn.

Walter clapped his friend on the shoulder in congratulation. "All you hoped for, then."

"Except that I would have had my lord live to return home," said Steven gruffly. "Sir Richard is not the man his father was."

Walter laughed. "As well I did not look to recruit him to the king's army for this campaign."

Giselle was turning her head back and forth between the different speakers, obviously confused by the quick-fire exchanges in an unfamiliar tongue. Walter was about to furnish her with a brief translation, but at that moment Rosamund and the lady Eleanor appeared, on foot.

"Eleanor!" Walter bowed deeply, but his use of the girl's Christian name confirmed his status as family friend, with enough years between them to make the relationship almost avuncular.

"Sir Walter." Her address, and her curtsy, made the greeting more formal, and placed greater social distance between them, but her voice was cordial, and she smiled upon Giselle kindly when Walter presented his wife to her, taking the guest's hand in welcome. "I am so sorry that I was not here when you arrived. I have been staying with my aunt in her anchorage at the church."

Nothing would be said, thought Steven, about her brother's desertion, or the reason for it.

"Come with me, pray," Eleanor invited Giselle gently. "You are tired, and it must be so uncomfortable to be in a strange land, even when it is your husband's and therefore you belong here. I will have rooms prepared for you, but for now come to my chamber where you may sit and rest a while. No one will disturb you." She turned her back on the others and led Giselle away.

Steven exchanged glances with Walter. It was masterly in its way, this hostessly competence, as natural to Eleanor as the sweetness and care she showed to ordinary folk in the village who were in trouble. Something about their need broke through her cool exterior and engaged the warm heart within.

"The kitchen staff have gone with Sir Richard, have they not?" asked Alys, practical as ever. "How on earth will the lady Eleanor feed guests without them?"

"There must be someone in the kitchen cooking for the few who are left," Steven pointed out. "And supplies on the shelves in the pantry, too, like enough, even if not much is being brought in fresh until Sir Richard returns."

"A scullion rules the kitchen at present, I suspect," put in Alan. "Fills the pots and pans as well as washing them and stoking the fire. And the fare is basic, by all accounts. But the lady Eleanor will manage something."

"I will go to the kitchen." said Alys with decision. "Even my lady cannot work miracles without help. Ros, do you find linen and prepare a chamber for Walter and Giselle, meanwhile. The household servants have gone with Lady Maud, too, remember."

Fifteen

The sisters hurried off together, and Alan went away to the stables to check on the guests' horses, leaving Steven and Walter alone.

"You chose well," Walter smiled. "Alys will match you wherever your ambition runs. A good wife is above rubies, they say."

Steven returned the smile, but somewhat wryly. "My father chose her, though I made my own decision to wed her, in the end. She's a mite too eager to rule the roast," he added. "Never short of a solution to any problem, and not shy of telling a man what he should be doing, either."

Walter's smile grew broader. "You'll settle down together in time. 'Twas not a love match, after all. You cannot expect too much to begin with. And she's a woman of character. It's not surprising she has her own ideas."

Steven looked at him. "A love match is not what I sought," he asserted. "But I'm also not the man to stay at home tied to a woman's apron strings, especially a woman who wants to run her own business. I have my self-respect."

Walter raised his eyebrows. "So what do you intend? As much as any of us can have plans, just now."

Steven cleared his throat. "You said the king was looking for reinforcements. I'm a free man now, as you know, and I had no chance to fight for my country when we were in the East. Is the offer you made me in Calais still open? Will you take me with you to Calais in your retinue?"

Walter stared at him for a moment. He knew—as surely so must Steven—that taking him on as a retainer would inevitably cement the differences in their status, and make it more difficult for the two men to be friends in the old easy way that transcended social class. On the other hand, he could not refuse the offer of service on the king's behalf from someone of Steven's experience.

"You puzzle me," he said. "Why should you want to leave the manor, newly married as you are, and free? Surely your life is here now? Haven't you had enough of adventuring?"

"No," replied Steven bluntly. "Tis my freedom that leads me to make this choice."

Wat looked at him. There was more to this desire of Steven's than met the eye, surely. "And Alys?"

"I will explain it to her. Until the weaver's business can be restarted—and I know not how that can happen in the face of the pestilence and its ills, never mind that trade is suffering from the war and the king's taxation—she is dependent on me. After that...we shall see. I have no wish to live off my wife's business, nor do I have a taste to learn weaving. Arms is my trade now, and by God I mean to ply it. There is plenty of opportunity, so far as I can see."

Wat sighed. It was a pity that Steven seemed to have decided to run away from whatever difficulties his marriage had run into. Clearly he had not found the loving relationship Wat had with his own wife, but it did not seem that he had given the marriage much chance. Perhaps, after all, some space was what the couple needed. Steven was not alone in seeing the opportunities for gain that war offered, and with his military expertise, he would be sure to find a captain ready to recruit him. But if he took service with

Walter himself, perhaps he could be prevented by ties of fealty from spinning off into less conventional adventures.

"I will take your offer," he said at last. "And thank you for it. The king needs every willing and able soldier he can get in the next few weeks, if we are to turn back French incursions into the Calais pale and keep our bridgehead for the next campaigning season—that is, if negotiations for a new truce fail, as well they may. But I cannot wait for you to get ready. Giselle and I will leave tomorrow and aim to reach my lands south of Oxford by evening."

Steven nodded his agreement.

"I have only a few days to muster my men and march them back to Sandwich to pick up the transports. We sail on the twenty-ninth and the king will not wait. I cannot return this way, so you must either come with us tomorrow or find your own way to the port. And I have no spare mounts, so you must provide your own. You will not arrive in time if you make the journey on foot."

Steven knelt before him, acknowledging his suzerainty and leadership. "I will speak with Alys," he said as he arose. "If I can be ready tomorrow, I will ride with you. Otherwise, I will make my own way. And God keep you, Sir Walter."

No longer 'Wat,' Walter noticed. He raised a hand in acknowledgement that their relationship was changed irrevocably. They were now lord and man-at-arms, and equality was impossible. Even the friendship they had enjoyed as boys would be subsumed into a different kind of loyalty and service. But it was Steven's choice, and he could not refuse him.

~ * ~

Alys heard Steven's plan with amazement and growing fury. "You will make me a laughing stock," she told him. "To marry me and then go off to fight in the king's army a few weeks later—what kind of husband does that make you?"

Steven made an effort to be patient. "It's a chance I have to take," he explained. "A chance to serve the king, and Sir Walter, and also to make some gains for myself. Money, Alys. Something we have little of at present, you may remember."

"My coin went to pay for your freedom," she reminded him, her tone sharp. "Once the weaver's business is running again, we will recover. 'Twould be better for you to stay here and work with me than run off after speculation."

He was silent for a moment, biting back the angry words that came to his tongue. "I've no mind to be a weaver," he told her. "Nor to replace James and perform labouring tasks on the land like a serf. I'm a soldier, Alys, you have to accept that. And remember what I have told you about questioning my actions," he added, sternly.

"Very well," she agreed after a moment, though her expression told him this submission was superficial. Beneath it she was still angry and resentful.

He saw that in deciding to leave her so quickly after their marriage, especially without being properly reconciled to her after their recent quarrel, he had done their relationship no service. Yet he had taken his decision, and made his promise of fealty to Wat. There could be no going back on that. She must make of it what she could.

"When must you leave?" she asked.

"Soon." He felt more comfortable with the practical logistics of the situation, and answered her readily. "Sir Walter will not come back this way, so I must either leave with him tomorrow or find my own way to Sandwich to join the transports."

"You'll need a horse. Sir Richard has taken most of the decent ones, so you won't find one on the manor here."

He ignored that. "I think 'twill be best if I stay here for a few days, while Sir Walter and his lady go on to Oxfordshire. That will give me a chance to get my equipment together, such as it is. I have enough of my lord's wages to buy a horse. I'm not asking you for more. But I must leave within a sennight."

She shrugged. "So be it, then."

~ * ~

Walter and Giselle were on the road early the following morning, leaving Steven to make his own way to Sandwich to join the muster as soon as possible.

Alan had a suggestion of his own. "As you are riding to Sandwich," he said, "I will ride with you. I must go to Kent soon to see where Rosamund and I will live, and our ways will lie together for much of the way."

"We will need horses," Steven pointed out, wondering whether Alan regretted selling his mare now he had to undertake such a journey. "And to be honest with you, Alan, I do not have the resources to buy more than a broken-down nag that may founder on the way. Sir Walter did not pay me any advance on my wages for such equipping, and I did not think to ask him."

He had put a brave face on his penury when speaking to Alys, but good horses were costly and he had had other expenses to bear such as a new leather jerkin and a swordbelt. "I guess when I get to Sandwich, I will be able to sell the beast again, for Sir Walter won't thank me for bringing another horse to transport across the Channel. There'll be riding horses to be had in Calais, if he wants me mounted."

Alan clapped him on the shoulder. "I still have enough left from my wages to buy us some horses. I took your counsel and told my brothers they must fend for themselves for the most part, though they did not like to hear it, I confess. I will buy us a couple of strengthy beasts. If there is nothing left in the village that can be spared, we'll go into Whitchurch and see what can be bought there."

Steven nodded. "Thanks, Alan. I'll repay you as soon as I can."

"Tis understood. Steven..."

"Yes? What's on your mind, friend?"

"I'd like Rosamund and me to be betrothed before we leave."

Steven looked at him, remembering his own and Alys's reservations but deciding now to reject them. "I've no objection if my lord countenances it, though Alys still seems to have her doubts of you."

"I'm aware. Your support will be enough for my lord, however, when Ros applies for his permission. She is his ward, and it is his decision. But until he is home, we cannot go ahead with the formal betrothal."

Steven grunted. "I take it she is willing?"

Alan smiled. "It is agreed between us. I would wed her as soon as may be, but I must arrange a home for her first. She will find it hard to leave her family and live so far away."

"I don't understand why Sir Thomas left it in his will that you must go so far." It was usual to appoint bailiffs from outside the manor, to ensure impartiality in their treatment of tenants, but the DeClercs owned other manors that were closer to Northchurch than the Kentish one. Why there?

"Beaconswell simply has a vacancy, I guess. Sir Richard must have chosen it, for as he said, Sir Thomas didn't expect to die on the journey." He laughed. "To be honest, I quite relish a fresh start in a new place among new people. But it will be different for Rosamund. She and Alys are close, are they not?"

Steven nodded. "They are. Never any knowing what's going on in their heads, either."

~ * ~

While this conversation was going on, Alys and her sister were hanging bed linen over the lavender bushes in the cottage garden to catch the breeze and the fleeting late autumn sunshine. Almost against their will, the conversation turned on the pestilence. There was nothing new to say, and their hopes and fears were the same as they had been for weeks as the scourge crept nearer, but because they were sisters, they spoke of what was on their hearts.

"Father Edward and Father Piers are doing all that they can to turn aside God's wrath from us." Alys was maintaining hope even in the face of contrary omens. "Though sins such as yours and Alan's," she added, glaring at her sister, "will hardly help."

"In God's eyes, Alan and I are already wed. We have plighted our troth, and that is enough. We are only waiting for Sir Richard's consent, as I am his ward, to make all right."

Alys knew as well as Rosamund did that the Church recognised as binding such pledges made between a couple, even privately without witnesses. But she refused to be placated. "Sir Richard's consent wasn't so important to you when you let Alan seduce you."

Rosamund glared at her in her turn. "Sister, you would not wish me now to risk losing my inheritance through not waiting to consult my lord, in whose wardship my marriage lies? Alan is everything I ever wanted. I love him and he loves me. But I think," she added, thoughtfully, "we should not wait too long to marry."

Alys stared at her with sudden suspicion. "Are you with child, Ros?" she asked, and held her breath.

After a moment, Ros nodded, her eyes lowered.

Alys opened her mouth to scold, and then closed it again.

"Don't say anything to anyone, will you?" begged Rosamund. "I have not even told Alan about the baby yet——it is too early to be quite sure. I've only missed one of my monthlies. But I know it for myself, that there is new life within me."

"But where will you live when you do marry? I suppose Alan's been too busy making love to you to think about the consequences! There's no room in his brothers' house for another couple, that's for sure. They're teeming like vermin in there as it is."

"Alys!" Ros exclaimed with some anger, for her sister's barbed comment had annoyed her.

Alys touched her arm in contrition. "I'm sorry, Ros. I had no right to say such a thing. Forget it."

Ros's face relaxed. "Indeed, I do not altogether blame you, for their poverty is a sore issue for us, as you can imagine. Alan knows not how much he should help them, for Steven says they will never be free of debt, and we should not let them bleed Alan of his new prosperity."

She straightened one edge of the sheet to prevent it from dragging on the ground. "Alan says that he must go to Kent soon to see about the rents, and about the bailiff's job. I suppose that is where we will live when we are married. But it is a long way away," she added sadly. "Still, if we could be married soon, perhaps I can travel with him."

Alys raised her eyebrows. Rosamund clearly couldn't bear the thought of being separated from her lover, even for a week or two. But as a pregnant woman, even early on, she shouldn't be setting out on a journey that would take several days in uncertain weather, especially with no knowledge of what situation they would find when they arrived.

She put her arm around her sister. "Of course, you and Alan must marry as soon as may be. But you shouldn't go to Kent with him yet, especially if you are with child. We will look after you until he returns."

If he returns, she added silently to herself. She shrugged off the worry, realising she was probably being unfair to Alan. Rosamund said they had plighted their troth, and Steven believed Alan wasn't the man to go back on his word. "Meanwhile we can send word to Sir Richard, and get his consent to your marriage."

She picked up the basket that had contained the sheets, ready to take it inside the cottage, but Rosamund detained her, indicating her mother, seated at the door with her distaff as usual. Clearly she didn't want Ellen to hear what she was about to say.

"Have you quarrelled with Steven, sister? Forgive my question, but he seems very cold towards you, for a man just married. Sir Walter was surprised he wanted to go with him to Calais, Lady Eleanor told me."

Alys resented this change of subject, but could not be surprised at her sister's concern. It was inevitable that the coldness between her and Steven would not go unremarked.

"Is it what happened over the bridge?" Ros asked her gently. "You were very annoyed with him, I know, and I think he with you."

Alys sighed. "To tell truth, we've hardly spoken since it happened. When we are with others, he is polite to me and I to him. But he has withdrawn into a shell that I can't penetrate. Tis best for him to go away for a while. Even five years' soldiering, and all those places he went to, haven't made him ready to settle down." She shook her head. "Mayhap I said more than was fitting. I forget to mind my tongue sometimes, you know that. Yet it seemed so wrong, what he did. It's still impossible to get a cart from one side of the river to the other, and you know how difficult that makes things for our folk. Steven is not popular, even though he was only obeying orders, and I know he meant it for the best."

"It must be hard if you can't talk to each other." It seemed to Rosamund that there was nothing she and Alan could not discuss, laugh over, share with each other.

Alys shrugged. "Let him go if he wants. Maybe we all need to grasp the things that matter to us, while we can. Who knows what the future will bring, or even whether any of us *have* a future?"

~ * ~

Two days later, in the early dawn, the two women watched their men load up their newly bought horses outside the weaver's cottage. They worked quickly and efficiently, in the automatic routine of departure that had taken them half-way across the known world and back. Nothing was said, but Alan held Ros to him for a moment, fiercely, as though to imprint the memory of her body upon his. She had not told him of her condition, fearing that the knowledge would tempt him to stay with her when he should not, but neither had she pleaded to come with him as perhaps he had half-expected. She could only hope he would return soon, and that the response from her guardian with regard to their marriage would be positive.

Steven did not even look at Alys, but mounted and waited impatiently for Alan to join him. Then they rode away eastwards towards Basingstoke, to pick up the London road. At the last moment Steven turned in the saddle and sketched a wave, but Alys did not see him. She had already gone back into the cottage, where she found Ros huddled in a heap, sobbing uncontrollably.

Sixteen

All the leaves had fallen and the trees were rimed with frost by the time Sir Richard's household returned to the village. Village life was settling into winter routines, but word went round quickly that the lord and his entourage were back, though the retinue was smaller than the one that had left in October, for the family had remained in safety, further north.

"I heard that we had guests," Sir Richard told his sister, when she came out into the castle wards to greet them. "The report of pestilence in the village was a false alarm, I understand?"

She nodded, unsure, in truth, whether to be glad or sorry for his return. What was not in doubt, however, was her contempt at its tardiness.

"Our guests have long departed," she told him. "They had business in Oxfordshire and Sir Walter had to return with his men quickly to reinforce the king's army bound for Calais. It was unworthy of you to run away," she added, more than a hint of challenge in her voice.

"I took thought for myself and my family." His eyes met hers like daggers. "It was prudent, no more. Have you no care for your own skin, Eleanor?"

She held his gaze firmly. "Not if it leaves others to shoulder a burden I am unwilling to bear. We have responsibilities to our people here, Richard. Have you forgotten that?"

He shrugged. "The world is changing, sister. Chivalry is a code for nobles and warriors, and has little practical benefit. Our father thought too much of the old ways, and would not see the need for change, even in our relations with the tenants and serfs. I look after my own, but my tenants should look after themselves. Indeed, I have asked Michael to calculate rent payments to replace the old labour services. Set at the right level, this can bring us in more revenue than the value of the labour. Let each man make of his life what he can."

"Now?" Eleanor asked, aghast at this attitude. "You are setting this change in motion now, with death and chaos all around us? It cannot be long before it reaches us, this terrible scourge, Richard. We cannot escape it. Even in our northern manors, it will come to threaten Lady Maud and your children. No one will be safe. And change will come of its own accord, unless indeed this is the end of everything."

He turned his shoulder on her. "I do not like this obsession with death and suffering. It will pass, like everything else. I have my eye on the future, whatever that may hold."

Trembling with fury and frustration, but finding nothing further to say, she watched him walk away from her into the hall.

~ * ~

For Piers, the arrival home of the parish incumbent was a welcome relief. Fortunately, only one death had occurred after poor Hayward Tom's, that of an old widow who was mother to a priest at St Martin. Her son had come to minister to her in her dying hours, and had conducted the funeral before departing to his own parish. Piers had assisted, and felt that he had learned something about the duties he might be called upon to perform later.

Father Edward had also brought with him messages from Bishop William. In retrospect, Piers felt glad that his own missive to the bishop detailing the incumbent's departure with Sir Richard had never been sent.

"You are to go to London for your priesting," the priest told Piers the first morning after his return. "An ordination will be held on twentieth December, as usual."

Piers was enormously relieved at this news. Apart from anything else, it would be good to spend a few days away from the troubles and pressures of living so near the plague-ridden south-west. Perhaps, his hopeful soul suggested, there was something in the drier air that had prevented the pestilence moving further north and east, and London would escape. The authoritative physicians in Paris were still of the opinion that the sickness was carried on miasma, and were advocating (among other things) the possession of therapeutic herb bundles to sniff from time to time so as to ward off the putrid air.

His herbalist mother, he reflected, would probably have agreed with them. The correct combinations of herbs were known to protect one against all manner of ills. But he had not paid enough attention when he was a child to her words of wisdom, nor learnt how to concoct her nostrums or grow the herb ingredients, and as he had been her only child, her knowledge had died with her.

At the time, he had rejected the ancient wisdom she represented, adopting the official Church view that such ideas were pagan and belonged to the past. Instead he had longed for the higher learning of the physicians: not for them the butchery of the surgeon who treated injuries or carried out operations, or the quackery of the apothecary who made up medicines. Grand theories based on the ancient learning of Galen and Hippocrates informed their practice, together with the movements of the stars, among which the symptoms of their hapless patients counted for nothing. Yet how could one quarrel with the ancient learning? *We of today are not fit to tie their sandals*, he thought.

Recently, though, a corner of his mind had developed doubts. What help had the physicians of Italy and France been, this last year, to those who died in their thousands in the towns and cities where they practised their medicine? Why did the ancient theories have no answer to this pestilence? Would his mother's herbs fare any better? He wondered how much he had hurt her in rejecting her nostrums so completely. Sister Margery, after all, seemed able to combine a knowledge of herbs and their potencies with a deep and orthodox piety.

He set out for Southwark in mid-December, mounted on a pony from Sir Richard's stables. The bishop was ordaining several candidates during the week before Christmas, and he would join them, then return after the feast to take up his chantry duties properly. It was pleasant to be riding along on a fine morning, cold but clear for once, with no responsibilities but to take care of himself along the way.

At Basingstoke he fell in with a group of merchants travelling east, who were happy to have a member of the clergy with them. They had hired a couple of armed guards for the journey against the lawlessness that current disruption to normal life seemed to have encouraged. A robed cleric should have no need of such protection, but Piers was glad enough to benefit. In return he said grace for the party before their meal at the inn in Egham, and prayed for safety on the journey before they set off again next morning. On the surface, it seemed a cheerful and friendly group, but he noticed how the men studied each other's faces as they broke their fast, clearly looking for any sign of plague symptoms. By now they all knew what to look for, even if they had never seen a plague victim themselves. No one showed any sign of sickness, nor did the countryside they rode through seem affected, but Piers couldn't help wondering what would have happened if they had.

He parted from his companions as they rode into London, and found a lodging in the bishop's palace in Southwark for himself and a stall in the stables for his mount. At table that evening, he recognised one of his fellow-students at Oxford who, a year or two ahead of him in the quadrivium, was being ordained to a benefice in Surrey.

"I hear you too are to be priested," his friend said. "Many are to be ordained, for the bishop is sending priests south to take up incumbencies that are vacant."

He did not mention why they were vacant, but the reason reverberated in the silence between them.

"I have heard that some are attributing the pestilence to comets and conjunctions that happened three years ago," Piers ventured, tentatively. "They have corrupted the very air we breathe, they say. Yet the Church teaches that the pestilence is a punishment from God for the sins of Christendom. Is that right, think you?"

It was a question he had asked himself often. So many pious folk across southern Europe had processed through their towns and villages crying out repentance for transgression, while others had blamed outsiders such as the Jews and driven them out from their midst. But to no avail. The pestilence had still visited them. They had still died. He had told the people in Northchurch that suffering was not always caused by sin, but the doubts were still with him.

The other deacon shook his head sadly. "I know not, Piers. Tis said that the pestilence began in Asia, where there are few Christians. Mayhap God sees little difference between us."

"Then how angry God must be to visit such a punishment on the whole world!"

His companion shook his head, refusing to continue the discussion. "There is much I do not understand." He sighed. "It may be the beginning of the Last Judgement, some say."

"But surely we can do something to turn away God's wrath?" persisted Piers.

A shrug was the only response.

"I wish John were here," said Piers. "He at least would have some ideas about all this."

The other man smiled rather grimly. "John has ideas about everything, you'd think. But I talked to him before we left Oxford––

he's gone back to Yorkshire, to his home village, and the halls are all closed now. He said he had no idea what to make of this disaster, nor its meaning. No doubt he will be ruminating on the matter while he's at home, but who knows when the university will open its doors again?"

Piers felt a deep sense of disappointment. If John Wyclif, the most brilliant student he knew, could make no sense of what was happening, then truly answers would be hard to find anywhere. He resolved to talk to Sister Margery when he got home. He knew she would have thought and prayed deeply on the matter. And perhaps being made a full priest would mean that he himself would find greater wisdom and understanding. He hoped so.

~ * ~

Steven and Alan returned in time for the Christmas feast. Alan had been expected—indeed Rosamund, who had returned to serve her mistress at the castle during his absence, had looked for him much earlier. She had begun to worry that he had been murdered on the road or fallen sick of the pestilence in Kent, even though from all accounts the east of the country was still unaffected, so far at least. But neither he nor Steven had sent word ahead, and when the two men arrived in mid-December, not long after Piers' departure, in a flurry of sleet and snow that everyone hoped did not herald the advent of freezing weather for the Christmas season, they slipped unnoticed into the village, leaving their mounts at the castle stables.

"There are rooms available for Ros and me in the manor house at Beaconswell," Alan told Steven, not without a hint of pride. "Stables too, where we can keep our horses."

"Horses, is it?" growled Steven. "I see Rosamund is to be a fine lady now. You should have kept the mare for her!"

Alan ignored him, for he'd seen his beloved and Eleanor walking across the wards towards them. Rosamund ran to him and was enfolded. "Alan! Alan! You're here. I was so afraid—

"Hush, dear one," he said, putting her away from him gently to make his bow to the lady Eleanor.

"Indeed," the latter said with a twinkle of amusement, "I am relieved that you are to take on my role of comforter, for your betrothed has been in need of it while you have been away."

He grinned, for Rosamund was still clinging to him.

"Go with him, Ros," commanded her mistress. "You will have much to say to each other. I must speak with my brother."

She bowed to them and turned, gliding away as cool and patrician as ever, not a thread or a hair out of place. With admiration Alan watched her go, and then turned back to his betrothed. "I too am glad to see you safe," he told her. "How is it here? I see that the pestilence still holds aloof."

"We go on as best we can," she smiled. *In truth*, she thought, *nothing much has changed since he left*. It was winter, meaning that traffic to and from the village was sparse. A few brave souls still went to market in Whitchurch each Monday, and one or two pedlars had come through from the north with their carts full of goods, across a bridge now passable, with care, to horse traffic. They had brought the welcome news that so far the towns in that direction had not fallen victim to the pestilence, though the whole of the west of the country from Dorset to the Severn valley was in its grip, and it had recently crept into the southwest of their own county.

"Sir Richard is returned," Rosamund told him, trying to make the statement sound factual rather than a matter for concern.

He seemed to hear nothing untoward. "You've requested permission for us to wed?"

She nodded. "He will wish to speak to you, but I think there will be no problem." Alan's status as franklin, bailiff to the lord's manor of Beaconswell in Kent, should be enough to ensure that. She felt a rush of pride in him and his achievement. While Sir Thomas had bequeathed him his promotion, it had been granted in return for service that she knew had been given well and gladly.

"The lady Eleanor will speak for us, I think?"

"I do not know how helpful that would be," she admitted after a moment. "They are...not at ease with each other at present."

He frowned. "Why is that?"

She hesitated, wondering how much she should divulge of her mistress's secrets, even to Alan. "Sir Richard desires her to marry to please him," she told him at last. "But she wishes to enter a convent."

He whistled. "I'll warrant that does not meet with his favour."

She shook her head. "No, but I think I should not say more, for she told me that in confidence."

He walked with her along the lane towards the bridge, then abruptly steered her towards the big barn where they had first made love to each other. There was no doubt of his intention, but Rosamund hesitated in the doorway.

"My love?" He held her at arm's length, studying her face. "It has been so long. Do you not want..." He stopped, wondering if she had her woman's curse. "We will wait until you are ready."

He took her into his arms and held her tightly, as he had when he left her six weeks before. She melted into him then, responding to his kisses with ardour, her hesitation forgotten.

Suddenly he drew back from her gently and looked into her eyes, which fell before his gaze. "Ros...are you...?"

"With child. Yes, Alan. Perhaps I should have told you before you left, but it was too early to be sure."

"We must marry as soon as may be," he declared. "Advent is upon us now, but we can arrange it for the Christmas season. When will the child be born?"

"At midsummer, I believe." She looked up at him. "I did not think my shape had changed, yet you felt something."

"How could I not, holding you as I was?" he laughed. Then the smile faded from his face. "When would you have told me if I had not guessed?"

She put her arms round him again. "As soon as I had the chance, Alan. Tis not news I wished to keep to myself. My sister knows, but no one else. I have not even told the lady Eleanor."

He thought for a moment, calculating the months quickly. She must have conceived very early in their relationship, perhaps even in that first week after Michaelmas when every day their meetings at the barn had ended in hours of lovemaking. He took a breath.

Her fecundity was a great blessing—it meant their marriage would be fruitful, and he would have a family to work and dream for. Fresh love for her welled up in his heart.

"You would wish to tell her?"

She nodded again. "Tis hard for me to keep secrets from her. I do not think she would condemn."

He held her closer. "No, I'm sure she would not. And she will keep her own counsel, I know."

She nodded. "She will be glad to know we are to be married. I can tell her that."

He nodded, pulling her closer to him again. "You are well, though?" he asked anxiously, amid the kisses.

"Very well," she assured him. "I have had no sickness or malaise. Alys says there is nothing to fear."

He snorted. "Much Alys knows about it. She's not with child herself yet?"

"I think not," she replied with caution. "But Steven has been away..."

Alan resolved to keep his thoughts about Steven and Alys's relationship to himself. If he read the signs aright, love had not blossomed between those newly-weds, and perhaps never would until Steven gave up adventuring and settled at home. And prosy Alys, with her business acumen and her practical bossiness, might not be willing to let him rule the roast even then. The outcome of that marriage was anyone's guess.

Seventeen

Steven walked along the lane to the weaver's cottage. He found Alys at work sweeping the floor industriously, while her mother sat in the doorway with her distaff as usual.

She looked up in surprise.

"Steven! Home already?"

He couldn't be sure whether she was pleased or not. "We'd hardly arrived in Calais with the king's muster when we were stood down."

"How strange!"

"Recruiting an army was bluster, I believe, ahead of the parley the king had called with the French." In the face of the plague's slow but inexorable passage across north-eastern France, he thought it unlikely that either side would have much leisure to plan further skirmishes in the face of that deadlier enemy. "Word is that the king signed a truce with the French early this month which will last until August next year. He has sent most of the recruits home, leaving the garrison to hold the town as best they may."

"Are you dismissed too?" Alys asked, bewildered. If the war was over for the time being, perhaps Steven would no longer be needed.

"I have returned for the feast," he explained. "The prince is summoned to his father's side at Otford for Christmas and Merton for the Epiphany, and Sir Walter goes with them. The king keeps away from the city now, on the advice of his physicians, I hear. They are afraid the pestilence may reach London, if it has not already, and they wish him to avoid contagion."

"Yes, indeed," agreed Alys, rather awed by this closeness to royal affairs.

"I was not invited to the festivities, of course, though I bore Sir Walter company on the road. Feasts and grand games with masks are planned, he told me. That's altogether too chivalrous for me! So I shall be here for most of the Christmas season."

He sounded more assured than when he had left a few weeks ago, Alys thought, but she wasn't sure whether to be glad or sorry that he would be gone again so soon. His willingness to spend his life across the Channel from her suggested that absence had not increased his fondness for her, and as a wife and a woman she felt the emotional loss—and the slight—that implied. A natural wifely existence with a loving husband and children at her side seemed further off than ever. But in another sense, she welcomed freedom from that very existence and its constraints, for in Steven's absence she had written a letter to the Weaver's Guild, asking them to recommend one of their members whose circumstances necessitated paid work, and who might be willing to help her run the weaving workshop and finish her training. She was determined to carry out this plan now that she was married and could respectably invite a man to work alongside her, even though she knew the practice would be far from conventional, if the man was not her husband.

She decided to say nothing to Steven about the letter, which the lady Eleanor had kindly arranged to send on her behalf last month with a messenger taking documents to the DeClercs' agent in London, for something told her that her husband would not approve. If he had been planning to give up soldiering and stay home, she would have had no choice but to discuss it with him now he had returned. But it was clear he had no such intention, and no interest at all in helping her to develop the weaving business. When the business was up and running again, he might be willing to change his mind, especially if the truce held and he was released from military service. She would wait until then.

"When does Sir Walter return to Calais?" she asked.

"At the end of the festivities. My lord asked me to rejoin him at Sandwich after Epiphany."

So, Sir Walter was 'my lord' to him now, not Sir Richard. She wondered what the implications of that might be for her business. Would he seek to take her away to one of Sir Walter's manors when military service was no longer required of him? She very much hoped not. This was her home and she could imagine no other.

They sat in silence for a moment, then Steven opened his saddlebags and drew out a bag of coin. "I've been paid my wages," he told her gruffly. "When I am with Sir Walter, my board and lodging is all found, so I have little else to spend money on."

To be fair to him, Alys reflected, he was not extravagant and wasted little on drinking and dicing. It was action he wanted, not pleasure for the sake of it.

"I will need to keep some coin to pay for a horse and its transport," he went on. "My lord has promised to find me a good mount from his own stables when we return to Calais, for tis a nuisance to be changing beasts every time I pass through Sandwich."

His current mount had been acquired in the horse market at the port, saving Sir Walter the expense and trouble of hoisting two horses rather than one aboard the transport from Calais. Sir Walter's favourite riding horse was valuable enough to travel with him rather than being left behind at the garrison's mercy. But even with the difficulties it entailed, Steven looked forward to having a mount of his own of better quality.

He counted out some coins and put them into her hand. "I know you will have some dues to pay," he said. "And while I am away you had better keep James on to do the heavy work. Is Widow Agnes still willing to give him a bed in her cottage at night?"

She nodded. She was uncomfortably aware that until she could reopen the business she owned only the assets represented by her father's equipment, together with the cottage and the adjoining workshop he had built. Whilst as her husband Steven in theory had charge of their assets, she meant to keep the financial reins of the weaving operation in her own hands. Steven's bag of coin would make it possible for her to proceed with her plans. When the workshop reopened, even if she had to pay the master weaver for his work and for completing her training, profits would begin to flow into their coffers again.

Weavers were few and far between in rural areas as yet, the main industry being concentrated in London and a few other major towns, but there was a demand for good country cloth in the southern counties. Most folk wove their own everyday garments on the simplest of looms, but the better-quality stuff needed a professional craftworker and a larger loom to make greater lengths of cloth, which could compete at town markets locally with city-manufactured textiles, especially where there was a ready supply of wool from local flocks. That had been her father's plan, agreed with Paul as the foundation of her betrothal to Steven, and she meant to carry it out, whatever Steven's objections. It was still Paul, not Steven, who owned the sheep, and she knew he would sell her as much wool as she could use, for it would suit him to avoid the Staple and government taxes as far as possible.

If Paul had been hand-in-glove with his son, it would have been more difficult to deal with him direct, but she knew there was little love lost between them at the moment. Better to present Steven with a *fait accompli*. When the business was making money, he would be less likely to oppose its continuation. She could only hope the Weavers' Guild would send her someone competent...if they sent anyone at all. Steven's news implied that London might as yet be unaffected by the pestilence, but news was always out of date by the time it arrived in the village. If London succumbed, who knew what chaos would ensue?

~ * ~

"I give you good morrow, brother." Eleanor bowed with polite hauteur as they passed in the hall. She had broken her fast early and was about to walk down to the anchorage to visit her aunt.

Sir Richard inclined his head coldly in his turn. Relations between the siblings had not recovered since his return. Once or twice she had been tempted to take advantage yet again of her aunt's hospitality, for it was a lonely existence at the manor house with no companion to talk to; and she missed Rosamund, whom she had released from her service as soon as she heard about her maidservant's impending marriage. Ros would need time, Eleanor told her, to prepare for her wedding, to which Sir Richard had given somewhat reluctant consent.

The ceremony was to take place on the first of January, and Eleanor was pleased to have been invited to join the villagers to celebrate the marriage. Father Edward had promised to take charge of the blessing at the church porch, and she was looking forward to seeing Rosamund married so suitably and, it appeared, so happily.

"I have decided not to employ another maid, for there is little reason," she told her aunt as they walked in the anchorage garden, which was cold, cheerless and damp now that the summer herbs had died back, though a few late rosebuds clung to their thorny branches. "One of the bond-girls can serve me for the moment at need, for I am resolved to enter a convent as soon as may be."

"Your brother will not wish it," Margery warned her.

"I know it well. Richard cares nothing for my wishes, but I am mistress of my own fate, and I will choose."

"Have a care, Eleanor," Margery advised. "Your brother has his own plans for you, and I think they do not include a convent. You are not of age yet to speak for yourself."

Eleanor returned no answer, though she acknowledged the truth of her aunt's comment. She was determined to have no truck with her brother's intention to marry her to his overlord, but she feared that battle might still have to be won. At least there was the Christmas feast to look forward to. It had always been her favourite time of year, a national time of rejoicing that brought people together, offering them opportunities to forget their troubles and the dark days and hardships of winter, and remember the 'light in the darkness' that could not be put out. In the north and east of the country, at least, where pestilence had not yet banished all thought of jollification. A fortnight's festivities would be enjoyed from Christmas Eve to the Epiphany, by king and courtiers at the Archbishop of Canterbury's palace at Otford, where lavish feasts and inventive games and masques would be laid on for the royal family and its guests, as well as by prosperous freemen with their beef, boar or swan roasts and lots of seasonal vegetables. Even the landless and the copyholders—at least those who had paid their Christmas dues of livestock and grain—would be rewarded by a feast at the lord's expense, more or less generously sponsored according to the temperament of the individual lord.

Northchurch's new lord was not feeling generous, but in the face of her brother's reluctance, Eleanor became all the more determined that the DeClercs would host such a feast as usual in the castle hall.

"They've paid their dues," she pointed out to him, her beautiful eyes dark with anger. "They deserve their treat."

"Very well. But it is the last year. Next year they will have all their and services commuted to a money payment, and will be owed no festivities from me."

She disagreed profoundly with this policy, but it was pointless to argue. Who knew what state they would all be in next year, or whether any of them would be alive to enjoy Christmas anyway? She focused instead on making this year's celebration the best she could organise, and attended it herself.

Steven, as a free man in another lord's service, was for the first time excluded from the villeins' feast that the rest of his family would attend. So Alys suggested they invite Alan and Rosamund to celebrate Christmas Day at the cottage. They were none of them too flush for funds, in spite of Steven's contribution to her coffers, but she had been saving a joint of salt bacon for the occasion, and surrounded it with pasties and winter vegetables and enough fresh-brewed ale to keep the men happy, though Rosamund took heed of the advice she had been given by her mother in one of her less confused moments, and drank sparingly of the ale. A jug of fresh milk from their house cow served to quench her thirst instead. Apples and plums from the barn had been baked into pies as a second course, with a piece of home-made cheese to follow, and although it couldn't rival the castle feast, there was a warmth about the gathering that cheered Alys. Alan and Rosamund's obvious love for one another would have brought happiness to any feast, and even Steven forgot to be dour for a few hours.

At last Alan left the house, whistling, to bed down in a corner of his brothers' cottage for the night, while Rosamund said goodnight to her sister and brother-in-law and accompanied her mother up the ladder to the smaller of the two bedchambers above. Alys banked down the embers, put the fire cover over the hearth, and stored the few remaining viands in the cupboard for the morrow.

Steven stood broodingly by the ladder to the loft, his mood changing as they were left alone. "I'm waiting for you, wife."

She looked up, surprised. "I shan't be long. You wouldn't want the house to burn down around us, would you? Or the vermin to get the end of the bacon."

He turned his back on her and climbed up through the hatch to their bedchamber, which was separated by a rough wall from Ros and Ellen on the other side of the loft. She hastened to finish off her chores and followed him. He was in his nightshirt, his day clothes folded on top of the press. His eyes raked her, and her heart sank. So far since his return he had shown little interest in her sexually and had merely slumped into bed at the end of each day and snored all night. Whilst this was unflattering, she had not found it easy to respond to the matter-of-fact nature of his lovemaking on their wedding night, and there had been no chance since then to develop more congenial relations. Moreover, the odour of their quarrel after the destruction of the bridge still hung around them and had not been dissipated by Steven's absence.

He began to unfasten her chemise, and having removed it, he put his hands into the coil of her hair and pulled out the pins that held it. It fell, a mass of brown curls, over her shoulders, half-covering her breasts. But somehow his actions felt more like domination than sexual foreplay or tender passion. It was as though she were a doll rather than a beloved wife, with no feelings or volition, a mere puppet to provide him with a sexual outlet that had been denied him in Calais—if, that was, he had chosen to remain faithful to her and stay away from the prostitutes. She shivered, and reached for her night shift.

He lifted her into bed and climbed in after her, clumsily but with intent. He pulled up her shift and lay on top of her, his weight an uncomfortable burden as he entered her and began the rhythmic movements that were directed towards his own pleasure but brought her none. She lay quietly, trying to relax and submit, knowing well that to resist him would bring not respite but anger. A wife could not resist her husband's sexual advances unless she wanted to risk violence. Perhaps when he was satisfied he would be more gentle, and try to satisfy her in his turn. But still she had no idea what that satisfaction would feel like, only that she longed for it, and during his mechanical lovemaking found herself weeping silently for the lack of it.

She felt a sudden pang of envy for her sister. Clearly it had not been like this for Rosamund.

Eighteen

"My lord Fitzwilliam is gracing us with his presence next week," Sir Richard told Eleanor the following evening as they ate a light supper together in the hall. "I expect my sister to treat him as the honoured guest he is."

"I will honour him as your guest," replied Eleanor coldly. "But I will not marry him."

"Your marriage is in my wardship. You have no say in the matter."

She turned her shoulder on him impatiently.

"Sister, you know well how important this is for our house." Richard's tone became more gentle, his voice persuasive as he tried to appeal to her sense of family obligation. "I will seek election as a knight of the county when parliament is summoned next, and my lord Fitzwilliam has the ear of the king."

"What has that to do with me, pray?"

"Do not pretend stupidity. He is my overlord, and an alliance between us will bring me closer into his counsels. You are not a child, Eleanor. You know how these things are done."

"I do," she retorted. "And I want no part of it. I will be no pawn in your game, brother. I have made a vow of celibacy, and will enter a convent as soon as I may. The Church will uphold my decision."

"Not while you are still a minor. You are no use to me immured in a convent. Tis bad enough that your aunt entered the anchorage, for she and our father had no brothers or sisters. Now I have no one but you, for my children are too young. I depend on you to bring political gain to our family, and marry where I bid you."

She rose to her feet and walked away.

"Do not defy me, sister," he called after her, without regard to the listening servants. "You will regret it an you do."

~ * ~

Lord Fitzwilliam arrived in the teeth of a winter storm, accompanied by a small group of retainers, all of them well mounted and equipped. A large man with large appetites, he soon had the castle household running around frantically in response to his commands. Sir Richard emerged from the solar to greet his guest, but his role as host was clearly minimal. If Fitzwilliam wanted something, he demanded it, and the castle servants instinctively responded directly to his air of authority.

Dinner was served soon after the Fitzwilliam party arrived, and was the most lavish spread Sir Richard could lay on. The castle cooks, supplied with carcasses aplenty of animals that had been slaughtered as feed grew scarce, had contrived a feast of beef, mutton and poultry, accompanied by rich sauces full of spices, the courses interspersed with imaginative subtleties. The best wine flowed, minstrels played, and Fitzwilliam's mood quickly became expansive as he partook of the spread with approval.

He was less pleased, however, by the absence of his host's sister from the board.

"Where is the lovely Lady Eleanor?" he asked as the first course was being removed. "Not sick, I trust?" He chewed the last morsels of meat off a bone and flung it in the direction of his favourite dog, who caught the delicacy deftly before any of the others could make a move on it.

Sir Richard hurried to correct this impression. "She has not left her chamber this morning," he explained. "She rarely eats very much at dinner. But it is her devotions that keep her in her chamber, my lord, not ill health. She is very pious."

Father Edward, sprawled beside him with an empty trencher on the table before him and an even emptier wine glass at his hand, nodded gravely. "She spends many hours in prayer," he confirmed. He helped himself to an apple from the dish in the middle of the table and leaned back again in his chair.

Fitzwilliam frowned. Lady Eleanor's piety clearly did not impress him overmuch, and chaplains who put themselves forward in conversation with their betters both bored and irritated him. "I have come with no other purpose than to see her," he reminded his vassal pointedly, reaching for a nut from the bowl and cracking it with powerful fingers.

"She will join us in the solar later, I am sure," Sir Richard assured him, hoping devoutly that she would.

Fitzwilliam frowned at him. "I should hope so."

"I will remind her of her obligations," her brother promised hurriedly.

The second course arrived, platters piled high with finely carved roast capons, geese and venison, and an enormous meat pottage was borne from the kitchen in its cauldron by two stalwart serving men and placed carefully before Sir Richard and his guest at the high table. Silence fell as host, guest and their retainers did full justice to the cooks' efforts.

The meal wound on, the lighter third course of small birds and their baked fruit accompaniment giving way to cheese and spiced wine. Fitzwilliam eased his tunic belt and belched with satisfaction, while the servants scurried to clear away the remnants and bring bowls of water for the diners to wash their fingers. As the trestle tables were folded away, Sir Richard rose and led the way to the solar.

Eleanor, in her small chamber half-way up the turret at one end of the manor house, could hear little of the feasting in the hall below. A servant had brought her a platter containing a selection of meats and a bowl of fruit and nuts, and she had made a good meal, though leaving a substantial portion to be shared among the servants and the poorer folk from the village, who would, she knew, already be gathering outside the castle gates for the leftovers. She liked to eat sparingly, and felt ill at ease with her brother and his guests when they partook so lavishly of wine and rich viands. She could not understand why they wished to fill their stomachs gluttonously until their faces shone with excess and they could hardly move, nor did she see the attraction of imbibing wine until one's mind was fuddled and one's actions wild. It was not fitting behaviour for Christians, and whenever she knew a feast was being prepared for guests, she retired if possible to her own chamber.

Village feasts like the recent Christmas one were different. There the lord was providing entertainment and good nourishment for his poorer neighbours and tenants, and this was, to her mind, an excellent act of charity, in which she was glad to take her part. Her brother did not often become inebriated at these affairs, and his sense of his own importance helped him to retain his dignity and act appropriately. At his own table, with his own retainers and private guests, however, he felt no such need, and often he disgusted her.

Today she had felt particularly keen to avoid the communal dinner, for Lord Fitzwilliam had even less interest than his host in decorum or restraint, and encouraged her brother to behave similarly. But she knew they would both expect her to grace the company with her presence in the solar after the meal, and as darkness fell it would grow cold in her chamber. There was a brazier, but she did not want to give the servants the trouble of bringing fresh wood to burn on it two or three times in the evening. She wrapped herself in a silk outer gown and waited.

The early winter dusk was already falling when a tap came on the heavy oak door.

"It is time, Eleanor," said her brother.

There was a silence. It was significant, she felt, that he had come to fetch her himself rather than sending a lackey, for the personal request would be less easy to refuse.

"I ask only that you conduct yourself in a manner worthy of my sister," Richard went on. "This matters to me—to our house, as I have explained more than once."

Eleanor looked at him, her expression full of stubborn defiance. "It seems that you are determined not to take my wishes into account. You know I have long planned to enter a convent and spend my life in prayer. It is God's work," she added indignantly, "and you have no right to stand in my way."

Richard sighed, and she could see his temper rising. "But you are my only sister. And you are of marriageable age. Our little Meg is too young even to be betrothed, though her time will come."

Eleanor shrank from the thought, but she knew her brother would betroth his daughter, young as she was, to some lord for political gain as soon as he decently could. *Surely even he, please God, would not choose a gross, lecherous forty-five-year-old for his little daughter to mate with.* Yet that was to be his sister's fate if she could not hold out against him.

"Lord Fitzwilliam asks formally for your hand. At least come and meet with him, hear his request."

"I will not marry him, but I will come down to the solar as you ask, and speak courteously to my brother's guest." She picked up her skirts in one hand and prepared to descend the stone spiral staircase to the solar.

As she entered, she saw Fitzwilliam sitting beside the brazier, drinking hot spiced wine and nibbling on sweetmeats. His laughter sounded tipsy and ribald, and unconsciously she straightened, wrapping her robe around her as though to safeguard her purity. To insist on her presence at this carouse was an insult in itself. She resolved to greet Lord Fitzwilliam courteously and withdraw.

Her brother, it seemed, had decided otherwise. At a signal, a servant closed the oak door behind her with a finality that aroused Eleanor's apprehension.

She bowed to Fitzwilliam gracefully, with all the cold nobility she could command. "My lord," she greeted him. "I hope I see you well?"

The bow was returned, steadily, as though the man had not consumed who knew how much wine at dinner and was drinking still. "Well enough," he returned. "Though I will be better still when my business here is finished."

"Your business, my lord?" she enquired, her eyebrows raised.

"Do not pretend to be obtuse," her brother said impatiently. "Lord Fitzwilliam has asked to marry you, and I have given my consent."

Fitzwilliam nodded. "I must be home for the Feast of the Epiphany, so I am leaving on Friday. The marriage will take place the day before." His tone was quite decided, without any expectation of argument.

Eleanor's face turned white with fury, but there was fear in her heart too. The two men turned implacable faces to her, and it was clear they were not about to listen to her excuses.

"I have had no time to prepare," she told them desperately, trying to steady her trembling voice. "And I have often told you, brother, that I have no thought of marriage."

"'Twould be a waste of such beauty to bury it in a convent," said Fitzwilliam, with an ugly laugh. "You will not find me so ill a bargain, madam. I believe I have a way with women—in bed at least."

Eleanor shrank from him. "How dare you, sir! Father Edward knows of my resolve, and he will support me, I believe." She looked around for the priest, but he had made himself scarce.

Her brother's lips stretched in that thin smile that she hated so much. "Father Edward will do as I bid him and stand witness to the marriage."

"But I do not consent," she said, her voice rising as anger overcame fear. "Without consent there can be no marriage in the eyes of God and his Holy Church."

"A secular marriage would be perfectly legal," Richard pointed out. "But there will be no need to resort to that. Father Edward has his instructions, and as my personal chaplain he will follow them."

"And who is to say that you do not consent?" sneered Fitzwilliam. "No one here will bear you out."

Eleanor looked round again wildly. "God will bear witness," she said after a moment, as steadily as she could, though her heart beat wildly in terror. "You will answer for this to Him, my lord, an you force me."

Fitzwilliam laughed. "I will make my contrition nearer to my death. For now, I will do what I will do."

He turned to his host. "This is your last chance, Richard. I will wait no longer for this obdurate bride. On Friday I leave here, and if you wish for my goodwill, the lady comes with me, bride or no."

"She will agree, my lord," Richard gabbled, in haste to reassure him. "I have no fear of the outcome. What else can she do?"

"I will not submit to this," Eleanor declared. "I will walk out of this door unwed and claim sanctuary at the altar in the church. Or my aunt will protect me. You will hardly storm the anchorage."

"Father Edward would give you up to me," said Richard. "And you will not go to the anchorage."

"How will you stop me?" she fired up.

"Like this." He took her arm and led her, struggling and protesting, out of the door of the solar and up the stairs to her chamber. Fitzwilliam followed behind, a heavy presence as rearguard in case she broke free.

"Until you have thought better of your rebellion, madam," said Richard. He pushed her into the chamber with enough force to make her lose her footing. As she sprawled on the floor in front of him, he laughed again, closed the door, and turned the key in the lock.

Nineteen

Alys stood with Rosamund in the church porch, blessing the unusually fine weather after the storm and enjoying the company who had gathered for her sister's wedding, and the prospect of a modest feast to follow for close friends and family. Alan was planning to start for Kent the following day to take up the reins of his new role as bailiff on Sir Richard's manor at Breckenswell. Although it meant leaving Rosamund much sooner than he would have liked, he had timed his journey to travel with Steven again, as their ways lay together that far; Steven could not await Alan's honeymoon, for he had promised to meet Sir Walter at Sandwich the day after the Epiphany.

As for Ros, she had agreed, though reluctantly, to stay at home until Alan returned to collect her. Alys knew he could not go on trekking back and forth to Kent, especially as wintry weather must soon be upon them, not to mention the threat of pestilence. When he next returned, she must, sadly, be ready to say goodbye to her sister.

But today was an occasion for happiness, and for putting aside any worries for the future. Alys smiled at the good-looking pair as they stood handfast waiting for Father Edward to join them in marriage, and marvelled that in the midst of the creeping fear of pestilence that held most folk in thrall, they seemed so much at peace, as though nothing could disturb the bond between them, not even the fear of death. They were looking into each other's eyes at this moment, the depth of their passion evident to all who watched them. She was uncomfortably aware, again, that she and Steven had never experienced anything remotely approaching this.

Beside her, Steven stood quietly waiting for the ceremony to begin. He was wearing a new suit of clothes, standing best man for Alan as Alan had for him, and charged with security for the ceremony and the celebrations to follow. But his mood was grumpy and, Alys thought, his bad temper threatened to cloud the joy of the matrimonial.

"Father Edward is late," he grumbled. "'Tis an insult, by the blood."

"No, it is not," countered Alys. "Father Edward will be here soon, I'm sure of it."

"And the lady Eleanor," Steven persisted. "She also promised to come."

It was as though he bore a grudge against both the DeClercs and their chaplain, and was determined to take any shortcomings personally.

"Perhaps the lady Eleanor is indisposed. I know she wishes to see Ros married, and Father Edward promised to escort her, since Sir Richard has decided not to come."

This latter defection had been a bone of some contention, as Rosamund was Sir Richard's ward and technically it was his role to hand her over to Alan in person. But they had accepted Sir Richard's decision, because having given his consent to the marriage, he had no legal role to play in person at the ceremony. Indeed, Alys thought the celebrations would be happier for his absence, and even perhaps for Steven's. She almost wished her husband had left for Sandwich before the ceremony, and allowed Alan to make his own way to Kent. Quite apart from his moodiness, there would have been more time to plan the marriage properly and less unseemly haste about it. It might even have been possible for Rosamund to go with Alan to Kent, suitably escorted. But she had no wish for either Steven or Alan to be waylaid by masterless men on the journey, and respected their decision to travel together.

She caught sight of one of the castle servants making his way through the small crowd of wedding guests. "Here's a message from Father Edward, perhaps."

Steven grunted. "I trust there is to be no further delay. We've waited on Father Edward's pleasure too long already today."

Alys looked up at the sky, where dark clouds were already beginning to ruin the promise of the sunny morning.

The servant bowed to Alan and Rosamund. "Father Edward's apologies, madam. He cannot come today."

Spoken clearly, his words carried to everyone gathered around the church porch and there was a collective groan of disappointment and dismay.

"What prevents him?" growled Steven.

The collective sound was this time closer to a gasp at Steven's temerity, and Alan made a movement of dissent. Even disliking Father Edward as much as she did, Alys also frowned. Alienating the parish priest was not provident.

The servant hesitated. "I do not know, sir," he ventured at last. "Other business, that is all he told me."

"What other business?" demanded Steven, his anger at the discourtesy to his friends spilling over. "The arrangement should not be easily set aside, for Alan and I must leave tomorrow without fail."

The servant shook his head. "My lord needed his services, I believe."

Alan put a hand on Steven's arm. "Thank Father Edward for sending us word," he said to the servant. "We will make what other arrangements we can. Do not fret, Steven," he added in a low voice. "At need, I can delay my journey, even if you cannot."

"What of the lady Eleanor?" Alys asked the messenger. "She was to have joined us for the ceremony."

"The lady Eleanor keeps her chamber," was the reply.

"She is well, I trust?" asked Rosamund anxiously. It was very unlike Eleanor to fail in her obligations to those in her employ. She was sure her lady had intended to come to the wedding ceremony.

"I know nothing to the contrary," the servant said. He bowed and made his way down the lane towards the castle.

"The man knows more than he's telling," said Steven angrily. "We're being fobbed off, that's what."

Alys turned away from him. The guests were discussing the situation, some voices showing anger that they had been let down by the priest, others concern for the lady Eleanor. Rosamund and Alan had moved away a little and were clearly trying to decide what they should do.

A new idea struck her. "Is not Piers due back today?"

Rosamund nodded. "Word came yesterday that he was planning to leave London on Tuesday. It depends if he met with any delays, I suppose, but he was mounted and need only stay one night on the road."

Steven looked at her in surprise.

Alys grasped his arm. "Steven, could we wait at your father's house?" she asked in a low voice that only he could hear above the murmuring of the guests. "Tis much closer to the church than our cottage, and we have the feast laid ready at home besides. I believe Piers will come, and if Father Edward is still busy about other affairs, we can ask him to marry Alan and Ros. If the marriage doesn't happen today, I fear Alan will still leave with you tomorrow, and as he said, we do not want to wait. Every day that passes it will be harder to hide the fact that Ros is with child."

Steven shrugged. "Most folk have guessed anyway," he said dismissively. "The two of them are betrothed, after all. If they choose to have lain together before the blessing, what matter? They are not villeins who can be forced to pay leyrwite for fornication."

Alys sighed with frustration. Trust Steven to focus on the differences between the obligations of the villein and those of the class of free tenants to which he now belonged. "But at least if we can wait at your parents' cottage, the guests will not be soaking wet by the time the wedding takes place."

Steven raised his eyebrows at this practical view, but after a moment he nodded his agreement. "I will arrange it."

He went over to Paul and Cicely, who were standing together among the other guests, and consulted with them quietly. Within a few minutes, the whole group began to make their way up the lane towards the reeve's house, Steven's young brother Jack running ahead to warn Mary the maid to expect visitors.

"We must set a watch on the road against Piers' return," suggested Alan's elder brother Peter, a big man in his middle thirties. "If necessary, we can send someone along the road to meet him, ask him to make haste." He spoke to his two half-grown sons, who ran off in their turn.

Alan matched step with Alys for a moment. "That was a good idea of yours. 'Twould go against the grain to put off the wedding until I return, quite apart from Ros's condition. But I must go with Steven tomorrow, if I can."

"Will Piers be willing to marry us at a moment's notice?" Rosamund wondered aloud. "It is an imposition, Alys, do you not think, after his journey?"

"Nay. The banns have been read. Piers is priested now. Surely he will see the task as a privilege and be glad to help, since Father Edward has failed us." She thought of Piers not only as a priest but also as a friend, and their contemporary, who could be relied upon.

~ * ~

In happy ignorance of the honour in store for him, Piers was singing to himself as he bobbed along on the pony Sir Richard had provided for his journey. He was a slender youth and carried little baggage in his saddlebags, and the pony responded to the light weight by trotting cheerfully down the road at a fair pace.

He had made good time from Southwark, and had fallen in with a little band of friars on their way west on a preaching mission from Greyfriars. He had lodged as their guest at a small friary overnight, so the morning was not far advanced when they turned off the main road towards Northchurch, and Piers' heart was light. It was hard to credit now how anxious he had been, on the journey north-eastwards a few weeks ago, about the commitment he was about to make, and how much it had felt like the total sacrifice of his young hopes and desires. But at the moment of ordination all his anxiety, doubt and apprehension had fallen away and he had known for certain that this was the path and calling for him. Priests were dying every day in the service of plague-struck parishioners, and this might, he knew, be his fate too, but suddenly he felt willing to give everything that was needful, even his life, in the service of God.

Ahead he could see the keep of Northchurch Castle rising above the river. "Nearly home, Rusty," he said, patting the pony's neck. "You've carried me well, and I'm grateful. A rub down and some hay is what you've earned when we reach the stable."

A couple of lads were sitting by the gatehouse as he trotted up to it. He vaguely recognized them, but thought no more of it until one of them rose to his feet quickly and accosted him.

"Father Piers," he began in an urgent voice.

Piers brought his pony to a halt beside them. "You're Peter's boys, are you not??" he said, remembering. "Eddi and Eric. Is aught amiss?"

"'Tis Alan and Rosamund's wedding morning," the older boy told him. "But Father Edward has other business, he says. Alys asked us to watch for you on the road, and ask you if you will stand in for him."

"They want me to take the ceremony?" He was flattered, but on the other hand he had no wish to tread on Father Edward's toes. "I had no word of this when I left for Southwark. Why are they marrying in such haste?"

"Alan is travelling to Kent tomorrow," Eddi explained. "They wished to marry before he leaves, so we must make haste."

Piers nodded. "Do you know what has delayed Father Edward?" he asked.

The boys shook their heads. "The message said only that he could not come."

Piers unkilted the skirts of his robe and stepped down from the saddle. "One of you take my pony to the stables. Rub him down and give him some hay. One of the grooms will help you, an you need it. I will walk to the church."

The older boy took the pony's reins willingly and walked off with him in the direction of the castle stables.

Piers turned to the other boy. "Eric, go and tell your uncle and his bride that I will come as soon as I can." He tried to sound knowledgeable and confident, but in truth he was far from either. He had never assisted Father Edward at a wedding, and could not remember even attending one as a guest, except possibly as a child, years ago. Moreover, the older priest was clearly not available to give him instruction. He was on his own.

The boy ran off, and Piers carried his saddlebags up to his cell in the keep. As well as the new underclothes he had purchased in Southwark, one of the bags contained a missal he had been given at his ordination, which he hoped might contain the proper questions that a bride and groom should be asked before they made their vows. It would not make the marriage invalid if the wording he used was wrong, for the couple's consent and vows to each other were all that was legally necessary, but he had no wish to upset or disappoint these folk, who were trusting him to get it right.

Twenty minutes later, his face and hands washed in the ewer in his cell, fresh sandals on his feet, and a little more idea of the rubrics required for the wedding preliminaries in his head, he trotted down the stone spiral staircase and out into the castle wards. Without thinking, he glanced up at the tower where lady Eleanor had her chamber, wondering whether she was already with the wedding guests, for it was a certainty that she would have been invited. To his surprise, she was standing at her window, and when she saw him she began to gesticulate wildly. He stopped in his tracks, staring, but she continued to gesture at him. She was clearly in distress, and he had no intention of continuing on his way out of the castle without knowing why.

Peter's older son emerged from the stables at that moment, and came over to him.

"May I walk down to the church with you, Father?" he asked respectfully.

Piers indicated Lady Eleanor's window. "Do you know whether the lady Eleanor accompanies us?" he asked.

The boy followed the direction of Piers' pointing finger. "I do not know, Father. We were told that she was keeping her chamber this morning and could not come to the wedding." He hesitated.

Piers looked down at him. What was going on? The boy had clearly heard something and was not sure whether he should tell the priest about it. Strictly, nothing that happened at the castle was his business, but anything that distressed the lady Eleanor was of great concern to him. He must find out whether he could help her in any way, even if it meant keeping Alan and Rosamund waiting a little longer.

"I think we should find out what is wrong before we leave," he said at last. "Are the wedding party waiting at the church for us?" He looked up at the sky, where rain clouds were gathering ominously.

"I believe they are at Reeve Paul's house," the boy told him.

"Good. Good. Go then, and tell them I will be there shortly."

The boy shook his head. "Eric will have already given them that message. I will come and help you to succour the Lady Eleanor. I am a good man of my hands," he added proudly.

Piers smiled. He hardly thought he would need a bodyguard or fighting champion, nor that Eddi would stand much chance against Sir Richard's men at arms, but it pleased him to see the young boy's chivalry. "Thank you, Eddi," he said. "We will go together. But we do not need to use violence."

The boy bowed his head and followed him into the manor house.

Immediately they could hear the sound of an altercation from the direction of the turret where Eleanor had her chamber. They turned towards the staircase and heard Sir Richard's raised voice.

"You will do as I bid you, sister, or by God, I will keep you on bread and water for a month. Have a care how you flout me or you will rue it!"

Piers glanced at his young companion and began to mount the stairs as fast as he could.

"Do what you will, Richard. Or what you dare," they heard Lady Eleanor retort hotly. "I am sworn to be celibate and I will not marry this man or any other, whoever bids me."

A gentler murmur reached them—Father Edward's voice, Piers realised. Perhaps he was trying to reconcile the siblings and find a compromise. It might be that the two priests could act together in this, for Father Edward surely could not wish to see Lady Eleanor married against her wishes. Full of zeal, he hurried up the second flight of steps, with Eddi close behind him.

As he reached the door of Eleanor's chamber, to his horror he saw Sir Richard take hold of her arm roughly, as though to compel her forwards. Father Edward was standing beside him, obviously complicit in whatever was going on rather than trying to mediate, and behind him a large, corpulent man in a fine robe waited impatiently. Presumably this was the bridegroom that Sir Richard intended for his sister. His face was coarse and red and bore obvious signs of dissipation. No wonder Lady Eleanor wanted nothing to do with him. Piers' skin crawled at the very thought of her having to consort with such a man.

He stepped forward, and at that moment Lady Eleanor caught sight of him. The expression of relief, even joy, on her face as she realised he had come to her assistance was something he would never forget. But even with Eddi's stalwart readiness to help, he knew they were no match for the men who confronted them.

He hesitated, and then inspiration came to him. Ignoring the men standing around her, he addressed her directly. "I believe they are awaiting you in the village for Alan and Rosamund's wedding, my lady. May Eddi and I escort you there?"

He held out his hand to her, and at once a chorus of dissent arose.

"Lady Eleanor herself is to be married this morning," Father Edward asserted. "She cannot come." The subservient clerk beside him murmured his agreement.

"You should mind your own business," Sir Richard shouted at him. "Go back to your chantry and your prayers for my father and do not meddle with matters of which you know nothing."

"Have you no control over your household?" thundered Fitzwilliam, his ire seemingly directed mainly at his host. "First your sister flouts you, and your chaplain cannot command her obedience to God's will. Now this young priest comes interfering in your private affairs. I'm out of all patience with you. Either she marries me now, or I leave and that's an end to it."

Lady Eleanor, in command of herself again now that she had been given the hope of succour, spoke in cool patrician tones that cut like steel through the hubbub. "I thank you, Father Piers, and you too, Eddi. I am sorry to have kept Rosamund waiting. I will accept your escort gladly." And she bestowed upon her rescuers a smile to crown all smiles, full of gratitude, and no longer afraid.

There was a moment's frozen silence, and before her brother or Fitzwilliam could move, she had stepped forward and placed her hand on Piers' arm. She bowed slightly to the two men, her face and voice calm but her hand trembling. "Your pardon, my lord, that I must go before you take your leave of us, but as you see, our business here is finished, and I am expected elsewhere. I bid you farewell."

Fitzwilliam shrugged and made no move to stop her, but her brother barred her way. His marriage plans for her were dead, but it was clear he could not bear to allow her to defy his will.

"If you leave this house, sister, you will not return. I wash my hands of you."

She bowed again. "After your behaviour to me this morning, I would rather die than share a roof with you again. I will lodge with my aunt until I can arrange my place at Wherwell Abbey."

She let go of Piers' arm and swept past him, her escorts hurrying after her as quickly as they could, trying to avoid Sir Richard's basilisk glare. Piers could not help feeling glad that he owed his job to the provisions of Sir Thomas's will, not to Sir Richard's favour.

In the courtyard he caught up with her. "My lady, do I understand they have imprisoned you!" His voice was full of indignation as well as concern. "Have you taken any hurt?"

She shook her head.

"Your brother deserves to be whipped!"

She smiled, slowing her step to walk beside him. "I thank you, Piers, for coming to my rescue. But I am well, and have taken no hurt, I assure you. I admit, I spent an uncomfortable night wondering whether they would try to starve me into submission. But I do not think truly my brother would have done more than threaten. I am sorry to have thwarted his plans, but beneath it all he is my brother." She sighed. "I cannot stay here, or he will try again to marry me to further his ambitions, which I cannot do. But beyond that I bear him no ill will."

Piers was amazed at her forgiving attitude. Truly she was as much above him spiritually as she was in social rank. He could not forbear to admire her, whether or not it was a sin.

Eddi hopped in front of them in excitement. "I will go and tell Alan that you are coming, both of you. We will meet you at the church."

Twenty

When Eric brought the message that Piers was on his way to solemnise the marriage, the wedding party made its way back to the church, to stand in the increasingly heavy rain for what seemed an interminable time. Alys for one, looking around at the bedraggled guests for whom there was no room in the porch itself, was beginning to wonder whether there had been some further hitch and her sister would not be able to be married after all, when she caught sight of Piers, accompanying a pale and haggard-looking Lady Eleanor.

"My lady!" Rosamund left Alan's side and moved swiftly to meet her mistress, taking Piers' place beside her. "What has happened? We heard you had kept your chamber this morning, and I feared you must be ill. Should you be here? You look unwell."

Lady Eleanor shook her head. "I am well, indeed, Ros. My brother has been...a little troublesome. But all is well now. Father Piers came to escort me, and here we are." She made an effort to smile, but her normal composure was obviously shaken.

"Ros," Alan called her gently. "All is ready, dearest. It is time to make our vows."

She went to stand beside him at the church door, Piers moved towards them and the ceremony began. But although she answered the ritual questions intelligently enough, and exchanged the proper vows with Alan, Ros's attention was clearly still at least half on her mistress, and Alys thought it was no wonder. Usually poised and serene, whatever the circumstances, the lady Eleanor looked so white Alys feared she might faint.

After the vows, and the Mass that Piers celebrated for them in the church, without regard for the rights of the incumbent who should have been there to solemnize the marriage, but pleasurably conscious that this was the first Mass he had celebrated in his home church, the wedding party repaired to the weaver's cottage to enjoy the feast Alys and Ros had prepared. Piers made to return to his chantry duties at this point, but was prevailed upon to join them, and he made little attempt to resist the invitation. Ros would, he knew, take every care of her mistress, but Ros's main duties lay elsewhere from now on, and her relationship with her mistress would be irrevocably altered. He needed to see the lady Eleanor properly recovered before he could put aside his anxiety.

"You will not go back to the castle?" he asked her, slightly anxiously, as they walked along the lane and across the bridge, the colourful procession being applauded by the villagers whose houses they passed on their way.

She shook her head. "I cannot. Lord Fitzwilliam will have gone home by tomorrow, if he has not already departed, but I fear my brother will never forgive me for my rebellion." She took a breath, straightening her back, holding her head high. "And I would never be able to trust him again. I will do as I have planned, and enter the convent at Wherwell as soon as may be. Until then, I must stay with my aunt at the anchorage."

He thought with a mixture of joy and trepidation how wonderful it would be to have her so close to the chantry, so close to him. Lady Margery used the Lady Chapel for her private devotions, so he would see them and perhaps speak to them every day. The days before she left to take her vows, however short, would be sweet.

He watched her move among these humbler folk, who in spite of her exalted status in the community she truly thought of as her friends. He saw her relax as she ate and drank the simple fare provided, the colour gradually returning to her cheeks. Only then could he remove his anxious gaze from her and pay attention to the other guests, some of whom came kindly to acknowledge his new status and wish him well in his duties.

"God bless you for coming to help us this morning," Alan said to him. "I know not what business prevented Father Edward from arriving as he had promised, but the women"—he indicated Alys and Ros—"would much prefer to have you take the ceremony than Father Edward, anyway."

He grinned encouragingly, inviting an explanation for the delay, but Piers decided to hold his tongue. Lady Eleanor clearly did not want it known how close she had come to being forced into marriage, nor did he think it would help anyone to accuse Father Edward of being complicit in such a plan, though it was difficult to see how his involvement could be explained away if it became known. But he at least would make sure no further attempt was made to constrain her tonight. He planned to escort her to the anchorage after the marriage feast. Lady Margery would not allow her to be taken from there without her consent, and by tomorrow Lord Fitzwilliam would be gone.

~ * ~

Afterwards, what Alys remembered most vividly about her sister's wedding was not the relief that it had taken place at all, nor the very real joy she felt at her sister's evident happiness, whatever her own reservations about the bridegroom, nor even her pleasure at Rosamund's agreement to stay at home when Alan left for Kent—but the nightmare that overcame them all at the end of the day.

The daylight was fading, the fresh-brewed ale was running low, and the dishes held only broken remnants of the meats and pasties they had originally contained. Piers had escorted the lady Eleanor to the anchorage, and taken himself back to his cell at the castle. It was time for Alan to follow his bride into the main bedchamber, where some of the other women were making her ready, and submit to the ribaldries of bedding her in their presence. He had just reminded Steven, jokingly, that it was not so long since he and Alys had submitted to the same indignity, when one of the women near him suddenly swayed and fell headlong to the floor.

There was a moment's stunned silence. The afflicted one, he saw, was Rosamund's aunt, who was married to a shoemaker and had come over with her family for the day from Newbury where they lived.

Her husband bent over her anxiously. "Emma? What ails thee?" He gathered the woman into his arms. Her head fell back rather grotesquely and she was clearly unconscious. He looked round for Alys, who had emerged from the bedchamber at that moment to tell him that Ros was ready for Alan.

"Alys, where can I lay her?"

She hesitated. It was impossible to lay the sick woman on the bed prepared for bride and groom, for Piers had blessed it before he escorted Lady Eleanor back to the anchorage, and both it and the bride were ready for its intended purpose. But her mother, pleading headache—though more likely, Alys thought, simply confused by the number of people crowded into their living room—had already taken herself off to her pallet in the smaller bedchamber.

"I will rouse my mother," she said after a moment, preserving the fiction that Ellen would be the appropriate person to consult, but intending to do no such thing. "We will lay a pallet for Aunt Emma here by the fire." It was no use trying to get the sick woman up the ladder to the chamber. If her aunt were seriously ill, it would fall to Alys to nurse her. The men, not to mention Ellen, would be worse than useless.

Her uncle waited while she laid a pallet closer to the embers of the cooking fire. His wife was flushed and sweating, and a livid rash showed at her neck as Alys loosened her clothing. She noticed that Alan had approached and was standing close to them.

"I will tend to her," she told him. "Ros is waiting for you. You should go to her."

He stood for a moment looking down at the sick woman as she lay turning from side to side uncomfortably.

"Alan, you can do nothing here. Do not let this spoil your time with Ros."

Ellen was climbing slowly down the ladder from her bedchamber. "Has everyone gone away yet?" she asked, plaintively. "Quiet is what I need. It is all too noisy." From the main bedchamber, the sound of the crowd gathered around Rosamund and Alan's marriage bed was all too noticeable, though those still downstairs in the living room had moved away to give the sick woman space.

"Aunt Emma is ill," Alys told her, trying to sound soothing. "I will stay and see to her. Go back to sleep, Mother."

But Ellen was having none of it. "If you are here, I must join our guests." She hardly looked at the sick woman, and Alys wondered whether she had heard everything that had been said to her, and how much her mother remembered of the reason for entertaining guests. But it seemed that Ellen's mind was clearer than it had been earlier.

"'Tis time to bed the bride," she went on, nodding. "I must be there for Ros if you cannot." She peered at the sick woman. "Bathe Emma's head with some rose water, Alys, if we have some. That calms a fever."

Alys nodded. "I will get some in a moment." She heard the sound of laughter from the bedchamber. "Do you go and join the others, Mother. As you say, Ros will be glad of your presence."

She filled a bowl with the jug of water that stood on a small table at one side of the room, and dipped a cloth in the water to bathe her aunt's face. Her bottle of rosewater was in the larder. While the sounds of merriment rose to a crescendo, she walked as quietly as possible across the living room to the store cupboard. As she returned, she saw that Steven had come to join her by the sick woman's pallet.

"Alys, may I help you?"

She looked up at him, grateful for the offer and forgetting the coldness that still lay between them. "An you will, certainly. Though tis women's work to care for the sick, surely?" She smiled at him to soften the irony, but the smile faded as she took in his grim expression. "What is amiss?"

"Alan has asked me to take a look at Emma," he said.

"But why?" she asked. "Oh, Steven. No. Not—"

"I fear so. I do not think Alan would be mistaken. But I said I would look for the signs as well. Tis best to be sure before we say anything to alarm anyone. Especially after what happened with Hayward Will and his wife."

Alys nodded, her chest tight with fear. She watched Steven kneel beside the sick woman and study her carefully. He smelt her breath, then pulled back the blanket that lay over her for a moment, before covering her again.

"Is it...is it the pestilence?"

"There can be no doubt. The later stages, I think. I'm sorry, Alys." His voice was gentler than she had heard it for a while.

"It has come, then. What we have all feared for so long."

He nodded soberly. "We could not escape forever, in spite of all Father Edward's prayers and processions. I will go and find Piers. We do not know how long Emma may have left in this world."

Alys nodded. The guests must be told, too, she thought. But not yet, not until the ceremony of bedding the bride was over. Let Ros have this one night of joy. Tomorrow they would all have to face whatever God sent.

She kept watch beside her aunt's pallet all night, while Steven slept on the floor within earshot. Piers had shriven Emma as best he could when he returned to the cottage, though she was barely conscious and not able to make a full confession. But he gave her absolution as though she had. Steven wondered how many more would have need of such mercy in the days to come. His mouth curled wryly as he thought of Father Edward's strict sense of propriety in such things. He would certainly not do as Piers had done and pronounce absolution without proper confession.

By morning Emma was fading, and she died soon after Ros and Alan emerged from their wedding chamber into the half-light of dawn. Rain was falling outside as Alys sent James for the village carpenter to fashion a coffin for the dead woman. There was an unspoken consensus that the corpse should be boxed and buried as soon as possible, and as her family were relatively affluent, they could afford a coffin rather than making do with a winding sheet. Her husband and sons waited to carry her to the churchyard as the carpenter set to work, and the sexton had already begun digging the grave, for there was no question of taking her body back to Newbury for burial. Alys told James to go and ask Father Edward to take charge of the burying, as Emma's family had requested. She hoped he would accept the younger priest's guarantee of the pure state of the dead woman's soul, for Piers was in the chantry, adding prayers for Emma to those he was duty bound to say for Sir Thomas daily.

As the coffin left her house for its final resting-place, borne with due ceremony by four of Emma's menfolk, the sun emerged from the clouds. It was nearly midday, Alys realised, and nothing done about dinner. Ros and Alan had disappeared along the lane, but she saw Steven filling his saddle bags with a few coins, some leftovers from yesterday's feast, wrapped in a cloth, and a leather bottle of ale. He had donned his leather jerkin and heavy boots, and his sword and scabbard were laid beside the door, ready for the journey.

"Steven, you're not leaving now, this morning, are you?" she asked, aghast. "Emma will not be the last victim, if the pestilence follows the path it has done elsewhere. We will need everyone to work together here in the village if we are to cope at all. Sir Walter would understand, surely?"

He shook his head. "Alan has gone for the horses. We must leave in the next hour."

"Both of you are going? What of Ros and me?"

"I must go, you know that," he replied heavily. "I have given my word to Sir Walter, and he will be expecting me at Sandwich in the next few days. I cannot let him down. Alan rides with me as far as the manor in Kent, to pick up his rents and check on affairs there. They are expecting him, and that journey too cannot wait on events. He will return as soon as he can. You will do whatever you must, Alys. You will cope. You always do."

Alys's heart sank. Like everyone else, she had heard the tales from other places that had been affected by the plague: the massive death toll, so great that churchyards were filled and new land had to be consecrated to take the bodies, piled up in great pits without even such ceremony as Emma had received—not to mention the devastation to livestock left untended, fields untilled, and the terror and grief of those left behind. Whatever the state of her relationship with Steven, he was her husband, and she had relied on him for support.

"And what about Ros?" she asked with an effort. "Ros is with child."

"She must remain here with you and help all she can. She wanted to go with him, but he has bidden her to stay."

"It would not be fit for her to travel at present," she agreed. Better to wait for a few weeks and prepare properly. Perhaps Alan would hire a litter or some other conveyance to save his wife the ride. They would need some kind of wheeled vehicle to carry their goods with them.

She heard hooves at the gate, and Ros came in, sobbing. "They are going, Alys," she wailed, "and I cannot prevail upon them to stay, or to take me with them. I may never see Alan again."

Alys laid a soothing hand on her sister's arm. "'Tis no use crying, Ros. The men must go, and we must stay. It is not so different from their going to war, as men have done through all the ages. We women must look after our homes and wait for the menfolk to return. You know that as well as I do. And you knew he would leave today."

"But it is different now," cried Ros. "Aunt Emma dying like that... what if it happens to you, or me, or Mother? What if James takes the sickness and we have no one to work the fields or tend the beasts? What if—"

"We will have to cope," Alys interrupted her, unconsciously echoing her husband. "Somehow. We can. We must. If we all work together. And Alan will come back as soon as he can."

Twenty-one

An hour later, while a distracted Alys was trying to prepare a meal, the lady Eleanor appeared, walking unescorted through village streets newly wet with rain. Over her arm she carried a basket of posies.

"My lady!" Rosamund greeted her, opening the cottage door with surprise and some consternation. "Alone? Come in and sit down, though we have little to offer you. Aunt Emma's death has put us at sixes and sevens. And Steven and Alan have gone to Kent..." her voice died away as the tears flowed again.

"My dear." Eleanor took her hand and patted it comfortingly. "Do not distress yourself, I pray. Steven had given his word to Walter, and he had no choice. Surely you do not blame Alan for keeping him company? The two will be safer together than either would be alone, with the roads as they are. He will return as soon as he may."

Rosamund nodded. "I know."

"It is hard for you, just married as you are. I understand. And your aunt's death must have been a terrible shock."

"Alan and Steven said it was the pestilence this time," Alys remarked. "We must be braced for more sickness, more death, I fear."

Eleanor reached into the basket and handed them each a posy. "Sister Margery sends these – and I am to go around the village with the rest. There is not enough for everyone, I know, but she says it is late in the year and most of the fresh herbs have died back. These came from her store. She said also to tell you to add crushed garlic to your pottage, if you do not already do so. It is protective against all kinds of ailments—who knows, but it may work against the pestilence too."

Alys accepted the posy with thanks and tucked it into the neck of her gown. "Should you not go with your brother to safety this time?" she asked. "I feel sure he will be leaving soon, as he did before."

Eleanor nodded. "He has already gone, I think, and Steward Roger and Father Edward with him. They will not return until all is safe. But this time they have left us Bailiff Michael, at least." She smiled wryly. "My brother does not mean to lose track of his dues this year."

Alys could think of nothing to reply to this.

"Will you return to the castle?" Rosamund asked. "With Alan away, I could come back to your service, at least for a time."

Eleanor smiled. "It would be wonderful, Ros, if you could find it in your heart to help me in this way. I feel it is unfair to my aunt to continue to stay with her at the anchorage if I do not need to. The space is small, and her calling is not to tend to me but to pray. I did not care to be at the castle when my brother is there, but if he is gone... I should perhaps go back and represent our family as I did before. Yet it is a lonely place without another woman. I would be very glad of your company, I admit, until I can arrange to enter the convent."

She looked at Alys. "I will take very good care of her, I promise, until Alan returns. And I will help her prepare for her new life, just as she will help me prepare for mine. It will give us both something to focus on."

Rosamund got up at once. "I will get my bundle together. Alys will not need me here, will you, Alys?"

Alys stared at her. *Not need you?* She thought of the care her mother required, of the problems with James which Steven had not taken much account of, of the help Steven himself had reassured her that Ros would give her, together with whatever extra burdens the pestilence might bring them all. Yes, it would have been wonderful to have her sister beside her, sharing the load. But then she realised that Eleanor needed Ros too—in a different way, perhaps, but equally— and more importantly that Ros wanted to go with her mistress. It would be better for her, perhaps, than staying here with her.

She took a deep breath. "If you want to go, then you shall. God speed, Ros."

"I will not be going far," her sister reminded her sister, her eyes bright. "And if you need me for anything, you have only to send word."

Alys nodded, but her heart was heavy as she watched Ros gather up her spare linen and her distaff into a shawl and tie it on her back for the walk up to the castle. Her sister tried to say farewell to Ellen, but their mother seemed even more distant than usual, pushing herself backwards and forwards in the rocking chair rather than standing in her usual place at the door. Her gentle murmuring sounded unhappy and restless. Perhaps, Alys thought, she was upset by all the coming and going, and her cousin's death had probably brought back all the emotion of losing her husband. To Alys, her father's death seemed a long time ago, but she guessed, looking sympathetically at her mother across the room, that in Ellen's mental twilight her bereavement was as raw as ever.

~ * ~

For several days after Steven and Alan had departed, no one in the village sickened, and some even began to hope the death of Ellen's sister Emma had been a coincidence, much like the death of Hayward Tom. She had brought the sickness with her from Newbury, they asserted, which was on the main road to London from the West Country, and therefore vulnerable to infection, but her menfolk had returned home and there was no reason to suppose that anyone from Northchurch would contract it.

On Friday, it was Piers who led the weekly penitential procession that sought to keep disaster at bay, since Father Edward had indeed departed with his lord earlier in the week without paying his fellow-priest even the courtesy of a farewell. More villagers took part in the procession than previously, and their prayers were noticeably more fervent, which was to be expected after their brush with the disease they all feared. The fact that none from Northchurch itself had yet sickened encouraged them to feel that the ritual was efficacious and to be continued at all costs.

Piers himself had little confidence that this small place was somehow deserving of a protection that it seemed God had denied everyone else. It was surely only a matter of time before they were overwhelmed. But to him even prayers and devotions that did little to stave off disease might yet give spiritual strength to those who believed in them, strength they would need for the future.

On the Saturday after Epiphany, three people fell sick in the hovels on the edge of the village to the west, and Piers' prayers at Mass on Sunday focused on endurance and hope for the future, rather than holding out any prospect of further escape from the plague's attentions.

By Monday the number of cases had doubled, and he had attended two deathbeds and, with difficulty, helped the dying through some sort of act of contrition. Both had expired in agony, while their families watched helplessly, and in one house he feared there would soon be two more deathbeds to attend, for the spouse and two of the children were clearly ailing. One of the younger children was old enough to look after her healthy siblings, but the burden of caring for the sick was clearly beyond her. On his way back to the castle he called on Goodwife Joan and asked if she could lend a hand.

"'Twill not be easy." She shook her head. "My man has just this morning complained of pains and fever, and taken to his bed. But I will do what I can. Mayhap Goodwife Martha will be willing to keep an eye out here while I go and help them."

Piers sighed, and thanked her. Whatever her reputation for bossy busybodying, she would do her best, he knew, in this situation. "Let me know if your man needs me to hear his confession, but please God he will recover." He tried to remember if he had heard of people recovering from the pestilence, once contracted, and wished he had thought to ask Alan or Steven.

Alys was feeding the hens as he passed her house, his head bowed and the cowl of his robe pulled up. She knew where he had been, and could guess the outcome. It was no wonder he looked miserable. This was not what his job was supposed to entail, and she wondered whether he still found time to say the chantry Masses he was paid for, or whether Sir Thomas had been consigned to a longer sojourn in Purgatory for the moment. She shook her head. Father Edward would surely not be in God's good books just now—and not in the bishop's either, when the latter found out what God already knew, that he had again left his parishioners for the sake of his own skin just when they most needed him.

The dusk was beginning to gather, and she picked up a few eggs in the lean-to barn at the end of the cottage, where the hens roosted and the house cow and the pig slept in winter. The livestock were beginning to settle for the night, and she closed the door and began walking along the path to the cottage door, not hurrying, for her mother had been fretful and difficult to please all day and it was more pleasant to be outside with the animals.

As she reached the door, an unfamiliar voice from behind her said quietly, "Are you Mistress Alys?"

She whirled round, startled, and found herself looking up at a tall young man with a heavy-looking pack on his back. Thinking he moved rather stiffly, as though his body were weary, she looked past him towards the gateway, but no horse stood tethered there. Clearly, he had walked, and from some distance.

"Alys is my name," she answered after a moment, as calmly as she could.

"Mine is Finn," he told her. "I have come from London, where they told me that you are in need of a weaver."

"You are a master weaver?" Her heart lifted suddenly, for this was what she had longed for ever since her father had died. Even the knowledge that in a moment she would have to tell him there was pestilence in the village, whereupon he would turn and leave immediately, could not prevent that moment of exultation.

He hesitated. "I am trained, yes. That is why the Guild have sent me. But I have not worked for myself as a master. My father is the master weaver in our household. He came to London from Bruges twenty years ago, and he has done well. But I have older brothers who run the business with him, and there is no work for me other than the simplest of journeyman tasks. So, I am seeking my fortune, Mistress, you might say. I am hoping I may find it here." His long, rather serious face broke into a smile that went straight to her heart.

She thought for a moment. It was growing darker, and she could not in all conscience send him away from her door at this hour, even if she wanted to. She hoped her mother's fretfulness would not turn into hostility, as it sometimes did when there were changes, even in the shape of visitors.

"Come inside, Master Finn. I have news that may send you back to London in the morning as fast as your feet will carry you, but for tonight at least we can give you food and a place to sleep."

He frowned, but he followed her into the cottage and put his pack down by the door, handling it carefully as though it contained something fragile. She looked at it curiously, but said nothing. She had no right to be inquisitive, and in any case, it mattered not what was in his pack, for tomorrow he would be on his way.

Instead she turned to Ellen. "Mother, this is Master Finn, a weaver from London. He has come hoping to help us start the looms again. It may be that is not possible. But I have invited him to stay with us tonight at least, for he has nowhere else to go."

Ellen was crouched by the fire, huddled in her shawl, but she looked up at this. "Tis time the business was started again," she nodded. "More than time, your father will say."

Alys thought better of trying to explain to Finn why it had taken so long after her father's death to send to London for help, and why her mother still spoke of her father in the present tense. She had not said much about this in her letter, so he must be puzzled. Instead she moved to the lamp to light the wick, then began to stir the pottage.

"What is this grave news?" he asked, his eyes troubled. "Do you not wish for my help as I was told?" He indicated Ellen with his hand. "Your father..."

"Died a year ago," she told him. "But my mother...forgets. And now there is pestilence in the village. You'd best go back to London in the morning and wait until we are clear of infection."

He shook his head. "We have had the pestilence in London for weeks." His tone was matter-of-fact, without the edge of fear that might have been expected. "I left there three days past, and on the way I have seen signs of it everywhere. I had to sleep under hedges and in barns because at the inns there are few healthy enough to serve guests, and I did not know anyone with whom I could lodge."

Her eyes widened. No wonder he looked tired and worn, if he had walked over fifty miles without any sustenance or shelter. Her first task should be to give him a meal, even if she couldn't offer him much hope beyond that.

"We will feed and house you tonight, no question. But as for the future, who knows? Already there is little time to do our own housework because of the number of sick folk who have no one to care for them and need our help. Mother is not strong," she added, loyally, "so she cannot do much. But I have spent most of today cooking and cleaning for those who are too sick to do their own work. And tomorrow will likely be the same."

"I cannot expect you to hire me properly, of course, until our work here can attract customers. There will be much to do, to set up the looms and buy materials, but I understand that we may not be able to do that while the plague rages around us. No one will be thinking of buying cloth just now."

He smiled wryly at her, and she met his eyes, waiting for him to continue.

"But Mistress Alys, it will all end at last, and life will go on again."

She stared at him, impressed with his confidence in the future, when so many were predicting the end of the world.

"Then, if we are spared, we will start weaving, and if you wish, you may complete the training that you began with your father. You see," he added, "they told me a great deal, at the Guild, about your circumstances. I hope you do not mind that."

She brushed this aside. "It is why I sent a message to them. I am glad the letter arrived, and if things were different, I would welcome your presence here, and your help in getting my father's business working again. But..." She spread her hands. "Just now...it is impossible."

"Then I will stay until it is possible, if you will allow me? I will work for you for nothing, fetch and carry for you, whatever you need, to pay for my board, until then."

She thought of Steven's absence—she had begun to think of it resentfully as his defection—and all the burdens she was carrying at this moment without help. The presence of a man, young, strong and willing, was very appealing; especially one whose eyes held none of the lust that had made her keep James at arm's length, nor the determination to rule the household that she \had encountered in her husband, but only a desire to build something—perhaps even a need to belong somewhere—for the future.

She met his eyes and nodded. "We will be glad to have you with us, Master Finn. Thank you."

Twenty-two

Alys had found Finn a pallet to sleep on overnight in the living room by the fire, promising herself that the following day she would sort out sleeping accommodation for him in the workshop. But her night was disturbed by her mother, who was restless, tossing and turning in the bed beside her and subject to dreams and terrors.

She came down rather wearily next morning to find their guest, clad in a fresh tunic with his shirt sleeves tied above his elbows, stacking a load of firewood against the wall. He had picked up his pallet, she saw, and stored it tidily in the corner beside his pack.

She gave him a faint smile of thanks. In the light from the doorway, she could see him more clearly than had been possible yesterday evening. He was rather older than she had thought, and leaner, almost gaunt. His hair was very fair, his skin pale, and his eyes a washed-out blue. But an answering smile lit his rather sombre face, deepening the creases around his eyes and smoothing out the lines across his forehead.

"Come and see the workshop," she said.

He brushed the woodchips off his hands and followed her through the door into the room where her father had spent most of his daylight hours.

She threw back the window shutters and opened the big door that led into the paved courtyard, where once the carts had stood waiting to offload bales of wool or take rolls of cloth away for sale. The morning light flooded into the room, revealing the dust and cobwebs that infested every corner of it, festooning the big looms themselves, which dominated the central space. One loom was still loaded with half-woven cloth where she had left it unfinished after her father's death, while scraps of wool were overlaid by droppings in one corner, and she could see that rodents had made a hole in the corner of one of the doors in order to get in.

"I have not come in here for many months," she admitted. "It will need cleaning, maybe repairs, too."

"You have enough to do already," he replied quickly.

She sighed. "True. But I should not have let my father's workroom be neglected in this way."

She looked around, remembering the room as it had been in her father's lifetime, stocked with spools of woollen thread on the shelves and rolls of cloth waiting for transport, the master and a journeyman or apprentice at the looms. In those days, there had even been a boy to clean and tidy the room, usually a village lad who hoped to be taken on as an apprentice when he was old enough, but in the meantime was learning what he could by observing and serving the master for a pittance.

Her father suddenly seemed closer to her, the memories wiping out the months of grief and loss.

"If you will spare me a broom," offered Finn, "I will put all to rights."

She stared at him. She had not expected this. "You are a master weaver," she protested, "not an apprentice to be given the scullion tasks. I will get a village boy to do the work."

"Mistress, I doubt you will be able to find such a person just now," he reminded her gently.

"No," she acknowledged. "If we wish to make a start here, we will have to do the work ourselves. But there is no hurry."

"I have no responsibilities here but to the workshop," he pointed out. "You must care for your mother, and lend a hand to those who are sick in the village. Nothing is expected of me."

After a moment she nodded. "If the pestilence overwhelms us here as it has in other places..." She stopped, conscious for a moment of the possibility that no one would be left to re-start her father's workshop as she had hoped. However she might ignore the prospect, she was just as vulnerable as anyone else.

Then she shrugged. "It is as God wills. If you banish the dirt from this room, you can bring your pack in and sleep here. I will ask James our labourer to fetch some more straw to make a thicker pallet for you. And you can make whatever start you can."

"I will create an inventory for you," he suggested. "When we can begin weaving again, we will know what we need to buy."

She looked around rather vaguely. "There must be unused spools left on the shelves from before my father died, if the vermin have not ruined them. At least they do not seem to have damaged the looms."

"I can repair the looms, or anything else, if need be," he told her eagerly. "Remember, I was the youngest in my family, and my brothers loved the weaving itself. I can turn my hand to anything."

"We might be able to finish the lengths of cloth he had begun, if I can remember what designs he was using. They are on the shelf there, closely wrapped, see? We put them there when he was ill, to keep them clean."

He nodded. "I will check everything."

She smiled and left him to it. From the living room she could hear the sounds of her mother laboriously descending the ladder from the bedchamber, complaints already marring her composure. It was time to prepare breakfast.

Finn emerged to eat the meal with them before disappearing into the workroom again, taking his pack with him. When she had cleared the table, she settled her mother on her stool in the doorway with her distaff, ignoring her protests, and set out to do what she could for her neighbours.

She stopped at Goodwife Joan's house for suggestions as to where she might be most useful, for Joan had taken on herself the organisation of relief efforts from the beginning, and although Alys slightly resented her unilateral assumption of authority, she was content to accept her leadership for the moment.

But Joan met her at the door with the news that her husband had died overnight and the orphan girl who acted as live-in servant had developed tell-tale symptoms.

"I doubt she'll be of any use in her present state, and I must lay John out and make him ready for burial."

"I'm so sorry, Joan."

She hesitated. Laying out was usually a task shared by at least one female relative, but she knew Joan had none nearby, and if the servant was ailing, she would need some help from outside. It wasn't an easy thing to do alone, from a practical point of view, quite apart from the emotional support the help gave a mourning relative. "Shall I stay and help you?"

Joan shook her head decisively. "Nay, you're best giving aid to the living while you can. But will you tell Father Piers, please, Alys? That is, when you see him. I don't like to disturb him, for he was here before dawn to give my poor man the last rites and with all the illness in the village I wonder how much sleep he's getting. He'll be out and about later, for sure."

Gossip she may be, and sometimes the interfering busybody her enemies call her, but she has a good heart, thought Alys, resolving to come back and visit her neighbour later. First, she must go and check that Paul and Cicely were well. She had heard no reports of sickness from north of the bridge, but while Steven was away she was their only kin in the village, and they were her responsibility.

She met Piers as she crossed the bridge.

"I must not stay," he called, as she gave him the news about John. "I've had word that Goodwife Martha is sick. She has been ailing for two days, and so there may be need for haste. But I will call on Goodwife Joan on my way back."

That was too close to home for comfort, and Alys shivered. She was glad suddenly that Rosamund had gone back to the castle to keep the lady Eleanor company, for she would be safer there, probably, than at the weaver's cottage. She hoped Alan would return soon. Ros was his responsibility now, not hers, and she would be glad to see her sister removed to Kent out of harm's way. Lady Eleanor would find a conveyance for her in the castle stables, at need. Even with Sir Richard away, there must be some kind of litter they could borrow for Ros. She walked on up the lane to the reeve's house thoughtfully.

Paul and Cicely were well, she was pleased to find, though they were keeping close to home. Hired men took care of the flocks, and in the winter there was little else to do, though it was Paul's job to organise the ploughing on the common fields, which should start by the beginning of February. Jack was out with friends, his parents said, but they confirmed that so far there was no word of sickness visiting the more sparsely populated part of the village on the castle side of the bridge.

Alys returned home in the late forenoon to prepare dinner and do the evening chores, for night would fall early. She had seen nothing of Finn all day, though she noticed as she fed the animals that her biggest broom and a wooden bucket were missing from the storehouse.

As she was putting the final touches to the pottage, the door to the workroom opened and Finn emerged, smiling.

"Mistress Alys, Mistress Ellen, come and see."

Ellen ignored him, muttering unhappily to herself, and Alys wondered with some concern what memories the re-opening of the workshop had evoked. She followed Finn into the room and looked around her. The transformation was extraordinary. Dust, cobwebs and the detritus of vermin had all been banished, and on the nearer of the two looms new spindles had been set up ready for warping, one in blue, the other red.

"I have left the half-finished cloth in place," he told her, indicating the further loom. "I was not sure what you would want done."

"When I have leisure," she promised, "I will look out my designs. It may not be worth finishing, for my father was too ill to supervise me when I was working on it." That was a memory she would rather not revisit—of the household in chaos, her mother distracted by anxiety as she rushed about trying by any means to avert her husband's death, the doctor they had summoned from Newbury worse than useless, and Father Edward perfunctory in his attendance on the dying man.

"I have looked at the workmanship, and it seems to me good," he encouraged her. "There are techniques you may not yet know, of course, but I will teach you. The basic skills are there. You have nothing to be ashamed of."

I have things to be ashamed of that you know nothing of, she thought. She had often escaped the household chaos during her father's illness, she remembered, to continue the piece of cloth she had begun under her father's tutelage. Abandoning his sickbed to her mother's care was a dereliction of duty that had deluged her with guilt when he died.

She looked up, meeting those light blue eyes which looked so kindly upon her.

"I can tell he was a good man, and a good father," he reassured her. "You are right to grieve for him. But he would be so proud of your desire to become a weaver yourself, Mistress Alys."

"Alys...just Alys, please, Finn. We will be partners in this endeavour. You cannot go on prefacing my name with 'Mistress'." This was a big step in their relationship, to see him as a partner, but it felt curiously right. Had she only known him since yesterday evening?

He bowed slightly. "It would be an honour," he told her in his calm quiet way. "But I feel that others will expect me to show you more respect."

She considered this for a moment, impatient of a convention that would not allow him to be informal in his speech with her. But there would be plenty who would view her mother, in her addled state, as an inadequate chaperon in Steven's absence. Perhaps he was wise.

She nodded. "For now, at least. But in that case, I must do the same—Master Finn." She performed an elaborate mock curtsy, spreading the full skirts of her workaday dress. Her smile invited him to make light of the conventions, in spite of the formality of her reply. But instead his face took on a serious expression, the ready smile banished.

He bowed again. "So be it. Good night, Mistress."

"Good night."

The next morning, such considerations had been banished from her mind. She came down from the bedroom barefoot in her night shift, forgetting there was a stranger in the house, with her hair still in its night-time plait, and a shawl wrapped around her against the cold.

Finn was encouraging the fire on the hearth to wake up, with small pieces of wood from the stack. The door was open and he had clearly already begun bringing in more wood to replenish it. He looked up as she came down the ladder, obviously pleased to see her, but surprised at her dishevelled state.

"Mistress, is all well?"

"My mother is ill."

The blunt statement made his smile fade, but he made no more of it than he had of the presence of plague in the village the evening he arrived.

"I am sorry. Is it the pestilence?"

"I fear so, but it is hard to tell as yet." She thought of her mother's misery the previous day, and how she had put the wrong interpretation on it. "I believe she must have been ill since yesterday, but we were too busy to notice."

He hesitated. "Do you wish me to leave? Go back to London? I wanted to help, but if it will be a greater trouble to you to have me here, I will go."

She opened her mouth to accept, to have one fewer person to look after and think for. But Finn was her only hope of restarting the workshop, of completing her training, of ensuring the future she wanted, supposing any of them had a future. She had no right to let him stay, no justification for putting him in danger. But on the other hand, where was safe these days?

"Please stay." She looked up at him appealingly, yet not wanting to put pressure on him. "That is, if you can bear to."

He bowed slightly and went back outside. She heard the sound of the axe chopping more wood as she put the kettle in its place to heat before going back to the bedchamber to dress.

By the next day, her mother was running a high fever and unable to get out of bed, and to Alys's dismay small hard lumps had appeared in her armpits and groin that were painful to the touch. She moaned and fought Alys off when she tried to help her into a fresh shift, and refused all food and drink. She was clearly in considerable pain.

All day she lay in a stupor while Alys tried to keep up with the daily chores, for the animals still needed tending and they were short of bread. She had no time to go out and see how Goodwife Joan was faring, though James put his head in to collect his orders for the day and brought the news that Joan was now ailing herself. Finn was nowhere to be seen, and she wondered whether he had thought better of his decision to stay.

Several times, as her mother's sickness grew worse, she was on the point of sending for Ros before it was too late. But each time she thought better of it, fear making her wilfully blind to the reality of her mother's condition, until Ellen, rousing briefly towards evening, asked for the priest.

Alys stared at her, for her mother's mind seemed clearer than at any time since her husband's death.

"Father Edward," the sick woman whispered. "Send for him, Alys."

"Mother…"

"My time has come. I must confess…make ready for the next world."

Alys's eyes filled with tears. "Father Edward is away with Sir Richard and his family, Mother. But I will get you a priest." Thank God for Piers. Her mother would probably not remember who he was, but the robe and tonsure would reassure her.

She ran down to the gate, looking for someone to help. James was at the door of Widow Agnes's cottage, a few yards down the lane. She had not allowed him into the house at dinner time, though without explanation, and hoped his landlady had fed him.

"James!"

He turned and ambled unhurriedly towards her. She nearly screamed with impatience, balling her hands into fists so tightly that her nails dug into her palms.

"Mistress?" He stood there before her, obviously hoping that the summons was an invitation, that she had thought better of her earlier refusal to allow him into the house. For a moment she almost felt sorry for him, but anxiety quickly replaced that feeling as she remembered the urgency of her mother's need.

"James, run to fetch Father Piers. And please get word to Ros that she should come. I fear..." Her voice broke, and she had to swallow tears. "I fear my mother is dying."

James blanched. "The pestilence?" he whispered.

She nodded. "Yes, I think so. She has the growths in her armpits, and the fever."

He nodded. "The sickness moves fast, they say. Healthy one day, gone the next." In spite of the horror, his tone was ghoulish. Was he relishing the drama?

Alys shook her head in disbelief and anger. "Please hurry," she commanded him coldly. "Run!"

After a moment her words seemed to penetrate, and he turned and made his way towards the bridge at a shambling gallop.

Twenty-three

With Ellen's death, their nightmare entered a new and diabolical phase. The weather turned colder, with heavy rain and occasional snow, and the symptoms of the pestilence seemed to change too. Increasingly the sick presented with a terrible cough that wracked their lungs until they brought up blood, while the trademark buboes that everyone had come to recognise—and dread—were seldom seen.

The first indication of this new phase came when Steven's brother Jack came running into the weaver's cottage to tell her both his parents were sick. They were coughing up blood and he thought his mother close to dying.

"I've told Father Piers," he said breathlessly. "But we need help. Alys, please will you come?"

Alys finished off the seam she was sewing and broke the thread. Her mother's body was still lying in the bed upstairs, with Rosamund sitting weeping quietly by her side, but then Rosamund, Alys thought with some bitterness, hadn't had to deal with her mother's vagaries over the last fifteen months. She herself felt nothing in the way of grief, only guilt that she did not. Instead she had taken on the task of making the winding sheet in which they would bury their mother. They had abandoned all hope of procuring a coffin for her. The village carpenter was occupied in trying to care for his own sick wife, and had had to suspend his craft activities just when they were most needed. James had reopened her father's grave, and they would bury her mother there as soon as the winding sheet was ready. It was the best they could do in the present circumstances, though the thought of such a mediocre burial had brought on fresh wails from Rosamund, with which Alys had felt little sympathy. What had to be had to be, and wailing would not change it.

She looked at Jack. If she went to help Paul and Cicely, it would mean leaving Rosamund to deal with her mother's burial alone. But what choice did she have? Jack was far too young to manage on his own, and his sisters were all miles away and effectively out of reach.

"Go back to your parents, Jack," she told him. "Help them where you can. We are preparing to bury my mother, but I will speak with Rosamund and come as soon as I can."

She climbed the ladder to the bedchamber and put a hand on her sister's shoulder.

"Paul and Cicely have sent for me, Ros. They are sick, and Jack thinks Cicely does not have long. I must go."

"But we have to bury Mother this morning!"

"I know. You will have to take care of it, Ros. I cannot leave Cicely and Paul to suffer without help." She hesitated. "Piers will come and say the prayers if he can. And Master Finn will help you, I'm sure, as well as James."

"B-but he is not kin. Why should he help?"

"Master Finn is...like that. When you know him better, you will see."

When she had arrived in haste to attend their mother's deathbed the previous day, Rosamund had seemed very shocked at Finn's presence in the cottage, in spite of Alys's explanations. Finn had spoken to her sister with his customary courtesy, and a sympathy Alys had not up till then encountered among men, but there had been no opportunity for any further conversation, and little time even for the two sisters to make their farewells to their mother before Piers arrived to tend to her spiritual needs. "He will carry our mother down and help you with the handcart. I will ask him that now before I go, and give James his instructions for today. Ask Master Finn for any other help you need and I know he will give it willingly."

How do I know that? she wondered. Perhaps it was the way Finn had become involved in their daily life so quickly, so easily, and always kindly and courteously. She was sure she could rely on him in this crisis.

"I doubt he can make pottage, though," she added with a gleam of wry humour. "You will have to take care of that when you get home. I will come back when I can, but I owe it to Cicely and Paul to help them now, and who knows how long I will be?"

She left Rosamund trying to master her tears and ready herself to take the leading mourner's role in whatever funeral ceremony Piers could arrange in the midst of his other duties. But when she arrived at the reeve's cottage, she found Piers at Cicely's bedside, already going through the ritual questions that would help her to make a full and final confession. On the table she could see he had already unpacked the blessed oil to give her extreme unction, and the consecrated elements so that she could take communion after absolution. She spared a thought amid her practical considerations for the poor young priest, faced with demand after demand for the wherewithal of a 'good death,' and driven by the responsibility to meet the needs of so many who feared damnation or a lengthy period in Purgatory. His dutifulness, she thought, might truly be the death of him, if he could not give himself some respite from it all.

On the other side of the bed Paul sat by his wife, who was coughing fretfully from time to time and flushed with high fever. He was clearly unwell himself, but he refused Alys's offer of a pallet laid on the floor beside his wife's bed so he could rest, and insisted instead on holding his wife's hand as she struggled to breathe. Her answers to Piers's questions gradually grew slower and quieter, until speech stopped altogether.

Piers admitted defeat, and administered absolution and extreme unction to the dying woman, before putting the consecrated elements away in his valise. Poor Cicely was too far gone to be conscious of these, and coughing too much to eat or drink anything anyway. But in any case, he comforted himself, the Church taught that someone who died suddenly without opportunity to confess to a priest was to be considered in a state of grace. He'd done his best, and so had she.

He tried to smile at Alys, whose own mother he had so recently shriven. He feared Ellen must have been buried without proper ceremony, for he had been too busy with the dying to attend whatever funeral the family had managed to arrange for that morning. From the speed of Alys's arrival in response to Jack's plea, he thought it likely that she had not been present at her mother's obsequies either. For all the good she could do here, he thought, looking at Paul's face, she might as well have attended. It would not be long before Jack was summoning him to another deathbed, and there might be others elsewhere in the village in between. In the last week, there had been at least one death every day, often more.

He rose to his feet slowly and left them to it. He wondered where Steven was, and whether Alys would try to fetch him back from Calais. However fast the messenger, he would not come in time to see his parents alive.

Alys was debating the self-same question. If Paul died too, Jack would be left alone. Another reeve would have to be elected, though the office on this manor, as on many others, was treated in practice as though it were hereditary. As a free man, Steven would be disbarred from taking over his father's role, but the only other son was Jack, who was much too young for the responsibility. She shook herself. These were no thoughts to harbour as she sat beside a deathbed. She should be comforting Paul, and laying out his wife for burial as she and Rosamund had done for her mother only the day before. She wondered briefly where Mary, Cicely's maidservant, had disappeared to. She should have been looking after her mistress and master, not leaving it to others. And Alys could hear the house cow lowing miserably in the field behind the cottage. She probably needed milking.

Jack was standing by the door, silently watching his mother cough her last few breaths, the blood from her mouth trickling down onto the covers as fast as Alys wiped it away.

"Jack, where is Mary?"

"Gone home. Said she feared to take the contagion."

Alys shrugged. Mary's family lived among the worst of the hovels south of the river. She would be just as likely to meet with the pestilence there as here. But fear made for poor decision-making.

"We must do without her," she told him briskly. "Do you go and fetch more wood for the fire, for tis cold in here and your father has a fever."

He went out at once, glad to have something practical to do. He wasn't sure whether his mother was still alive or not, but she had had the priest, which was the most important thing. There was no need to hang over her, waiting for the end when there were chores to be done, chores that might help his father. He had taken his parents for granted all his life, he realised, and never understood how much he owed them. He had respected his father, of course—Paul had made sure of that—and he had loved his mother dearly, but he had never thought until today that he might lose them while he was still a child. He could not understand how he could have been so foolish, for even without the pestilence that was carrying off so many, his parents were getting older and could not be expected to live forever. Steven and his sisters were all much older than he, and several siblings born in between had died in infancy. Jack was the child of their old age.

In the end, Alys was unable to return home until the next day. As soon as she and Jack had found a cloth to act as a winding sheet for Cicely and a neighbour had helped Jack carry her away to the graveyard—where no doubt the unfortunate lad would have to dig her grave himself, with or without help from the neighbour—Paul consented to crawl into the bed himself. She cleaned up the coverlet as best she might, but she could find no spare bedding in the linen chest, and Jack did not know where it was kept. It would have to do.

She wondered where the reeve's hired men were. The neighbour who had helped Jack had been loud in his protestations that it was they and not he who should have been carrying the reeve's wife to her grave, and she thought, with a wry smile, that they would meet with a berating from Steven when he came home for their dereliction of duty. It was possible that they were out with the livestock, for Jack had mentioned sickness among the sheep that mirrored the human pestilence, but it was more probable that, like Mary, they had abandoned their allotted tasks and gone to ground.

In the early hours of the morning, she sent Jack for Piers to repeat for Paul the rituals for the dying that he had followed for Cicely. The old reeve managed to retain consciousness long enough to complete the seven prescribed questions and take the consecrated elements, and also to reassure those beside him that his affairs were in order.

"I have made a will," he told Alys near the end, in a thread of a voice between violent paroxysms of coughing. "Piers wrote it for me when I was first sick, before Cicely died. He will take it to the court for probate, when that is possible."

She nodded, tears in her eyes at the old man's self-possession in such straits.

"What I have is divided between Jack and Steven, for there is no one else," he went on hoarsely. "My daughters had their dowries and are well provided for. Send for Steven, Alys. Get him to come home, and to stay. Tis not fit for him to leave you and go off soldiering like this when we are all dying."

"He went to serve the king," she ventured, not wishing to argue with him so close to death, yet feeling he wasn't being altogether fair to Steven.

"Went to serve himself, more like," was the uncompromising reply. The venom in the words brought on another fit of coughing. She looked helplessly at Piers.

"You have declared that you wish to be reconciled with all," the young priest admonished the dying man. "That includes your son Steven, surely?" Alys was surprised to hear the authority in his voice.

Paul nodded, his face ashen. "Forgive me, Father."

"You are forgiven," Piers reassured him. "Have peace now and trust in God's providence."

For a moment, Alys thought the reeve was going to cast the pestilence and its attendant deaths in the priest's face as poor evidence of divine providence, but he restrained himself, or perhaps he no longer had the energy for such disputation. An hour later, the final breath rattled in his throat and he died, to follow his wife to the grave before it had been properly filled in, and with a similar lack of ceremony. Alys used the stained coverlet as a winding sheet in the absence of anything more suitable. She doubted whether it could be cleaned sufficiently for re-use as bed linen, even if anyone had had the time to spend on laundering it. It had been beautiful once, embroidered for her wedding by Cicely herself nearly thirty years before, and laundered carefully ever since. At least, she thought, it is fitting that it would be buried with those who had slept under it all that time.

~ * ~

Rosamund sat sobbing quietly in the big wooden chair in the living room. Alys had not long returned from Paul and Cicely's with the news that both had died, and she had brought Jack with her, for he was too young to be left alone in the house.

"Jack is going to make his home with us for now," she told Rosamund. "He and I will go and shut the animals up for the night, while you stir the pottage for me. Have you seen Master Finn?"

Rosamund shook her head. "Not since yesterday. I think he slept in the workroom last night, but I can't be sure."

Alys wondered whether Finn had in fact found other lodgings for the night, perhaps mindful of the proprieties of sharing a house unchaperoned with a married woman. Strangers had been driven out for less, rumour being what it was, though possibly the gossips were otherwise occupied at present.

"He has been very kind," Rosamund added.

Alys hoped that, wherever he was, he would return soon. She could do with some kindness herself.

"Come, Jack. Those animals need feeding." She looked back as she went out. "Don't forget the pottage, Ros, or we shall all go hungry."

Rosamund gave the mixture in the pot a desultory stir and went back to her seat. She wondered where Finn had gone, and hoped he had not run into any trouble on her account. He had helped James convey Ellen's body to the graveyard on the handcart, and the two men had lowered the woman into her husband's grave with as much ceremony as could be managed without a priest in attendance. She had not seen either of them since, and assumed James had gone back to whatever farm work Alys had assigned him. She had not given Finn a second thought until Alys asked his whereabouts, being far too occupied with her own unhappiness, and her own failures.

Lady Eleanor had accompanied them to the interment, and walked back with Rosamund to the cottage afterwards, but Rosamund was all too aware that the house smelt of death and the bodily decay associated with the pestilence, and would not ask her in.

"Tis not fit for you, my lady. Forgive me for my lack of hospitality. Until Alys returns from Paul and Cicely's, we are all in chaos here."

The excuses were pathetic, she knew. She should have cleaned the house and opened the shutters, closed to keep the sick woman warm, and banished the odour of death from the living room so she could invite her dear mistress in to keep her company, a comfort she was badly in need of. But it had all been too much for her. Alys was the anchor, the lynchpin that held the household together. Without her presence, Rosamund had allowed herself to become submerged in an overwhelming grief that was at least partly made up of guilt. It had been too easy for her over the past year to leave the care of their mother to Alys, to throw herself into her work for Lady Eleanor, in whose company she had always blossomed and felt valued, or latterly to spend clandestine hours with Alan—hours of lovemaking which had led to her pregnancy and marriage.

She longed for her husband to return with an almost physical yearning, and had begun to look out for him secretly, for she had hopes that he might arrive any day, if he had spent only a week or so in Kent as he had intended. That was, if he could come at all, with the country in the grip of this terrible calamity. She shivered. Supposing he never came, or she died of the pestilence while he was gone and they were separated forever? The dark thoughts spiralled in her mind and she began to sob again.

Twenty-four

Alys showed Jack where the food was kept for the hens, and shooed them into the barn that was attached to one end of the cottage. The days were still short, and she wanted no twilight foxes to capture her best layers while the family were eating dinner. She hoped Rosamund was keeping the pottage stirred. She didn't want to find a sticky lumpy mass stuck to the bottom of the cooking pot when she went inside.

She picked up the bucket of household food waste and went into the barn to feed the sow. Jack had finished giving the hens their grain and was shutting them into their coop in one corner of the barn.

"Shall I look for eggs, Alys?"

"I usually pick those up in the morning. There aren't many this time of year anyway."

The boy nodded and put the bag of grain away on the shelf. "Is it dinner time yet? I'm hungry."

You wouldn't know both his parents had just died, she thought. But on the other hand, one wailing mourner, in the shape of

Rosamund, was enough for the household to deal with at present. Jack might feel his loss later, when the first shock had passed.

Finn came up the path as they went in. Alys introduced him to Jack and told him the boy would be staying with them for the present. He said nothing, but clapped the youngster gently on the shoulder.

"That's good. Alys is so busy that we shall need lots of help."

Jack smiled, his face relaxing. "I'm good at helping," he said.

Alys ushered them both inside. "Let's get some food on the table. Jack is hungry, he says. God willing, Ros has the pottage ready, and there's the end of a loaf from yesterday."

Alys sighed. Fresh bread should, she knew, have been prepared this morning and taken down to the bakehouse in time for dinner, but she had arrived home late in the forenoon, in time to make the dough but not to get it baked. Rosamund had obviously failed to notice they were running short. Perhaps it was her fault for taking charge of things like baking and cooking since their father died, instead of sharing it with her dreamier sister.

They sat together round the table, spooning up the pottage— not as good as usual, Alys thought critically as she tasted it, but what could you expect? At least Rosamund had not allowed it to burn. Jack was eating ravenously, she was glad to see, and she wondered suddenly how long it had been since he'd had a proper meal. His parents had wanted nothing to eat while they were sick, and so she had not cooked anything while she was there, existing herself on snatched crusts and the remains of a cheese in the pantry when she had a moment to spare from nursing them.

She glanced at Rosamund. Her sister looked pale, and was picking at her food without appetite. "You're eating for two," Alys reminded her. "Alan will expect you to be looking after that baby of his."

Rosamund shrugged.

"I think Alan is your husband, and he is away on business?" Finn enquired.

Alys realised she had had little chance to explain Rosamund's circumstances to Finn. She wondered whether the weaver had noticed that Rosamund was pregnant, and thought he probably had. Not much missed his observant eye.

"He is in Kent," explained Rosamund, roused to a shred of animation. "He has been appointed bailiff at Sir Richard's manor at Beaconswell, and we are making ready to travel there together, when we can. He will return soon, I hope."

"It must be hard for you without him. Especially at the moment."

Rosamund's eyes filled with tears at this well-intentioned sign of sympathy, and Alys wished Finn had not offered it.

"You should go back to the castle, Ros, while you wait for him." she suggested. "The lady Eleanor will be missing your company. My sister is maid-companion to the lady Eleanor, Sir Richard's daughter," she added for Finn's benefit.

"I had the honour to speak with my lady yesterday," he admitted. "I did not like to see her walking alone when she left here, so I gave her my escort back to the castle."

Alys smiled at him approvingly. "I'm sure the lady Eleanor appreciated that very much, Master Finn."

"Lady Eleanor said she can manage without me," Rosamund told her listlessly. "There are servants still at the castle. My lord did not take so many of his household with him this time."

"Tis not the same, though, surely? There will only be kitchen maids and laundrywomen, and they are not fit company for my lady."

Rosamund shrugged again. "We will talk of it tomorrow," was all she would say.

After the meal was cleared, they sat in silence for a while, each busy with their own thoughts but no one wishing to share them. Alys lit the lamps and put ready the candles that would light them to bed. The dim room was filled with a sense of melancholy, but at the same time there was a reluctance to go to their chambers, as they often did after dark in the winter. At length Finn took a candle, lighted it at the lamp, and went through into the workshop, letting in a cold draught from the unheated room.

Alys went to find a pallet for Jack to sleep on, thinking Finn was intending to make ready for bed. It was in her mind to ask him to let Jack sleep in the workshop near him, in case the boy had night terrors and needed comfort. She had seen the way he responded to the young weaver's courteous welcome, and thought he might find it easier to sleep near him rather than to be left alone in the living room when she and her sister went to bed.

She was about to suggest this to Jack when Finn reappeared, pulling the workshop door to behind him. He was carrying a leather bag shaped like a wineskin. He put the candle down carefully on the shelf, snuffing it as he did so, and seated himself on a stool. Out of the bag he drew a pot-bellied string instrument, and began to tune it.

"Some music will lift the spirits, I believe."

So that was what he had in his pack that he had treated so carefully! Alys had never played a musical instrument, nor had much contact with those who did, except for listening to the band at village dances or feast day celebrations, or occasionally in church. But Rosamund sat up at once, her eyes aglow, remembering evenings in the castle hall when visiting musicians had entertained the lord's guests, or the family; or when the lady Eleanor herself had played the harp for them to sing.

He unpacked the bow from the case, and ran it through his hand. "My bow has not travelled very well," he told them rather sadly. "Sometime I will have to make another one. But it will do for tonight."

He began to play an Epiphany carol that commemorated the death of the Holy Innocents. The melancholy tune struck the right mood, yet the sound was soothing, and after a few moments Rosamund began to sing the words quietly.

Finn smiled at her as the song finished. "You have a lovely voice, Mistress. What else can you sing? Mayhap I can accompany you."

She shook her head. "We were singing that one not long ago at the castle, before Sir Richard went away. I do not remember many others, and I have not been taught to sing."

"Music is much more than techniques that can be taught," he told her. "Especially song. The voice is a person, and expresses the feelings the person holds inside."

Rosamund looked at him, and her eyes filled with tears. "I think I will go to bed now." She picked up a candle and lit it, her back to them. "I'm sorry...thank you so much for the music, Master Finn."

He bowed slightly and began to put the instrument away. "Another evening, we will try again, perhaps. Though I think Mistress Alys is right. You should go back to the castle while you wait for your husband to return."

To her surprise, Rosamund nodded. For some reason, his advice seemed to carry an authority that Alys's had not, though in truth it was no business of his. Alys felt a momentary irritation about this, but it was not directed at Finn personally. Men could say the same things as women, but say them so that others would obey without question. On this occasion, she supposed she should be grateful.

She furnished Jack with a pallet and suggested he might be happier in the workshop.

"Of course," agreed Finn, picking up his candle. "Come with me, Jack. I will show you the least draughty corner."

Alys wondered how much he himself had had to experiment to find out where the draughts were, and hoped he had not been spending cold uncomfortable nights in the makeshift sleeping accommodation.

He smiled at her, reading her thoughts. "I have filled the gaps in the wall," he told her. "And we will mortar them properly in the spring, when we have leisure."

It seemed so speculative an assertion—that spring would come, and they would have leisure to make repairs to the workshop wall—that Alys could only marvel at the quality of his optimism. She said goodnight and sat for a while wearily by the fire, watching the flames die down, her mind full of fearful images of death and disease, until it was too cold to sit there any longer. Then she covered the embers, lit her own candle, and went to join her sister.

The next morning Rosamund, unbidden, declared her intention of going up to the castle.

"I have no spare linen here," she gave as a reason. "At least I must go and replenish that, and make sure the lady Eleanor is well."

Alys nodded. Neither of them wanted to explore aloud why in this season of sudden death such checks were essential. "That puts me in mind of something. I must go and see Goodwife Joan this morning. I heard she was ailing when I was at Paul and Cicely's, and I've had no chance since then to check on her. Can you wait for me to return? I do not mean to be long."

Rosamund opened her mouth to protest that there was no knowing how long Alys might be, if Joan were ill or some other emergency claimed her attention. But Finn forestalled her.

"It would be an honour for me to escort you to lady Eleanor," he said, with that slight bow with which he punctuated so many utterances. "Since Alys has other calls on her time."

"Will you let the chickens out and feed them while I'm next door, Jack?" Alys did not want to take the boy with her to Goodwife Joan's, where who knew what horrors might await. But she didn't want him brooding alone, either. Finn could be relied on to return as soon as he could and take charge of the youngster, but she really felt she should not delay her visit to Joan.

Jack nodded. "Of course, Alys. Shall I fetch in some more wood, too?" He looked up at Finn, for it seemed to him—a justifiable assumption, Alys thought rather ruefully—that Finn was acting as man of the house in the absence of Steven.

"Good boy. If you take in some of the small stuff and stack it in the corner there, then when I come back we will take an axe to the bigger logs."

Finn waited patiently while Rosamund put her cloak on and donned her pattens, for the lanes were slippery with icy slush. Then he tucked her hand into his arm and walked away with her in the direction of the bridge.

"I think Master Finn admires Rosamund very much, don't you, Alys?" observed Jack.

"Most men do," Alys replied drily. *Finn had best not turn his eyes in that direction, or he'll have Alan to deal with.* Yet she had no real doubts of Rosamund, whose heart was armoured by her love for her husband. Alan had nothing to fear. So why did she feel slightly jealous, as though Finn belonged to her and should not be letting his eyes stray to her sister?

She shook herself. *Tis just that he is to be my weaver,* she thought. *He will be no more than a hired man, even if he is teaching me.* But it occurred to her that that wasn't how she had spoken to him when they discussed re-starting the looms and getting the business going again. Then it had sounded more like a partnership of equals rather than mistress and man.

She watched Jack set off for the barn and then turned up the lane towards John and Joan's cottage, a few dozen paces away.

Goodwife Joan met her at the door of her cottage, very much alive but looking rather pale and weak.

"I am so glad to see you!" Alys exclaimed involuntarily. "Not many seem to recover from this sickness once it has them in its grip."

"Takes a lot to kill me," the other woman declared. "Them growths, they just grew and grew and then burst on me the second day I had the sickness, and once I'd cleaned myself up and put on a fresh shift, I was champion. Not just as strong and dandy as I used to be, maybe, but 'twill come in time, I expect."

"You should rest," advised Alys. "Who knows, the sickness may return if you do not. Sit down and let me make up the fire and bring you some food." The cottage was a small one, with one room only downstairs, and a single loft for sleeping, but today it was cold and cheerless, and the hearth empty except for charred embers.

"I've not much food in the cupboard," Joan told her, sinking gratefully on to a bench by the wall. "I didn't have the strength to make bread dough this morning, and I think my flour bag is almost empty."

"I will bring you some of ours," Alys offered. "I have some more proving. Tis easier than setting about making a fresh batch for you here, by the time we've sent the dough to the bakehouse."

Joan nodded. "Don't know what I will do now, without John. Mayhap my son-in-law will take me in. But he's nosing around Widow Mary Buckley, over Whitchurch way, and if he's planning to marry again, he may not want me interfering."

"Wait and see," Alys advised, feeling some sympathy for Joan's son-in-law. "We will look after you for now. Get your strength back and then God will provide."

She went back to the cottage for a loaf of bread for her neighbour, and found Finn and Jack in the workshop. Jack seemed fascinated by the looms, and Finn had set up some spools and was showing him how to warp the threads to make a simple woollen rug.

"A new apprentice, Mistress Alys!" he declared in delight as she looked in through the door. "Jack would like to work with us, wouldn't you, lad?"

Jack turned a beaming face to her. "I would! Better than farming and organising the manor work rotas like my father did. Can I truly be a weaver's apprentice, Alys?"

She frowned at them both. "I don't know," she replied. "Wait until life is back to normal and your brother is home. We can't decide anything until then."

Jack's face fell, but he turned bravely to Finn and thanked him for showing him the process. "If I can, later, Master Finn, I would like to learn the weaving trade."

"Then you shall," Finn promised him, ignoring Alys. "As soon as may be."

"Come with me, Jack," said Alys, in a gentler tone. "I need you to run an errand to Goodwife Joan. She is recovering from the pestilence but she is weak and I have promised her some bread. You can take a morsel of cheese, too, and some of my winter apples. I don't know what store she will have of fruit, and they will help her to grow strong."

When Jack returned, she was busy laying her mother's bedding over the bare lilac bushes. There had been no chance to launder it, but the heavy showers would probably do the job for her, or at least rinse and freshen them up. Ellen had not coughed up blood and phlegm like Paul and Cicely in their death throes, but even so Alys could not stomach the thought of sleeping in the sheets where her mother had died. The spare bedding was airing by the hearth, and she would use that until she could clean her mother's linen properly. The shutters were open and the breeze was blowing through the house, for the atmosphere had seemed foetid to her this morning. Having the shutters open had made the rooms cold and she had had to cover the fire to stop the flames from blowing dangerously in the wind across the room. That would mean dinner would be late again, by the time she had got the heat in the cooking fire up to temperature, but it couldn't be helped.

She had a hand on the cottage door latch to go inside when a voice hailed them from the gate.

"Good day, Alys."

She turned. To her amazement, Alan was standing in the gateway, his hand on the rein of his cob. Both horse and rider looked travel-stained and tired, but at least they had returned safely.

"Alan! I'm glad to see you. How was your journey?"

"Tis worse than a war zone out there," he told her. "All the inns are closed from Reading to the Kent border. I had to sleep in barns and outhouses all the way back, and tether the cob where I could. There was no fodder for him, either, and that delayed me because I had to stop so often to let him graze. I kept away from the towns as far as I could, but everywhere there are folk wandering and dying by the roadside, their wits gone. Bodies lying unburied out in the open, cows unmilked, livestock on the roads. And the smell! Tis a foretaste of hell, I tell you."

"Tis not so good here either," observed Alys quietly.

Alan seemed not to hear her. He had caught sight of Jack. "Hey, lad, what brings you here?"

The boy looked at him. After a moment, he told Alan quietly, "I live here now." He opened the cottage door and went in, closing it after him.

Alan looked at Alys. "What's all that about? Where are Paul and Cicely?"

"In the churchyard. My mother too. The pestilence has been rife here since you left."

"Ros?" His face was white. "Where is Rosamund?"

"She is safe, Alan, with the lady Eleanor at the castle. Do not worry. The pestilence has not touched her."

"And the child she carries?"

"All is well." *For now.* The words hung between them for a moment, unspoken.

He put his foot in the stirrup and swung up into the saddle. "I will go and see for myself. But as long as Rosamund is well, that is all that matters to me."

Twenty-five

As January gave way to February, in spite of a run of cold and snowy weather that made walking about the village difficult and brought hardship to many, particularly those who were sick, Alys found herself in a state of surprising contentment, though she had a tussle with her conscience about this. Was it wrong to have a sense of ease—even joy—in the midst of all this calamity? Walking home from the castle, where she had been visiting her sister, she could not help feeling she had many blessings to count. Alan and Rosamund had been offered rooms at the castle by the lady Eleanor, who was reluctant to say goodbye to her maidservant, even if she was no longer expected to stay in her service, and with Alan at her side Rosamund was blooming.

Meanwhile she, Finn and Jack had begun to create an efficient if unconventional household. Jack was still somewhat withdrawn and tended to sit silent during any conversations that took place, but he was clearly very attached to Finn——indeed, Alys wondered whether he did not have a better relationship with the weaver than he had had with his own father, who had been a dour, hard task-master and an overbearing parent, as she knew from Steven.

He helped Finn with the heavier household tasks, and under Alys's instruction, had taken on feeding the chickens and the pig and keeping an eye on the house cow, who lived most of her life in the paddock behind the cottage and was brought into the barn only in bad weather. Cooking, cleaning the house, milking the cow and preparing dough for the bakehouse fell to Alys, along with any laundry, and although she thought Rosamund better off with Alan at the castle she sometimes found herself wishing for another woman to share the load with her. Still, the household had enough wood in stock to keep a good fire in the hearth, and plenty of salt bacon, corn, beans and pease remaining in store, together with feedstuffs for the animals.

Jack and Finn had taken the handcart and fetched what provisions remained at the reeve's house before the mice found a way into the store cupboard or it was looted by the destitute. In spite of the loss of her mother, her parents-in-law, and so many others, and the disappointment she felt that re-starting the weaving business seemed as far off as ever, she felt an unwarranted lightness of heart as she went about her daily tasks.

"Is it wrong, think you?" she asked Finn one day as they set out along the snowy lanes to help an elderly widow whose daughter and grandchildren had died the day before. "To feel cheerful rather than despairing, in the midst of all this misery?"

He looked at her gravely. "Is that how you feel?"

She nodded. "It's all so awful, and yet..."

"We can find small kernels of joy even in the most terrible circumstances. I think it is good to let those moments come. Otherwise we would truly despair, would we not?"

"Do you feel them too?"

He smiled down at her. "Indeed. Every time I see you, caring for everyone, so practical, so resourceful, you bring me joy."

She said nothing, but her heart hammered in her chest. She stole a glance up at his face, but he was looking straight ahead as he strode along. What did it mean, this confession of his? Why did it cause her breath to quicken and her cheeks grow hot? All she knew was that this was a dangerous conversation, and one that she would not like anyone else to know about. What on earth would Steven think?

She wondered what Steven was doing, and how long he would be away. No doubt he would return when it suited him, or when Sir Walter had no further need of him. With some feelings of guilt, she had to acknowledge to herself that she was perfectly happy without him, but she was conscious that he would not approve of her sending to the Weavers' Guild for a master to finish her training any more than he would be tolerant of the friendship that was growing between herself and Finn.

Every day the two of them went out to help their neighbours, though Finn tried to ensure Alys did not go into any dwelling where he had reason to believe there was sickness. But he encouraged her in the rest and worked alongside her, whether it was summoning Piers to a deathbed, clearing paths so as to bring food or fuel to the poorer folk, arranging for bereaved children or grandparents to be cared for by extended family, tending beasts that would otherwise be neglected, or giving practical counsel and encouragement amid the stench of fear that stalked the village.

Gradually they had become almost inured to the suffering they saw, no longer commenting to each other on the rumours of communities deserted further afield, nor dwelling on the symptoms of the sick, nor even lamenting the spread of the pestilence into every corner of their own village. Yet everywhere they walked they saw signs of decay: dead and dying animals scattered across the flooded pastures near the river, unploughed arable fields at the southern edge of the village, and in every lane empty houses whose doors hung open, inviting wild creatures and vermin to make use of them until a new tenant found the wherewithal to pay the heriot owed to Sir Richard and take possession.

Though they seldom spoke of it, both had ceased to be anxious about contracting the pestilence themselves. Either they would die, or they would be spared—it was all in God's hands, as Alys observed several times. There was no time or energy to think further than the immediate needs of the day, but they were both certain the world would not come to an end, whatever others might fear, and in unspoken accord were determined to do whatever they could to make sure that those who survived in Northchurch would have a chance of putting things to rights again when the pestilence had passed. And at the end of each day, whenever the needs of their neighbours permitted it, there was supper around the fire with Jack to look forward to, and the feeling of work well done and comfort and companionship at the end of it.

"Another reeve must be chosen to replace your father, Jack," Alys remarked, as they sat by the hearth in the gathering dusk one February evening. "For tis more than time to apportion strips in the fields and organise the ploughing, even if we cannot make a start until the thaw sets in."

Jack nodded rather absently and Alys wondered whether she had been tactless in mentioning the matter in front of him. Electing the reeve would normally be done at the manorial court, though it might be some time before the next one was held, since Steward Roger, its usual chairman, was still with Sir Richard in the north. The bailiff could take his place at need, but reeve or no reeve, ploughing must be done as soon as the snow thawed, or they would none of them eat come autumn.

At last Jack spoke. "Most of the ploughmen are dead."

Alys put a comforting hand on his shoulder then turned to Finn, a teasing smile on her face in spite of the sadness of the subject. "I suppose ploughing is not another of your unknown accomplishments, Master Finn?"

He made a deprecating gesture. "Unfortunately not. I have lived all my life in London, and the womenfolk bought food for the most part in the markets. I have never seen a plough, to my knowledge. But..." He paused.

"You can learn?!"

"I told you. I can turn my hand to anything, if someone will show me how."

She nodded, becoming more serious. "I will speak to Matthew Ploughman. He is old now and no longer leads the work, but he was the best in his day. And Jack can supply the oxen." Although Reeve Paul had kept mainly sheep on his pastures, he had traditionally provided some oxen for use in the village ploughs.

"I will ask the hired men tomorrow," promised Jack. "There has been a murrain and much death among the beasts, I know, in this cold weather, but surely there must be enough oxen for at least one plough, maybe two."

The murrain had been caused by neglect, Alys thought privately, for several of her father-in-law's hired men had departed from the village early in the outbreak, leaving his animals to fend for themselves. She suspected the men had taken the opportunity to escape their unfree status and find work in one of the towns, a few of them even leaving their families unprovided for. Not that it would help them if they fell sick on the journey with no one to look after them. But that was their affair. She could understand the temptation.

"I fear we will not have as much need of ploughed land this year as last," she said aloud. "For there will be far fewer mouths to feed." Already the village population was heavily depleted, and who knew where it would end?

Finn said nothing, but he took his rebec from its bag and began to play. He had taken to doing this every evening if they were all sitting together by the fire, for comfort and, Alys thought, something more than that. The music seemed to lift them above the everyday terrors they were facing, and remind them that better times would come, if they held on to their faith, to their humanity. Even if they themselves did not live to see those times, others would.

~ * ~

Piers lay on his narrow bed and tried to sleep. After supper, which had been brought to him in his cell, he had been called to Bailiff Michael's suite of rooms, and there had shriven the bailiff's wife and seen her make as good an end as possible, though she coughed her lungs up in the process, just as Cicely had and a dozen others. He had long gone beyond the point where he could relax enough to sleep except when he was completely exhausted, and sometimes not even then.

Often, as now, his mind turned round and round like an animal in a trap, seeking answers to doubts and questions and finding none. He had been taught by Father Nicholas, when learning his catechism as a child, that God was all-loving, all-merciful, and forgave sins in response to repentance. Punishment was reserved for the wicked, those committing mortal sin, and anyone who refused to repent. But where was that all-loving God now? The pestilence had no favourites. It did not single out communities where religious ritual was missing, or where priests failed to do their duty, or reserve its attentions for the wicked and lewd, the lechers and prostitutes, or even those whose moral laxity might be shown up by their more pious neighbours. It was indiscriminate, making no exceptions for the righteous or dutiful, sparing only a few, and then according to some unfathomable logic that left him reeling.

Over the last fortnight Piers had found himself attending two or even three deathbeds every day, at all hours of the day and night, and still he could hardly keep up with the demand for his ministry. He had long given up even attempting to offer any kind of funeral ceremony to the bereaved, who had to manage as best they could with the resources to hand. He had seen biers pushed through the snow by grandfathers in their seventies, tears flowing down their aged cheeks and into their beards, who had never thought to be burying their own children instead of the other way round; and by round-cheeked children in groups, too young to look after themselves, who had somehow wrapped their one remaining parent in a shroud and heaved the body on to a handcart to push up the hill to the churchyard, slipping and sliding in the icy slush.

How they would dig a grave or what words they would say to send their father or mother on their way to the next life he knew not and had no time to worry about it. As long as the dead had made their peace with God, it was all he could do. So far he had managed to attend every deathbed, but some of the dying, he was sure, had not understood the confessionary questions he asked, and yet others were in too much of a stupor to make proper responses, leave alone those whom the pestilence seemed to have turned mad, and whose staring eyes saw nothing of the real world but had retreated into a nightmare somewhere within. He daily thanked God that Holy Church did not condemn those who failed to make a proper confession because circumstances did not allow them to do so.

A long queue of penitents had come to him in the last few days, as Shrovetide began, to confess their sins and be given absolution ahead of the forty-day fast of Lent with its tradition of self-criticism, self-abnegation and preparation for the glorious celebration of Easter. Given that it would give comfort to those who might die suddenly of the pestilence before a priest could reach them, Piers had been keen to interview all his Shrovetide penitents, but the process took a long time, since they were comprehensive in their confessions, and he worried that at any moment there might be more urgent calls on his time. He comforted himself that if anyone was at death's door, a neighbour or family member would certainly summon him to their side. He had been woken more nights than he could remember from his slumbers to go out to someone on the point of death, while his days were spent trying to comfort the bereaved.

It was frustrating that none of this was truly his job, though of course in the circumstances he would have helped the parish priest and taken some of the load off him. But to be left bearing the whole burden, while Father Edward put his chaplaincy to Sir Richard above his responsibility for the parish, was too much.

As for poor Sir Thomas, his time in Purgatory must be getting longer and longer, as Piers' ability to keep up with the Masses he was supposed to say for his lord became more and more curtailed. Somehow he must find help.

Next morning he entered the hall for breakfast to find Alan seated at table with Rosamund, and the lady Eleanor with them. No high table was set up, and they sat in a group in the body of the hall, being waited on by a motley collection of menials, some of whom clearly had little or no training in such work. This condescension on the part of Lady Eleanor was typical, though Piers knew her brother would not have approved. Yet why should she be condemned to sit alone on the dais, he thought, and the few remaining servants be asked to do the extra work of serving her special food?

He greeted the lady reverently, lowering his eyes as he spoke to her as a conscientious priest should, and took his place at the board beside Alan, who was tucking into beef and bacon pie and washing it down with the castle's best ale. Rosamund beside him ate more moderately, and the lady Eleanor, who had broken her fast earlier, toyed with a few sweetmeats and a small loaf.

Piers noticed that the bread was coarser than usual, and the ale seemed to him weak, though Alan was making no complaint. No doubt the castle kitchens were as understaffed as the rest of the manor, whether owing to sickness or to so many being absent with their lord in the north. He murmured a grace, crossed himself, and consumed his own meal in silence while conversation went back and forth merrily across the table. Alan was regaling Rosamund in particular with rosy-tinted details of their new home. Piers wondered whether his newfound prosperity and status was not going to the archer's head.

"Alan," said Eleanor after a while, "may I ask something of you?"

"My lady," acquiesced Alan in his best franklin's voice. "What is your pleasure?"

"Pleasure it is not," she replied. "But I hear Bailiff Michael has sickened this morning, and I am concerned that he will be unable to keep the records of those who have died, and the heriot payments their successors have made. It is so easy to lose track of everything, and we should do our best to take note of the deaths and new tenancies at least, ready for the manor court."

Piers had noticed, as he went about his duties, that the lord's animal pound was becoming uncomfortably full. Here the best beast owned by each incoming villein tenant was kept until it could be checked and allotted to a herd, earmarked for slaughter, or, in the case of the horses and mules contributed by the better-off families, taken to the castle stables. It was probable that as many as thirty beasts had been brought there over the last few weeks, in some cases representing multiple deaths in the same family as brother or son followed the original tenant to the grave. It wasn't surprising Bailiff Michael couldn't keep pace with recording them all. Piers couldn't imagine what would happen if he died, for appointing another bailiff at this juncture would be impossible. It would have to wait for Sir Richard's return, and who knew when that would be? No wonder the lady Eleanor had appealed to Alan for help.

"And while you act as deputy to Bailiff Michael," Eleanor went on, "Rosamund will help me with the Shrovetide food."

To cheer her people, Eleanor had decided to provide some festive food to mark the end of Shrovetide in late February, since the normal feast on Shrove Tuesday could not realistically be held. Dishes were to be available in the castle grounds for those who came to the manor court to register deaths or new tenancies. She knew that many who had no business at the court would come and partake too, but that did not matter. Like all housewives, she hated to see waste, and with a reduced complement to feed at the castle there was plenty of rich food—meat, eggs and dairy produce—that needed using up before the Lenten fast. The castle kitchen was still shortstaffed, but when approached, a number of the villein women had volunteered to take charge of cooking the traditional foods, an offer which she was glad to accept. The castle would, she promised, provide the ingredients for pancakes and pastries and other seasonal dishes. All those of the unfree manor tenants who had made their Shrovetide confession would be invited as of right.

As the days passed, Alan was glad to see Rosamund occupied with these arrangements, for his wife had been showing signs of anxiety. Now in the fifth month of her pregnancy, she felt well and the baby had quickened, but she was terribly sensitive to the horrors going on around her, even though Alan did his best to keep the worst from her.

"I cannot bear it," she said to him one evening as they made ready for bed. "Every day I hear of some new case of sickness, or a death. Piers looks exhausted. And yet Alys goes round everywhere visiting everyone, and telling them what to do, as well. How does she cope?"

Alan smiled. "Alys is different from you, my love."

"Is she? Perhaps she just doesn't care as much. Perhaps she doesn't *feel* as much."

In spite of Alan's own reservations about Alys's behaviour, particularly the presence of the weaver in her cottage and by her side as she made her helpful way around the village, his natural sense of fairness couldn't let this pass.

"She's no fool to take unnecessary risks, Ros. Everyone knows the sickness seems to pass from person to person, whatever Piers' Paris physicians may say. If she didn't care about her neighbours, she wouldn't put herself in danger the whole time as she does." Steven would put a stop to it if he were here, but who knew when Steven would come home, and Alan had no authority over Alys, brother-in-law though he might be. He wouldn't for the world have wanted to check Alys's actions, anyway, even though he felt worried by the ubiquity of Master Finn, for the two of them were holding the village together during this crisis. It was just as well Steven had stayed away.

"No, I suppose that's true. I wish she would think of my feelings if she were to take the sickness, though. Tis bad enough as it is. I just worry all the time."

He kissed her and helped her into her night shift. He had been surprised and concerned how the pestilence seemed to have affected his wife, making her anxious and panicky where she had once been confident and hopeful. Perhaps it was the effect of losing her mother, or because she was with child herself. Pregnant women often seemed to have odd fancies, and a sensible man ignored them as best he could.

Twenty-six

For once, on Ash Wednesday Piers lay undisturbed in his bed the whole night, after returning quite late from a deathbed. But sleep was again slow to creep over him, and when it did come it was troubled by dreams of the flames of hell, from which he was unable to snatch all the souls who were crying out for help. He slept rather late the next morning, and stumbled down to the hall to break his fast just as the servants were clearing the table. But they found him some cold meat and bread to satisfy his hunger, and one of them told him that he had a visitor.

"Alan Archer has asked him to sit in the solar for the moment," the man told him. "The lady Eleanor is there with him, for she broke her fast early as usual. But he bears messages for you, and as he is a priest she is suggesting we make up a bed for him in your cell, or perhaps in Father Edward's quarters, while the house at the church is made ready for him."

Piers frowned. A visitor with messages was welcome—perhaps the bishop had written to tell him what he should do about his chantry duties while he was filling in for Father Edward, since there was no sign of the incumbent's return. But the house at the church that was supposed to be used by the priest had not been lived in for several years, because Father Edward, like Father Nicholas his predecessor, had held the living in addition to his role as family chaplain. In theory both priests should have found a vicar for their parish duties, but what point was there in paying out even a vicar's pittance if they could do the job themselves? If the church house was being made ready, it sounded as though this clerical messenger was planning to stay for a time, which in the circumstances was very good news.

Excited at the prospect of help, Piers hurried through his breakfast and trotted up the stairs to the solar. The brazier had been lit in honour of the guest, for the lady Eleanor rarely used the room in her brother's absence, and the two were seated on each side of it in cheerful conversation. Piers could not help a tiny pang of jealousy at their ease with each other, though he quickly suppressed it.

The visiting priest was young, like himself, but short and round and beaming. Looking at him, Piers understood why Eleanor had responded to his smiling converse and bore him no more ill will.

"This is Father Robert," Eleanor told Piers. "He has come from the diocese of Bath and Wells with messages for you from Father Edward and from Bishop Ralph, in whose service he has recently been." She got up gracefully from her stool. "But he will tell you all himself. I will leave you two to talk, for I must speak with the bailiff."

Piers looked up. "Is he recovering?" Perhaps what ailed him had not been the pestilence after all. He hoped so, for Bailiff Michael was well liked by all.

She shook her head. "I do not know yet. We will send here for you if you are needed."

Left in the solar together, the two young priests sat for a moment, sizing each other up. "What a woman!" Robert exclaimed. "Never met her like before, in cottage or castle."

Piers regarded his cheerful rubicond countenance with disfavour. This enthusiasm was too worldly for his taste. "She is a saint," he told Robert austerely.

"I'm sure she is. And beautiful with it."

"She has the grace of an angel. The other day she spent hours in a hovel in the village, comforting a dying woman until I could get there to shrive her."

Robert's eyes opened wide with amazement. "And she a lady born!"

"As I told you, she is a saint."

"She explained to me that her brother is away in the north with his chaplain and the family, but I can't say I really understand why he has left her here in charge of his affairs. Seems scarcely fitting."

Piers hesitated. It seemed ungracious for him to acknowlege Sir Richard's failings, although he agreed that it was outrageous of him to leave Lady Eleanor to deputise for him while he saved his own skin. "What messages do you have for me?" he asked instead.

"I am part of the message in my own person. Father Edward has appointed me his vicar here while he is away with his lord."

"That is good news." This was no doubt why the church house was to be put in order for the visitor. That mystery at least was solved.

"The second is from Ralph of Shrewsbury, whose clerk I have been until recently."

Piers raised his eyebrows. Ralph of Shrewsbury, being bishop of Bath and Wells, had little to do with the Winchester diocese. But Father Edward could appoint as vicar whomever he chose.

"Sir Richard and his entourage rested a night with Bishop Ralph on their way north after Christmas," Robert explained. "Father Edward gave thought to his responsibilities here, and asked me to come and take over his duties until he could return."

"That was weeks ago," said Piers indignantly. He thought of his own struggles to give pastoral care to the parishioners all that time while this little robin of a man had dallied. "What took you so long?"

The other man smiled cheerily. "I had affairs to settle before I left Bath and Wells. Tis no light matter, to take up an incumbency at a moment's notice."

"We could have used your help," Piers replied.

"The pestilence?" whispered Robert, as though it might hear him if he spoke louder.

"That was why the lady Eleanor was at the bedside of one of the villeins. The village here has some three hundred souls, and of those we have lost nearly a hundred in the last few weeks. Is the pestilence not raging in your diocese, too?"

Robert hesitated. "I believe so. But I have been with Bishop Ralph at Wiveliscombe, his country retreat. The manor there has not been affected, or not yet."

"Well," replied Piers after a moment. "You have a lot to learn."

"You will help me, though?" The other priest's face had paled somewhat from its normal rosiness. "As you say, I know little of the situation here, and you have been dealing with it for some time—most competently, I must say, from all I have heard from the lady Eleanor, who speaks highly of you."

Piers hid the glow of joy that welled up in him at his lady's appreciation of his efforts. "My true work is in Sir Thomas's chantry, to ease his soul through Purgatory. I have neglected the task that he educated me to do in order to help the people of this manor during these trying times, in Father Edward's absence. Now that's your job, and I wish you joy of it. I believe instructions have been given to make the priest's house ready for you. It has been out of use for years, but if that takes a day or two, short-staffed as we are, you are welcome to a pallet in my cell." He rose to his feet and gathered his robe around him.

"There was another message," Robert added quickly. "Bishop Ralph said to tell you the Holy Father has declared that non-priests can take confession, *in extremis*. Even a woman can hear confessions if there is no priest to do so, and they are to keep the secrets just as we do."

"I have heard of such ideas before. But never from the Holy Father. That is news indeed." Piers wasn't sure how to take this new departure.

"I believe we may yet be glad of such permission. But while we can, we priests should do the job, do you not agree?"

Piers rubbed his face. "If it continues as bad as this, it may well be necessary to take advantage of the Holy Father's permission by the end. I will help you an I can, but I must fulfil my responsibilities towards Sir Thomas as well."

As he left the castle, he saw a servant running from the bailiff's quarters towards the solar and concluded that Father Robert was about to have his first taste of a plague death. Dourly, but with dogged perseverance, he trudged off to his own cell before making his way down to the chantry.

As he passed through the church, he saw Sister Margery on her knees at the lady chapel altar. She had a small altar in the anchorhold itself for her personal use, but she preferred to pray in the chapel when it was quiet. He felt a slight lift to his own spirits as he passed her. However dark the hour, her prayers would be heard by God.

And so, for the next fortnight, as February drew to an end and March brought the first signs of spring, Piers pursued—not without a guilty sense of relief—his appointed task of prayer in the chantry, leaving Father Robert to struggle with the demands of the parish. What people had begun to call the Great Mortality continued to stalk the lanes of Northchurch, visiting almost every household. One or two villagers, like Goodwife Joan, had survived the disease early in the outbreak, when the buboes had burst, or shrivelled up before the fatal rash developed, but none survived the coughing version of the disease, and most died quickly.

Unfortunately, Piers' respite from it all, and with it the time to give Sir Thomas's soul its help through Purgatory, was short-lived, for at the end of the fortnight Father Robert was found dead in his bed, and the burden fell on him again.

He took his problem to Sister Margery the morning after the young priest's death, and asked her advice.

"I must have help, Sister," he told her wearily. "Managing on my own almost killed me last time, and now it has killed Father

Robert too. God forgive me for my laziness, for I could have helped him more. But I cannot do this alone."

"Then I will help you," she replied at once, as though she had already thought the difficulty through and determined upon a course of action. "I will leave the anchorhold and hear the confessions of the dying. After all, the Holy Father has said that it is acceptable for a woman to do this, has he not?"

"Yes, that's true, but Sister," stammered Piers, taken aback, "you are sworn to remain in the anchorhold. You cannot break your vows—you will be forsworn."

"Not in these circumstances. You have said yourself that there are too many deaths for you to deal with all properly. If I could hear their confessions, you could give the dying extreme unction and the viaticum, and also you could bury the dead with the proper prayers, rather than the makeshift arrangements that are being made at the moment."

"Yes, but..."

"I cannot see any other way," she said firmly.

"Well..." An idea came to him suddenly, clearly, as though by inspiration. "Let me try one thing first. I would not wish to see you out in the world again, if it can be avoided, when your calling is as an anchoress."

"What thing is that?"

"The brothers at Whitehill Abbey. Some of them are priests. Surely one at least will come in our need?"

"Perhaps. That is a good thought. But Father Piers..."

He had turned to go, but he stopped at the concern in her voice. "Yes?"

"I counsel you, do not go alone."

~ * ~

Alan and Rosamund were breaking their fast in the hall with Eleanor when Piers arrived.

"So will you ask the clerk to prepare the ledgers for the manor court, Alan?" Eleanor was saying. "We will need to hold another one soon, to register the deaths that have occurred in the last few weeks."

"Certainly, my lady."

He felt excited about presiding over a court for the first time, if also a little apprehensive; and proud to have been asked to stay on as deputy bailiff after Michael's death, given that no new appointment could be made in Sir Richard's absence. He was unwilling to take his pregnant wife on a long and uncomfortable journey in these uncertain times, and the appointment offered a way to avoid that. Moreover, as Northchurch was Sir Richard's most prosperous manor, and the head of the DeClerc honour, he would be temporarily richer for the change, marking a heady rise in his fortunes since he returned from his travels. Letters had been sent to apprise the Kentish manor of the new arrangements, and to make sure that someone was doing the work of bailiff there. The young groom sent by Eleanor on this errand had not, however, returned, so Alan could not be certain the messages had actually arrived. All he could do was to learn the work here and await events.

"If we can hold the court as usual, next week, we should try to do so," went on Eleanor. "And of course it will be Lady Day soon, and we must have the accounts ready for that. Perhaps Steward Roger will return then. He would normally be going round all my brother's manors at this time." He heard her sigh a little, as though the effort of trying to keep the manor running normally was becoming burdensome.

"Before you go, Alan," Piers put in quickly, as Alan rose to do the lady's bidding, "might I—with your permission, my lady—ask your help?"

They all turned to look at him, in varying degrees of surprise and disfavour.

"What is your need?" asked Eleanor after a moment. "What I have asked Alan to do is important for the manor, but I know you would not have countermanded it without good reason."

"Indeed, I do not wish in any way to cut across your wishes, my lady," Piers protested. "But I am worried that soon I will not be able to keep up with the demands of those who are sick and dying in the parish. Already I cannot bury them all properly or even give them the viaticum. There are too many, and the calls for my attendance come too quickly. With Father Robert dead and Father Edward still away with your brother…"

"You are perhaps being too conscientious," Alan suggested. "Perhaps not all can be accommodated, with the situation as it is."

"No, I will not have any denied their spiritual rights," Eleanor said quickly. "Be they high or low, all are equal in God's sight, and in their need of a blessed death. How can we help you, Father?"

"I wish to go to Whitehill Abbey," he answered. "Many of the brothers there are ordained priest, even though not all of them practise their calling. But in these terrible days, surely at least a few of them would come to our aid? If, that is, they have not been called upon by others already."

"That is an excellent idea. And you wish for Alan's company?"

"I would prefer not to go alone, for I don't know what we will find. Sister Margery thought it best."

There was a silence for a moment.

"What say you, Alan?"

The archer nodded. "Aye, I will go with you. You have done much already to help people here in our parish, and tis only right that you should have some assistance from the brothers. Will they have horses there? Or should we take mounts for them?"

"They have their own stable," Piers assured him. "May I take a pony for my own use from the castle stables, my lady?"

"Of course," said Eleanor. "Take what mounts you will. There is little of any quality there save my own mare, but indeed, Alan, I have no need of her today, nor have had for some days. Why don't you ride her yourself? She will be the better for some exercise." she smiled. "I feel sure she would welcome you on her back again."

And so it happened that Alan, riding his own beloved mare, followed Piers and his pony up the hill from the castle towards Whitehill Abbey, a few miles to the north. It kept to itself well away from other human habitation, as Cistercian monasteries were wont to do. It might be that the brothers would reject Piers' request, since it would mean rubbing shoulders with everyday life as it was lived in the sinful world, but Alan thought they would probably respond to the necessity. No one of priestly status ought to hold back in these dire circumstances, and only those with good excuse—or a malleable conscience, like Father Edward—would find ways of doing so. Alan had never shared Steven's cynicism about the Church and its sincerity. To him, priests were the godly servants of God and the people, from whom the best might be expected. So far, Piers had not disappointed him. Indeed, he viewed the young priest with a great deal of respect. Much had been demanded of him without preparation or experience, and he was young yet, younger by a couple of years than Alan himself, and by his own admission only half-trained.

They trotted sedately along the muddy unpaved road that led up into the hills where the monks had built their abbey, Alan holding in his mare to keep pace with Piers' pony, who was old and fat but the best Sir Richard's stable had offered with his master absent. The rain had let up for the moment, and the sun peeped through the clouds and cast an encouraging beam on them. Their spirits lifted a little. For both, the ride through open countryside, even a late-winter countryside of mud and flooded fields, had proved a welcome relief to the sickness and suffering they had seen so much of in the past few weeks. It was still God's world, even if he seemed to have forgotten the human inhabitants of it.

As they approached the abbey, they saw no one stirring abroad, though usually lay brothers and servants would have been hard at work in the fields or the woods, or gathering fish from the ponds for the monks' dinner. Instead a pall of silence lay heavily over the abbey grounds. The two men glanced at each other.

"Something is amiss here," commented Alan, dismounting by the gateway.

"We'd best go and see," agreed Piers briskly, but his heart sank.

They led the horses into the stableyard and tethered them. Here too was an unearthly hush where normally all was bustle. Alan peered into the horse barns. The horses stood in their stalls, though the fodder in the troughs was running low.

"Where is everyone?"

Neither of them pursued this thought.

"I'll go inside," volunteered Piers bravely, lifting his valise down from the saddle. "Do you go and see if you can find any of the lay brothers. Someone must be in charge, whatever has happened."

"Nay, Piers. I'll not let you go alone." Alan unlatched the door into the cloisters and held it for Piers. He had faced danger and horror before, on the battlefield and in many an adventure on the way, but even he shrank from what they might find here.

Twenty-seven

They walked through the cloisters silently. The carrels where the scribes copied books for the library showed no sign of life, nor did the central grassy square around which the pillared cloisters ran. Piers pushed open the door into the warming room, but it was cold and empty.

He looked at Alan with consternation. In winter, even under the austere Cistercian regime, the warming room would always have a brazier burning.

Alan shook his head and walked on along the cloister to the chapel. He opened the door and looked in, but the same silence and stillness met him. Together, with a chill at their hearts, they mounted the dorter stair to the dormitory where the monks slept. At first this too seemed empty. But then Piers saw what appeared to be a bundle of white robes on one of the beds towards the far end of the dorter. As he approached, he realised it was a monk, sprawled across the bed, his feet still touching the floor.

"Brother…" He put his hand to the monk's shoulder, and turned him over on to his back. A face ravaged by sickness turned its sightless eyes up to him. The body was stone cold.

"He's been dead some time," Alan commented, coming up behind him. "Long enough even to be limp again."

Piers knew about rigor mortis, where the dead became stiff and difficult to handle after a few hours' death; then it passed off again and you could move their limbs as you wished. He might attend death beds, but he had had no experience of handling the dead. He couldn't remember whether he had ever seen a body after the stiffness had passed. They were usually in their winding sheets by then, laid out by the women, hands folded and limbs straight, ready for burial. Why had no one cared for this man's body in the proper way?

"The infirmary," he said. "That is where the living must be, if any there are."

They moved more quickly, running down the dorter stair and across the cloister to the infirmary. Alan flung open the heavy wooden door, and a terrible stench hit them. Piers felt his gorge rising and he retched, turning back into the cloister for some fresher air. Alan waited a moment and then went in, the end of his sleeve pulled across his face.

An appalling scene met his eyes. White-robed bodies lay everywhere, in the beds, on the floor, some in their own excrement, others blood-stained or soiled with the release of bodily fluids at the point of death. Some had clearly been dead for days and were showing the first signs of decay. The body nearest the door was still warm, sprawled across the infirmary desk with his face half-pillowed on his arms.

After a moment Alan reached out a hand and closed the staring eyes. "My God!" he exclaimed. "What has happened here?"

"They have taken the sickness one after the other." Piers looked around the scene with horror. "The infirmarian tried to care for them, I guess, but then the sickness came upon him, too."

"And there was no one left to care for him."

"No." Piers tried to make sense of it. "But these are all robed monks. Where are the lay brothers?"

"Would they come to the infirmary if they were ill?"

"I don't know, but I would have thought so. They live here, after all, at least most of them do. Where else would they go for help?"

Alan turned for the door. "We'd best go and find them. There's nothing we can do for these poor souls."

"They may not have been able to confess, or receive extreme unction," said Piers anxiously. He could see no sign of consecrated bread and wine, though possibly a priest might have taken those away with him. But if so, where had he gone? Were there more bodies somewhere else that they hadn't looked?

"I will say the prayers for the dead, if you will go and look for the lay brothers, Alan. Come back here and tell me what you find." Ignoring the stench and mastering his nausea, he knelt down among the dead to offer up the prayers the Church provided for such times.

Alan went outside into the cloister, relieved to escape the charnel-house atmosphere of the infirmary. He left the monastery buildings and went out into the grounds. The two horses still stood tethered in the stableyard, and he spared a moment to find them some fodder and a bucket of water. His sharp ears picked up the sound of an axe which seemed to be coming from behind the stables. A lay brother, clad in homespun and apparently in good health, was calmly chopping logs in the lea of a woodshed piled high with them.

He straightened up when he saw Alan.

"Good day," he said.

"Good day?" replied Alan incredulously. "*Good day?* What in God's name are you doing?"

The man indicated the pile of logs, incredulous in his turn at the question. "Why, chopping logs for the abbey, sir. What else?"

"Have you taken a look inside the abbey lately?" asked Alan.

The man looked shamefaced for a moment and then shook his head. "'Tis no business of mine what goes on inside. My jobs be all outside. Chopping wood, clearing and coppicing. Most days I see none of the brothers. Except on Sundays when we are in chapel," he added. "Though they didn't hold no services this Sunday past. I reckon," and he lowered his voice confidentially, "I reckon maybe they have this pestilence that everyone is telling of. But tis the infirmarian's business to care for the brothers. I stay out' way." There was a pause. "What be ye doing here, master?"

"I came with the chantry priest from Northchurch. We are overwhelmed with the pestilence in the village and hoped one of the priests here could be persuaded to come and help us."

"And would they not come? Tis unlike the brothers not to help others in need, though they live retired in general."

"They're all dead, man. Every one. Unless there's some we haven't found yet, but if so they must be ailing too. The place is as silent as...as the grave." He stopped.

The woodman nodded. "I'd noticed that."

"You'd noticed something?" Alan spoke sarcastically, for he was becoming impatient with this conversation, as well as with the woodman himself.

"The silence. Tis not usual. I don't go into the cloisters, of course, and there is a rule of silence mostly, within, but still we hear sounds from the kitchen and the warming room sometimes."

"You did not think to check what was happening?"

"Nay, why should I? Like I say, tis the monks' business what happens inside. I've my own tasks to do."

"Where are the stablemen?" demanded Alan. "The gardeners? The kitchen servants?"

The woodman shrugged. "I dunno. Ain't seen the stablemen since yestere'en. Be the horses all right?"

"For the moment, but they will need fodder and water very soon. You can deal with that," he added.

The man bowed his head in acceptance of the instruction.

"Where do the other lay brothers sleep? Not in the dorter with the monks?"

"Nay. We have our own sleeping quarters." He waved in the direction of outbuildings on the other side of the monastery herb garden.

"Is there anyone there?"

"Not this time of day," the man replied. "Nor should there be. Though, truth to tell, I been on my own there for the last couple o' nights."

There was nothing more to say to someone who had so little curiosity, not to mention so little human compassion. Alan abandoned him and went back into the cloisters.

He found Piers still kneeling among the bodies.

"Piers, I found a lay brother. But he's a woodman and stays outside. He didn't know what was going on in here. Nor did he care, curse him. He says he has not seen any of the lay brothers since yesterday, but if they have died too God knows where the bodies are."

Piers got up from his knees. "We must bury these men at least before we go."

"Impossible. There isn't time. We have to get back to Northchurch and tell them what has happened here. Get word to the bishop, to the headquarters of the Cistercian order, wherever that is. Abroad somewhere, I expect."

"Burgundy."

Alan sighed. "Not much chance of getting word across the Channel at the moment. But the bishop should know. He can send folk to clear up here. Tis not our job."

"Yes, it is," Piers persisted doggedly. "I am not leaving them here unburied. It would not be Christian."

Alan thought of the lay brother he'd spoken to, and his litany of tasks that were not his business. Piers was right. They could not shuffle off this duty so easily. "I will go and find that damned woodman. He can lend a hand."

By the time the woodman had been convinced that it was appropriate for him to dig graves, and Alan and Piers had, with the aid of a handcart, transported all the foetid corpses in their filthy robes down to the abbey graveyard and disposed of them, indiscriminately, into the pit he had dug, accompanied by the prayers that Piers insisted on saying for them all, the day was well advanced. No sign had been seen of anyone else on the estate and they decided the lay servants had probably fled. The abbot, too, was unaccounted for, and his cell looked suspiciously tidy for one overcome by sudden mortality.

They searched the entire monastic complex looking for more bodies before they told the woodman to close the grave. Then, exhausted and depressed, they collected their mounts from the stable yard and set off home, hoping the woodman would at least have the sense to turn the monastery horses loose if there was no one to look after them.

"I hope no one in Northchurch has died while I've been away." Piers' mind was turning at last from the immediate imperatives of burying the monastic dead. "It'll be dusk by the time we get home."

Alan frowned. Throughout the burial proceedings, he had been trying to persuade Piers to leave the monastery as quickly as possible, unhappily aware of the worry and distress their prolonged absence might be causing at home. Also, he was hungry. They had put their heads in at the abbey kitchen to check for bodies, but neither of them fancied eating anything that plague-infected monastic hands had touched, even though there were loaves on the table and a dried-up haunch of meat grown cold on a spit in front of the dead fire.

It seemed crass and unfeeling to desire food in the face of the total disaster that had befallen Whitehill Abbey, and he felt sure Piers did not share his hunger pangs. But the fact remained that he was a healthy man who had put in a lot of hard work that morning, and it was past dinner time. He hoped the castle kitchens had saved something from the midday meal.

~ * ~

Eleanor and Rosamund had busied themselves about the manor house during the morning and had not given much thought to Alan and Piers and their errand. Two of the kitchen servants were ailing, though still at their posts before the cooking hearth, and Eleanor gave orders for them to be sent to their beds and hot gruel supplied to them whenever meals were being served to the healthy. The remaining staff could prepare a simple meal for everyone else without too much difficulty.

"After dinner I think I should go and visit Alan's family," Rosamund said as they walked across the wards to the solar. "Eric brought word yesterday that his mother is sick. Alan spoke last night of visiting them today, but I am not sure when he expects to return from Whitehill."

"It is but a short ride to the abbey. I suppose they may wish to wait for the brother-priest to return with them, but even so I would expect them to return for dinner. I expect there will be time after that to visit his family." She thought for a moment. "But will Alan want you to go where there is sickness, Rosamund? You have a child to consider now, and should not court danger."

"Where is there not danger, in these days, my lady?" For the first time for some weeks Rosamund felt brave and strong, and ready to emulate her sister. "When Bailiff Michael took the sickness, I did not hear you refuse to go near him in case of danger."

Eleanor nodded. "That is true. Well then, if Alan does not return for dinner, we will go together."

Rosamund was aghast. "That is not what I meant at all, my lady! Alan would certainly not want you to court sickness for the sake of his family, for they are nothing."

Eleanor smiled. "They are as worthy of care as anyone else, Ros. If you are going to see them, then I will give you my company. Unless you would prefer to go alone?"

Rosamund hesitated, but the thought of taking the journey on her own did not appeal. "I could ask Alys..." she faltered.

"No." Eleanor had clearly made up her mind. "Alys has enough to do. You and I will go if Alan has not returned. We cannot leave them without succour, if there is sickness."

It was no use saying more, but Rosamund knew that no one, not even her sister, would be happy at the idea of the lady Eleanor sick-visiting in the hovels of West End. Alan might even be angry with her for allowing it. She hoped he would be back for dinner and could take up the cudgels himself. But if not, she resolved to make the journey by way of the weaver's cottage and see what Alys could do to make Eleanor see sense.

The two women ate dinner in the hall alone, for Piers and Alan had not returned. Rosamund felt a little anxious about this for, as Lady Eleanor had said, it was only a few miles to the abbey and surely, they would have concluded their business by this time? But she said nothing, trying to talk sensibly of trivia as dinner conventions demanded. She had, of course, not grown up with such etiquette, but the dais was no longer used at mealtimes, since Sir Richard and his family had departed, and although Eleanor sat below the salt with the higher servants such as the bailiff and Rosamund herself, she clearly expected conversation to follow the same subjects as would have pertained at high table.

The second course had just been removed by the servants when Toby came in. He addressed himself to the lady Eleanor.

"My lady, forgive my disturbing you. There was a message to Father Piers, from one of the villagers, but as he is not in his cell, I thought…"

"Indeed, you did right to come to me. Father Piers had to go to Whitehill Abbey today, though we are expecting him hourly. What is the message?"

"The boy is here, outside, my lady. Will you speak with him?"

"Bid him come in."

Toby went out into the courtyard, and Eleanor took a seat on one of the benches along the wall. Rosamund stood beside her, a feeling of dread at her heart which was not relieved by the sight of Eric, Alan's young nephew, creeping into the hall in the wake of the groom.

Eleanor turned an encouraging smile upon him and an enquiring eyebrow on Toby.

"This is Eric," Rosamund told her, trying not to feel sick. "Alan's nephew, his elder brother's son."

Eleanor's face lit up. "Of course. Eddi's brother. What is your message, Eric?"

"If you please, my lady, we can't find Father Piers, and…and my mother is at death's door. My father, too, has been desperate sick since yesterday. The Father must come at once."

There was silence for a moment. Then Eleanor rose to her feet. "Father Piers will be home soon, and we will leave a message for him to come to your cottage as soon as may be. In the meantime, I will come myself."

The boy looked dazed. "You, my lady?"

"I too," added Rosamund at once. "Alan and I had heard that there was sickness in your household, and we had planned to come today. But we have been delayed, like Father Piers."

"But we need a priest! They are dying!"

"Have a care, boy," put in Toby, who was still standing in earshot. "That's no way to speak to the lady Eleanor."

Eleanor made an impatient movement. "This is not a time for the niceties, Toby. We will come, Eric, as soon as we have put on cloaks and boots. Run back home and tell them help is on its way."

Twenty-eight

At the weaver's cottage, Alys had finished clearing dinner and was starting to check the stores. The crock of flour was getting low, she noticed, and she was aware that James had not come to the door for the day's instructions at dawn, nor at midday in the hope of dinner. Indeed, she couldn't remember seeing him for several days. So much was taking place so quickly that the days seemed to run into each other, leaving no space for reflection, or even for noticing anything untoward, and Finn had unobtrusively taken on much of the heavy work that James would normally have done.

She wondered whether the labourer had decided to take his chances elsewhere. Landless he might be, and impoverished enough to take what wages she had been able to afford for his services—perhaps in the hope of gaining her hand in the days before Steven came back, perhaps only because there was no better option—but he was a free man, not tied to the manor by villein status, and could go where he pleased. She hoped he was not lying in a ditch somewhere in his death throes, far from help or succour.

Perhaps later she would find a moment to go across the road to ask the Widow Agnes whether she had heard anything.

Wherever he was, the flour crock was getting low, and someone would have to take grain up to the mill before it ran out altogether. Yesterday, at least, the mill wheel had still been turning and presumably the miller was at work as usual.

She looked round and saw Jack hovering in the doorway of the workshop, which seemed to exert an enormous fascination for him.

"Is Master Finn within, Jack?"

The boy nodded. "He is checking the stocks of wool, I think."

"Ask him to step through here when he has a moment, please."

The request was forwarded, and within seconds Finn was before her, his tall figure swathed in short but voluminous overalls. She could not help laughing, and was glad to see the blue eyes crinkle at the corners with amusement in response.

"I found your father's working tunic in the chest," he said. "I hope you do not mind. I did not have room in my pack for my work clothes and it is the best I can manage for the moment."

Laughing had made her feel better, she realised. "Of course I do not mind. It is just that it fits so badly! I am sorry we have no time to alter it for you, or to make you a new one."

He smiled. "That time will come. May I use it for the moment, to save my own clothes for other purposes? If you will forgive my ridiculous appearance, Mistress Alys. Perhaps it will double as a ploughing apron. Ploughman Matthew has promised to give me my first lesson this week."

"I have a task for you outside now, if you will be so good."

He took off the overalls, revealing his workaday shirt and tunic beneath, and handed it to Jack. "Please put that back in the chest, Jack."

"We are running short of flour," Alys told him. "It is James's task to replenish it, but James has not come near us today, so we will have to manage without him. There is a sack of grain in the barn. Will you take a bag of it down to the mill and get it ground for me, if you please? I would be so grateful. The miller will take a fee, of course, but I will find you some coin."

"Of course, Mistress," Finn replied simply, as though there were no greater pleasure or satisfaction for him than to do her bidding.

"Jack!" she heard him call. "Will you come with me to the mill to get some grain ground for Alys?"

The boy appeared at once, and the two figures, the one tall and lean and well-knit and the other half-grown, small for his age and stocky like his father, went out into the chilly air together. Extraordinary how the orphaned boy had taken so easily to the stranger from London. Was it admiration for Finn that led him to favour the weaver's trade, or had weaving interested him for some other reason?

Finn shouldered the grain bag and steered the boy out of the gate in the direction of the mill. He and Alys had agreed it was best to keep him busy, so that what had happened to his parents did not dominate his thoughts too much. Grief was a necessary part of loss, of course, but it would come when it would, and Finn thought Jack was not yet ready to face the full force of it.

He wondered for a moment what was happening in the Flemish community in London, whether his family was suffering loss like so many others. It seemed all too probable, but he put it out of his mind. He had chosen to leave the city and settle in this rural place, far from all he had known, and this was where his concerns must be. Sooner or later, word would reach him as to his family's wellbeing, and there was no point worrying about it until then.

Jack ran on ahead of him along the lane, and as he reached the bridge, Finn saw him encounter another lad about the same size. The two evidently knew each other and stopped to exchange news for a moment. Then Jack came flying back along the lane.

"Eric says his mother and father are sick of the pestilence. His mother is dying, and they cannot find Father Piers! But the lady Eleanor says she will come, and Mistress Rosamund with her, and that the priest will come later when he returns. Master Finn, what should we do? Surely it cannot be right for the lady Eleanor to go to the West End, with only Rosamund for company?"

Finn considered. He had quickly conceived the same admiration for the lady Eleanor that was held by everyone else in the village. She was a pearl beyond price and should not, he agreed, be put at risk in this unfortunate manner. Moreover, Alys's sister, he had noted, was expecting a child. She too should not go unescorted to the hovels of West End.

On the other hand, the destitute poor were as entitled to spiritual comfort as anyone else, especially in the face of death. He could imagine this was the line the lady Eleanor would take, and he could not quarrel with it. What on earth was Father Piers doing, to make him unavailable when needed? The poor young man was struggling with burdens he was not ready to bear, that was clear. But he did not give the impression of one who would quit a task easily.

And where was Rosamund's newly returned husband in all this? He had heard a great deal about Alan and his exploits, but he had not seen much of him since his return, as he was being kept busy as acting bailiff. Finn was not altogether sure whether he might not turn out to be a vain and shallow popinjay. On the other hand, Alys's beautiful sister was clearly on fire for him in a way Alys herself was not for her own husband. Alys had said nothing to imply fear or dislike of Steven, or indeed any other emotion, but that was all. What would it take to awaken her, he wondered, and who might do it, if her husband could not?

He looked at Jack, who was standing waiting for him to pronounce upon the immediate problem. "Go and tell Mistress Alys what Eric said. I will deliver the grain to the mill, as she asked, but I believe you and I should meet the lady Eleanor and Mistress Rosamund and give them our escort. Do you agree?" He waited for Jack's nod. "Then come back to me at the bridge as soon as you may."

Finn watched Jack set off at a run towards the weaver's cottage before continuing down the lane to the bridge and the mill beyond it. His errand was quickly done. There was a new miller, for Matt had died in February, and his more amiable brother was now in charge. Coins changed hands and the flour was promised for later. Meanwhile Finn had kept an eye on the bridge and was sure the ladies had not passed by. He found a milestone near the bridge and perched upon it comfortably, ready to wait for as long as was necessary.

~ * ~

When asked, Widow Agnes confirmed that James had indeed decided to take to the road with his few belongings. He had, Alys was glad to hear, paid his landlady for the food he took with him, and for the breakfast she had made him the day before, but he clearly had not wanted to take the time to bid Alys farewell. The widow was clearly unhappy about his disappearance, not least because what little prosperity she had depended on Alys paying her a few pennies for James's accommodation, which would no longer be forthcoming.

"What am I to do now?" she asked Alys, who did not know what to say in reply.

She was returning from the widow's tiny cottage, the woman's laments still ringing in her ears, when she saw Jack running frantically towards her. The story streamed from him, breathless and garbled, and she had to make him stop and start again before she could make head or tail of it.

"Master Finn is waiting for me at the bridge," he finished. "But he bade me tell you first, that we will go with the lady Eleanor and Mistress Rosamund. He said they should not go to the West End unescorted, though truly I do not think he has ever been there himself."

"Probably not," agreed Alys. She was privately as horrified as Finn had been that Eleanor and Rosamund had taken it upon themselves to fill the priest's place. Quite apart from the danger to their own health, it was impossible for them to do for the dying what he could do. She could only think the lady Eleanor wished to give comfort, whatever else she could not give. And remembering Rosamund's desire to accept Alan's brothers as her own flesh and blood, quite apart from the responsibility she felt towards her mistress, it was not surprising that she had thought it her place to go with her.

She picked up her cloak and pushed her feet into pattens. "I will come with you," she said. She followed Jack out on to the path and latched the door behind her. It still felt strange not to have to make provision for her mother, or reassure her before she left on an errand, as she had been accustomed to do for so long. But those days were over, and in time the strangeness would pass.

Finn sprang to his feet as she approached.

"There was no need for you to come, Mistress! Jack and I will take care of the lady Eleanor and your sister."

"I will do my best to persuade them first that they can do no good," she said. "Or to let me go instead of Rosamund. It would be better for her to go home and wait for Alan, as she is with child."

But when the two women arrived, it proved impossible to move them from their purpose, and in the end the whole party set off for West End together. There they found Peter and his wife sharing a sickbed, both struggling to breathe and exhausted by coughing. They needed Piers, and not even the lady Eleanor's presence could comfort them.

"Father Piers will come," she assured them. "As soon as he may. Meanwhile you may have confidence in the mercy of God who forgives sinners. And at need, I am permitted to hear your confession. The Holy Father has said so."

She took the wooden cross on its chain from around her neck and held it before the dying couple. "Remember that he died for you on this cross, as we hear in the Mass every day. Ave Maria..." And she began to say the Rosary, still holding the cross up high.

Rosamund sat mesmerised. *She will be made a saint one day,* she thought. *So far above me that I can hardly reach and touch her.*

Alys, meanwhile, was looking into the practical matters at hand. It was clear that it was not only Peter and his wife, Martha, who were ill, though as yet the sickness had not taken serious hold of any of the others. In such crowded conditions, it was difficult to care for anyone properly, and if all the adults were to succumb, the surviving children would need looking after. She checked the food cupboard and found it almost empty, the crock of flour down to the last inch or two, the apples half-rotten and some of the onions going soft. Apart from some peas in a jar, there was little that was edible.

"Fi... Master Finn." She caught herself just in time and added the formal title.

"Mistress? What is your will?"

"They need food. When you fetch our flour from the mill, could you bring it here instead of taking it home? Ours will last till tomorrow at least and there is more grain in our store."

He nodded. "What else is needed?"

"The children must be hungry, for I doubt anyone has had the energy to prepare food today."

He nodded. "Even the fire is cold, but I have put kindling ready if you wish it lit. They have a tinderbox on the mantel there."

"Yes, please. I will make some pottage while we wait for Piers. We cannot put any meat in it, because of Lent, but it will be better than nothing, and I can use some of these onions to give it flavour–– they can't all be rotten. At least the folk here, that are well enough to eat, can do so. It will strengthen them."

"I think it is not good for Jack to be in this house," Finn commented. "It will remind him of his parents' death. We will go and fetch the flour, he and I, and perhaps then I will send him home. Do we have enough beans in our larder to spare some for your pottage?"

"That is a good idea." She smiled at him. "Tell Jack you need his help to carry the provisions and I'm sure he will go very willingly."

The pottage was soon simmering as the fire heated up, and she shepherded the younger children away from the sickbed and sent them outside into the fresh air to play while the meal cooked. She left the door open so she could keep an eye on them, and hoped the fire would create enough warmth to keep those who were sick from taking cold. A quilt was keeping Peter and Martha warm, but the grandmother was shivering in a threadbare shawl and Alys feared her fever was mounting.

Not long before dusk, Finn returned with Jack and the supplies, which she added to the pottage. The aroma of hot food was appetizing, and acted as an antidote to the foetid smell of sickness. She found bowls in the cupboard and set them ready on the table.

"Father Piers is on his way," Finn told her. "And Alan. They will be here soon."

Eddi, who was hovering nearby savouring the prospect of a hot meal, overheard this and at once went to his parents' sickbed with the news. There were general cries of relief, but Eleanor kept her seat.

"There is something else," Finn said.

Alys looked enquiringly at him.

"When you can leave the pottage, I think you should come next door."

"Why? What has happened?"

He hesitated. "I'm not sure. But we should look."

Mystified, she went over to Rosamund. "Ros, Piers is coming and you and the lady Eleanor will be able to go home. Will you look after this pottage for me for a few minutes? Master Finn thinks we should check next door. Who lives there, do you know?"

Rosamund thought for a moment. "Timothy the cottar and his family, surely. His daughter Mary was Cicely and Paul's maid."

Alys remembered that the girl had disappeared home when her master and mistress became ill. She had not seen her since.

"Perhaps they too are ill. As Finn says, I should go and see."

"Do you want me to come with you?"

"No, you stay here. Master Finn will not let harm come to me. There is nothing for you to worry over."

They went out together, unnoticed, into the street. Timothy's tiny cottage was set at an angle to Peter and Zack's, almost abutting it at one corner. As they drew near the door, Alys became aware of a strange droning noise, on a single wavering note. Otherwise there was silence.

Apprehensively, she put her hand to the latch and pushed the door open. The dusk was already falling and the single room was almost dark. No lamps had been lit, and the brazier gave out no glimmer of light, but the droning sound was louder. Finn opened a shutter, which even in the dusk let in a little more light into the cottage, and as her eyes grew used to the dimness, Alys could see an old lady sitting in a chair, rocking herself to and fro, to and fro, incessantly while she keened her mourning dirge. Beside the bed, in which Timothy and his wife lay, long past any help, were Mary and her five younger siblings, huddled together on the bare floor.

"Are they all dead?" Alys asked, horrified.

Finn nodded silently.

"Oh Finn..."

He stood there for a moment as she wept, letting out her grief at last for all the deaths of the last few weeks—the loss of family and friends and neighbours, the fears for the future which she had till then kept at bay. She had been so brave that he had even thought her unfeeling, focused so much on the practical that there was no room for much human emotion. But he saw now that it had not been so.

A sob caught in his own throat as he gathered her into his arms and held her tightly, to shut out the grandmother's dreadful keening, to try to shield her from the horror and the fear of it all, longing to protect this young woman whom from the very beginning he had revered and loved, at first with the kind of respect and affection that arose from a shared enterprise, but more recently with something much deeper that ironically threatened all he had hoped to achieve in this place. For Alys already had a husband, and Finn's love for her was all in vain.

Twenty-nine

When Piers and Alan arrived at the castle to hear that Eleanor and Rosamund were down at West End visiting the sick—news that Toby seemed pleased rather than sorry to give them—both men were aghast, and Alan was angry. With his wife, not with the lady Eleanor, he hastened to explain to an affronted Piers.

"She's with child," he told the priest furiously. "What is more, I told her I would go this afternoon, and she knew I wasn't planning for her to accompany me."

"That's probably why they went," Piers pointed out reasonably. "The lady Eleanor would not let her go alone, and you and I were not here."

"We should have been here." Alan's voice was savage. "God rot those brothers at Whitehill."

Piers was shocked. "Tis hardly their fault they are dead! What could we do but give all of them a Christian burial, if you can call it that?"

Alan shrugged. "I told you the needs of the living should come before the needs of the dead who can no longer suffer."

Piers hesitated. In one way, he could see Alan's point, but in another his priestly office made him aware that the dead had needs that could not wait, and they could not cry out for help.

"I must go at once to your brother's house," he told Alan. "Eric's message said Martha was on the point of death. And that was hours ago." He looked at the sky. The sun had set and heavy clouds hung above them, threatening rain. There would be no moon to light them on their way.

"I'm coming with you," said Alan. "I must get Rosamund out of there as soon as may be. I will escort the lady Eleanor home as well, while you are ministering to the dying."

Without further conversation, they turned their mounts and set off down the lane. Better to ride than to walk, as the horses were already saddled, for horses' night sight was better than humans', and these two knew the village roads well. They would be unlikely to stumble even in the gathering dark. Besides, Alan thought, it might be useful to have mounts to carry the women home. Rosamund would be exhausted by emotion, if by nothing else.

As they reached their destination, Finn and Alys emerged from Timothy's cottage.

"There has been great tragedy," Finn told Alan, to save Alys from having to speak. "This whole family has been wiped out by the pestilence, except an old grandmother, poor soul."

Alan peered at Finn in some bewilderment.

Alys pulled herself together. "Master Finn and I came to help Ros and the lady Eleanor, but we heard this strange keening…" Her voice faltered as she tried to control her tears.

Piers had dismounted as well and tethered his pony to the branch of a tree on the far side of the lane. "Alan, will you see to these beasts? I must go to the sick."

Alan hitched his horse to another tree branch. "I'll fetch my wife out of that house first. The mare can carry her home and then the horses can go to their stalls. Unless you wish me to leave the pony here for you?"

Piers shook his head and lifted his valise down from its fastening on the saddle.

"Master Alan, I need your help," Finn said.

Alan had taken a couple of paces towards his brother's house, following Piers. He looked round. "Why so?" He was already regretting responding to Piers' appeal for help that morning, and was growing tired of being delayed and placed in awkward situations.

"There are eight bodies in that house, and an old lady whose wits have been turned by their deaths. I want them out of there."

Alan stared at him.

"What shall we do about the old granny, Mistress?" Finn asked Alys. "We can't leave her there alone."

"She'd best come home with us," suggested Alys. She smiled wryly. "'Tis nothing new for me to look after an old woman whose wits have been turned by grief."

Finn made to lay his hand comfortingly on her shoulder, but just in time noticed Alan's eye upon him. He let the hand fall to his side.

"I must go back to Peter and Zack and the family," Alys said. "I'll tell Ros you're here, Alan."

"I'll tell her myself," he said, moving to follow her.

"When you've helped Master Finn with those bodies," she reminded him. She paused for a moment, then added prosaically. "I think you should leave them in the street, out of sight if you can. We can't bury them now that night is falling."

"Aye," Alan agreed. He had no mind to start ferrying corpses to the graveyard while Rosamund was still in danger, though he looked surprised at Alys's apparent lack of emotion. "They'll come to no more harm there, God knows."

Finn said nothing. He knew what he knew about Alys's true feelings and how she hid them.

In silence, he and Alan manhandled the eight bodies outside the door, four of them so tragically small and light, and stowed them as tidily as they could in the small gap between the two cottages. For Finn did not want the old woman to see them on her way out of the door. For now, she had better be left where she was, until Alys had finished what she needed to do at Peter and Zack's. In any case, Alys was more likely than a stranger to convince the old woman to leave the house.

Alan brushed off his hands. "Why did you come to Northchurch, Finn?" He deliberately omitted the courtesy title Alys had used. He was suspicious of the stranger who had arrived unannounced in their midst and taken root in his friend's house in his friend's absence, and had wanted to question him ever since Alys had first mentioned the weaver's arrival, but had had no opportunity.

"Alys sent to the Guild of Weavers in London for a master weaver," the other man replied after a moment.

"Did she indeed?"

"I am a master, but I have no business of my own, for my father is still alive and my brothers are older than I. There is no room for another master weaver there. Mistress Alys wishes to finish her training and start the looms again, and I am here to help her."

"And what does Steven, who is Alys's husband and my friend, as you probably know, say about all this?"

Finn shook his head. "Mistress Alys has not told me anything, but I have assumed he gave her permission. Do you think he may not have done so?"

"He has been away soldiering with the king's army in Calais the last few months. I have not seen him since before the Epiphany, and neither has Alys. When did this message to the Guild come?"

Finn hesitated. "Forgive me, Master Alan, but I think this is Mistress Alys's business and I should not be talking even to you about it. She will tell you everything, I am sure, if you ask her, as Steven's friend as well as her sister's husband, but it is not for me to divulge what she has not."

Alan threw him a look of scorn and strode over to his brothers' house. Finn watched him go thoughtfully, then picked up a half-broken bucket from the cottar's yard and dipped it in the well. He set it down beside the horses and loosened their tethers in turn so that they could drink.

The horses had had no time to do more than quench their immediate thirst before Alan emerged from his brothers' cottage, accompanied by a reluctant Rosamund.

"Alan, I must not leave the lady Eleanor on her own here. Surely you must see that?"

"However much you feel you owe the lady Eleanor," Alan replied implacably, "our own child must come first. I will take you to Alys's cottage for the moment, if you wish to wait until the lady is ready."

"Yes, please, Alan. I would be much happier to feel that I had not abandoned her altogether. I'm sure she will come soon, and then you can escort us both home."

He nodded. "Mayhap Alys will have some hay I can give to these two beasts. They have had nothing to eat since we left Whitehill Abbey."

He left the horses tethered and walked slowly along the lane with Rosamund.

"What happened at the abbey?" she asked hesitantly. Nothing had been said about what had delayed Piers, but from the demeanour of both men she had the feeling it was something terrible.

"The brothers are all dead. We had to bury them and it took time. I'm sorry we were home so late." There was no way to give her the news less bluntly, much as he would have liked to do so.

"Poor Martha. She was desperate to confess before she died. Thank God Father Piers came in time. I heard the lady Eleanor say that even women can hear confession when someone is at death's door, but 'twas clear Martha wanted the priest."

Alan said nothing. This continual harping on confession, absolution and a good death irritated him. A focus for pious women and clerics, he had always thought, but his brother Peter seemed as bad as the rest, now that he was sick. Perhaps, he reflected, using an imagination that was underdeveloped from lack of employment, it was different when you were actually facing death. He had suffered a light wound or two on his journeys with Sir Thomas, but never anything that put him in mortal danger. It was easy to scoff at other folks' fears.

He looked at his wife, glad that she seemed to have stopped moping and regained her confidence. On the other hand, almost the worst of today's incidents was the danger she had put herself in by insisting on visiting his family. What on earth Steven would make of Alys's current habit of going in and out of plague-ridden houses to help the inhabitants he dreaded to think, though in truth it was hard to know, sometimes, what Steven would think about anything. Alan still didn't understand why his friend had been so keen to leave the village and go soldiering with Sir Walter, when they were so recently returned from years abroad, especially so soon after his marriage.

But one thing he was sure of was that Steven would not take kindly to Finn taking up residence in his house, even though the weaver was apparently sleeping in the workshop and by his own account was in residence only for the purpose of re-starting the weaving business. But if the latter were true, what was he doing at Timothy Cottar's house with Alys that evening?

He walked with Rosamund to the weaver's cottage and left her there while he took an armful of hay back to the horses. Jack seemed pleased to see her and at once went to the cupboard to find some food for her. Alan had hoped to return almost immediately so they could reach the castle before the twilight faded altogether. But Eleanor refused to leave Martha's side until Piers had administered extreme unction, and in the end it was not Alan but Piers who escorted her back to the castle. She protested first that she was not dressed for riding, and that with the priest's arm for support if she should stumble, and the light of the moon that was by then shining faintly behind thin clouds, she would do well. Alan could lead the pony back to the castle stables, or let Rosamund ride it.

"You should focus on Rosamund's wellbeing," she told him in her imperious way, which yet had such sweetness behind it that no one ever resented it. "I will see you on the morrow."

But by the time Alan reached the weaver's cottage with the two horses, Alys had put Rosamund to bed in her own lavender-scented sheets, and Finn and Jack had retired to the workshop for the night. There was nothing for Alan to do but accept as graciously as he could the bread and cheese Alys had prepared for him—for however angry he was with her for letting his wife visit his brothers' family, courting infection, he was too hungry by that time to do other than take what was offered—and then make his own way back to the castle in the dark with the horses.

Alys closed the door behind him with some relief. She had decided not to mention that, while Rosamund slept soundly in Alys's bed, Timothy's bereaved mother Christine lay in the other bedchamber, though whether she was actually asleep or not Alys wasn't sure. She knew Alan wouldn't approve, and would no doubt have some pungent things to say about harbouring the destitute old lady under the same roof as his precious wife, but she hadn't the energy to argue with him about it tonight.

Thirty

Piers went to his cell full of conflicting emotions. On the one hand, he was exhausted from the day's events and longing for his narrow bed and the rest it offered. Yet on the other hand, walking back with the lady Eleanor in the faint moonlight, her hand tucked into his robed arm, had been a heady delight, and the sense of being her protector and escort and confidant along the dark road filled him with a deep satisfaction. When they arrived at the castle, she had insisted on his joining her in the family solar—an unheard-of honour for any member of the castle staff—for a late supper served by one of the kitchen maids, who had waited up for her mistress. Eleanor was obviously tired, and had fallen rather silent, which Piers understood and respected, so they had spent much of the time in quiet prayer, but the hour of companionship they enjoyed that evening, before she courteously bade him good night and went up the stairs to her own chamber, was infinitely precious to him.

As he lay in bed waiting for sleep, he found his mind wrestling with the kind of reflections he would have preferred to tackle in daylight. Bewilderment at the horrors he had encountered that day (where was God in all this—could he really be punishing all these people, including the good brothers at Whitehill and Timothy Cottar's innocent children?) mingled with joy that it had fallen to his lot to spend time with the lady Eleanor and be of service to her (yet how could this be right, when he was a priest and she a prospective nun, between whom even friendship might be suspect?). He found himself asking why some took the sickness and others not? And why had he been spared, when he knew many other priests, like Father Robert, who had carried out their spiritual duties faithfully and ministered to the sick and dying yet had died of the pestilence within days?

Piers felt he had no special gifts or attributes, nothing but a sense of duty. Was it just chance? But if so, why did people pray for deliverance? Why did he pray, daily, for that deliverance for himself and for others? For the lady Eleanor, in particular. He groaned inwardly and turned over in his cot. Every time he thought of her, he prayed she would take care, and even if she would not, God would take care of her Himself and not let her fall prey to this terrible sickness. The thought of her sick and dying turned his heart cold. If there were any justice, God would not let this pestilence touch her.

He fell asleep at last, but awoke early, tense and anxious, with an ache behind his eyes. He knew that since his errand to the abbey had failed, and failed spectacularly, his first task that morning was to apprise Sister Margery that there was no help to be had from Whitehill. He knew she would give him all the assistance in her power, but at what cost? For an anchoress to leave her dwelling and go out into the world again was like a woman leaving her husband. Yet how could he prevent her, if she conceived it to be her duty?

"Of course I must help," she said briskly, when he told her what had happened the previous day. "How could I sit here and do nothing while folk die unshriven for lack of someone to hear their confession? If the Holy Father has said that even a woman can do this, then I of all people must respond."

"But your prayers..." faltered Piers.

"My prayers can still be said in-between times. Sometimes prayer alone is not enough, and there must be action. So if there is need, send for me at once. Promise me, Piers."

So he promised, though with a heavy heart. It would not be long, he knew, before her aid would be required.

Thirty-one

Over the next few days, cases of plague continued to bring their blight of sickness and death to Northchurch. But as though to cheer them, the equinox passed in a blush of new warmth and sunshine that felt like a blessing after the winter, and reminded the villagers that Lady Day, and the new calendar year it heralded, would soon be upon them.

Eleanor awoke slowly to the sound of birds singing in the trees whose bare branches reached out almost to touch her tower window. Her brother had had the window glazed, so the shutters could be left open without the room being prey to draughts, but she often left the casement slightly open to let in some air while she slept. This irritated him, as the glazing had been expensive and done for her benefit, but it was a small piece of independence she had clung on to. In her convent, if ever she was able to go there, the windows would probably be unglazed and the shutters draughty and she could have as much fresh air as she wished without defying those in authority over her.

She twisted the end of her plait uncomfortably. When this dreadful time was over, and God smiled on them again, would she still be happy to follow the calling to the conventual life she had always believed to be hers? Like everyone else who had suffered this crisis and survived it—and who knew, yet, how many would survive it to the end, for the pestilence showed no signs of loosening its grip on them—she was not the same person she had been before it had befallen them. In earlier years, self-discipline had curbed the laughing playful child as she grew into a woman, but she was aware that the cool serenity that others saw and valued was still little more than a mask, a mechanism to curb the exuberance that seemed inappropriate for one of her rank and future vocation.

She had cultivated it, almost she had believed it had become part of her true personality, until the pestilence came and broke that illusion. Beneath the mask she was as terrified as anyone else, and wracked with grief and a sense of inadequacy that was mitigated only by the service she was occasionally allowed to give to others. And she could not share her fear with anyone, for they depended on her for guidance and leadership.

Except Piers. The walk back to the castle a few nights ago, in which she had found herself opening her heart to him, and the quiet hour of prayer in the solar that followed, had been such a balm to her. For a man only a little older than she was herself, he had so much knowledge, and he seemed to care for everyone, tireless and selfless in acting as parish priest simply because there had been no one else to do the work, apart from that brief period when Father Robert had come as vicar. She knew a message had gone to Father Edward to let him know Robert had died, for she had sent it herself, along with the last report Bailiff Michael had written for the steward, but no reply had come back. Whether the message had arrived, of course, was another matter.

She was beginning to find the responsibility for manor affairs a heavy one in the absence of her brother, whom she still found it hard to forgive, not only for the wrongs he had done her in trying to force her into marriage, but also for his dereliction of duty to his dependants.

But she thanked God for Alan, who was finding his feet as acting bailiff, and no doubt learning skills that would stand him in good stead in Kent later on. She should arrange new quarters for him, she reflected, for he had asked permission to take into his own household the three surviving children of his brothers after all the adults in the household had died. Eric, his sister and Zack's daughter Beth were sleeping with the servants in the hall at present, and making themselves useful in the stable and kitchen. But it would be good for them to be brought up by Alan and Rosamund in their own quarters, which at the moment consisted of no more than a chamber above her own in the tower. Perhaps she would ask one of the servants to make ready Bailiff Michael's rooms for Alan and his family, and the children could help.

She suddenly became aware of the tumult of feet hurrying up and down the tower stairs past her door. Alan and Rosamund's quarters were above hers, and she sat up immediately, full of concern. Was the baby coming early? Or, God prevent, had Alan or his wife sickened with the pestilence?

Her blood running cold at the thought, she thrust her covers aside and threw on a robe over her night shift. There was no time to summon a maidservant to help her dress, and it sounded as though everyone was busy anyway. Some crisis had occurred, and she must go at once to see whether she could help.

Alan looked up when he heard her voice at the door of his chamber. "My lady, Rosamund is sick, as you can see. What should we do?"

She stood there for a moment, irresolute. "Is it the pestilence, think you?" Ordinary ailments sometimes responded to the basic herbal remedies she had learned from her aunt, but the pestilence took no heed of remedies and went its own terrible way. Yet Rosamund...she could not let Rosamund die, without a struggle.

He nodded, and she saw the anguish in his face. "The fever

comes first. But the growths have begun in her armpits. I fear we do not have very long."

"I will go and ask Sister Margery," she decided. "With the spring sunshine we have had in the last week, the herbs are putting forth new leaves. Perhaps she will have something to give us."

She ran down the stairs to her chamber, calling for someone to send a message to the stables. The mare could be saddled while she dressed, and riding would be quicker than walking now that the lanes were clear of snow again.

She met her aunt as she rode to the church. It was strange to see Sister Margery walking the lanes instead of keeping to her chosen anchorhold. Her robe, so clean and fresh, would soon be muddy, Eleanor thought, as she drew the mare to a halt.

"Rosamund has taken the sickness," she told her bluntly. "I need your advice, Aunt. What should we do for her?"

Sister Margery looked at her. "I cannot come myself, for Piers has sent word of a villein family in need of help down the road towards Micheldever, and he is busy elsewhere. One of the manor tenants, I believe…Simon is the name of the father, but I believe it is others of the family who are sick."

"I do not know the man." Eleanor shook her head with impatience, serenity deserting her. "What should I do for Rosamund? Please, Aunt. I cannot bear to lose her."

Sister Margery nodded wisely, her eyes on Eleanor's face. "I know how much she means to you. And she is with child, is she not? When I return, I will see what herbs we have that may help. Some have some spring growth, though others will slumber for a while yet. Wait, though, do you have garlic?"

Eleanor frowned, for garlic was a home-grown peasant accompaniment to food, used to give pottage flavour when there was no meat. The castle cooks despised it, she knew, in favour of more expensive and exotic flavourings. "I remember you recommended it to Alys."

"It keeps away sickness, certainly, though little seems to bring respite from this pestilence. But it might be good crushed as a poultice, for the chest if she coughs, or for the buboes if she has the growths. Maybe mixed with vinegar."

Eleanor stared at her. These were unfamiliar remedies. "Alys will have garlic, I am sure," she said at last. "I must go and tell her of her sister's sickness, anyway. She will want to come."

Sister Margery nodded and set off again towards the bridge and the southern part of the village. After a moment, Eleanor trotted after her, passing her before the end of the lane. She rode carefully over the still-fragile bridge and down the lane to the weaver's cottage.

"My lady!" Finn was chopping wood with Jack outside the cottage, for a few warm days had not deceived anyone into thinking spring had arrived for good. "What brings you here?" He came down the path and took the mare's reins.

"Please hold her for me, Master Finn," she said. "I must see Alys."

"She's milking, my lady," he replied. "Let me go with a message, for she is in the paddock and the ground is still muddy from snow melt."

She hesitated. "Tell her..." She swallowed. "Tell her Rosamund is ill."

He dropped the reins, and turned and ran across the garden to the paddock gate.

~ * ~

Alan sat helplessly beside his wife's bed while her fever rose and her discomfort increased. He neither knew nor cared that beneath his hastily donned robe he was still night-naked. He was only dimly aware of others coming and going, of Eleanor returning with Alys, of the servants running to and fro with cool water to bathe his wife's face, or weak ale for her to drink, or pungent herbs recommended by Sister Margery to banish the poisoned air of the sickroom.

Rosamund occupied his every thought, and as the day wore on, he sank to his knees and began to pray with a fervour he had never thought possible. His careless past sins weighed heavily upon him, for he had allowed himself to be occupied with manor business during Shrovetide and had not gone to confession with everyone else, thinking it would wait until Holy Week. Surely God's anger should have been turned on him rather than on his wife? He feared not only for her but for her unborn baby...his child, so innocent but so vulnerable. He prayed that God would spare them, and strike him instead.

In the early afternoon, Rosamund began to groan, a dreadful sound that tore at his heart. He saw that the buboes were growing larger, and the lumps were hard to the touch. She cried out in pain when his fingers probed them, and he desisted.

"We have prepared a poultice," Alys told him, laying her hand on his arm. Of all of them, she had stayed the calmest, though her white face told of inner turmoil. Even the lady Eleanor had seemed distraught, rushing from kitchen to buttery like the servants following Alys's instructions. "They will bring it as soon as it is cool enough to lay on. Sister Margery said to treat the buboes with it. 'Twill hurt grievously, I fear, but mayhap it will ease her. If not, we can lance them."

But when the poultice came, laid on the table in its cloth by one of the kitchen maids, it was ignored, for Rosamund had gone into labour. In anguish, Alan watched as her body bore down on the helpless infant, expelling it from her womb with terrible speed and agony. There was no time to summon help, and Alys, trembling, received the bloody foetus in her own hands and cut the cord with the knife Alan mutely held out to her. It was a boy. For a moment the child seemed to breathe, and a faint sound came from his lips; but then he fell back, limp and lifeless. Eleanor, in tears, brought water from the bowl on the table to baptise him before his soul departed.

For a while after the birth, Rosamund lay torpid, unmoving, and Alan feared she was dying. "Where is Piers?"

Eleanor shook her head. "I do not know. My aunt has left her anchorhold to hear confessions if he is not available."

Alan nodded. He had heard about this from Piers himself, along with all the religious and theological doubts it had engendered.

"I will call her." Eleanor got up from her knees.

"Let us try the poultice first," said Alys. She had wrapped the tiny corpse in a cloth and laid it on the cool stone of the big window-sill. When Piers came, they would arrange for the child to be buried.

"The mixture has cooled," Eleanor pointed out. "Mayhap it should be warmed again?"

"I think we should use it now," Alys told her, and in spite of Alan's preoccupation, he marvelled at her calm assumption of authority. Even Eleanor was deferring to her, and yet it was her own sister who lay inert and perhaps dying. It was unwomanly, in his eyes, but it was magnificent too. "Let the kitchen prepare another for later."

This was defiance in the face of death, thought Alan, that she should look to a future for Rosamund even of a few hours.

Eleanor nodded and went to give the instructions.

"If you need more garlic," Alys called after her, "send word to Finn. There are bulbs in my store cupboard. He or Jack will bring some."

No longer any pretence of formality, Alan noted. He was 'Finn' not 'Master Finn.' But he did not want to think about this now, nor the implications for his friend's marriage. If Rosamund died...

They spread the garlic and vinegar poultice on the hard growths in Rosamund's armpits, and she moaned, which was at least a sign that she had not gone beyond pain. Alys did not know in detail what recipe Eleanor had given to the castle kitchen staff, and it seemed strange to use garlic as a poultice rather than a flavouring for food, but she had faith in Sister Margery. Besides, in the face of death anything was worth trying.

The hours passed, and Rosamund still lived. Alys persuaded Eleanor to go and eat a belated dinner, though she herself would not leave her sister. She felt no hunger or thirst, though she drank some small ale when it was brought her and felt the better for it. Alan sat silent, responding to nothing, ignoring even the ale that was offered. It was as though he had gone into a trance, his mind engaging with nothing but his wife's struggle for life. Piers came and blessed them all, and carried away with him the baby for burial, but Alan gave no sign of noticing his presence.

"I will return later," the priest said. "If she is sleeping now, we should not rouse her to make her confession. I do not think she will die yet. But I will not be long." He did not suggest that anyone should come with him to bury the baby, Alys noticed. No one was willing to leave Rosamund's side, even for that. She felt the grief as an almost physical pain, constricting her heart with pity for her sister and Alan, as well as for herself. But newborn deaths were not uncommon. It was as nothing to what she and Alan, and the lady Eleanor, would feel if Rosamund should die.

Thirty-two

But Rosamund did not die. Whether it was the effect of the poultices applied to the buboes, or Alys's quiet competent nursing, or Alan's fervent prayers and promises to God, they would never know. Her fever broke that night, and she began to recover as the buboes shrivelled up and her strength gradually returned, though Alys, remembering Goodwife Joan's recovery in January, warned Alan that she would probably be weak for some while.

"It matters not," he muttered, smiling down at Rosamund lovingly. "She is alive. She is still with us. Nothing else is important."

He said nothing of the lost baby, and, Alys thought, probably at this moment that was not important either, though perhaps in time it would become so, especially if Rosamund's weakness meant she could not conceive again.

She left them together and went, at last, to take care of her own needs. Eleanor insisted that she ate something before she went home, and offered her a bed so she could rest, but she refused. "I must go and look to my own family," she said.

Eleanor looked puzzled. "What family is that?"

"My own household, I meant," Alys explained. "Master Finn and Jack, and Christine, Timothy Cottar's mother—we took her in after her family died. I must go home and see to things there. I have a responsibility to them, now that Rosamund is safe."

It was not, she realised, that she was truly worried for their wellbeing. Finn would have seen to that. Whatever needed to be done, he would be capable of making it happen, and Christine would be more than willing to cook and clean. Indeed, part of her was looking forward to going home and being cared for herself, after the long hours of sick nursing at the castle.

She smiled at Eleanor. "Look after Rosamund for me."

"Indeed, we will do that."

She walked slowly back to her cottage, savouring the sunshine and the birdsong. It was too early for the trees to put forth new leaves, but some of the fruit trees in the castle orchard were showing their first pink and white flowers, and the shrubs in the hedgerows were greening up in the warmth. And next week it would be Lady Day, the Feast of the Annunciation, traditionally the marker of the new year. *The year of our Lord thirteen-forty-nine—what would that bring?* she wondered. Was it too much to hope that the pestilence would magically vanish, or at least relinquish its hold on their every minute, their every thought?

For the first time since the plague laid hold of Northchurch in January, she felt glimmers of optimism that the new year would bring better things.

~ * ~

The first manorial court of the new year was, by contrast, dispiriting, like the weather, which, after promising so much in mid-March, had turned cold and wet again. New cases of the pestilence had decreased in number over the past week, but the court was mainly concerned with the deaths of the previous month, which were many. Alan, acting as the steward's deputy, sat numbly hearing—and recording for the manor roll, with the help of the clerk—the register of deaths, the proving of rights to take up a tenancy, and the list of holdings that at present had no tenant to take them on.

There was also the presentation of wills that had been drawn up, often at the last minute with Piers the only witness to the deceased's wishes for the distribution of their few belongings. How the priest had found time to make notes of these impromptu benefactions, Alan could not imagine. Most had little or no legal foundation and would not have to be proved formally. But they were an indication of intent that he wished the manor authorities to honour if possible, and there were few objections to them from the villagers present as the clerk read them out.

There were inevitably some minor infringements of the law to take note of, though these would have to wait for the return of Sir Richard or his steward to sort out. But it was depressing to hear of the looting of empty houses, theft of valuable animals, and even one or two breaches of the peace where the thieves, in competition for booty, had come to blows. The more serious cases would require a jury, and no one was suggesting they could find twelve men ready and willing to undertake that duty just now.

Piers came up to Alan as the court was dispersing and requested a private word with him.

"Come into the solar," Alan suggested. "We won't be disturbed there, for the lady Eleanor is with Rosamund."

"How is she?" Piers asked. "Still recovering well, I hope?"

Alan nodded. "She was asking whether she could go out for a walk today, which must be a sign that she is feeling stronger, though of course we told her to wait a few days longer, till the sun shines again. Tis not long since she left her bed, and she still spends most of her time in our chamber. The lady Eleanor has been so good to her, spending much time sitting with her, encouraging her. They pray together often."

Piers nodded his approval, noting the change in attitude of Rosamund's husband towards spiritual matters. Alan had made a full confession after Rosamund's brush with death, and in the wake of that had become one of the most stalwart supporters of the Church the village had. He had also donated a substantial sum this week to help the poorer tenants to pay their tenancy entrance fees, as well as providing for his nephew and nieces, all of which Piers had much appreciated.

The matter the priest had to discuss today, however, was a sensitive one and he wasn't quite sure how to approach it.

"Goodwife Joan has brought something to my attention," he began cautiously. "Mayhap you can settle it, one way or another."

"That meddling crow. I can't think of anything she might have to say that would be worthy of a moment's consideration."

Piers rubbed his face. Clearly Alan's change of heart did not extend to a charitable view of Goodwife Joan. "At least it must be spoken of between you and me," he replied. "Or she will make it public."

"What can this be, Piers? Spit it out, for God's sake."

Piers frowned. He could think of no way of broaching the subject delicately. "She makes out that you and Rosamund are not legally married."

"What? God's teeth! You married us yourself at the church door."

"It is a question of consanguinity."

This gave Alan pause. Church rules governing the degrees of relationship within which couples could marry were notoriously complicated. He knew of no reason why these should affect Rosamund and himself, however. "What consanguinity is she alleging?" he asked. "I know of none—truly, Piers."

"I did not imagine you had flouted the rules deliberately. But it will have to be looked into, nevertheless."

Alan checked an explosion of wrath with an effort. "Please explain."

"Do you remember your mother?"

"She died when I was a baby. I have no recollection of her at all."

"I have been looking at the register kept by Father Nicholas. Goodwife Joan says your mother was first cousin to Paul's wife Cicely, though I can find no record of it."

Alan shrugged. "I know nothing of this, though Steven may have heard something from his mother. But if tis so, what of it? That would make Steven and me second cousins."

"Within the prohibited degrees," said Piers.

Alan laughed. "But as I haven't married Steven, what does it matter?"

"There is the question," went on Piers rather apologetically, "of the relationship of the two sisters. Steven married Alys in October, and thus created a situation where, as Alys's husband, he would be considered Rosamund's brother."

He stopped, to let the implications sink in, and saw Alan's face blanch. "God in heaven protect us."

"Goodwife Joan says, quite rightly, that this means, through Steven, you and Rosamund will also count as second cousins."

"Can that be maintained? Surely—"

"I don't know. But Goodwife Joan is demanding you and Rosamund refrain from taking communion at Easter. She says your incestuous relationship will profane the rite and the marriage should be annulled."

Alan swore. "I'd like to get my hands round that busybody's neck! My innocent wife to be accused of incest...And just now, as well, when she has been ill."

Piers waited a moment for the other man to calm down. "I understand how you feel, Alan, and I know neither of you has done wrong knowingly. But still..."

"As soon as Rosamund is well enough," declared Alan, "I will take her to Kent where no one will know us or say anything about any consanguinity."

"But now," Piers pointed out, "you will know."

"It may not be true. You said yourself, Piers, that you didn't know whether it would stand. Even if it's true."

"You could speak to Goodwife Joan yourself," Piers suggested.

"Maybe. Or I'll ask Steven when he comes home." He gave a wry grin. "I'm feared to speak to the old besom myself, or I might forget to practise Christian forbearance. We've had enough death these past weeks, without me putting her underground."

He looked so grim that Piers could almost believe he meant it.

"Have you had word of Steven's coming? Will it be soon?"

Alan shook his head. "I've heard nothing. But mayhap he will be home for Easter."

Piers sighed. "Will you keep this news from Rosamund?"

"I should think I will! Would you suggest I tell her that she may not be my wife at all, that all these months we have been living together in mortal sin?"

"No, no. But it must be resolved, Alan. One way or another. Perhaps a papal dispensation..."

"Dispensations are for the rich and noble," retorted Alan. "You know that as well as I do. The pope won't be interested in folk like us."

"You could talk to Sir Richard," suggested Piers. "He might take up the case for you."

"And where is he?" Alan's voice was sharp with sarcasm. "As absent as Steven, and like to stay that way as long as the pestilence still dogs us. Besides, why should he care? He didn't want me appointed bailiff to Beaconswell by his father's will, and he'll be quick to get rid of me from this manor once he returns."

"I've often thought tis strange that Sir Thomas was so keen that you should leave the manor. Steven, too, if you remember. In his will, Sir Thomas offered him free manumission if he went elsewhere."

Alan shrugged, too preoccupied with this new dilemma to revisit an old mystery. The problem worried at him all day, as he wrote up the manor records from the clerk's notes. He had been hard at work for several days before the manor court hearing, and was looking forward to spending some time with Rosamund on the morrow, but Piers' revelation had soured his anticipation. What on earth was he to say to her? Was there really a possibility the Church would not see their marriage as valid because of some extraordinary calculation of consanguinity that made no sense at all?

He decided in the end that he must speak to the source of the rumour, and get Goodwife Joan either to make good on her accusation or abandon it. With Easter on the horizon, less than a fortnight away, the matter was urgent. Whatever he felt, he must endure her probable gloating without violence, if not with equanimity.

Having made his decision, he was able to eat dinner with Rosamund cheerfully, and converse companionably afterwards as they sat in the solar. The lady Eleanor was visiting her aunt that afternoon, and they were alone. Rosamund was leaving her bed earlier each morning, though she still returned there soon after dusk and sometimes took a rest after lunch, as she had done when she was expecting the child. He knew that wound was raw for her still, and he sometimes found her weeping when he came into their chamber unexpectedly during the day. But she tried to keep a smiling face for him, taking pains with her appearance and showing interest in his work.

"Tis a far cry from being an archer on your pilgrimage with Sir Thomas," she teased him as they sat with a dish of preserved fruits between them.

"Indeed! I never had sweetmeats to nibble on whenever I wished. I marvel that the castle cooks are still managing to produce such delicacies."

Rosamund picked up her embroidery, an occupation which she had taken up since they began to live at the castle. She had never been very handy with a distaff, but her stitches were neat, and the lady Eleanor had encouraged it as a pastime suitable for the wife of a franklin.

"You have no need to sew your own clothes now," her mistress had told her, smiling. "Alan will have enough money to pay for a seamstress from the village, either here or in Beaconswell."

"But I like to sew," Rosamund had replied, showing Eleanor the exquisite christening gown, she had begun for the baby. "Is this fine enough work for a franklin's child, think you?"

Remembering this, Alan wondered what had happened to the christening gown. He did not think she had finished it, but it was too soon to ask. Perhaps another child would wear it, in later years. But Rosamund was still bleeding after the birth, as well as weak from the sickness itself, and he wondered whether she would ever be strong enough to carry another baby. If indeed there was to be another chance—for if Goodwife Joan had her facts right, there might be no future for them together. He almost groaned aloud at the thought.

Rosamund looked up from her sewing as though she had heard the inner groan. "Something is troubling you, Alan, I can see. May I know what it is?"

"Nay, sweetheart. Tis nothing. Nothing for you to trouble with. I want you to concentrate on recovering your health as soon as you can."

~ * ~

Two days later, Alys arrived home from visiting Rosamund to find pottage simmering on the hearth, but to her surprise Finn, looking rather out of place in the role of cook, was stirring it.

"Where's Christine?" she asked.

"Her daughter's man came over from Whitchurch to fetch her. They have asked her to make their home with them now that Timothy and his family are dead."

Alys nodded approvingly, although she felt disappointed not to have seen the widow and bid her farewell. "That is good. I would have been happy for her to stay here with us, but family is best."

Finn smiled to himself, enjoying the irony that Alys's own household had not for some weeks contained any of her blood relations. But he thought it best not to point this out to her. "In truth, I think she was not very willing to go," he said. "But her son-in-law persuaded her."

Alys raised her eyebrows. "But why would she not want to go?"

"Well," replied Finn, unable to contain his laughter this time, "we are well found here with you, you know. Very well found."

Alys stared at him, and then smiled. "I am glad you feel that," she replied. "And tis best in another way, too, for Steven would never have put up with having another man's mother living with us. He was willing to house mine, but only for my sake."

There hung between them the unspoken thought that Steven would not relish Finn's presence in the workshop either.

"Now that we have a spare bedchamber," suggested Alys, taking up the subject boldly, "I can offer you that, instead of a pallet in the workroom. It is time you had proper sleeping quarters. You have been here for nearly three months."

"Nay, Alys. You know that cannot be. I'm best to stay where I am. The pallet is well-stuffed, and comfortable enough. Besides, I would not want to leave Jack to sleep alone, young as he is. He still has bad dreams some nights."

As do I, thought Alys. She dared not tell Finn that some nights she also felt unutterably lonely...and often, in wintry weather, cold to the marrow. Until her marriage she had always shared a bed with her sister, and it felt strange to sleep alone.

There was a step on the threshold, and Jack appeared at a run. "Alys! I saw the lady Eleanor by the bridge. She says will you come to the church? Sister Margery is ill."

Alys and Finn looked at each other. "Please God not the pestilence," said Alys in horror. "I had hoped there would be no more."

Finn sighed. "I know you did. But I fear the sickness is not finished with us yet."

Alys reached for a basket and her cloak. "Have we still some garlic?"

Finn opened the cupboard. "It is sprouting, but some cloves may still be of use."

"I don't know whether we can make up a poultice there, but I must go at once. Finn, please would you crush some cloves and send Jack up to the anchorhold with them in a cloth as soon as may be? Some vinegar, too, if there is some."

"This is what was in the poultice that helped Rosamund recover?"

"Sister Margery recommended it. It is worth trying."

But when she arrived at the church, she found that it was not growths that ailed the anchoress, but the terrible cough.

Thirty-three

The room was silent, apart from the painful wheezing of the dying woman. Eleanor leaned forward to wipe the blood away from her aunt's mouth. They were alone now. A storm was brewing outside and she had sent Alys home as the light began to fail. For thirty-six hours the two women had done everything they could, applying poultices to Sister Margery's chest, and cooling cloths and herbs to her brow, but to no avail. Piers was praying in the chantry, and would come in a moment if Eleanor called him.

A single candle flickered by the bedside, but there was no one to see her tears.

"Why do you weep, child?"

Eleanor looked up. Her aunt's eyes were open.

"Why has God allowed all this, Sister Margery?" she burst out. "What have we done—not just here in England, but in France, in Italy...? Are our sins so terrible, all over Christendom?"

There was a long pause. Then her aunt sighed. "Nay, my dear niece. No more terrible than those of any other time, I believe. Christ died for our sin. That is the meaning of the Mass, that He is broken for us. That he became sin for us. He did not suffer because he sinned but to obey God, to the uttermost. When we suffer, we follow in His footsteps. God is in our brokenness, too."

Eleanor thought about this for a long time. "If that is so, what need is there of penance for sin? Is not ordinary suffering enough?"

Sister Margery moistened dry lips with her tongue and the cough rattled in her throat. "I'm thirsty."

Eleanor brought her a drink and held the mug for her while she gulped some down.

"For some sins," her aunt went on after a moment, "penance proves repentance."

This reminded Eleanor of something she had long wanted to ask. It was unfair to a woman who was so ill, she knew, but she might not have another chance.

"What did my father do to earn so severe a penance? He told me before he left that it was Father Nicholas who sent him on pilgrimage, to spend all those years in foreign lands. But when I asked why, he would not say. It must have been something serious, something secret that none of us knew about. But you knew, didn't you? Aunt Margery, you have to tell me."

The old anchoress paused a moment, coughing again and wincing as pain tore through her chest. Then she said, in a hoarse, strained voice quite unlike her normal sweet tones: "He killed your mother."

"No!" Eleanor gasped.

Margery nodded, inexorably. "Yes, he did. He strangled her in a passion one day, because she threatened to cause a scandal."

"A scandal?" Eleanor was incredulous. Her pious, devout mother? The one whose voice never rose above a whisper, who spent half her life in church, even when it meant neglecting her children? "Dear God, what kind of scandal?"

There was a long pause while Margery struggled for breath.

Eleanor was suddenly conscience-stricken. "I ask your pardon, dear aunt—dear Sister Margery. I should not question you thus."

The anchoress shook her head. "Nay, tis not fitting I should go to my grave and leave you in ignorance, if you desire to know the truth." She paused, gasping for breath. "There was a young steward, the one who was here before Steward Roger. Joanne wanted to leave your father, and go away with him. Thomas couldn't bear it."

"Father Nicholas knew, because he was my father's confessor," said Eleanor, light dawning. "But Father Edward wasn't told."

Margery nodded.

"Then that's why…" She paused.

"Yes. That is why Father Nicholas was sent away. Thomas found another benefice for him, up in the north. It's why Piers, who knew nothing, was educated to be the chantry priest."

"But surely Piers should know now. How can he pray for my father's soul if he is in ignorance?"

Margery shook her head. "Your father did not want him to know. No one was to know. Richard still does not, and I…I did not mean to tell you. But…"

She sank back on to her hard bed with its straw mattress, and Eleanor saw that she was flushed and drowsy. *She is sinking*, she thought.

She rose to her feet and went to the chapel door to call Piers. Then she returned to the bed and knelt beside it, taking her aunt's hot feverish hand in hers. "Dear aunt, regret nothing. It would have been wrong for there to be no one left who knew. Surely my father's path through Purgatory will be slow and painful. At least I may now pray for him, as I know you have done."

Her aunt's eyes were closing, and she heard Piers come into the anchorage and begin the questions that would bring about confession and absolution before the end. He looked tired, and hardly acknowledged her presence. She gathered her cloak about her and withdrew into the church, where she knelt in the lady chapel to pray, not only for her aunt in her passing, but also, vehemently, for her father's soul.

~ * ~

Finn and Jack had spent all day on the land. They had ploughed the field behind the cottage and sowed grain in it, part barley and part wheat as Alys had instructed, to give an early crop of barley and a late crop of wheat to store for the winter. Last year's harvest had been so poor that Alys thought her grain sacks might be empty before the wheat was ripe, though the rye crop James had planted in the autumn could be harvested soon, and that would keep them fed for a while. The surviving villeins, Finn knew, were out in the common fields he and Matthew had ploughed, sowing what seed they had.

Finn found himself wondering how much of all this would have been achieved if Alys had not driven them all on. She was everywhere, now that the worst of the pestilence seemed to be over, either suggesting what might be done––but tactfully, so that they did not notice a woman was giving them instructions––or facilitating whatever action was required, just as she had by finding a way for him to learn how to plough. He was proud of her, and knew he would be prouder still when he worked with her on the looms.

He sighed. As Easter drew nearer and spring made travelling easier, he had become convinced that Steven would soon return. He was in no doubt as to what would happen then. His lovely easy companionship with Alys would be lost, and it was doubtful whether Steven would even allow him to carry on the weaver's business with her, as they had planned. Perhaps, Finn thought, he might suggest to Steven he be allowed to work the looms on her behalf, to bring in some income... even if Steven would not allow Alys herself to take part in the work. That would be hard for her, but better than closing the business for good; and it would at least give him some opportunity to see her, even from a distance. He smiled to himself. He doubted Alys would stay in her conventional place among the pots and pans for long, whatever Steven said.

He put the tools away in the barn, while Jack untied the house cow and let her wander out into the paddock, well fenced off from the arable.

"How are your beasts, Jack?" he asked, as they walked towards the cottage.

"We've fewer than before," the boy answered ruefully. "The house cows both died when the hired men abandoned them. But there are enough sheep for a decent wool clip, I think, if we can find someone to do the work." Both his father's expert clippers had died during the pestilence, and there was no one left who had the necessary skills to stand in for them.

"We have a few weeks before they will be needed," Finn comforted him. "By then things may be easier, and maybe folk will be on the move and looking for work."

"Think you that the pestilence will ever come to an end, Master Finn? It seems to go on and on."

Jack's voice faltered, and he stumbled as he walked. *Poor boy*, Finn thought. He must be exhausted, for they had been out all day, and while Finn was ploughing, he had gone up to his father's holding to check the sheep.

"I promise you it will pass," Finn said, with more conviction than he really felt. "Already there are fewer cases in the village." Though this had been no help to poor Lady Margery, he reflected. God grant that the garlic and vinegar he had sent up to the anchorhold with Jack would have been some use.

He wondered when Alys would be able to come home. He was concerned that she would be exhausted after nursing her sister and then Sister Margery in quick succession, and did not want her to come back and be immediately immersed in caring for her own household. Perhaps the Widow Agnes would come in and look after them at need, though the meals would not be up to Alys's standards.

Yet he could not quarrel with Alys's priorities. The anchoress was a village institution, a fount of wisdom and prayer on whom the whole community depended. She deserved the best of care in her own hour of need, and who better to deliver it than his beloved Alys?

The cottage felt cold when they went inside, for the fire had died down under its cover. He had left kindling ready, however, and soon had the fire sparking brightly on the hearth to warm them. He pulled the shutters closed against the dusk and lit the lamp, served

Jack some bread and cheese from the cupboard, and sent the boy off to bed with a candle when he had finished his portion.

While he ate his own supper, Finn listened to the wind growing stronger, with squally gusts that beat about the cottage and rustled in the thatch. He closed the roof vent as far as he dared, and kept the fire tended so it burned in flame rather than smoke. He looked into the workshop and saw that Jack was already fast asleep, his candle still alight beside his pallet. Finn snuffed the candle for safety and took it back into the main room.

He sat down again on a stool and took his rebec out of its bag. It seemed strange to be sitting here playing to himself rather than to the others; but it was comforting just the same. Darkness had fallen, and he could hear rain dripping from the thatch. Alys was clearly staying at the anchorhold tonight as well. That must mean, at least, that Sister Margery was still living, still needing care. But he did not want to bar the door and go to bed yet, just in case.

~ * ~

By the time Alys left the church, the sun had long set and it was dropping chill and dank. She knew that the lady Eleanor, preoccupied with her aunt's sickness—and, she thought, at last despairing of the outcome—had not realised how late in the day it was. She clearly wanted to be alone with Sister Margery, which was her right as the anchoress' closest relative. Unless Alys wanted to spend time on her knees in the chapel until she was needed at the bedside again, there was no alternative but to set off home as soon as possible.

In any case, she was exhausted and thought she would fall asleep if she tried to pray. Besides, she was conscious that she had left Finn and Jack to fend for themselves for thirty-six hours with no woman to care for them. No doubt they would manage—Finn was clearly very capable of cooking a simple meal, if needs must. But it was her home, and she wanted to be housewife in it.

The wind was rising as she walked down the lane, and clouds raced across the sky, hiding the moon that might have given her some light. Picking her way in the gathering gloom across the planks of the bridge, she slipped near the southern end and half-fell into the surging, icy river. She had no breath to call for help, nor was there anyone within earshot to hear her. Only a desperate grab at the nearest pier had saved her from being swept into the current, and as her skirts became waterlogged, she struggled with all her strength to pull herself on to the bank before the swirling waters bore her away.

Thirty-four

Finn put the rebec away in its bag and stretched his muscles. It was full dark now and time for bed. He had gone to bar the door, for surely Alys would not come that night, when he suddenly remembered he and Jack had left the cow in the pasture, rather than bringing her into the barn. She had been tied up while they were ploughing and sowing the field, and they had thought to let her have a little time grazing before evening. But he had been so busy making supper for them both that he had completely forgotten to go back. In good weather, it would not have mattered, for over the summer she often stayed out grazing all night. But he could not in all conscience leave her out in a storm.

He covered the fire, put on his boots and wrapped a cloak round him, pulling the hood up over his head. A torch would blow out in no time, but he found the covered lantern they used sometimes if they had to go out for any reason during the long winter nights. With luck, it would not catch a gust and plunge him into darkness.

He opened the door and closed it again behind him against the wind. The squall passed, and a full moon appeared behind the scudding clouds. He put the lantern down in the shelter of the hedge and started along the path towards the paddock.

In the distance he could hear cries down the lane. He turned and found his way to the gate.

"Ho there! Help, someone!" It was the new miller's voice, he thought. There was something afoot down by the bridge. He opened the gate and ran.

The miller was kneeling on the bank, leaning out rather dangerously into the stream, his hand grasping the sodden skirts of a woman who was, Finn saw, in danger of being swept away in the raging current. It was only after he had stepped on to the bridge to grasp her hand and pull her to the bank that he saw who it was.

"Alys! What in God's name..."

"Hold your tongue, man, and let's have her out of there." The miller, burly and muscular, was hauling on Alys's skirts with a will, and between them they managed to pull her out of the river and lay her on the bank.

Finn rubbed her hands in a frenzy of anxiety, while the miller pulled her body unceremoniously further away from the river, which looked ready to flood.

She pushed them both away and sat up, blinking, while her hair, robbed of its coif, which the river had stripped away, fell loose around her, streaming with water. "I thank you both," she gasped.

Finn put his arm around her and helped her to her feet. "Are you injured? What happened?"

"I slipped into the river as I crossed the bridge, and it was difficult to get out again," she explained. "But I have taken no hurt, I assure you."

"'Twas as well Master Finn came along when he did," the miller told her. "We'd have lost you else. I came out to check the bridge in this wind, weak as it is, and saw you struggling. Still, all's well, as they say."

Alys nodded. "Do not stay out in this wind on my account, I pray, Miller. Master Finn will look after me."

"Jack will be wondering what has happened," put in Finn quickly, to remind the miller that he and Alys were not alone in the cottage. He devoutly hoped Jack was in fact still asleep and had not wakened to find the cottage empty. "Come, Mistress Alys."

They walked together along the lane, Alys limping a little. Finn felt her shivering and his arm tightened about her. "I have a good fire burning," he encouraged her. "We will soon get you warm again."

The clouds had thickened again, and he heard a rumble of thunder further up the valley, while another squall blustered about them as they reached the cottage. The storm was clearly still building.

"Go inside." He unlatched the door for her and gently guided her over the threshold. "I must go and bring the cow into the barn. To my shame, I forgot earlier."

"That is Jack's job, not yours," she protested.

"He has been out all day," Finn told her. "He is in bed already, and fast asleep. Go you in, Alys, and warm yourself. I will be there in a few minutes."

He picked up the lantern and walked round to the back of the cottage. The cow was standing by the paddock gate, bellowing to be allowed in. She made no resistance as he opened the barn door and took her inside, scattering the slumbering chickens. He chased them into their coop and closed the door. There was hay in the trough, so he left the cow to eat it and latched the barn door behind him.

In the cottage, Alys had taken the cover off the fire and set the kettle to heat on the hearth. Finn went to the cupboard.

"Honey water?" he asked. It was her favourite specific for cold and chills.

She nodded. "I think there's only one jar of honey left, but I'm sure there are a few spoonfuls there, and the bees will make more soon."

"You should take off your kirtle, Alys," he suggested, his anxiety for her banishing his normal concern for the proprieties. "I will find a robe to wrap you in. You will catch your death else."

Without waiting for permission, he mounted the ladder to her bedchamber and came back with a soft woollen robe that she rarely wore. She thought the last time had probably been her wedding night.

She laughed at him softly. "That is my best robe, Finn. My father wove it for me."

"He would want you to wear it now." He helped her with the sodden kirtle, and hung it up to dry. She was still shivering, and he saw that her undergarment was wet through as well, the loose folds hanging limply around her. Without thought, filled only with loving care for her wellbeing, he unhooked the fastenings and took it off, slipping the robe around her shoulders as he did so.

Alys looked up at him, colouring deeply, and drew the folds of the robe more closely about her.

"Your pardon. I did not mean..."

"I know you did not. But another time," she added gently and, he realised, with a touch of humour, "I can unfasten my own chemise."

The kettle began to sing, and he stirred a spoonful of honey into a mug of hot water and brought it to her. "If there is a small apple," she said, "that would make it even more delicious."

He found a wizened apple in the cupboard and cut it up for her with his knife. She stirred the pieces into the honey water, and took a seat beside the fire, her hands round the cup to warm them.

As she sat there in the firelight, her damp hair curling across her shoulders, her dark eyes veiled beneath shadowed eyelids, and the lovely rose-coloured robe hugging her shoulders, she was so nearly beautiful that he could not take his eyes from her.

"How is Sister Margery?" he asked, trying to give his thoughts a safer direction.

She shook her head. "She still lives, but we do not know for how long. The lady Eleanor would not let me stay. Piers is close by, and she says they will do all that is needful."

He sighed. "I am sorry. The village will miss her, an she dies."

"'Twill be worst for Lady Eleanor. Sister Margery's friendship has been so important to her."

"But she has your sister still," he reminded her gently. "They are good friends, as well as mistress and maid, I think."

Alys nodded.

"I should leave you," said Finn, recollecting himself. "You are tired and must rest." He picked up the candle and lit it from the lamp. "Have you all you need?"

She heard the thunder rumbling, closer now. "No, Finn!" She looked up at him pitifully. "Please...please stay a while."

He stood still, unsure what she was asking.

"I am afraid of thunder," she whispered. "It is the only thing..."

He led her to the bench and sat with his arm around her, her head against his shoulder, while the thunder rumbled and crackled all around the house, and she shook with fear. How strange, he thought, that the horrors of the pestilence had not daunted her, nor weariness, nor bereavement, nor even tonight's near-disaster in the river. She had faced them all with fortitude and offered help and guidance to all. But a simple thunderstorm had undone her.

There came an enormous clap immediately overhead, and at the same moment lightning blazed through cracks in the shutters and lit up her white face with its terror-stricken eyes. He drew her closer until he could feel every curve of her body against him, and his breath came short in his chest. "Alys, mijn lief—my love!"

She raised her hands to clasp his face, and suddenly he knew she desired him as much as he did her.

He hesitated, holding her closely but scared to go further, fearing to take her irrevocably into the unknown.

"Do you not want...?" she asked him shyly, her breath on his face, her eyes appealing.

He bent his head to hers. "More than life itself."

"Then come."

She rose from the bench, and as she did so, she let the robe fall from her shoulders to the ground. He gazed at her in the soft firelight, his heart beating wildly. Her breasts adorned her chest like ripe apples, and her waist and hips curved and swelled beneath them, drawing him in. He groaned as a great wave of hunger for her swept over him, then followed her blindly up to her bedchamber and lay with her in exultation as though it were their wedding night. And their mating was not only hunger satisfied and desire sated, but a feast of delight and joy and passion that lasted the night long, until the thunder faded away and a great calm fell.

~ * ~

After Piers had shriven Sister Margery, he and Eleanor sat one on each side of her bed as the night hours wore on and her life drained away. Her paroxysms grew gradually weaker, until she had no strength even to cough and the breath rattled coarsely and slowly in her chest. She made no other sound and Piers realised she was already gone far from them into the hinterland of heaven, where he believed she would be welcomed with open arms.

Would she even need to pass through Purgatory, he wondered, on her way to the realms of God? A holy life, dedicated to prayer, and then given freely in the service of others—surely she would have few sins left to purge. It was some small comfort to him in her passing, for he had revered and valued her. He would miss her counsel when she was gone. But for her niece it would be a much greater loss. He watched the lady Eleanor's face as the emotions crossed it, anger and despair and grief, ending with a smoothing out of expression, a retreat behind the barriers that always enabled her to keep her serenity in the face of tragedy.

Sister Margery slipped away without either of them being aware of the moment of her passing, the rough thread of breath fading as she left them. Her eyes were closed, her face peaceful.

"My lady, I believe she has gone." Piers spoke quietly and wished he had happier things to say.

Eleanor gave a deep sigh. "So much death," she said sadly. "So much suffering. Even a saint such as my aunt. I do not understand it, Piers."

"Nor I," he replied after a moment. "I gave up trying to make sense of it many weeks ago. And yet...I believe God is just. Whatever sins we have committed, this is surely a punishment beyond anything we have deserved. It cannot be His will. Yet who can stand in His way?" He shook his head, too weary to think further about it.

"You should go back to the castle," Eleanor told him. "You have had no rest since my aunt became ill, and little enough before that."

"Nor have you, my lady," he pointed out. She looked white and strained, and he wondered when she had last slept.

"Nay, but you will have others to minister to. I have only my aunt. When you go back to the castle, will you take a message to Rosamund when she wakes? Ask her if she will come and help me to lay out my aunt and make her ready for burial. We cannot have the funeral she deserves, with so many still dying, but she shall have what care we can give her."

Piers hesitated. "Should Rosamund deal with the dead, think you, when she has newly survived the pestilence herself?"

"Of course, you are right. I should not ask it of her. Alan, too, would not wish it."

"Mayhap Alys will come back," suggested Piers.

"That is a good suggestion," she said warmly. "Please, will you send for her—in the morning, for I guess she will be asleep now? I am sure she will help me, as she did yesterday and the day before. Such a good woman, Father, do you not agree?"

"Indeed. I will fetch her for you."

"Ask a servant to go, when you get back to the castle," she insisted. "You need to rest, or you will not be able to meet the demands of others, especially now that you do not even have Sister Margery's help. Although..."

He waited.

"We will speak of it later," she said at last. "After she is buried. That is the most important thing now."

Piers drew his cloak around him and went out through the church into the cold clear dawn. Ignoring Eleanor's instructions, he took the fork down to the bridge. It would be quicker and more appropriate, he thought, to go down to the weaver's cottage and escort Alys himself than send a messenger boy or a groom.

But at the bottom of the hill his intention was frustrated, for the bridge had fallen victim to the wind and the flooding river. Its piers askew, the makeshift planks that had repaired it swept away with the fast-running water, it lay in ruins. No one would be crossing from one side of the village to the other that day.

The miller came out to speak to him as he stood disconsolate, uncertain what action to take next.

"Ho, Father!" he called, above the sound of the fast-flowing stream. "What is your will? As you see, none can cross today. But I will watch for someone passing over the other side who will take a message, an I can."

"It is Alys I need," the priest told him. "Sister Margery died early this morning, and the lady Eleanor asks her to come and help lay out the body. But if I cannot get across to her, then clearly she will not be able to go to the anchorhold."

"That is sad news," the miller said, his face falling into lines of grief. "I will get word to her. Then tis for her to decide what she should do."

Piers acquiesced in this, and turned back towards the castle. At least he could pass on the news, and the lady Eleanor's need of help, to Alan. As bailiff he was in charge of the castle in her absence, and would arrange something. As the lady had said, he himself must husband his strength for the next onslaught of demands. But it must end, in time, he told himself as he trudged up the hill to his cell. The deaths, the suffering. *Nothing can go on forever. If it is not the will of God to destroy us, this can only be a testing of our faith, our courage, our love for one another. It will pass.*

Thirty-five

Alys awoke slowly, stretching langorously and sensuously. It was already light, and far past the time when she should have been up and busy, but for once she didn't care. Finn had long arisen, for the bed was cold beside her, but she needed a few minutes to muster her chaotic thoughts before she faced the day's work. Her body felt heavy and warm with his lovemaking, but her mind was racing. What they had done had felt so right—was so right, she was sure. It had consummated a relationship that had grown gradually, without her being aware of it at first, but that was, in its mutual support, companionship and tender commitment, so much closer to the ideal of marriage than that formal bond that existed between herself and Steven. Yet according to the Church's teaching, she and Finn had committed adultery, a mortal sin that should be confessed by them both immediately, with a heavy penance to follow. Failing that, they could not take part in the Easter Eucharist, the highlight of the Christian year, and in the long term risked permanent exclusion not only from the earthly community of believers, but also from the kingdom of heaven. Many would draw back from them and predict the fires of hell.

She shivered suddenly and pulled the covers over her.

In the room below, she could hear movement, and Finn's light tenor voice speaking to Jack quietly. They must think her still sleeping. She pushed the covers aside and got up. She wondered whether her chemise was dry. The clothes press by the window held a spare one, and she dragged it out and pulled it over her head quickly. Her workaday robe was there, too, and she pulled that round her, remembering with a blush where the one she'd worn last night must still be.

With care, she descended the ladder to investigate the skirts of her kirtle. They always took ages to dry, even near the fire, and on the wall where Finn had hung the garment they would be wet for even longer. Too bad. If the top of the skirts were dry, the kirtle would be wearable.

Finn had built up the fire and the kettle was already beginning to steam. Jack was sitting on the bench with a hunk of bread, and she felt guilty that she had not arisen earlier to make the men porridge. They had clearly both been out working already, and had probably done what they could of her chores, too.

Jack looked up as she arrived at the foot of the ladder. "Alys! I hope I see you well, sister? Master Finn said that you had a near escape last night. Thank God you are safe."

She gave him a faint smile. It was the first time he had had the confidence to call her 'sister,' but the greeting reminded her that he was her husband's brother, and she and Finn would do well to be careful in front of him. She hoped he had slept deeply all night and seen and heard nothing.

"Where is Master Finn? I will heat you both some porridge." The oats were soaking in the food cupboard, she saw, put there last night, no doubt, by the handy Finn. It would not take long to cook them now that the fire was hot. She transferred the sticky mixture to a cooking pot and stirred it well before she put it on the hearth near the hot coals.

"He has gone to help at the bridge. I have seen to the animals," he added proudly.

She thanked him, smiling. "What is happening at the bridge?" she asked, idly, adding hot water to the porridge mixture.

"The storm destroyed it."

She gasped. "Not completely, surely?"

"The repairs that were put in place before Christmas have broken. I have not seen it myself, but that is what Finn says."

"Go and tell him, if you please, that the porridge will be ready in a few minutes. He should break his fast soon."

Jack got up from the bench obediently. "Oh—and he said to tell you that Sister Margery died early this morning. Father Piers sent a message."

He went out quietly, but without much sign of grief. *He is young*, she thought, forgiving him. *And glad to be alive himself, I expect.*

And I am immersed in a mortal sin that does not feel like a sin, God help me.

She wondered whether the lady Eleanor needed her help to prepare Lady Margery for burial. But with the bridge destroyed, would it be possible to cross? She would ask the menfolk when they returned for breakfast.

It was some while before they returned, and she had to pull the pot away from the fire to stop the porridge from burning. She heard their footsteps on the path with a sudden tightening of the nerves. How should she behave with Finn when all was different, and yet could not be seen to be?

She heard voices outside and the door opened to let them in, Jack first, his curly hair ruffled, and Finn behind him. The air that came in with them was cold and fresh. Finn's eyes met hers briefly as Jack put aside his outer garments and hung them up. Then she bent to fill the bowls. Jack took his and sat down, spoon in hand, hunger focusing all his attention on the food in front of him. Finn's hand touched hers as she gave him his bowl, and the contact sent shockwaves into her heart, making it leap and then race.

He regarded her calmly. "You are recovered this morning, Mistress?"

She nodded, unable to trust her voice. Was there a double meaning behind his words?

"I told Jack what happened last night, that you fell into the river. I am glad you have taken no hurt."

"You must have been very late home," Jack observed, a spoonful of porridge held ready to go into his mouth. "I woke sometime while it was still dark and Master Finn wasn't there."

"There was thunder last night," Finn explained quickly. "Did you not hear it? Mistress Alys does not like thunder, and I did not want to leave her alone until it abated."

We should tell the truth where we can, thought Alys, approving. *Please God, we do not have to tell too many lies to add to our mortal sin.*

"I will have to join the others repairing the bridge this morning," Finn told her. "There are so few able-bodied men in the village now that we should all help as we may. I have some skill with woodworking, and must use it."

"I will come too," offered Jack. "Men are coming from the castle side of the river. I expect Eric will be there, if he can be spared from other work."

"How long will it be before we can cross? They will be preparing Sister Margery's body for burial this morning, God rest her soul. Perhaps I should be there to help?"

"Some hours, I think," Finn replied. "Stay here and rest, Alys. You have done enough for now. Let others help the lady Eleanor."

"I'm worried that my sister will feel she should go, if I cannot. She may not be well enough yet, and I fear that the sickness may return."

"Alan will not let her do anything that she should not," Finn reassured her. "You can trust him to do what's best for her."

That was true, and she said no more.

"Come, Master Finn," Jack called impatiently from the door. "They will be needing us for the work."

She watched them depart together happily, and wondered what wreck knowing the truth about her relationship with Finn might make of Jack's hero-worship. She was his brother's wife in his eyes, after all, if no longer in her own.

She swept the house and opened the shutters to air it, wrapping herself closely in her robe to keep warm. Then she set a rich pottage simmering on the stove for their dinner, with pease and barley grains and some crushed garlic and dried herbs to flavour it.

She had not seen Widow Agnes for a few days, and while the pottage was cooking, she dressed in her damp kirtle, covered the fire and went along the lane to the tiny cottage. The widow was at her door, watching the activity at the bridge.

"You are well, Agnes?"

The old lady nodded. "Tis lonely, though, without James sleeping here at night. I sometimes fear to be robbed."

"Why should you be robbed?" asked Alys, puzzled. Apart from anything else, the widow had virtually nothing of any value worth taking.

Agnes shook her head. "You hear these things," she said.

"What things?"

"Widow Joan was telling me that in some places people cannot sleep safe in their beds for robbery and violence."

Alys had to think for a minute before she realised she meant Goodwife Joan, whose marital status, and therefore her village appellation, had been altered by her husband's death. Joan needs a ticking-off, she thought. Since surviving the pestilence, the woman seemed to think herself above normal conventions. This was not the first time Alys had heard of ugly rumours originating with her in the past few weeks.

"I have heard of nothing like that happening in our village," she reassured the older woman. "You can sleep peacefully in your bed, truly." She hesitated. "I could ask Jack to come over and bring his pallet, if you want. He sleeps in the workroom with Master Finn, but there is no reason why he should not bed down by your fire instead."

Agnes looked at her. "You've no thought for your reputation, Alys?"

Alys felt herself blushing. "What do you mean?"

"I say this for your good, Alys, not to criticise. You know I mean no harm—I am not a gossip like Joan. But while Steven is away, you should have a care for what folk will say. It was different when Christine was with you, but now that she is gone... If Jack, Steven's brother, is there and sleeping in the workroom, he is a protection for you, if you get my meaning."

Alys got her meaning very well, and she could not blame the widow for the observation. "Perhaps we can think of someone else who can stay with you at night," she suggested instead, returning no answer to the woman's warning. "There are orphans who might be glad to have supper and a bed here."

Agnes nodded. "That is a good idea. Alan has taken in his brothers' children, I hear. But there are others from West End who cannot afford the heriot to take on their tenancy, or are too young to work their strips without help. There is room for one here, perhaps two, but no more."

Alys looked round the single room where the widow lived. A rickety cupboard stood against one wall, and a table with a single chair against another. By the small hearth where an inadequate fire burned, there was a stool, and in one corner a ladder led up to the sleeping loft, open to the room below. As a wheelwright's widow, her status was free, but she had no sons and the business had died with him, threatening her with penury as once Alys and her mother had been threatened. Yet the cottage was clean and tidy, and on the table Alys could see a lump of dough set to rise, covered with a cloth.

"I'll have some dough ready to go to the bakehouse later," she said. "I will take yours as well, if you wish."

"Thank you, Alys. That is very kind." There was a payment due for using the bakehouse facility, and the old woman clearly understood Alys's implied offer to pay for her bread to be baked.

Alys went home and mixed the dough. Although her cottage was larger, the supply of wood for the fire was greater, and consequently the room was warm, especially with the shutters part-closed against the wind. The dough would rise more quickly than Agnes's, and would be ready for the bakehouse after dinner.

Finn and Jack came in briefly to eat their meal, and reported that work was going well on the bridge. "By tomorrow we will be able to cross," Finn told her. "Maybe even later this afternoon, though I would not trust a horse to go over it safely. I have heard no more about Lady Margery, but I suppose she will be buried tomorrow—it may be a private ceremony, perhaps."

Alys nodded. An anchoress would not want a showy funeral, even in normal times. "Have you heard of anyone in need this side of the village?" she asked, mindful of the fact that Piers might not be able to cross the bridge until the next day.

"I believe they still have the sickness down in the south," he answered. "But no one has tried to send for Father Piers, so I think it is not mortal, or not yet."

"I will go and see to them," she said, "when I have taken the bread for baking."

He looked anxious, but said nothing, for which she was grateful. Knowing now that he loved her, she could understand that he was concerned she might go into danger. But it pleased her to see he would not stand in the way of her doing what she thought was right.

She visited the house where there was sickness, a poor single-roomed villein's hovel the size of Widow Agnes's yet housing a family of five. All, it seemed, had been sick with the buboes, but one had survived it and was recovering, though she was still too weak to look after the others. Alys cooked them some food and promised to bring bread on the morrow, but she thought the mother of the family and one of the daughters at least might not survive beyond that. She would tell Piers to pay them a visit when the bridge was passable, in case no one was able to fetch him in need.

She hurried home as the dusk was creeping in, passing the workers on the bridge who were packing up their tools for the night. It was still cold, but her heart lifted to see the light lasting longer as the spring advanced. It gave her a feeling of hope for the world, even if her personal life was a maze through which as yet she could not see her way.

There was no time to speak to Finn until the evening, after their usual supper of bread and cheese and apples. Jack was ready for bed, tired with his efforts repairing the bridge. "He and Eric did men's work," Finn told her proudly, almost as though Jack were his son, and they a conventional family.

She smiled at Jack. "Well done. I won't keep Master Finn from his bed too long this evening, I promise."

He nodded, accepting and unsuspicious, and took his candle away into the workroom.

"Is it well with you, my love?" Finn asked, taking her hand. "After last night?"

She felt her body responding deeply even to that gentle touch, and her face grew hot. "It is very well."

"I ask your pardon," he went on, rather diffidently, "for my impudence."

"Impudence?"

He nodded, his eyes not meeting hers. "You are another man's wife, and I am your employee. I should never have raised my eyes to love you, and I should certainly not have taken advantage of your accident last night, and your fear of thunder. Forgive me."

"No, no!" she cried, and he raised his finger to his lips to quiet her, lest Jack heard. "There is nothing to forgive!" she went on more quietly. "I invited you—you did not importune me or beg or seduce. I wanted you. I still do."

He bowed his head humbly before her. "God bless you, Alys. That must not happen again, though, whatever we feel for each other. We took no thought for Steven, and his rights as a husband to have a faithful wife to return to. We took no thought for our immortal souls, either."

"You are my true husband," she declared, eyes bright and defiant of what the world, the Church or anyone else might think. "All these months you are the one who has been my companion and helper, the one I have relied upon, and I have come to love you, though I did not know it until last night. When have I lived with Steven? A few days here and there over six months of marriage. I hardly know the man. And that's the life he wants. If he does return, it will not be for long."

She laid her hands on his chest and looked up into his face. "In these days when death can strike at any moment, Finn—my darling Finn—let us take what we have been given, while we can."

"And Jack?" he asked after a moment. "What will Jack feel when he finds out? If we go on sleeping together, Alys, he will find out. There will be no way we can stop that."

She told him of her offer to Widow Agnes, but not entirely to her surprise he vetoed it for much the same reason the widow had done.

"If it is to be...our love," he said, as he rose to follow Jack to the workroom to sleep, "it will come without our taking what is not ours to have. I too believe we belong together. If God wills, there will be a way. If not, we must part, for I could not endure to stay here and work with you if you are married to another. But never doubt that I love you, that I will always love you."

He took her in his arms and held her briefly, kissing her chastely upon the brow. She yearned for him as she had not believed it possible to yearn, yet to beg might be to prevail...and if she prevailed against his better judgement, against his deeper convictions, she might in the end lose him altogether. And that she could not bear.

Thirty-six

After much thought, Alan sent word to Widow Joan that he wished to speak with her. It felt strange to have the status to summon a villager to the castle rather than walking round to her cottage, but he was growing used to being a manor official and franklin instead of an out-of-work, landless archer.

She came all of a fluster, stringy grey hair awry but wearing her best gown, and clearly uncertain why she had been summoned.

"I've paid all my manor dues," she told him sharply. "Even down to the eggs last week. But there, tis not surprising a jumped-up fellow like you can't keep track of things properly. Not like Bailiff Michael, who kept tabs on everything."

"Payment of your dues is not in question," he reassured her quickly, ignoring her insults so as not to engender more malice. "Tis a personal matter."

She gaped at him, and then light dawned. "Aaah! You've been talking to Father Piers."

"I have. And I'd like to know what reason you have for even making the suggestion that our marriage is invalid. Consanguinity,

Father Piers told me, were the grounds you gave. Explain yourself, please."

His banked-down anger made him sound haughtier than normal, and Widow Joan quailed a little. "It's within the fourth degree," she told him, but more politely than before.

"I cannot see how my wife and I can be related within the fourth degree, however you calculate it," he replied. "Be more plain, if you please, Widow Joan."

"We-ell," she began, clearly relishing the opportunity for discursive explanation. "Your mother—you won't remember her, of course, for you were jest a baby when she died and your father married again within months—poor man had no choice, with a parcel of brats in the house and none of the girls old enough to keep house."

Alan said nothing to this. It was true, as far as it went, but his stepmother had been a good woman, a childless widow who had mothered them all.

"Your mother didn't come from Northchurch," Widow Joan went on.

Alan frowned. "I think that's correct, yes, but I don't think I have ever known where she did come from. My father never spoke of her."

"Your stepmother wouldn't have liked it," Joan explained. "Terrible jealous woman, she was. Never let him even think of either of his previous wives. You'd think they'd never existed."

"She was a good mother to all of us. Get on with your tale, woman, and stick to what you know."

She bristled slightly, but continued: "Now this is where Steven's family comes in. When he was a youngster, Cicely's uncle...Mark was his name...'ran' to Newbury and stayed his year-and-a-day to become a free man, see? Then he apprenticed himself to a cobbler and made a living from it, though he died not long after the famine, poor soul."

"So? You are making a very long tale of this, Widow Joan."

"'Tis necessary," she insisted. "Cicely's Uncle Mark had a daughter, see? An only one, she was, for all her brothers and sisters died young, and then Mark and his wife died, too. But when Cicely found out about the girl, her father—Steven's grandfather—arranged a marriage for Mark's daughter with your father. That's how you and Steven are second cousins. Both of you are great-grandsons to Cicely's grandfather."

He was silent for a moment. To make her accusation stick, she must have done the further calculation Piers had explained to him about the relationship between Steven and his wife's sister creating a consanguinity that neither of them had known of. But he wasn't going to tell the story for her.

"I haven't married Steven," he pointed out robustly instead. "So where's the consanguinity to prevent me marrying Rosamund? She and Alys aren't related to either of us."

"Ah, but that's not the end of it, is it?" she went on, malice in every word. "Steven marries Alys, all right and proper, in October, and beds her too—I was one of the witnesses."

What had possessed Alys and Steven to invite her? he wondered. *Alys wasn't that keen even to invite me!* "And ...?"

"So, I was talking with Sister Margery, God rest her soul. Maybe around Christmas it were, after you and Mistress Rosamund were married."

"Sister Margery?"

"I used to go and talk to her sometimes. She knew her herbs, see, and so do I."

Alan strongly doubted whether Widow Joan's knowledge was anything approaching Sister Margery's, but the statement wasn't worth challenging. "And what did Sister Margery say?"

"Well, I was telling her about your mother and Cicely's uncle and all, and she said—clean out of the blue, she did—'that's consanguinity.' So of course, I asked her what she meant."

Sister Margery had said nothing to him. Was that because she thought, on reflection, that the consanguinity was too marginal to worry about, or merely because wisdom and observation told her that he and Rosamund should not be separated? Perhaps it was the news of Rosamund's pregnancy that had stopped her. He would never know now.

"And she said?"

"Father Piers told you...he must have done," she shouted at him triumphantly. "He couldn't have kept it to himself, as a priest, could he? Not when he has to give you the host at Easter."

Alan knew what Piers had said. Could it really be true? He decided Joan probably did not understand as much as she thought she did, and he might be able to shut her mouth before she spread the suggestion more widely.

"Father Piers believes that the consanguinity is not clear enough. Steven and I are only just within the prohibited degrees anyway, and it is not he and I who are joined. Marrying two sisters doesn't bring us within the prohibition." This might not be true, for Piers had merely said he wasn't sure, but surely the priest would not gainsay him in public?

Her face fell, to his satisfaction. "No?"

"No," he confirmed ruthlessly. "You have made up this vile calumny against my wife and me, and it is nonsense. I don't expect to hear any more about it, in the village or anywhere else, Widow Joan. Is that clear?"

She cowered slightly, which gave him a great deal of satisfaction. "I'm sure I beg your pardon, master, if I have said aught amiss."

"I will say no more about it, if you will do the same. And you must never mention it to my wife. Understand?"

She nodded, and to his surprise dropped him a little curtsy. "I'm never one to spread rumours," she told him, piously.

Alan snorted. "Make sure you do not."

But after she had gone, he was more than ever unsure whether what he had said was actually true. What if he and Rosamund really were not married, after all? What was even more frustrating was that Steven and Alys had hardly lived together at all, over all these months. Steven clearly had not found married life to his liking, and he had never heard Alys complain that her life was the poorer for his absence. Indeed, Rosamund had said just the other day how worried she was that Alys was getting too close to Master Finn.

"They share a love of weaving," she had told him, as they lay together before sleeping. "And he is—forgive me, Alan, for I know Steven is your friend—he is a much kinder, gentler person than Steven. Alys likes that."

"She can do what she likes and Master Finn won't gainsay her, is what you mean," he had replied, but he smiled to soften the words.

"Well, perhaps. But she is such a strong person, Alan. She will never be happy with someone who tries to dominate her all the time."

"If anyone can do it, Steven will. He's not one to take orders from a woman, and after all, she is his wife. She'd better not get too friendly with Master Finn."

"I'm sure she would never do anything wrong," Rosamund hastened to reassure him. "She is always the one who tells me off for my misdeeds!"

The conversation had ended there, and Rosamund had drifted off to sleep. But it would be horribly ironic, Alan reflected wryly, if his own marriage was the casualty of consanguinity, rather than Steven and Alys's. Whatever the truth of it, he would have to speak to Steven.

~ * ~

The opportunity arose sooner than he had expected, for on the Monday before Easter, Sir Walter rode in to the manor with a small retinue that included Steven. They arrived just before dusk, having ridden a long stage from London.

"We avoided the city itself," Steven told Alan, who had come out of his office to greet them. "'Tis terrible there—folk being buried in great pits, hundreds each day, and the survivors fighting over provisions."

Alan nodded. "'Twas starting to go that way when I came through on the way back from Kent in January. It must be much worse now, if the pestilence has been raging all that time."

"How are matters here?" asked Walter. "I will stay only to rest the horses overnight, then I am going to collect Giselle from our manor in Oxfordshire, for the pestilence has reached them too, I hear; and she is with child. In Calais things are getting better, so it will be as well for her to come home now."

"They are easing here too," Alan told him. "But we have lost many—almost every household has been affected, and in some most or all have died."

Walter shook his head. "Tis the same story everywhere." He handed his reins to Toby, who had come out of the stable to take charge of the horses.

"I apologise that I am the one to greet you," said Alan rather awkwardly. "But the lady Eleanor should return soon. She is out with Piers in the village."

Walter frowned. "Is that safe for her?"

"Safety is not her first concern, Wat." He sounded exasperated rather than admiring, though in truth he felt both emotions. "Sister Margery died last week. She left the anchorhold to help Piers shrive the dying, but before long she took the sickness herself. Since her aunt died, the lady Eleanor has taken on her role with the sick."

"Why cannot the priest manage on his own?"

"Give the man his due, Wat! He is paid to be chantry priest and pray for Sir Thomas's soul, remember? But first Father Edward followed Sir Richard north, and then the vicar he sent us in February died of the pestilence within days. Piers has been carrying the load ever since. Sometimes there are two people dying at the same time, and he cannot be close by to shrive both of them. The Holy Father, as you may have heard, permits even women to hear confessions if a priest is not available and the end is near."

Walter shook his head. "Strange times we live in, when a woman can do a priest's work."

"I will have a chamber prepared for you." Alan remembered suddenly that he was in charge of the castle's domestic arrangements as well as the manor accounts. "No doubt Steven will be sleeping at home tonight."

He looked at his friend and wondered suddenly what trouble he was sending upon Alys, unwarned.

"Aye," agreed Steven, who had been listening with interest to the conversation. "I won't trouble you for a bed, my friend." He remounted and turned his horse, a big powerful cob well up to his weight, southwards towards the bridge. Clearly private speech with him about this consanguinity business would have to wait.

"Have a care, Steven!" Alan called after him. "The bridge is in poor repair after a storm. Pray lead your horse over it. Do not try to ride or you may end in the river."

Steven acknowledged the warning with a wave and rode on. Now he was here, he was keen to return to the cottage and see how Alys had been faring while he was away, though in truth he had not thought of her very often while he'd been in Calais.

No word had been said by Alan to the contrary, so he was assuming all was well with her and she had not fallen prey to the pestilence. He realised he had not asked after his parents, either. But he had had no stomach for the niceties of lordly living at the castle, on which it appeared Alan was flourishing. Dressed like a franklin, and airs and graces to go with it, he thought with disgust, and wondered where his friend the simple archer had disappeared to.

He let his tired horse settle into a quiet walk, resting him after the journey. He still felt a simmering anger at all they'd seen on their journey. Their road had taken them through the outlying streets of London, and the sights had shaken him. Not only the bodies piled up awaiting burial, some of them inadequately protected against vermin, or the wandering madmen, driven out of their wits by grief or horror, or the lewd activities of men and women who sought oblivion in drink or sexual excess, but the starving survivors picking over refuse heaps, and fighting over what little had come into market from the countryside. It was clear either the food producers were dead, or they dared not venture into what had become a city from hell. Calais had suffered badly from the pestilence, but the presence of the garrison there, well led and well organised, had saved them from social dislocation. And Northchurch seemed a haven of peace by comparison with other places. For the present, at least, he was glad to be home.

He negotiated the bridge circumspectly, leading his horse, and remembered suddenly that there was nowhere at the weaver's cottage to stable the beast. He could hardly put him in the barn with the livestock. He would have to beg stable-room at the castle for the big gelding when he'd offloaded his saddlebags. No doubt Alan would arrange it, as he seemed to be in charge of such matters.

It was only a short distance from the bridge to the weaver's cottage, so he did not bother to remount. As he came up to the gate, to his amazement he saw his brother chopping sticks in the garth. "Jack?"

The boy looked up from his task and his face lit up. "Steven! You're home!"

He ran to his brother and Steven gave him a rough, awkward hug and let him go. "'Tis good of you to be helping Alys."

"I live here now, Steven." The boy's face clouded over. "You have not heard, I see. Mother and Father died of the pestilence, weeks back. I have been here with Alys ever since."

"'Tis good of Alys, then," amended Steven. The thought of his mother's death wrenched at his heart, though he would not have shown such emotion for the world. But he could not grieve for his father.

"Nay, it has been good for both of us. And there is Master Finn..." his voice trailed away, remembering that Steven knew nothing of the weaver's arrival. "Alys will explain."

Steven frowned. Who was this Master Finn? An outlandish name and not one he recognised. His face darkened. What had Alys been up to while he was away?

"Hold my horse, boy, if you will. I must unload here and then take him back to the castle. Unless you'd like to do that for me? He's a devil to ride when he's fresh, but you can lead him if you go carefully, for he's too tired to give you any trouble."

Jack looked at the big horse in wonder. "Yes please. I would like to take him for you." There was something ugly and angry about Steven suddenly, and he preferred to be out of the way if there was going to be trouble. It reminded him too much of his father's quick temper, and the fist that had often laid him on the floor as a result.

He unbuckled the saddle bags and handed them to his brother, before taking hold of the reins to lead the beast back to the castle. He stroked the horse's nose, and it whickered at him in a friendly way. He turned it towards the bridge and set out, walking slowly, one hand on the rein, the other stroking the smooth coat.

Steven watched them go for a moment, to check that Jack could manage, but the cob walked along quietly with him, giving no trouble. He remembered that even as a small boy Jack had had a way with horses. He turned from the gate and went down the path towards the cottage door.

Thirty-seven

Piers and Eleanor had left the humble cottages that straggled along the road out of the village towards Micheldever, and had begun to walk back towards the bridge. Eleanor's skirts, Piers noticed with dismay, were muddy and soiled around the hem, and he wished again that, if she felt she must help him—and God knew he was grateful for the help itself, as well as thrilled to have her company—she would consent to have her mare saddled and ride. But when he had suggested it earlier, she would have none of it.

"I would not ride and have you walk beside me," she had said. "How haughty you must think me!"

He had disclaimed hurriedly.

"So it would mean saddling you a pony, too, and the stablemen have enough to do as it is. Trotting down to the bottom of the village and then being tied up for hours would not be good for the horses, and you know well, Father, that my lovely mare would not put up with it."

He nodded, agreeing with her reasoning, but still feeling it was inappropriate for such a lady to be walking around the dirty lanes like a peasant maiden, even if she wore her oldest dress for the purpose.

He had had as little success in trying to stop her from accompanying him in the first place. "What my aunt could do, I can," she had told him implacably. And then, more moderately: "Father, please indulge me in this. You know what a loss Sister Margery was to everyone, not just to me. This is one small way in which I can fill her place."

And so they walked side by side along the dirty lanes. That morning they had watched two women in two separate households meet their end, leaving grieving comfortless families behind them—families where there had already been losses, one of an elderly grandfather, the other of two of the youngest children. In both, the older girls would have to take on the burdens of their mother.

There was no question that Eleanor's presence had made a difference to the families. In one she had heard the dying woman's confession while Piers was occupied in the next-door cottage, and then given place to him to provide absolution and extreme unction. In both, she had encouraged the girls who had to look after their father and the remaining children, and had given them advice and offers of assistance if needed, though where this assistance was to come from, Piers did not know, for the castle staff were already stretched to the limit, and even village neighbourliness seemed to be in shorter supply than before. Poor folk, he thought compassionately. So many families had lost loved ones that those who remained had their hands full caring for their own.

"I will tell Alys," Eleanor said, unconsciously answering these thoughts. "She will help, or she will get someone else to do so. Dear Alys, what would we have done without her?"

He nodded. "It is a miracle that she has not been touched, all through this. But it seems the pestilence works that way. Some are taken from us, some are not. And a few, like Rosamund, take the sickness and yet survive."

"That was a miracle indeed. And you too have been spared, Father Piers." She beamed the sunshine of her lovely smile on him, and he felt his face warm in response.

"And you, as well," he replied softly.

He wasn't sure she had heard him...indeed, he had not particularly meant her to do so, for what right had he to make personal remarks of any kind?

"Then we can still believe in miracles, can we not?"

He agreed, but cautiously. "Rosamund seems still drained and unhappy. Perhaps it is the loss of the child. That was a hard blow to bear."

She nodded. "I hope she will come through it soon. Another child to fill the gap would help her," she added wisely. "And would bring Alan joy, too."

There was a pause as they negotiated the bridge, whose new planks seemed to be holding. "When all this is over, I must persuade my brother to rebuild this in stone," Eleanor commented, pulling her skirts together so they did not catch on the piers as they walked through.

He followed her, watching her footsteps carefully, for word of Alys's narrow escape had reached them, and he was fearful lest Eleanor might slip as Alys had. But her leather-soled boots gripped the wood better than Alys's pattens, and all was well.

"I have wanted to tell you, Father," she went on as they started up the hill to the castle, "how grateful we all are for your work these past weeks, in the place of our parish priest. I hope that soon Father Edward will return. There are fewer cases of pestilence now, and we must hope it will move on and leave us," she added. "Or at least perhaps he will send another vicar. Your work in the chantry saying Masses for my father is important and should go on as soon as possible, but I know you cannot manage both."

There was something behind her words that he could not grasp, some personal concern for her father, perhaps. "With the help you have given me, I have had time to keep up with the chantry Masses as well."

"That is so good of you," she exclaimed, smiling warmly. "My father would be grateful. He has such need..." she added to herself.

Piers looked at her. "What do you mean, my lady?"

"It is something my aunt told me before she died. But she said my father did not want it known, and I hesitate to say more."

"I am not your confessor," Piers acknowledged, "for that is Father Edward's privilege, I know. But if you have things on your heart, even if they are the sins of others and not your own, you should tell them to someone." She had no confidante, he thought, now that Sister Margery was dead. Rosamund was not her equal, even as the bailiff's wife, and she was not well besides. Who could she turn to? Perhaps she had confessed to Father Robert, in Father Edward's absence, but he did not want to put himself forward as a substitute unless it was necessary. She was above him in every way, spiritually as in all else. What could he offer her other than, perhaps, a listening ear?

"I thank you." She hesitated for a moment. "If I ask you to come and hear what is on my heart, I know you will honour anything I say as if it were a confession, although the sins I would speak of are not my own, but my father's."

"Indeed, my lady. Anything you say to me in confidence will go to my grave with me. Have no fear."

My father did not want you to know, she thought, remembering her aunt's words. But she knew she would tell him nevertheless.

~ * ~

While Jack was chopping wood outside, with promises that he could join them in their endeavours when he had finished, Finn and Alys were busy in the workroom. With the reduced need for their help in the village, they had turned their efforts, with some enthusiasm, towards preparing the looms for work. They had hunted out the stored spools, "for it will be a while before we can get fresh supplies of spun wool," Alys commented, and discussed the designs they would use.

As they worked together, she suddenly felt a sense of closeness to her father. These were the very tasks that she had done with him when he was master of the workshop. But for the first time she was glad he had died when he did, that he had not had to suffer the terror and grief of the pestilence. Even Purgatory, she thought, could surely not compete with the horrors that had come upon them in the past months. She still grieved for her mother, but the loss had become dulled by the overlying grief she felt for so many deaths. Yet Rosamund had survived, and was gradually growing stronger, and she herself had not been touched, though she did not understand why. And Finn...her heart chilled for a moment at the thought of Finn becoming sick and dying. Finn had come in their very hour of need, and helped them through it all.

"Some of this wool is very fine," commented the weaver, unaware of her complicated train of thought. He felt a thread from the spool judiciously. "Your mother was a good spinster."

"We used to do all our own wool preparation. We bought fleeces from Paul direct, you see, and processed them here."

"That must have been a great deal of work. There are so many processes. What help did you have?"

"We had a journeyman who sorted the wool, but of course Paul's fleeces were always very good. That is why my father bought from him. Paul was skilled at breeding sheep to produce high quality wool, which is the reason his fleeces brought in such good prices. He sold to us at a discount, because we are local. We must get Jack to understand that it's important for him to make sure the quality of the fleeces remains high."

Her thoughts ran ahead. Since Jack was keen to take part in the weaving, perhaps Steven would be prepared to take charge of wool production. They could keep the family connection in place and perhaps he would be happier to stay now that his father was no longer there to put him down. But that might mean she would have to continue as his wife...She sighed. She had no idea how the complicated relationship among herself, Finn and Steven might be worked out, and she could see that Finn would refuse to discuss it with her. He seemed to think it could all be left to fate.

"And the cleansing?" he asked. "In London, we bought ready-spun spools from the traders, so it was a very different business. I will have to learn."

Alys smiled at him. "My father had so many plans for this place. Few workshops carry out all the processes through from the raw fleeces to the finished cloth, but he wanted us to do that. He thought it was the way the industry would go in the future, especially in the countryside where it isn't so easy to specialise. James was employed to do the heavy tasks, washing the fleeces, and beating and greasing them too. That's mainly seasonal work, so he tilled the land as well usually, though we sometimes had a boy from the village to help with that." She paused. "I wonder whether he'll come back now that the pestilence is no longer so severe. We shall have to find someone else if he does not."

"I think it may be hard to find new workers. They will have plenty of choice now and will not have to take whatever is offered them."

Alys thought of the much-reduced numbers of men, women and children in the village compared with a time before the pestilence had come, and could only agree with him. "There are still some youngsters old enough to learn the work, those who are not needed to till their own fields because their fathers and older brothers are dead. The girls, too, may be interested in coming to work here, for Rosamund will have to be replaced. She used to do the carding. She only went to work for the lady Eleanor when my father died."

"It was a big operation, I can see. There are dyes on the shelf here. Did you dye in the wool or in the piece? Because we didn't have the raw wool to deal with, in London we often bought natural threads and dyed them in the piece, which works for a plain garment, or one with solid-coloured panels, but for designs, of course, we'd need coloured threads."

Alys nodded. "We died in the wool and warped it on to separate spools. But of course, sometimes we dyed in the piece as well."

On the other side of the workroom wall, the sound of Jack's chopper ceased. "He must have finished," said Alys. She put down the spool she was holding and brushed her hands on her apron.

"He'll be hungry, as usual. I'd better go and find him something to eat before he comes in here. I need to check the pottage and give it a stir, anyway."

Finn smiled. "You must get someone to do the housework, Alys, if you are to work on the looms. No one can do everything, not even you."

She shook her head at him. "All in good time, Finn. All in good time!"

She pushed open the door into the living room and went to wash her hands in the ewer. She stirred the pottage, which was simmering nicely and would soon be ready to eat. Her stomach rumbled at the aroma of food. It must be nearly dinner-time. Perhaps she should serve the meal at once instead of giving Jack a bite of bread and cheese and expecting him to wait.

There were footsteps outside, and the door was flung open. Surprised, for Jack usually entered the house quietly, sidling in as though trying to escape notice, she looked up. "Steven!"

He watched her eyes open wide at the sight of him. She blanched, and for a moment he thought she might faint. Then she steadied herself, a hand on the chair back, staring at him as though she'd seen a ghost.

He stood in the doorway, his body in its travelling cloak almost filling the gap between the doorposts, and stared back, his face set rather grimly. She was thinner, he saw, and there were lines on her forehead that had not been there before.

The door to the workroom opened, and a tall, lean figure appeared. "Alys..."

Steven turned towards him. "Who are you? And just what are you doing here?" He could guess, but he wanted the man to give an account of himself. His face was thrust forward belligerently, and Alys hastened to explain.

"Master Finn is a weaver come to help me start the business again." She glanced briefly at Finn. "This is my husband, Steven."

Finn bowed courteously. "I am glad to meet you, Steven. Mistress Alys has of course spoken much of you."

"Get out!"

"Steven! How dare you?" Alys's eyes blazed.

"You're not welcome in this house," Steven told Finn furiously. "I don't know where you came from or what your intentions are, but I don't want to see your misbegotten face again."

Finn silenced Alys with a gesture, and then spoke, quietly as usual. "I should explain that Mistress Alys invited me, months ago. I am a Flemish weaver from London, and I have come to assist her, as she says. To set up the looms again, and to finish her training. I have been glad to help her with other work during these difficult times, in return for my bed and board. Now that you are here to serve and protect your wife, I am no longer needed for anything but the business. I will, of course, take my belongings and find somewhere else to sleep."

He bowed to Alys. "I thank you, Mistress, for your hospitality all these weeks, and for your kindness to a stranger. If your husband permits, I will come by the day to work as we agreed."

Steven was about to say that he did not permit, but Finn gave him no opportunity. Having delivered himself of his courtly speech, he dived back into the workshop, and after a few moments came back with his cloak, his pack and the rebec in its bag. "I bid you good-day, sir," he said to Steven. "Until tomorrow, Mistress."

Reluctantly, Steven stood back from the door of the cottage, and Finn shouldered the pack and went on his way.

Thirty-eight

Outside the cottage gate Finn met Jack, running up the lane having finished his errand. "You should have seen Steven's horse, Master Finn! He is a wonderful beast, and so friendly. He walked with me up to the castle, as quiet as you please." He stopped and took in Finn's appearance. "Why do you have your pack and the rebec, Master Finn? Where are you going? You are not leaving us...?"

"It would not be fitting for me to stay in the house now that Steven is home," Finn explained. "I must find somewhere else to sleep for the meantime."

Jack was aghast. 'But where?"

Finn shrugged. "There are holdings waiting for the heriot to be paid. I can take one of those, mayhap. I will come back to work, so you will see me again tomorrow, I hope. I have known for some while that this might happen, when Steven came home."

"You cannot take on an unfree holding," protested Jack. "You're a free man, a craftsman. It would be..."

"Unwise? Inappropriate?"

"Nay...unfitting, I'd say."

339

Finn smiled, for Jack was himself a villein like his father. "What would you suggest then, Jack?"

Jack's face lit up. "We could live in my father's house. I haven't given the lord my best beast yet, for Alys said to wait and speak to Steven before I did that, since I want to be your apprentice weaver. But 'twould be easy to do it today, and then the holding would be mine and you could come and stay with me."

He sounded most enthusiastic, and Finn had to smile. Then he bowed, with a flourish. "Master Jack, I thank you. Shall we go?"

"In a minute," said Jack. "I will speak to Alys first, and bring my bundle."

"Wait. It may be that Mistress Alys and her husband will want some privacy."

"But I can't leave without telling her!" objected Jack. "When she's been so kind to me, too."

Finn nodded. "I understand. I will wait for you in the lane, if you want." He thought it best not to be within sight of the cottage while he waited, in case Steven were to step out into the garden.

"I won't be long," the boy promised.

He pushed the door open and stopped. Alys and Steven were standing six feet apart, the tension between them palpable. He hurried to explain what he and Finn were planning, then went into the workroom to pick up his few belongings.

"I forbid it," Steven snarled at him. "You're my brother, and who's he? Nothing to you, when all's said and done."

"That's not true!" Jack shouted. "You weren't here. You don't know what it's been like. James deserted Alys, and Master Finn has done all the heavy work for her ever since. He learned to plough, and we sowed the field. He's done everything and you send him away? Why shouldn't I invite him to my house, now that Mother and Father are dead?"

Steven looked flabbergasted, as well he might. This was not the diffident boy he had left behind.

"Do not worry, Jack." Alys spoke quietly. "It is good of you to help Master Finn in this way. Do you want to take some food from the cupboard to cook for your dinner, as it seems Steven is not inviting you both to share ours?"

There was a bite to this comment which was not lost on Steven, who scowled at her.

She measured out a cup of pease and some beans and barley and wrapped them in a cloth. "Here you are. Master Finn will know what to do with them, and there are cooking pots at your house. Tis time you went home to your own property, now that you have someone to go with you. You have livestock to see to, and hired men to command. Steven will come to talk to you later about it all, I'm sure."

Jack took the cloth and stowed it in his bundle carefully. "Good morrow, brother," he said as politely as he could.

Steven nodded briefly but did not reply. When Jack had gone, he shut the door and barred it. "And now you can tell me, wife, what you have been doing while I have been away. What is all this about inviting a master weaver to come down from London, and having him live in this house with you?"

Alys had opened her mouth to tell him it was no business of his. But there was a threat in his voice that gave her pause. "Have some dinner, Steven," she suggested, going to the cupboard for some bowls. "It's ready, and there's no call to let it spoil, since there's no one but you and me to eat it. You must be hungry."

It had been a long ride since early morning, and the pottage, as always in this house, smelled good. Steven decided to eat first, and call his wife to account afterwards. But when she had cleared the dishes and wiped them, and covered the fire, he could wait no longer.

"I'm ashamed of you," he told her. "Living here with that man like a slut with no decency, and my own brother aiding and abetting you. What will people say of you, Alys? Did you give no thought to that? No thought to my feelings? You lied to me back at Christmas. You must have known this man was coming, even then."

"I did not know," she answered sharply. "No word was sent from the Weaver's Guild in reply to my request. Master Finn simply arrived, shortly after you and Alan had left in January. There have been no lies, and no gossip either, to my knowledge. You are away and far off, husband." She crossed her fingers and tried not to think of Widow Agnes's words.

"Away and far off is where I've been, aye," he countered hotly. "In Calais, manning the king's fortifications." Her defiance had stoked his anger, bringing it to boiling point. He neither knew nor cared whether she was telling him the truth about the weaver, though his brother's defence of the man made it seem less likely that he was truly the interloper on the make that he had feared. But defiance he would not stomach.

Alys said nothing, suddenly fearful of this angry man in whose power she was. He had barred the door, and as her husband he had the right to beat her, or otherwise discipline her in any way he chose. Unless he maimed or killed her, nothing would be said or done by anyone. She was powerless, and her conscience told her that he had rights here that she had flouted. But her instincts still led her to fight.

"Your brother is right. Master Finn has worked here for no payment, only his board and a pallet in the workroom. His behaviour has been above reproach." Though mine has not, she admitted silently. You have a right to be angry with me. "It is despicable of you to turn him out at a moment's notice when he has done nothing wrong."

"I'm the master here," said Steven. "And my will is what counts. You forget yourself, Alys. You are my wife, and must do my bidding. I see I must remind you of it."

He pushed her towards the ladder up to the bedchamber and, shrinking, she climbed it in front of him, borne upwards by his hand at her back. At the top she tried to stop, to argue. But he was inexorable. He shoved her into the room ahead of him, and forced her on to the bed.

~ * ~

"I will come back next Tuesday, if all goes well," Walter told Steven the next morning, as he and the reduced retinue set out for

Oxfordshire. "I'd not ask you to travel the roads east on your own, but we should be safe enough as an armed band."

Steven nodded. "God speed, Sir Walter. I will be ready when you return." Already the prospect of a week at home seemed like penance rather than relief. He was not proud of his actions the previous day, and had left Alys on her own for the morning to recover. She had been white and silent when they awoke, but he was not sure whether this arose from hurt or anger. The obligations of marriage meant that he could demand conjugal rights of her at any moment, and in theory it worked the other way, too, though he couldn't visualise Alys asking for sex. But it would have been better to be gentle than overbearing and violent, and he regretted it, though pride prevented him from saying so.

As for this business of reopening the workshop, and employing Master Finn to train her and operate the looms, he was at a loss what to make of it. He had never taken it seriously when she had first suggested, back in the autumn, and could not believe she had gone so far as to send to the Guild as she had done.

"Tis a wild idea," he remarked to Alan as they sat in the bailiff's little office later in the morning, drinking ale and catching up with each other's news. "Have you seen much of this Finn character? Looks and speaks foreign, and as confident as you please. I gave him his marching orders, as you may imagine."

"I hope you didn't literally throw him out," said Alan. "I was a bit dubious about him when he first arrived, I admit, but he's proved his worth over the weeks. If Alys wants to do this weaving, then why not let her? You aren't going to be here to see, by all accounts, and it seems a bit unfair to the woman to make her keep house when there's no one to keep house for. Tis not as though you have children for her to care for."

"They've turned my brother against me, too," grumbled Steven, ignoring this. "Jack took Master Finn's part, would you believe?"

Alan did not reply. There was little point when his friend was in this mood. "Come to the solar and see Rosamund," he suggested instead. "She's a bit down, poor love, what with losing the baby and still feeling weak after the sickness."

"You're lucky still to have her."

"I know, man. Believe me, I know. But…"

Steven raised his eyebrows. "But what? What are you keeping from me, Alan? I can tell there's something."

Alan shrugged. "Goodwife Joan—Widow Joan she is now—has been saying to Piers that Rosamund and I are not legally married. There's consanguinity, and it involves you and me being second cousins and Rosamund and Alys being sisters. Because you were married before we were, you're considered Rosamund's brother, so that if you and I are second cousins, so are she and I. That's within the fourth degree, and it would make our marriage invalid. I haven't dared tell her."

Steven thought about this complicated explanation for a moment. "Why are we second cousins? It's the first I've heard of it."

Alan explained. "It sounds incredible, doesn't it? But I think she's right about your great-uncle. Did you know anything about him having a daughter?"

Steven shook his head. "We didn't have any contact with him, as far as I know. He disappeared and that was that. How the devil does Joan know anything about all this, anyway?"

"I never thought to ask her."

"Now you mention it," Steven said, rubbing his chin thoughtfully, "I do remember my father saying something about kinship. It was the reason he helped your father out, after the Great Famine. Because they were kin. But I never worked out how. That was probably what he meant."

Alan tried to remember how long his mother had been married to his father before he himself was born. "The Great Famine was thirty years ago." he said. "That's a while before my mother married my father."

"The effects went on for years afterwards, though," Steven pointed out. "And my father went on baling your lot out."

Alan shrugged. "Tis no matter. The relationship exists, it seems. Steven...I'm afraid."

"Of hellfire?"

"Seriously. I'm afraid 'twill kill Rosamund if she knows. To think that we have been unwed all these months, and that we can't be married. Church law won't allow it."

Steven grimaced. "I see your point. Poor maid. What will you do? You can't hide this away, man. Especially if Joan the Gossip has the details."

"She is keeping silent because Piers asked her to. God knows what retribution he promised her if she gabbed. I certainly promised plenty."

"I wish it were the other way round," said Steven thoughtfully. "I wouldn't mind being rid of Alys, to be honest."

"Steven! You should not undervalue her so."

"I can see her strengths. I know she has made a difference to people's lives these last months. Everyone tells me so. But she and I cross swords too easily. She wants to be independent and run things her own way, and I expect her to be submissive. We shall always be fighting if I am home." He got up and stretched. "Well, I guess I can stay away soldiering. I always meant to do that—serving Sir Walter at Calais while I'm needed there, then maybe signing up with one of the other captains as a mercenary. There are plenty of local wars on the continent, and booty to be had, what's more. I could make my fortune!"

Alan went to the solar on his own, leaving Steven to mooch off about his own affairs. He was rather concerned about his friend's marriage. He had come to appreciate Alys over the months he'd been back in Northchurch, particularly since he'd become bailiff, and felt sad that she and Steven were at odds.

Rosamund was sitting rather listlessly with her embroidery, a brazier alight in the centre of the room to keep her hands warm. Alan put off his cotte and sat down near her.

"How are you, my love?" he asked.

She looked up with a faint smile. "Better, I think. But tis a slow process."

"Never mind that. There is plenty of time." *But not much time for us,* he thought, *unless I can find a way through this maze.* He decided he could not keep the problem from her any longer. Steven might mention it to Alys, and Alys would want to discuss it with her sister. He had not sworn Steven to secrecy, knowing he would not spread the story about. But it was a different matter between husband and wife, especially when Alys's sister was involved.

"Sweetheart, there is a matter I must talk to you about."

"I thought something was troubling you. I know I seem wrapped up in my own health, my own sadness. But tis not so. I notice when you are burdened."

"I have been told there is cousinship between myself and Steven."

She raised her eyebrows enquiringly, and he tried to explain as clearly as he could what the situation involved.

"But, Alan! That would mean we aren't really married at all." She began to sob.

Cursing himself for his decision to tell her, and wishing the telling could have been less blunt and stark, Alan knelt beside her, rubbing her hands and kissing them. "We will find a way through this, I promise."

"Is there a way? Oh, Alan, surely there must be a way. I love you so much!"

He took her in his arms and promised a way would be found. But in his heart there were many doubts.

Thirty-nine

Alys wandered about her cottage in her robe, sore both in body and mind, and glad that Steven had taken himself off early. She would have been hard put to it to know how to act towards him after yesterday's events, and wanted some time to think. Finn and Jack did not put in an appearance in the workshop, which was not surprising. Probably they had enough to do making Jack's home fit to live in, not to mention selecting a suitable beast to take up to the castle as a heriot for the holding.

She wondered what Steven would think of Jack taking on his father's land with help from Finn, and decided she did not care. Finn was perfectly capable of looking after himself, but she was glad he had gone away graciously in the face of Steven's animosity the previous day, rather than staying to make a fight of it. Finn was not the man to use violence for his own ends, and she liked him the better for it.

Nothing Finn could have done would have prevented Steven from using the sexual act to punish her and establish his own dominance. It was something elemental, to which his own need had driven him. She had hated it, crying herself to sleep afterwards with thoughts of the contrast with the beauty and love with which Finn himself had taken her, so recently, in that same bed. But even as she wept, she had accepted that it was the way Steven might have been expected to respond to the situation. The question was, what to do now?

At length she dressed herself in her workaday clothes, saw to the animals and the basic chores, and walked up to visit her sister. They had seen little of each other in the past couple of weeks, and Alys wanted to make sure she was still recovering well. Whether she would burden her sister with her own problems remained to be seen. She would decide on that when she arrived.

She met Alan as she walked through the castle grounds.

"Alys! I'm glad to see you. Rosamund has had...some distressing news. She is upset, and I do not seem to be able to comfort her. Maybe you can do better."

"It must be bad, if you cannot cheer her! I will do my best."

She did not ask what news had troubled her sister so much. Her sister would tell her whatever she needed to know.

Rosamund ran to her when she reached the solar, and threw herself into her sister's arms. "'Tis dreadful, Alys, what Alan has told me. What are we to do?"

She drew Alys to a stool near the brazier and explained.

"Consanguinity!" exclaimed Alys. "But that's extraordinary. I have never really understood those degrees of relationship, I must admit. But you did not know you would be seen as second cousins. You and Alan did not mean to do wrong."

"No, and Piers knows that, he says. No one is accusing us of anything deliberate. But we will not be able to take communion at Easter unless we separate and make confession of sin, and how can we do that? It is all wrong, Alys. Of course, we are married! How could I feel this way and not be? I have loved Alan since he first returned home from the East, in September. And I carried his child..." She began to sob.

Alys held her, but her thoughts were racing. "Ros! You slept with Alan long before Steven and I were married, didn't you?"

"Yes. The first time we lay together was after the Michaelmas feast."

Alys dimly remembered hunting for her sister after the feast, and concluding that she had gone off somewhere with Alan. She had worried about it at the time, and worried even more when she found her sister was with child. But Rosamund had not told her about the pregnancy until after she and Steven were married, so she had not been quite sure when the relationship began.

She stood up briskly. "I've had an idea, Ros. No, don't ask me right now. I have to check something with Piers. I will tell you as soon as I'm sure. But I think there is a way out of this unholy mess— for both of us."

"B-both?" queried Rosamund.

Alys nodded with decision. "Both. You need to be married to Alan, of course you do, and I hope you will have more children when you are fully recovered. You two have a life to live together. But I do not wish to be married to Steven any longer. He is brutal to me when he's angry, and—keep this to yourself, Ros, and do not judge me, please—Finn and I love each other. I belong with him, and I will not give him up."

Rosamund put a hand to her mouth in horror. "Alys!"

Alys shook her head at her. "No more now, I beg. But do not give up hope."

She left the solar and walked down to the church. With the recent decline in cases of sickness, Piers would probably be in the chantry. She would go and find him there. She wondered whether she should make her confession to him, and decided it would be a good idea. Piers would not condemn, and she would accept whatever penance was imposed.

~ * ~

Eleanor had awoken early, her mind turning over her aunt's revelations, her heart still full of grief for her death. She must go and speak to Piers. More than ever, she was convinced it was right to tell him her father's secret, partly so that he could pray more effectively for Sir Thomas's soul, partly for reassurance that her father's penance would be enough to lead him through Purgatory. She could not bear the thought that he might find his way only to Hell, not only for his sake but for her own. The hope of a reunion with him in Heaven had helped her through many a sleepless night last autumn. She did not want to be robbed of it now.

Piers was eating breakfast when she went down to the hall, and she joined him at the table, choosing her own simple meal from the viands the servants had laid on the trestle boards. "Father Piers, I want to talk to you about my father. My aunt told me of sins that had been kept secret from all the family, and they burden my conscience. I know he was given a heavy penance for them, and he carried it out, but still..."

"You would like assurance of his absolution."

She nodded, glad of his quick understanding.

"Then, when you have finished eating, we will go down to the church, and to the confessional. That is the proper place for such revelations, and you will feel comfortable there that no one will disturb us, or listen to what you have to say."

She rose obediently and went with him.

It was a silent walk, for each was occupied with private thoughts. Piers felt an even greater exultation than usual in her company, for the honour and responsibility of confidant was to be his, and the sharing of secrets Eleanor felt she could share with no one else. As always, she walked freely on a long stride—reminding him a little of a young pony—and kept up with him without difficulty.

As for Eleanor, she felt a sense of freedom already, even before the confidences had been made, as though her burden for her father was lighter for the prospect of sharing it with another. And for the first time she found herself enjoying Piers' company for itself, because he was a friend, a human being with whom she felt a deep connection, quite apart from revering him as an ordained priest cognisant with the holy mysteries of her faith.

They sat in the confessional together, separated by the grille, and he waited in silence for her to speak.

"As I said, it is my father whose sins I want to tell you about," she began at last. "I knew nothing of them till the other day, nor, I believe, does my brother yet know. But my aunt told me on her deathbed." There was a pause for a few moments, and he knew she was trying to hold back her tears.

"Take your time," he reassured her.

"Sister Margery told me..." She paused, swallowing down tears. "She told me that six years ago my mother fell in love with our steward. His name was Peregrine, I think. Do you remember him, when we were children?"

"A young man," Piers said, thinking back. "Well set-up, with black hair. I suppose I can see that he would be attractive, and your father was a lot older than your mother, wasn't he?"

"Yes," she agreed in a small voice. Clearly the idea that her father's attraction for her mother had failed due to age was a hard one for her to accept.

"It happens, my lady," he told her, thinking of the marriage she had narrowly escaped.

"Eleanor," she corrected gently. "We are equals here, and you should use my name."

His heart swelled and choked him for a moment with the enormity of the honour she was bestowing on him. "If you wish it, then...Eleanor."

"It seems," she went on, "that my mother wished to leave my father and run away with Peregrine. I cannot...I cannot understand how a woman would want to do that, but perhaps, if she loved him so much that...that..."

"Mayhap she could not help herself," suggested Piers compassionately.

"Yes, I think that is how it was. And my father," her voice rose on a sob, "my father killed her."

Piers was silent with shock. He had not imagined this.

"I think it was because she threatened to leave. He could not bear the shame of it. I have thought so much about this, for my aunt told me only the bare bones of the story before she died. But I think he could not bear to lose her to another man. He preferred her to be dead. I remember only that she died suddenly, and her child with her, and that we all grieved. My poor mother..."

Piers sighed. "You do not know whether mayhap they had committed adultery, your mother and Steward Peregrine. If the child was not his own, I imagine your father would have found that intolerable, as most men would."

"Sister Margery did not say. Perhaps that is not something she knew, for she was vowed to the anchorage by then, and was not living at the castle. If my father did not tell her, she would have no knowledge of it. And perhaps he would not wish to, for her sake as well as his own. She loved him dearly." She paused. "It is a great thing to love one's brother. Mine has not made it easy to do that."

Piers remembered only too well. "I do not excuse his behaviour in trying to force you into marriage."

"From which you saved me!" she put in quickly. "God be praised, and I thank you again, Father."

"If I am to call you Eleanor, even if only now, as we talk together, then I am a friend, not your confessor, and you must call me Piers, as you did when we were children."

"If you wish," she answered.

"Try to forgive Sir Richard," he went on. "For he was doing what seemed best to him, for the family...perhaps even for you. Not everyone can understand the call to celibacy, to God's service."

"But you understand."

"Of course."

"I will try, then." She was silent for a moment, her lips moving in prayer. He waited patiently for her to continue her story.

"I do not know whether it was discovered that my father had committed murder, or whether he confessed to Father Nicholas. But I understand now everything that has always puzzled me: why Father Nicholas was given another benefice, why Steward Peregrine left so suddenly, why my father sent you to be trained as a chantry priest, and built the chantry on to the church, why he went off for five years on a kind of crusade. He went to serve the Teutonic Knights in Germany for a while, didn't he? Alan and Steven spoke of it. And I think they visited the Kingdom of Jerusalem before they returned."

"In his will, he tried to make sure that Alan and Steven did not stay in the manor either," suggested Piers thoughtfully. "But in fact I don't think either of them knew anything of your mother's murder."

"We were all so young then. Steven is a few years older than Alan, but Alan was only sixteen or seventeen when he followed my father on his pilgrimage, and you and I were younger still, hardly more than children. The secret must have been kept very close, if no one but my aunt and Father Nicholas knew of it."

"I am honoured by your confidence, Eleanor," said Piers, his heart very full. "But I think you wished for reassurance?"

"I want to be sure my father's soul will be saved through his penance."

"It is not penance that saves," Piers pointed out gently. "It is repentance. You and I cannot know what was in his heart, but to undertake such a heavy penance so willingly suggests that he wanted to find peace for his soul, that he was repentant."

"I hope so. I hope so with all my heart. I loved my father very much."

"I wish," sighed Piers, "that you had not been burdened with this secret...that Sister Margery had taken it to her grave, as she promised."

"But I do not wish that. It is always good to know the truth, even when it hurts. I will understand others better, because of this. But it must go no further, Piers. Whatever happens."

"Of course. As if it were your own confession, I will hold it secret." He was grateful for the honour she had bestowed in confiding in him, glad of the trust she showed, but he also felt as though the burden she spoke of had been transferred and he was now carrying it for her. That was a joy also, of course, but the burden was a heavy one, especially the promise to tell no one—for that would hold, he thought, even for his own confessor, if ever he had one again.

At her request, he blessed her, the relationship shifting again to priest and parishioner. But the underlying friendship had not changed, and they parted warmly, with a curtsy from Eleanor that proclaimed their equality in her eyes.

She walked back to the castle slowly, enjoying the feeling of lightness as the burden of her father's sins was lifted, and relishing freedom from it. And she found, suddenly, that as Piers had helped her to understand her father as a man with a man's needs, she herself was appreciating Piers as a woman might appreciate a man, though it felt strange and alien to her, used as she was to seeing no difference between the sexes, to relating to both men and women only as pure souls.

She had always known she would be a nun, and that sexual congress would be forever outside her personal experience. She did not desire Piers in a carnal way, for such base thoughts could have no room in her lofty idealistic existence, among the pure love and devotion she held for God and his saints. Indeed, she thought, Piers himself would be injured if she entertained such a desire...for his own vows, already taken when he was ordained deacon, were similar to those she would take in her turn, and he would be a lesser man if he did not hold to them.

But she understood now that a woman might love a man in truth and purity, with tenderness, as a special individual given to her by God, without relinquishing her chastity. It was a joy so unexpected and so welcome that she savoured it all the way home. Best of all, she knew Piers had that same feeling for her. Although nothing had been said, she had felt it, sensed it in the way he looked at her, in the tenderness with which he had counselled her. That love would sustain her in everything she did, in her life in the convent, in her service to others and to God. Nothing could spoil it, if she held to her purpose, as she knew he would hold to his.

Forty

Alys found Piers on his knees beside Sir Thomas's tomb. He rose stiffly when she spoke to him, as though he had been there for some time.

"Alys? Does someone need me?" She thought he looked pale and tired, and felt some compunction about disturbing him.

"No, there is no one dying. Not even anyone sick, as far as I am aware. Could we really have come to the end of it, Piers? All this horror and death…has it finished, think you?"

"No one knows," he replied, rather helplessly. "Suffering and death are never finished, are they? Nor sin."

He sounded so sombre that she laid a gentle hand on his arm. "Is there something new?"

He shook his head. "It is just something the lady Eleanor shared with me. Nothing I can tell you, but it has grieved me."

"Will you hear my confession, Father? For I have sinned."

The formal words, and the formal mode of address instead of his given name that she normally used, brought him out of his abstraction.

"Of course I will." He led the way to the little confessional and sat down.

Afterwards he absolved her and gave her his blessing. "Your penance shall be not to have speech with Master Finn for a week," he told her. "Not for any purpose. I will speak to him myself, for he too needs to confess if you are both to receive the bread on Sunday at the Easter Mass."

She bowed her head. "I wanted to speak to you about something else, too. This is not a sin...or at least not mine. My sister told me of the doubts that have been thrown on the validity of her marriage. She is sore distressed, Piers. Tis pitiful to see."

He nodded. "But I cannot see how it can be resolved, unless by dispensation."

"I had an idea," she said. "Tell me if I'm correct about this."

He listened, and then nodded again. "That sounds logical enough. Though whether it would stand in a court of law, I know not. And if Steven opposes it, you will stand little chance, I fear. For you would be relying on Alan and Rosamund as witnesses, and they would have their own reasons to lie...not that I believe they would be doing so, you understand. But courts, even ecclesiastical courts, are places where judgement relies on evidence."

"Thank you, Piers. I will speak to Steven."

"God speed, Alys. And may He prosper your cause."

She smiled and left him.

He stood silently for a few minutes after she had gone. It was such a burden sometimes, to be confessor and hear about people's sins and wickedness. One more thing that went with parish ministry, for which he felt so unfitted. The revelations Eleanor and Alys had brought him weighed him down. Alys could be absolved, and he hoped she and Steven and Finn might find their way to a solution along the lines they had discussed, without further sin. But where there was love, he knew, almost always there was desire for physical closeness. Even a priest was not immune, however much his vows forbade it.

Which brought him to Eleanor. What sweetness it had been for him to hear her confidences, though he was concerned at the weary strain in her face as she spoke to him. She would not bring him her sins, unless in extreme need, for he was not her confessor and, in her piety, and deep love for everyone, he felt she had little need of shriving. But honouring him with the secret her aunt had told her of Sir Thomas's sins was appropriate, for was he not responsible for the Masses for Sir Thomas's soul? He had seen, too, that his love was not despised or rejected by her, that rather it was welcomed, without an ounce of her purity lost. He hoped, desperately, that he would be able to keep his own feelings chaste, that they might not in any way corrupt hers.

~ * ~

On her way home, Alys met Jack and Finn, leading one of Paul's horses. In the ranking of the value of beasts, horses came above oxen, dairy cows, and pigs, and it was clear they had decided the lord was due a horse as heriot, fulfilling the requirement of 'best beast.' It was a fine animal, too, the better of the two Paul had possessed, young and vigorous and strong, in normal times a valuable beast, though who would be buying horses just now? Perhaps Sir Richard would take it into his own stables.

Jack left the horse's reins in Finn's hands and ran forward eagerly to greet her. "Alys, we have mended the door and the shutters and Finn cooked us pottage almost as good as yours!" He turned admiring eyes on the weaver. Alys was glad to see that he, at least, did not despise a man for doing woman's work at need.

"That's good," she said. "And this is your heriot payment, I take it." She indicated the horse.

Jack nodded.

Her eyes met Finn's, and he smiled, a secret kind of smile that assured her of his continuing love. He bowed formally, however, and gave her a conventional greeting. She remembered suddenly that Piers had laid penance on her for her sin that she was not to speak to Finn for a week. She had not foreseen a casual meeting like this, and he would surely be hurt and confused if she did not say anything.

Besides, had it truly been a sin, in any case? She was sorely tempted, but respect for Piers held her back.

"Jack, you and Master Finn should stay away from the workroom for a while. I do not wish Steven and Finn to come to blows over me, and tis what may happen if he sees Finn there."

"I was not minded to come while he is here," Finn answered, as though she had addressed him and not Jack. "There is enough to do at Jack's for a few days, as it seems those hired men who survived the pestilence have disappeared. No doubt there are better livings to be had in Newbury or Winchester, now that the plague has run its course. But never fear, we will have enough fleeces by summer for us to take our pick, as well as sacks for the Staple to earn Jack some income."

She smiled at him, but did not reply. "We will speak again when Steven has gone," she said to Jack. "All of us. There is much to say, but it will be better to wait." When Steven left again for Calais, the week of silence would almost be up.

She curtsied to them both and went on her way, down the lane to the bridge, while Finn, looking rather puzzled, took the other branch of the fork up to the castle with Jack.

As she walked, for the first time she saw the spring wildflowers in the banks along the roadside. How long had they been blooming without her noticing? The sun was shining, but she was sure they had not put forth blooms since she walked in the other direction that morning. She smiled, turned her face to the warm spring sunshine, and allowed joy to well up in her heart.

When Steven came home for dinner, she was sitting by the door in the sunshine with her mother's distaff in her hand. Her skill was not as great as her mother's had been, but the task was a coded message to her husband.

"Good morrow, Steven," she called to him as his burly figure turned in at the gate. "I have a good dinner waiting for you."

He hung up his cloak on a peg and sat down on the bench expectantly. Soldiering undoubtedly had its advantages over home life, but generally the cuisine was not one of them. He remembered

Alys's dinners from the last time he had been home, although he had been too angry to taste much of what she had given him the day before.

She handed him his bowl. "May I speak with you about what happened yesterday?" she asked.

Immediately he was on the defensive, and she saw the geniality engendered by the good pottage fade from his face. "I am sorry if I was importunate," he said. "It has been a long time since I was with you."

She wondered whether he had been faithful to her all those months in Calais. If so, perhaps that would go some way to explain his urgency, if not his brutality. Maybe long abstinence had mingled with a desire to punish her. "I ask you that you will not treat me like that again."

"You are not proposing to deny me my conjugal rights, Alys?" He could find more congenial sexual companionship in Calais, but that was not the point.

"No, but I will not put up with being forced. If I submit to you, I do it of my own free will."

This smacked of an unseemly insubordination, but he let it pass.

"I ask also that you allow Master Finn to come and work my father's looms. I invited him here for that, and with the pestilence arriving soon after he came here, so far we have done little. The weaving business would bring us an income, which I know you wish for," she added as a small incentive.

"I don't want him under the same roof...," he began.

"Not while you remain here, of course. He understands that you should be given some peace and privacy. But when you go back to Calais, then I would like to work with him. He can sleep at your parents' cottage with Jack, as he will be doing while you're here this time, or have a pallet in the workroom, as he has done up to now."

Steven shook his head like a tormented bull. "Why do you have these ambitions, Alys? I am earning enough as a soldier to keep us both. I have a bag of coin for you that I plan to leave with you when I go."

"Who knows when you will return?" she asked. "Or even *if* you will? Soldiers get killed, and in these uncertain days, I would not give much hope of a messenger bearing a bag of coin reaching here alive. I need to have funds I can rely on here, where I can use them. This is my house, Steven, and it is my business. Both of them belonged to my father, and now they belong to Rosamund and me. I gave you my dowry to pay for your manumission, and you promised me dower lands that your father held. I have never seen any income from those."

"My father said he would administer them for you, and give you the income."

"I have never seen a penny of it."

"My father would not cheat you!" he exclaimed.

"That's true," she admitted. "I do not accuse him of trying to do that, and besides he is dead. These last few months neither he nor anyone else will have gained much income from the lands anyway. But you see what I mean, Steven. And also," she added, taking a deep breath, "I owe it to Master Finn to keep to the bargain I made with him, to complete my training and work the weaving looms with me."

He stiffened, but reluctantly agreed. "But I want your promise, Alys, that you will have no carnal relations with the fellow. No sweet words, no kisses. Well set up, he is, and I can see the temptation when I am away. But I'll not put up with being cuckolded. Be warned!"

There was a flash of yesterday's anger in his eyes as he said it, and she thought it best to deflect that. "I will always be faithful to my husband," she said submissively, though her meaning was deliberately different from that which he would hear. "That is the essence of the marriage contract, is it not? You have my word."

There was more to say about that, but it was not the time. Not yet.

He slept in the second bedchamber that night, freshly made up by Alys with her best lavender-scented sheets as recompense. He grumbled at his banishment, but showed her more respect than he had done the previous evening. Alys herself lay awake for many hours, turning over in her mind what Piers had said to her, and decided penance given for adultery that turned out to not to be adultery after all was not binding. On the morrow she would go and speak with Finn.

She found him in one of the barns at the cottage she must now think of as Jack's house, and promised him that if he would be patient, all would be well.

"If so, that will certainly be a miracle. But I have faith, Alys, in you and my love for you...and in God."

She looked around, but the barn door was closed. She leaned closer and kissed him, and his arms engulfed her. "Was it bad for you, with Steven, after I left you?" he asked anxiously.

She hesitated, wondering what effect the truth might have on him. Then she pressed herself against him. "Yes, it was," she replied, keeping her voice calm and quiet. "But I will survive it, and I believe better times will come, for all of us. Steven does not love me, Finn, any more than I love him, and I do not believe that will change."

She thought of her father and Paul, arranging her marriage with the best of intentions, believing that love would come with intimacy as it so often did, that they would rub along together as a married couple, and the business would prosper. None of it had happened as they had hoped, but that was often the way with life.

He kissed her and let her go. "Without loving each other, you will be unhappy, both of you, whether Steven stays or goes. And he will take out his unhappiness on you, Alys. Truly, I fear for you."

"You do not need to do so. After the Easter feast, we will see what we will see. Have patience until then, my love."

Forty-one

It was Maundy Thursday, and Piers had said the Tenebrae service in the darkening church, the growing twilight outside mirroring the spiritual evocation within. After it, the altars would be stripped and the building prepared for the solemn commemoration of Good Friday on the morrow. He looked around the congregation, standing silently as the service finished. Almost everyone who had survived the pestilence was present, high- and low-born together. Alan and the lady Eleanor stood in front of the others, and their faces were clear to him in the dwindling light. Behind them were Steven and Alys, and he thought he caught sight of Finn with Jack, and Widow Joan with her son-in-law, while Toby stood alone near the back of the church. The Tenebrae service spoke to them all of the darkness they had suffered over the past few months, but also of the hope brought by the symbolism of Easter of a fresh beginning on Sunday.

The congregation watched while Piers removed the embroidered altar coverings and folded them carefully. He had never taken the priest's role in this ceremony, but he had seen it done often enough in his youth and knew what was required. He dismissed the congregation and blessed them, inviting them to return tomorrow for the solemn service to mark the crucifixion.

Eleanor moved from her place after the blessing, swaying slightly. She had felt strange since dinner time, hot and shivery at the same time, and exhausted, and it had been difficult to persuade herself to come out to the church. But not to do so would be unthinkable. She had attended every Holy Week service here in the church since she was a child. Rosamund had wanted to come with her, but at the last moment she had felt too weak, and Eleanor had walked down to the church slowly on Alan's arm, followed by those of the castle servants who could be released from their duties. Piers had spoken the service beautifully, and it was a pleasure to hear the Latin sentences pronounced with such meaning and understanding.

If only she did not feel so ill. She could not believe it was the pestilence, for she had seen enough of it over the past weeks to know the symptoms. Either a cough or the bubonic growths were consistent signs of that malady and she had neither, just a terrible lassitude. Mayhap she had an ague, but if so it would soon pass. She pressed her hands to her head.

"My lady." Alan spoke beside her.

"I am sorry..."

"Alan, take my lady's arm," said Alys urgently from behind him. "She is faint."

Eleanor leant heavily on Alan's arm and tried to walk. Her head spun and suddenly blood poured from her nose on to the stone pavement beneath her. Piers leapt forward to catch her as she fell, and the last thing she felt was the rough woollen texture of his robe. As her senses failed, she slipped like a dead weight through their hands and tumbled to the stone floor.

At once there was pandemonium. The remaining congregation, seeing their beloved lady fall to the ground in spite of the efforts of the bailiff and the priest, ran forward to her assistance, surrounding her with well-wishers who had the greatest devotion imaginable for her but no idea what to do.

"Father, she is ill. What should we do? What is wrong?" The questions peppered Piers as he tried desperately to clear space around the lady.

"Back!" commanded Alan with all the authority he could muster. Steven stepped to his side, and between them they thrust away those who pressed too close.

"Please," put in Alys firmly, stepping into the gap they had created. "Move back, for my lady needs air. She cannot breathe with all of you around her. I know you want to care for her, but please let us find a litter for her so we can take her up to the castle, to her bed."

Her words were heeded immediately. "A litter for my lady," was the call, and some began to run for help.

"I will carry her," offered Steven.

"I will send to the castle for a conveyance," Alan told him.

Piers, kneeling distractedly beside her, rubbing her hands, looked up at them both. "There is a mat in the anchorhold," he said. "We can bear her home on that." He did not want to offend Steven, but Eleanor, though slight and fine-boned, was tall, and she should be carried home as comfortably and with as much dignity as possible.

"I've carried my share of corpses on the battlefield," returned Steven grimly, but he stood aside and waited for the litter to come.

In a few minutes, a makeshift litter had been created out of poles and the sleeping mat, and the melancholy procession set off.

Halfway up the hill Jack came running down from the castle. "They are bringing a hand-cart," he called breathlessly.

Alys thought the hand-cart too reminiscent of those that had taken bodies to the graveyard in the past few months, but any conveyance was better than nothing, and there was no time to harness horses to a litter.

Jack looked at the silent form on the mat with horror. "Alys, she is so still!"

She put her arm round him. "She lives, Jack. Do not worry." She straightened up. "Go back and get the cart to hasten. We must bring her home as soon as may be."

They saw the hand-cart approaching as they reached the fork. They loaded their precious burden into it, and everyone pulled with a will. But the lady did not stir from her torpor, and her skin felt dry and burning to the touch as they helped to move her from the mat to the litter.

"She is hot as fire," Alan muttered to Piers.

"I know," Piers answered, and went back to his prayers, while his brain whirled madly. What herbs might they give her? What would Sister Margery or his mother have advised? Why was everyone dead who might have helped her? And in his heart there was a wrenching fear, constant beneath these surface thoughts: *God, where are you in this? Why have you not answered my prayers? She of all people should be spared to serve You in her longed-for convent, as she has always lived here in Northchurch to serve others in Your name. Please God, may she yet live!*

But by the time they reached the castle, and put her to bed in her own chamber in the tower, she was clearly dying. Blood ran from her nose and mouth, and dark bruises spread under her skin, while her fever still mounted, in spite of the cooling damp cloths Alys applied to her forehead and hands. And through it all Piers knelt beside her, praying, praying, but knowing all the time that it was to no avail.

When it was over, and she was cool at last, they left him alone with her, and he said the prayers for the dead. There had been no time for shriving, no time for extreme unction or the viaticum, for she had died within an hour of their reaching the castle, and had never regained consciousness. But Piers was sure there was no need. Even now she would be with Christ.

When he had finished, he left Alys, weeping at last, to sit with the body, and took the news to the solar, where Alan sat with Rosamund, holding her hand and trying to persuade her to eat the food the servants had brought.

"The lady Eleanor?" she asked. "Is she...?"

"God has taken her," Piers told her, in a harsh voice quite unlike his own.

Rosamund shrank back, and Alan leaned to put his arm around her.

"Was it the pestilence, or some other malady?" asked Alan. "I have not seen anyone die like that since the siege of Kaffa. And then rarely. With the plague, they do not usually die so quickly. I wonder how long she had been unwell."

Piers shook his head. "I know not. And truly, it matters not. She is gone."

Rosamund gave a little sob of fear. "Father, will I die, too?" she asked. "I am so weak still, though it is many days since I had the sickness. I am afraid that I will...fade away."

With difficulty Piers turned his attention to her. "I think not, Ros. You have fought the sickness and overcome it, where others, like our dear lady Eleanor"—his voice broke on the name—"were defeated and died. So few take the pestilence and recover, that to do so is achievement in itself. I pray you will regain your strength, though it may take time, and care. But I believe you will live now."

She turned her head towards Alan's shoulder and shed tears of relief into his cotte.

Piers sighed. "God has preserved your treasure," he said to Alan, in a tone full of grief. "But he has taken mine. May I be forgiven."

Alan raised his head and looked at him with sudden understanding, and the eyes of both men were wet with tears.

~ * ~

The two sisters laid her out...Alys dry-eyed and calm, but Rosamund weeping so bitterly that she could hardly see what she was doing, while Finn, turning his hand to anything as he had once boasted to Alys he could, raided the castle wood stores and crafted a beautiful coffin for her. Not for the lady Eleanor a naked berth in the common pit, amid the humblest plague victims, whatever her own wishes might have been. She would lie in state in the church during the Good Friday service and in the chantry during the Easter Vigil and the Sunday celebrations, and they would bury her on Monday.

The villagers filed past her in her open coffin on its stand in the parish church, mourning for her as for their own flesh and blood.

Perhaps, Piers thought, watching them from the altar as he waited to take the final Tenebrae service with its long readings from St. John's Gospel and Psalm 51, she in her purity and her self-negation, as well as her beauty and status, had come to stand for all that was best in their community, and for all they had lost in these last weeks. For every person in that congregation, which included every surviving villager, she represented the virginity of the blessed saints, unsullied by carnal contact with men, untouched by sexual feelings; high above them all, an angel given to them to light up their own crude humanity. A virgin pure, like Our Lady.

He led the service without thought, conscious of nothing but her body lying in front of the altar. How often he had feared that his sinful love for her might somehow contaminate her purity, and had therefore striven to hide it from her. But lately he had seen a different Eleanor, one who had valued him as a friend and confidant, as well as a priest. He thought of her distress, almost panic, in the face of her brother's efforts to arrange a marriage for her, and its contrast with her ability to give a pure and steadfast love to anyone who came her way, man or woman, even to himself, a boy thrust into the priesthood with no maturity or understanding, floundering among the demands it made on him like a fish in the shallows. Yet she was even younger than he, at least in years. Her loss went deep into his soul and changed it forever.

One by one the candles were extinguished, and only the central candle remained in the holder, illuminating the darkness, reminding them all of the light that shines in the darkness, a light that even in the midst of great suffering the darkness cannot put out. He recited the final prayer from Psalm 51 with tears in his eyes: "*Miserere mei Deus secundum misericordiam tuam...*"

Then slowly the congregation moved away, leaving her there in the darkness, alone except for Piers. He sat beside her through the night and into the morning. Others would bear him company the next night, for the Easter Vigil. But on Sunday there would be no feast, and no joyous ending of the Lenten fast as normal. Everyone would dress sombrely, as befitted bereavement rather than the joy of the resurrection. And on the Monday they would bury her.

Piers wept quietly as he thought of the Easter Sunday celebration they had planned, a service full of hope and thankfulness that the pestilence had passed on and might leave them hereafter in peace—a celebration of their survival. But how could they celebrate in the face of this tragedy? He could only trust that the words of the Easter service, and the sharing of the eucharistic bread with everyone, high and low, would suffice, for the liturgy was so well known that even in Latin the meaning would be conveyed. If they did not find comfort in the Lord's resurrection, what hope was there for any of them?

Forty-two

Sir Richard watched the keep of Northchurch Castle come into view ahead of him with some relief. He and a small retinue had pressed on ahead of the family, leaving Steward Roger to superintend the larger, slower party. The original plan had been for all of them to arrive home for Easter, but various delays along the way had disrupted this, and he had decided to take an advance party on ahead. His wife had been plaintive in her objections to this, terrified of armed robbery and murder by lawless gangs, but he had eventually allayed her fears by leaving most of the armed retainers to accompany her and the children, while he and a chosen few servants led the way. They soon left the main party behind, and travelling with few stops except to rest their horses, they made good time. It was only in the area south of Oxford that they had come upon the tell-tale signs of the pestilence: abandoned holdings and closed inns, and a few vagrants too scared to challenge their swiftly moving and well-horsed group.

It had been a difficult few months, but broadly his plan to evade the pestilence seemed to be working. The north was still unaffected, but he had heard that the sickness had ceased to plague the south and was moving on, up the main roads through Oxfordshire towards his northern manors, so he had decided they would all be safest back home in Northchurch. It had not been easy to convince his wife that it was better to pack up and move back home than sit out the epidemic where they were, and he had had to pull rank on her as her husband and lord, but in the end she had given in and done her best to get ready quickly.

He swung down off his horse in the yard outside the stables, expecting grooms to come running to attend to the mounts. But there was an eerie silence, and no one appeared.

"God's bones!" he cursed. "Pack of lazy good-for-nothings. What do I pay them for?"

"Tis the Easter Vigil, my lord," one of the retainers pointed out respectfully. "Mayhap they are all in the church."

"Leaving none to tend the horses or cook the dinner?" Sir Richard flung his reins to one of the esquires. "You'd best do the job yourself, Martin."

The esquire bowed and led the two horses away, followed by one of the other retainers with the third horse.

Just then, a little maidservant ran across the grounds from the kitchen buildings on the far side. "Sir, the grooms are not here."

"So I perceive," agreed Sir Richard acidly. "Where is everyone?"

"Why, in the church, my lord. Tis the Easter Vigil."

He nodded impatiently. No doubt Eleanor would be there, too. She hated to miss any of the religious rituals. "Prepare some food for us immediately," he told the kitchen maid. "I will speak with my sister later." He wondered whether Eleanor had taken up residence again in the castle in his absence, or whether she had continued to stay with their aunt at the anchorhold.

The maid stared at him and then burst into tears.

"What ails you, wench?"

"The lady Eleanor died on Thursday," she wailed, and pulling her apron over her head, she ran away.

There was a dreadful silence for a moment, while Sir Richard and his retainer looked at each other, aghast. "May the Virgin forgive me," said the lord in trembling tones quite unlike his normal decisive whiplash. "I thought the pestilence was over. We had word not long since that she was well."

"In these times much can change quickly, my lord."

Sir Richard said nothing more but walked up to the solar and sat silently, his hands gripped between his knees. A terrible sense of guilt came over him, as he remembered his unkindness to his sister, his intolerance of her contrary opinions and what had seemed to him her wilfulness in her plans to enter a nunnery rather than comply with his desire to see her marry well and to the benefit of the family as a whole. He had left her here on her own, twice, to take on the responsibility he had chosen to abjure, and because of his neglect, she had died. It was true that she had defied him, that she had herself insisted on staying to look after their people, in the face of danger, but did that absolve him? It was his responsibility, not hers. She had told him so, and he had brushed it off and thought only of his own safety. And she was dead...dead! He literally tore at his hair in a passion of self-recrimination.

~ * ~

They buried her on Easter Monday, as planned. Sir Richard had wanted to wait, to organise elaborate and expensive ceremonies like those held for his father, but he had been over-ruled, an experience he did not enjoy but had had to accept. For the bailiff's clerk, backing up Piers and Alan in their conviction that this was not what the lady Eleanor would want, confirmed that in her will, which he had drawn up for her in February, she had demanded to be buried 'with no pomp', and in the graveyard rather than the tomb in the church her brother had suggested.

"A will?" exclaimed Sir Richard. "But she was planning to enter the convent at Wherwell. Why would she draw up a will?"

"Perhaps," Alan suggested delicately, "she felt it might be wise, in the circumstances. We have suffered many deaths here in

Northchurch over the past three months. She knew she was in as much danger as anyone else."

Sir Richard muttered dire imprecations about the rent roll, and then seemed to recollect himself. "If that is what she wanted," he said, "then that is what she shall have."

He himself spent a few minutes alone beside her coffin, but what he said or thought was never told. His wife, having arrived early that morning after an uncomfortable night on the road, was prostrate after her journey, and he had consigned her to bed.

"We will do better without her," he told Alan, whose status as acting bailiff of the manor of Northchurch he seemed to have accepted, at least for the present. The children, too, were left behind in the castle, though Alys thought that hard for these young ones who had loved their Aunt Eleanor. But perhaps it was best for the sake of the village, all of whom had turned out to say farewell that chilly April morning, that Sir Richard should represent the family alone.

Alan was waiting in the chantry with the other bearers—Steven and Sir Richard among them as well as four of the poor tenants of the manor—to carry her into the church for the ceremony, and then to her final resting place in the graveyard. He wept openly as he said, speaking for all who had known her, "We shall not see her like again."

Piers' voice faltered and stumbled as, left behind in the chantry after the coffin's departure, he said the first of many requiem Masses for her. He had been glad to hand over the main role in the funeral service itself to the returned Father Edward, for his great fear had been that he would break down during the ceremony and betray the depth of his love for her.

Finn was in the church, though he had no part to play in the obsequies. He had his own memories of the lady Eleanor. In addition, his mind kept returning to Alys's promise to him, that if he was patient, all would be well. She had not spoken to him since, and in any case what could have been said, in the shadow of Lady Eleanor's death? He wondered what scheme she had thought up to rescue them from the pains of her unhappy marriage to Steven and their own forbidden love. She had mentioned telling Father Piers about it, so perhaps it was not anything too dreadful she had in mind. But he would be glad to know. "After the Easter feast," she had said. But when she made the promise, she could not have known what tragedy that feast would bring.

~ * ~

The following day, Sir Richard seemed to set aside his grief—though who knew what was hidden beneath that smooth, confident exterior—and take command. As soon as he had broken his fast, he demanded of the clerk where the will was kept, and had it brought to him.

"Read it to me, man," he instructed. "And explain it if need be. Translate it. I've no patience with all your Latin legal turns of phrase."

"It is very simple, my lord," the clerk reassured him.

"Good. Get on with it then. I must carry out my sister's wishes as soon as I may."

"First, the burial, my lord. We have done as she asked. She wanted you to know..." The clerk hesitated for a moment. "She says that she forgives you all wrongs."

Sir Richard turned pale for a moment, but quickly recovered his composure.

"She leaves her books to the young chantry priest, Father Piers."

The lord raised his eyebrows. "A surprising bequest, perhaps. And a valuable one. But they were hers to give where she pleased. I thought she would endow the Wherwell Abbey library with them, and perhaps she would have done, had she lived. I will tell him he must not sell them, for that would be a travesty of her provision."

"I do not think he will want to do that," the clerk told him. "For he is a scholar, my lord, who left his studies in Oxford to take up his duties here in the chantry. I feel sure she knew that he missed having books to read."

Sir Richard frowned at the temerity of this comment, but waved him to continue.

"Alan is to have her riding horse."

"The mare she bought from him?"

"Indeed, my lord. Alan has served her well in your absence and I believe this will be a welcome gift."

"H'm." Again, the bequest did not seem to please Eleanor's brother. But he let it pass.

"Rosamund, Alan's wife, is to have my lady's gowns."

Sir Richard nodded. "That is sensible. Rosamund has worn her old gowns before." She had looked well in them, he remembered. Rather too well for his own peace of mind, though of course he had never indulged himself too far in that direction. Not often, at least. His sister had stood in his way. "Is that all?"

"It is. But I have a request from Alan, that you receive him and his wife in the solar when you have leisure. There is a problem they wish to discuss with you." The clerk bowed and left the room.

Richard tutted to himself in irritation. He wanted nothing so much as some respite, and the company of his own family. His sister's will was an urgent matter he had had to deal with. His bailiff's problems were of considerably less concern.

He stretched his legs. He would allow himself a few minutes, and then he would send for them. Better to get the matter dealt with, and then he could relax.

Forty-three

The message came to Alan as he sat with Rosamund and her sister in the bailiff's suite of rooms, to which they had moved as soon as Sir Richard and the family returned. They had remained in the main building after Bailiff Michael's death only to keep Eleanor company, sharing the family solar with her at her request, and continuing to sleep in the tower in the bedchamber above hers. He did not know whether Sir Richard would expect them to leave for Beaconswell as soon as they had word that it was safe to travel. Perhaps it depended on what came of this interview, for if he and Rosamund were in truth not legally married, it might be better for both of them if he left Northchurch alone, never to return.

"Ask Father Piers to join us in the solar," he told the messenger.

"And Steven," added Alys quickly. "We need him there, too."

Alan looked at her. "Why is that, Alys?"

"You will see."

In the solar they sat around the brazier, which had been lit against the chill, for intermittent showers were keeping the warmth of the sun at bay.

"What is the business you wish to discuss, Alan?" Sir Richard asked when they were all assembled.

Alan explained what had been revealed about his family connection with Steven, and how this brought about consanguinity between him and Rosamund.

"Perhaps we should ask Father Edward for a ruling."

"We have already had such a ruling, from Father Piers here," Alan told him, indicating the chantry priest, who was sitting beside him.

Sir Richard's face showed his instinctive contempt for Piers' youthful opinion.

"However, we can ask Father Edward if you think it right," Alan added diplomatically.

"I think it would be wise. He has a great deal of experience."

Piers went to the door and called one of the messenger boys. "Sir Richard asks Father Edward to come," he said. "I believe he is in his cell."

Alys spoke up, not waiting for Sir Richard's permission. The matter was too important to wait for Father Edward's arrival, and the priest would not be sympathetic to her plight, she knew. There had never been much love lost between them. "There is something more to it than you have been told, my lord."

Steven stirred restively. Alys had obviously had wind of the matter from Rosamund and had got the details confused. He had little faith in women's ability to understand complex issues. They were simple creatures, and generally needed male guidance. Though Alys did not, he admitted, fit comfortably into such a conventionally gendered model.

"I think, and I believe that Piers agrees with me, that it is Steven and I, in fact, who are not legally married."

Not only Steven but Alan and Rosamund stared at her speechlessly.

"Nonsense, woman," exclaimed Steven after a moment. "Tis as clear as a pikestaff. You and I were married first, so it's our marriage that creates the consanguinity between Alan and Rosamund, not the other way round...and sorry I am to say so, Alan, my friend," he added, remembering the wish he'd expressed to Alan that it might in fact be his and Alys's marriage that was affected.

"But I checked with Piers," she told him. "It's not the legal marriage that creates the consanguinity, it's the consummation of it."

Steven's face expressed his bewilderment. "We consummated our marriage," he reminded her, irritated at having to discuss such a personal matter in front of others, particularly Sir Richard who, he felt, had always belittled him.

"Indeed," she agreed, not wanting to dwell even in her own mind on the quality of that consummation. "But the point is that Alan and Rosamund consummated their relationship first, before you and I were married. And *therefore,* it is not they, but we, who are within the prohibited degrees of consanguinity."

"That is the legal position, my lord, I believe," Piers put in. "The sexual relationship between Alan and Rosamund created a situation where Alan is in effect Alys's brother, and that means that if Alan is Steven's second cousin, she cannot marry Steven, though this case may be difficult to prove in a court of law. If your child had gone to full term, Rosamund," he added, gently, for it seemed brutal to remind her of the loss, "it might have been clearer."

"You spoke to me of the child," Alys reminded her sister, "not long after Steven and I were married. You were not quite sure then that you were pregnant, but it seemed to me clear that you and Alan had slept together some weeks before our marriage."

Rosamund nodded. "That's true. The first time," she blushed, embarrassed to admit so openly to their premarital affair, "was at the end of September, after the Michaelmas feast."

Sir Richard looked at Alan. "Do you confirm this, Alan?"

He nodded. "There is no question. In Reeve Paul's barn." He smiled ruefully. "We met there a number of times before we plighted our troth, I'm ashamed to say. And then we waited to marry until you came home, my lord, because Rosamund was your ward. That is why Alys and Steven were married first. Their betrothal was already in place before Alys's father died."

Sir Richard nodded. "The chronology seems robust. If Father Edward confirms Father Piers' reading of church law, then I think it is clear that it is your marriage, Steven, not Alan's, that is in question, and an annulment may be necessary. What say you about that?"

Steven drew a breath as everyone's eyes turned to him. "I am a soldier," he said, "and I will often be away from home. Alys has a business to run. We have no children so I am happy for her to live her life as she thinks fit. If Alan and Rosamund's relationship pre-dates ours as they say, then I am willing to give way."

He turned to Alan. "We have been friends a long time, and travelling companions for many months and through many adventures, and I know you very much want to remain married to Ros. If Alys is happy to be a maid again..." He looked anxiously for a moment at Alys, for this fate was one that many young women would fear, but receiving a decided nod he went on: "I will agree to applying for an annulment of our marriage, on grounds of consanguinity. I would be grateful for your help, Piers," he added, glancing at the young priest, "in preparing the application for the court."

There was a general sigh of relief at Steven's acceptance of the situation, and Alan and Rosamund clasped hands with joy. Rosamund looked at her sister and mouthed, "Thank you, Alys."

"That is well," Sir Richard pronounced with some relief. "Subject to Father Edward's agreement, I think we can declare this matter satisfactorily resolved. What say you, Alan?"

Alan bowed. "Indeed, my lord. This is a great relief to me, as you may imagine. My wife and I have been in great distress."

"And your position here as bailiff? What of that?"

"Tis for you to decide, my lord," Alan answered cautiously. "My lands that were granted in Sir Thomas's will are in Kent, as you know. And he intended me to be bailiff there, too."

Sir Richard shook his head impatiently. "I know that, of course. But you have been working here, and doing a good job, by all I hear. What think you of remaining in the post? Your lands will generate an income, but that can be paid here instead of in Beaconswell. I am offering you the post of bailiff here in Northchurch."

"Yes, my lord, I understand that." He looked at his wife. "Ros?" Northchurch was her childhood home, and also the place where her sister would continue to live and work. But it was also where she herself had been sick almost to the point of death, and as a result had lost her baby. He did not know what she would feel about living here for ever.

"I am happy to stay, my lord," she replied at once, "if Alan wishes it."

He smiled at her. "I do wish it. This is where we were born, and where you at least have always lived. I have no desire to go elsewhere if we do not have to." He met Sir Richard's eyes and then bowed deeply to him. "I thank you, my lord, and I accept."

He looked across the room at Alys as Sir Richard rose to his feet to leave, and his eyes were full of gratitude.

~ * ~

Steven and Alys left the Castle together, walking amicably side by side down the lane towards the bridge. When they came to the fork, Alys halted. "I am going up to your father's house."

"I'll come with you. I should talk to Jack."

They turned into the lane and walked a few paces. Steven looked down at her. "I must be on my way at dawn tomorrow. Sir Walter has commanded me to break my fast with the rest of his retinue at the castle before we leave, so I had better find a berth there tonight. But for this one evening, it would be good to be at the cottage with you."

To say goodbye, she thought. She nodded. "Mayhap we will have things to say, and only this chance to say them. But I must go and speak to Finn now, and let him know what has been decided."

Was there a moment's hesitation, a stiffening of Steven's spine, as he heard this? She wasn't sure. Whatever his instinctive reaction, he nodded in his turn. "Tis fair enough. Jack and I will check the stock and the fodder crops. While I am away, he will be running my lands as well as his own, and I'd like to be sure he can manage."

As they turned the corner of the lane to the barn, he asked suddenly: "Did you lie with Finn, while I was away?"

She glanced at him, wondering why it was so important to him. "I was not married to you, Steven, as it turns out, so it matters not, and tis better for you not to ask."

He laughed, but there was an edge to the sound. "That is answer enough for me. If you had stayed chaste, you would have said so and berated me for my insinuations! Tis more than just a business arrangement to you, then."

She nodded. "I want the annulment for Ros's sake, partly. But also for my own."

Forty-four

Finn was stacking logs in the woodstore close to the front door of Jack's house. He looked up as Alys and Steven entered the curtilage, and his expression became wary.

Alys smiled at him. "I would speak with you privately, Finn."

He looked surprised, as well he might.

Steven held out a hand. "I misjudged you when we last met," he said. "But I hope we may be on better terms in the future."

Finn looked at Alys, and received a tiny nod. He shook the outstretched hand, firmly though without much warmth.

"Jack is out in the pasture trying to milk the cow," he told Steven. "But he needs lessons from Alys."

"I'm sure that can be arranged," said Steven, his voice grave but with a smile crinkling the corners of his eyes. "Alys, I will wait for you at your cottage when I've talked to Jack." He grinned. "Don't take too long, though. I'm minded to have one last sup of your pottage before I leave."

She shook her head at him, smiling. "Good pottage takes time to cook, you know. You may have to wait a while for your dinner."

"I'll wait."

"Come into the barn, Alys," Finn suggested. "We can talk undisturbed there." He opened the door of the barn for her and she went in.

As soon as the door closed, he took her in his arms. "My love, what are you about? Tis surely tempting providence to come so openly to see me. What will Steven think? I do not want you exposed to more of his brutality."

She smiled and put her arms round him, pulling him close to her. "You do not know all. Did I not tell you not to despair?"

"I have been patient, as you asked." He put her away from him gently. "Alys, do not tease me. I cannot bear it, nor to have you close like this when our love is unlawful."

"But it is not unlawful, Finn. Steven and I are seeking an annulment." She told him about the meeting with Sir Richard, and that they had Piers' support. "Tis true, my love! I am not married, and we have done nothing wrong in God's eyes. You said, did you not, that if it is to be, we would find a way. And this is the way."

He looked troubled, and moved away from her. "It is not certain, though. The court might decide against you. Consanguinity is an uncertain matter at the best of times." His hands found the hinge he was fashioning on his workbench and began to fidget with it.

Alys watched him in dismay. "It is a possibility, but unlikely. Alan and Rosamund are concerned in this as well, and they will bear witness for us. I truly believe it will be as we hope, my love."

She stopped, worried suddenly that he was regretting his involvement with her, after all. "Finn...you haven't changed your mind?"

He turned at once and enfolded her in his arms again. "Never! I have loved you since the first moment you spoke to me when I was a stranger at your gate, a weary traveller with nowhere to lay my head." He kissed her, tenderly, but with passion just below the surface. "To live with you, and work with you—forever—would be bliss beyond anything I looked for when I set out from London."

"Do not fret, then. It will be as God decrees, but I believe we will be together."

It was nearly noon when she left him. Jack was in the house putting together a meal, but she did not dare to stay and help them, for Steven was waiting, and she had promised him a final dinner.

"We are becoming quite good at cooking," Finn reassured her with a smile as she said farewell. "But we will break our fast with you tomorrow, after Steven has gone. God speed, my love."

"You will explain to Jack? I have not time now, and…I am not sure what to say. He thinks of me as sister, because of Steven. I do not want him to feel rejected."

He smiled at her, and she felt her whole being grew warm in response. "I will explain. Jack will understand, and I think he will be glad for us. The three of us will be together, in the way that we have been this spring, which has made him happy. You need have no fear."

He bent and kissed her, and she left him to go back to her cottage and say her goodbyes to the man whom she had thought of as her husband, but from whom she might now be free.

She made the best pottage she could for Steven, flavouring it with a piece of meat he had brought her, as well as herbs, and they ate it at the table together. But now that there was time to talk, it seemed there was little to say. Steven's concerns were mostly with his brother.

"He'll be all alone when I'm gone," he said, frowning. "Tis a lot to ask of a boy his age, to take on a holding that size and make it profitable. Our sisters are all wed, and settled in their own places."

"Finn has it all in hand," she told him. "He speaks of finding reliable hired men to help. And Jack can live with us until he is old enough to wed." She said nothing about Jack's desire to be a weaver. It might all come to nothing once he tried it, after all.

"Thanks for looking after him, Alys." He handed her a bag of coin. "Your dowry," he explained, slightly awkwardly. "If our marriage is to be annulled, it should be restored to you. And I have been paid my wages, so I can afford to do so. Your dower lands will revert to me. Perhaps I will sell them, when times are better."

"Will you come back when the war is over and settle here? Jack will miss you."

He shrugged. "I don't see an early end to this war. The truce is already halfway run, and the king wants to rule France...or says he does. I'll be at Calais with Sir Walter for a while yet. But when we are riding this way next, I will come to see you."

He smiled suddenly. "Send me word when the annulment is approved. I might even ask leave of absence to come to your wedding."

She shook her head at him, glad they were parting on good terms. "Nay, there's no need for that. But thank you, Steven, for accepting the situation. I am grateful."

He waved that away. "It suits us both. Thank God for Alan's inability to keep his cock in his drawers when there's a pretty woman to make love to. Else it would have been his marriage that is to be annulled, and ours that stands."

She thought of Finn's words. "It was meant to be."

He laughed. "Mayhap. Or you and I are lucky. Well, I was ever one to ride my luck."

She smiled at him. "It's served you well so far."

As he set off along the lane for the castle in the fading light, she wondered whether she would ever see him again.

~ * ~

"Mount up, Steven. Tis time we were on the road." Sir Walter clapped his liegeman on the shoulder. "I've had no word yet as to whether the king and the Prince of Wales mean to celebrate St George's Day at Windsor as they did last April." Last month the king had prorogued parliament indefinitely, but Walter did not want to be caught idling here in Hampshire if his lord needed his services further east.

He had intended only to stay one night in Northchurch, but Lady Maud had struck up a friendship with Giselle that promised much, and had begged them to stay another day to allow the pregnant woman to rest. Walter had been adamant, however, that they must be on their way this morning and they had broken their fast very early so as to make the most of the daylight.

He handed his wife into the litter just as Lady Maud came out to see them off, accompanied by two servants with stirrup cups. The postilions mounted the horses harnessed to Giselle's litter, and the little entourage formed up around her. When the stirrup cups had been emptied, Walter doffed his riding cap to his host, and the troop moved off, with a clink of harness and a creaking of leather. They rode slowly and carefully over the bridge and turned eastwards along the road to Basingstoke.

At the weaver's cottage, Alys was standing at the gate to watch them pass. As the little cavalcade trotted past, she waved to them and Steven raised an answering hand.

It must be terribly uncomfortable for Giselle in that litter, she thought, watching the contraption jounce and sway between the two horses that carried it. She had never learned to ride, except pillion behind her father when they went to market, but a litter looked more uncomfortable even than that. *If I had to travel, I'd rather walk, even if it takes longer.* But thankfully travel was not something she had to worry about for the moment. Maybe one day, she and Finn would go to London to see how his family had fared during the pestilence, but it was too dangerous to go anywhere near the city at the moment without an armed guard.

She caught sight of Finn and Jack crossing the bridge in the wake of Sir Walter's retinue. They came to stand beside her as the cavalcade picked up speed along the road. Finn rested his hand on her shoulder. "Good morrow, Alys. Jack wanted to say farewell to Steven, so we waited by the fork and followed them down."

"I'll miss him," said Jack. "But when the workshop is in business again, and you have finished your training, I will become Master Finn's apprentice. He has promised me. Others can look after the land and the sheep until Steven returns. Life is good, is it not, Alys?"

"It is enough for me even that we are alive," Alys told him soberly.

Finn looked down at her, and his heart lifted at the thought of new beginnings—a workshop to run together, love and laughter and perhaps children to bring light to their lives. Yet across that sunny landscape there lay a deep shadow. At the back of his mind was the fear that the pestilence might return, that it might become an intermittent backcloth to the weaving of their lives together. As he had walked past the churchyard that morning, the scar of raw brown earth against the green of the pastures beyond had been a reminder of all those who were alive no longer, cut off before their time by a catastrophe at once so dire and so little understood. And nothing would ever be the same again. Even if the pestilence were over, the past months of agony, terror and death, and the images of suffering and fear they had engendered, could not be altogether banished; those who had experienced them would never forget. Nor would they take each other for granted. Every day they had was to be treasured.

His fear faded, and practical matters reasserted themselves. The horsemen had vanished round a bend in the road, and there were chores to be done. He gave Alys a quick hug.

"Come, my love," he said. "They have gone, and there are hungry mouths to be fed here. Mine among them."

Epilogue: 1399

The old man dreams a little in the warm sun, seated in his carrel in the cloisters. His quill sits idly in his hand, the ink drying on the nib. He has begun colouring the capital on the last page of his illustrated chronicle. It is beautiful—full of gold and scarlet and blue, but it tells of a life lived among momentous events.

He recalls the time it all began, when he came back to the village of his birth as a half-trained young deacon, to live and work among the companions of his childhood. He came to pray for his patron in the chantry, but he stayed to serve them all as the Great Mortality swept over England. Strange to think this monastery where he is to end his days is now flourishing, where once he knelt and prayed among the dead.

Grim times, they were, when fear and death stalked the land and loss and grief came to everyone...yet shot through with moments of joy and selfless altruism, as men and women found strength they did not know they had in giving love and care to family, neighbours and strangers. He remembers the lady Eleanor and is glad to have survived it all and lived his life for God.

He stirs a little, dipping the quill again, and completes the final capital. Soon it will be time for supper, and then vespers. His own span of life is close to ending now, and his work is finished. He lays down the quill and dozes while he waits for the end of the day.

Historical Note

Northchurch, its people and its immediate surroundings, are fictional, but many of the other people, places and situations mentioned actually existed, and I have woven them into my story as accurately as I can. For example, King Edward III and his bishops did send out letters to priests to read to their congregations in October 1348, with the information I have presented, and people's reactions to them in Northchurch are typical of reactions at the time. The pope did give permission for lay people to hear confessions, 'even women,' and reactions to this generally represented—as such reactions do—the pre-existing attitudes of individuals. Most priests stayed with their parishioners and many paid with their lives, like Father Robert, but some fled like Father Edward, and so did many noble families, like the DeClercs, moving from one to other of their various estates in an effort to escape the plague (in many cases successfully).

The pandemic we now call the Black Death moved across England in a single prolonged wave, but its trajectory was complex; that is, it did not enter in the south and pass uniformly northwards across the country. Instead, it followed major transport routes, spreading first westwards along the south coast, with separate nodes of infection in major ports such as Bristol on the major inlet below the Severn estuary. This almost certainly represented transmission by ships, some directly from the continent of Europe. For several months after what were probably the first infections in Dorset in June 1348, the interior of southern England was almost untouched, but Dorset, Devon and Somerset suffered badly in the early months. In November or December 1348, the disease came to London, with devastating effects not only medically but also socially and economically; but the route of transmission is uncertain. Again, it may have been direct infection by sailors or passengers on ships from the continent, or possibly by returning soldiers from Calais after the truce that halted the Hundred Years War, albeit briefly. King Edward III's decision not to close the ports in October 1348 may have been costly. But as the disease raged across the rest of Europe, moving ever northwards and eastwards, until 1350, the ports would have to have been almost permanently closed, with dire effects on an economy heavily dependent on wool exports. Edward's war expenditure meant that he needed taxation, primarily on exports, to keep his ambitions to be King of France alive. It was a matter of national pride to which national safety from disease was sacrificed. In the light of the sketchy understanding of disease transmission at the time, it is perhaps unfair to blame him.

Thus, rather surprisingly, the disease did not hit northern Hampshire until January 1349. The evidence from the turnover of parish incumbencies, which is one of the main ways in which the statistics for this pandemic were compiled, shows that the bulk of the deaths were in the period January to March 1349, though people did continue to die of plague in much smaller numbers for the rest of the year. The records of the Bishop of Winchester are extant and have been published (by Hampshire County Council).

There is evidence from chronicles, letters and other descriptions of the incidence of the disease both in England and on the continent of Europe that three different types of plague were present, in differing mixes in different places and at different seasons, which is one of the reasons why it was so devastating (the other is that there had been no similar outbreak of plague in Europe since the 6th century and few people had any immunity to it). The most prevalent type in the early part of the pandemic, in Italy and France, was bubonic plague, which had a death rate of something around 60 or 70 percent of those infected. But in England, partly because of the colder weather experienced during winter and spring, 1348/1349, many cases were of pneumonic plague, which affects the lungs and is very much more deadly. A third and rarer type, septicaemic plague, in which the bacillus enters the bloodstream directly and overwhelms the patient extremely quickly, is almost always fatal. Today all these types can be treated with antibiotics, but without them it was (and is) untreatable. Over Europe as a whole, the death rate from the disease probably approached 40 percent; in England it was more like 50 percent—in some places higher. On the basis of the transfer of incumbencies, Hampshire was one of the more badly affected areas. The plague returned in 1361, and periodically throughout the next three centuries, never quite as destructive as the 1348–1350 outbreak, but deadly enough to keep the population lower than its pre-plague maximum.

If you want to read further on the subject of the fourteenth-century pandemic, there are a number of more-or-less accessible books on the subject. I've included here a list of those I found particularly helpful:

Philip Ziegler, *The Black Death* (Penguin, 3rd edition, 1982, first published in 1969), is the first and still a classic treatment of the pandemic.

Benedict Gummer, *The Scourging Angel: The Black Death in the British Isles* (Vintage Books, 2010) gives a very coherent and readable account of the movement of the pandemic across the British Isles.

Sean Martin, *The Black Death* (Pocket Essentials, 2007) is a concise survey of the pandemic across Europe from 1347–1350. Its small size obviously reduces the amount of detail, but it is a good introduction if you don't want to engage with anything substantive.

John Hatcher, *The Black Death: An Intimate Story of a Village in Crisis* is an imagined or fictional account of an English village in the throes of the pandemic. It is not a novel, but seeks to examine the history of the plague from the point of view of those who suffered it, without the reflections of historical hindsight.

John Kelly, *The Great Mortality: An intimate history of the Black Death* (HarperCollins 2006) surveys much of the same material as the other books, but includes the historical speculations that emerged in the early 2000s as to whether the Black Death was actually bubonic plague or not. This is of academic interest, although subsequent archaeological investigations of plague victims seem to have concluded that these speculations were in fact unnecessary because traces of *Y pestis* have been found in the bones of plague victims of the time.

A good selection of primary sources is included (and translated) in Rosemary Horrox's edition of documents, *The Black Death* (Manchester University Press, 1994).

On the Hundred Years' War, and in particular the situation around Calais in 1348, Jonathan Sumption's monumental work, *The Hundred Years War*, is invaluable, especially Vol. I, *Trial by Battle* and Vol. II *Trial by Fire* (Faber & Faber, 1997 & 1998).

For a very useful and accessible general introduction to medieval life, I recommend Ian Mortimer's *The Time Traveller's Guide to Medieval England* (Bodley Head, 2006).

Meet Jane Anstey

Jane Anstey has been writing since she was a child and had her first story published in the school magazine at age 12. This is her fourth book published with Wings ePress. She studied history at Oxford University and has maintained her interest in medieval history ever since—hence this novel. She is married with two adult daughters and lives in Cornwall, UK, with a cat and three guinea pigs.

Other Works From The Pen Of

Jane Anstey

Beauty for Ashes – When Hollywood actor Luke Carson falls for English college student Samantha, he finds himself on an emotional roller-coaster ride to disaster.

St Martin's Summer – Reverend Jeremy Swanson investigates an unpopular farmer's death and its connection with an abortive village love affair and a small boy's disappearance.

You Owe Me Five Farthings – A failing marriage and a mysterious ancient book keep Reverend Jeremy Swanson busy in this sequel to *St Martin's Summer*.

Letter to Our Readers

Enjoy this book?

You can make a difference

As an independent publisher, Wings ePress, Inc. does not have the financial clout of the large New York Publishers. We can't afford large magazine spreads or subway posters to tell people about our quality books.

But, we do have something much more effective and powerful than ads. We have a large base of loyal readers.

Honest Reviews help bring the attention of new readers to our books.

If you enjoyed this book, we would appreciate it if you would spend a few minutes posting a review on the site where you purchased this book or on the Wings ePress, Inc. webpages at: https://wingsepress.com/

Visit Our Website

For The Full Inventory
Of Quality Books:

Wings ePress.Inc
https://wingsepress.com/

Quality trade paperbacks and downloads
in multiple formats,
in genres ranging from light romantic comedy
to general iction and horror.
Wings has something for every reader's taste.
Visit the website, then bookmark it.
We add new titles each month!

Wings ePress Inc.
3000 N. Rock Road
Newton, KS 67114

Printed in Great Britain
by Amazon